THE GIRL OF MANY CROWNS

THE GIRL OF MANY CROWNS

D. H. MORRIS

The Girl of Many Crowns © 2024 D. H. Morris

New Classics Publishing, LLC, Liberty, MO, USA

FIRST EDITION

Library of Congress Cataloging-in-Publication Data
Names: Morris, Deborah L., author.
Title: The Girl of Many Crowns / D. H. Morris.
Description: Liberty, MO: New Classics Publishing, LLC, 2024.
Identifiers: ISBN: 979-8-9908280-0-1
Subjects: LCSH Judith of Flanders, 843-870--Fiction. | Civilization, Medieval--Fiction. | Europe--History--
476-1492--Fiction. | Great Britain--History--To 1066--Fiction. | Queens--Europe--History--Fiction. |
Historical Fiction. | Love stories. | BISAC FICTION / Historical / Medieval
Classification: LCC PS3613 .O67 G57 | DDC 813.6--dc23

ISBN (Paperback) 979-8-9908280-0-1

Library of Congress Control Number: 2024912767

Ten percent of the net proceeds from the sales of this book will be donated to OUR Rescue, a non-profit organization dedicated to rescuing young boys and girls from exploitation and sex trafficking. Please go to https://ourrescue.org/ to check out this special organization.

CHARLES THE GREAT (CHARLEMAGNE)
|
LOUIS (EMPEROR LOUIS "THE PIOUS")
|

PIPPIN I   LOTHAR I   LOUIS THE GERMAN CHARLES

| | |

PIPPIN II   LOTHAR II   1. **JUDITH**
              EMPEROR LOUIS   2. LOUIS
              CHARLES OF PROVENCE   3. CHARLES
                                            4. LOTHAR
                                          5. CARLOMANN
                                          6. ROTRUD
                                          7. ERMENTRUD
                                          8. HILDEGARDE
                                          9. GISELA
                                        10. GODEHILDE

AETHELWULF - KING OF WESSEX
|

1.   AETHELBALD
2.   AETHELBERHT
3.   AETHELRED
4.   ALFRED (ALFRED "THE GREAT")

Charles the Great's Empire Divisions
856 A.D.

N

(Britannia)

Bruges
Flanders
Aachen

Worms

Lothar

Louis the German

Brittany   Neustria

Burgundy

King Charles'
Holdings

Emperor Louis

Mont Cenis
Pavia

Charles
of
Provence

Luna

Aquitane

Septimania

Via Francigena

Leonine City
Rome

Tyrrhenian Sea

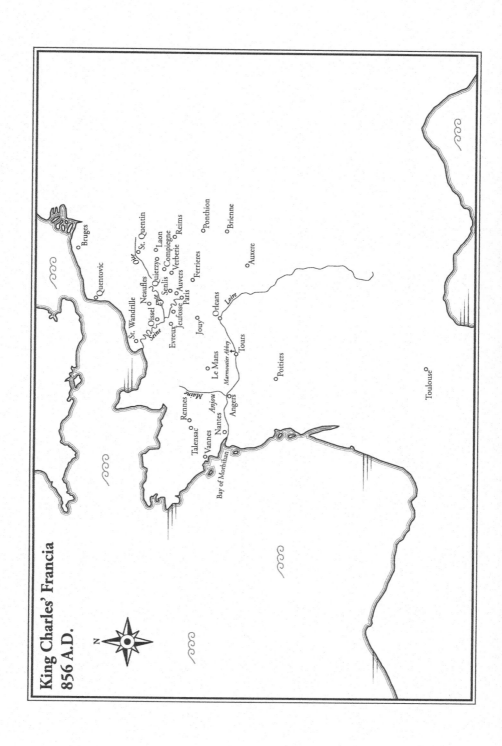

King Charles' Francia
856 A.D.

N

Bruges
Quentovic
St. Quentin
Oise
Neaufles
Laon
St. Wandrille
Oissel
Quierzyo
Compiegne
Senlis
Verberie
Reims
Ponthion
Seine
Eyes
Auvers
Brienne
Evreux
Jeufosse
Paris
Ferrieres
Orleans
Auxere
Jouy
Loire
Tours
Marmoutier Abbey
Le Mans
Poitiers
Rennes
Maine
Anjou
Talensac
Nantes
Angers
Vannes
Bay of Morbihan
Toulouse

PART I

JUDITH OF FRANCIA

CHAPTER I

MARCH 856 – Flanders, the Kingdom of Francia

Emerging from the dense forest separating his family estate from the road leading to his future, sixteen-year-old Baldwin Iron Arm ran his fingers through his ebon locks before donning his helmet. He grinned at Marius, his childhood mentor and companion on this journey before urging on his mount. Passing Bruges—the sorry little trading settlement frequently overrun by Viking Danes—made Baldwin glad that his widowed mother, Countess Guinhilde's manor lay on the opposite side of a forest inhabited by wolves and bears who discouraged many who would otherwise invade their holding.

"Someone should really do something about this nasty little bump in the road," Baldwin remarked as they moved beyond the ruins that had once been the thriving community of Bruges.

"Would that someone be you?" Marius laughed.

"Perhaps," Baldwin shot back. "Once I have made my fortune in King Charles' service."

"It never hurts to dream," Marius chuckled, pushing his horse into a canter, forcing Baldwin to catch up.

Countess Guinhilde's final words to her son upon his departure ran through Baldwin's mind as they made their way across Flanders. "God has blessed you with many gifts, including great strength and intelligence. And where much is given, much is expected. Use your gifts in His honor and in faithful service to your king. Remember that goodness and loyalty are the essence of nobility," she cautioned before kissing his cheek and sending him on his way.

Brutal March winds made Baldwin glad of the leather tunic and chain mail he wore, passed down to him through several generations of knights and warriors. Broad of shoulder and taller than most men, Baldwin had earned his moniker of "Iron Arm" by the time he was fourteen as he fought side-by-side with the men of Flanders, defending their lands against the vicious Danish raiders. His reputation in battle had brought him to the notice of the king of Francia's seneschal, Gauzlin, and had earned him the prized letter of invitation to join the king's elite forces. Excitement pumped through his veins as surely as blood as he began his five-day journey to Senlis and King Charles' court.

Most of the Belgae, Baldwin's people, supported King Charles over his half-brothers, Lothar I and Louis "the German." The three royal brothers had been at odds with each other since the death of their father, Louis the Pious, had fractured the kingdom into three parts. Kings Lothar and Louis the German did not succeed in taking Charles' territory. But, with the recent death of King Lothar and his son's ascension to his throne, Louis the German yet remained a threat to King Charles' kingdom.

At midday, Baldwin and Marius gleaned bits of news and gossip from a group of knights resting by the side of the road.

"Francia is quiet for now, but that will not last," the captain of the group assured Baldwin. "Between Brittany, Louis the German, the Danes, and the rebel lords of Aquitaine, you will see plenty of action before long."

"How goes the conflict in Brittany?" Marius wondered.

"The war is over, but the Bretons are terrible negotiators," the leader shook his head as he prepared to resume his journey. "Although they defeated the king at Jengland, they did not insist on complete independence from Francia. In the capitulation treaty that King Charles signed with Erispoë, leader of the Bretons, Brittany will be largely autonomous. And, I might add, a thorn in the king's side."

"Then, we are at peace," Baldwin concluded.

"Only for now," the captain nodded his farewell as the knights mounted their horses. "This kingdom has too many ambitious leaders for peace to last."

Baldwin and Marius pushed ahead, finding accommodations before nightfall in a poorly kept inn. They knew they might have to share their room, tiny as it was, with other guests, but Baldwin and Marius were glad of rest for their horses, shelter for themselves, and hot stew to warm their bellies.

Two other travelers joined them late in the evening. Only floor space remained, Baldwin and Marius having claimed the lone, dusty straw mattress. However, as soon as the new guests curled up—each in his own corner of the room—they began to snore. The cacophony of snort, gasp and wheeze and the sour smell of unwashed bodies, made Baldwin lie awake longer than usual. All part of the adventure, he reminded himself wryly as he eventually nodded off.

Reaching the forest of Cuisia on the fifth day, a light fog and drizzle made the going miserable. "We've but a few miles to Senlis," Baldwin called to Marius. "I say we push on rather than seek shelter. In fact, I am sure that I can reach the town before you can, old man."

"Hah! Old man, is it now?" Marius smiled broadly, gave Baldwin a playful cuff, and spurred his horse forward to take the lead.

The last vestiges of daylight were fading fast when they eagerly approached the wall surrounding the village of Senlis. Baldwin was impressed by the wall's size—more than three times his own impressive height. The missive he bore from the king's seneschal gave them ready entrance and the watchmen directed them to the palace surrounded by its own impressive wall. A guard admitted them to the torch-lit palace grounds and bade them dismount and wait while he summoned Gauzlin, King Charles' seneschal.

The position of seneschal, Baldwin knew, was one of distinction and importance in the royal court. King Charles' first seneschal, Adalard, had set a high standard for all who would come after him. He had not only managed the recruiting, housing, assigning, and compensating of those who served in the royal household, but he had also arranged the marriage of King Charles to Adalard's own niece, Ermentrude of Orléans. After five years Adalard had moved on to serve King Charles' brother, King

Lothar I. However, his legacy was a system that ensured King Charles had a steady stream of young noblemen ready to serve in whatever capacity the court required.

Gauzlin, the current seneschal, appeared to be around thirty years old and carried himself with easy confidence. He approached, eying a restless Baldwin shrewdly.

"Ah, Baldwin Iron Arm. I have heard much of you. King Charles needs knights with your skill. And this is your man?" he inquired, looking at Marius. At Baldwin's nod, Gauzlin continued. "You are both hungry and tired after such a journey, and your horses need attention. Let us see to them first."

They followed Gauzlin to the massive stables, which easily held some two hundred horses. Gauzlin introduced them to Martin, the hefty, grey-bearded Marshal of the Stables. At Martin's command, several grooms took charge of their mounts and helped them remove and carry their packs. Across from the stables were several long barracks. In one of the buildings Gauzlin found two unclaimed beds for them and room to stow their saddle packs.

"Where are the other knights, sir?" Baldwin ventured as they left the empty barracks.

Gauzlin smiled. "We encourage our married officers to invite the younger knights into their homes for food and conversation in the evenings. You will not want for company when Marius leaves, I assure you."

Gauzlin led them through a side door in the palace to the kitchen, where they enjoyed a hearty supper of venison, cabbage, cheese, and bread. As Baldwin and Marius ate, Gauzlin filled them in on what to expect.

"As to employment," Gauzlin addressed Baldwin, "I cannot say more without conferring with King Charles. Most young noblemen begin in military service and train with the hope of becoming officers. With a name like 'Iron Arm,' you might expect to be used in such a capacity."

Gauzlin laughed when Baldwin blushed at the mention of his nickname. "Your reputation has preceded you, my young friend. The court always needs skilled fighters. But I have two other traits

I am also seeking. How patient are you, Baldwin, and what of your loyalty?" Gauzlin's gaze was piercing,

"My mother taught me, sir, that loyalty is the very essence of nobility. But, as for patience, it is a trait I am still pursuing," he answered carefully.

"Me too!" Gauzlin admitted ruefully. "We may have a special assignment for you if you are as loyal as you say and if you are willing to pursue patience as well. I will speak with the king tomorrow. I hope to have a specific assignment for you by the afternoon."

Gauzlin rose to his feet as Baldwin and Marius finished eating. "Return to the barracks and rest tonight. If you need anything, ask the other knights. Some of them should have returned by now. Rest well, Baldwin Iron Arm." Gauzlin left them to find their own way.

The barracks gradually filled with young knights ranging from Neustria and Aquitaine on the west to Septimania in the South, from Burgundy in the east, and from Flanders in the north. Each region in Francia was represented. The knights welcomed Baldwin to their ranks and offered good advice. But, when he had finally quenched his oil lamp and sleep embraced the others, Baldwin's mind remained unsettled. What special assignment is Gauzlin considering for me?

Rising before dawn, Baldwin and Marius followed the other knights to chapel, afterward breaking their fast with bread and cheese. When the knights went to their various assignments, Baldwin and Marius turned to the stables. Martin led them to find their horses, which had been well cared for.

"Feel free to explore the palace grounds," Martin encouraged them. "You will probably not hear anything from Gauzlin until after the king's morning council."

The palace grounds were quite extensive and included several other barracks, an armory, as well as a chapel, a monastery, and kennels. Baldwin and Marius visited with the royal hunters, returning with their lively hounds after bagging a large buck and several rabbits. Gauzlin approached as they started back toward their barracks.

"I trust you are being well provided for, young Baldwin." Gauzlin clapped Baldwin on the shoulder.

"We are, sir," Baldwin assured him.

"Good! I am to bring you to the throne room. King Charles would like to speak with you personally. Marius, can you find your way back to the barracks?" Gauzlin questioned.

At Marius's nod, Gauzlin led Baldwin through the main palace doors into the impressive reception area and up a grand marble staircase. They passed guards as they moved along a corridor deeper within the palace.

Baldwin admired the beautifully colored mosaic floor tiles arranged in intricate patterns. Sculptures and exotic objects of art adorned niches while rich and colorful tapestries graced the walls. He ran his fingers appreciatively over the elaborately carved, gold-accented handrail on the sweeping staircase leading up to the throne room. King Charles, like his grandfather, Emperor Charles the Great, was clearly a connoisseur of fine things.

Gauzlin gave valuable instruction as they walked. "The king is consulting with John Scotus, an Irish scholar and adviser to the king. They are discussing the upcoming summer assembly. Every summer, nobles from all over the kingdom gather to discuss current laws and vote on any changes proposed by the king."

Gauzlin paused before a double door with a posted guard. "We will enter when admitted by the keeper of the door and wait at the back of the room until we are summoned forward. This is no time for cowardice, young Baldwin. Do not speak unless the king speaks directly to you. But if he asks you a question, speak boldly and clearly. Speak your mind and speak truth. It is what the king expects and what he admires." They presented themselves to the keeper of the door for admittance.

The throne room was long and spacious, with a large table off to one side. Mirroring the detailed carving of the throne itself, the ceiling was arched with intricate wood inlay. Behind the throne, the wall displayed Francia's royal banner—blue, with gold embroidery and fringe. From Baldwin's vantage, King Charles appeared to be in his late thirties, tall and slender. His brown hair and beard had a reddish tint, and he wore a pale blue tunic with purple leggings denoting his status as king.

King Charles' demeanor was thoughtful but confident as he deliberated with his silver-haired counselor. Whether sitting or pacing restlessly about the room, it was evident that the king was in command. When the discussion concerning the next assembly ended, King Charles beckoned Gauzlin and Baldwin forward. The aged scholar, John Scotus, examined Baldwin with eager curiosity. Determined not to reveal his nervousness, Baldwin followed Gauzlin's lead, bowing deeply until the king addressed them.

"So, this is the 'Iron Arm?'" King Charles stood and approached Baldwin. "You are accomplished in all forms of battle?"

"Yes, Sire. I have experience in fighting the Viking raiders." Baldwin spoke with what he hoped was the right amount of boldness.

"Have you learned to read?" the king wished to know.

"Sire, my mother saw to it that I was well instructed in reading, arithmetic, military tactics, history, manners, and music."

"Excellent. I wish all in my kingdom were as well educated. Perhaps, someday, we will be able to spend more time on learning and less on war." The king exchanged a meaningful glance with John Scotus.

"And your mother, how does she fare?" King Charles inquired.

"She fares well, my King," was Baldwin's reply.

"Has she kinsmen to look out for her interests?"

"Yes, Sire."

"Then, I hope you will stay and serve our court for some long time, Baldwin Iron Arm," the king continued, seemingly pleased. "Will you pledge loyalty to me, Baldwin?"

"I will gladly, Sire," Baldwin answered confidently, placing his closed fist over his heart.

"For that, I thank you, young knight. I have seven children, and the queen is even now great with child. Will you also pledge to defend my family?"

"I pledge to defend them with my life, Sire." The conviction in Baldwin's voice rang true.

"Many dangers threaten our kingdom, demanding all our cunning and resources to keep them at bay. I need someone with your talents to help my son Louis prepare to someday lead an army in battle—and survive. Louis will shortly be crowned king of Neustria. I will appoint administrators for him over Neustria until he is prepared to assume control. In the interim, he will need to become a leader of men, on and off the battlefield."

The king paused as if considering and then spoke with decisiveness. "I desire you to play a role in my son's development. I offer you the position of companion, defender, and arms instructor of Prince Louis. Will you pledge to faithfully train Prince Louis in the very arts of battle you have mastered and defend him with your life, if necessary?"

Baldwin was momentarily stunned into silence. This was neither what he had expected nor wished for when he had set out on his journey. He had been trained to fight, and he was eager to prove himself in battle against his king's many foes. What did he know of teaching a child prince? But this was the employment he was being offered. Baldwin was wise enough to know that this assignment was not only a great responsibility but also a great honor. He could do nothing but accept it.

"Sire," he promised with all sincerity. "I will devote all that I am to achieve the result you desire."

"Well spoken, Baldwin Iron Arm," the king looked pleased. "Gauzlin, give Baldwin every resource necessary to accomplish his assignment. Dress him as a member of the royal household. If he is to be the future king's companion, he must look the part. Oh, and find him quarters within the palace, readily available to Prince Louis."

The king moved toward his throne and then turned back, "Serve me well, young Baldwin Iron Arm, and you may become a count in your own right, as your father was before you."

Gauzlin appeared pleased as they left the palace and began walking back toward the barracks. "You acquitted yourself well, young Baldwin," he grinned. "King Charles likes you. What are your feelings after meeting the king?"

Baldwin considered his jumble of emotions. "Why would the king entrust me, a raw recruit, with such a weighty matter? He has more-experienced knights able to instruct Prince Louis. I had hoped to learn from them, myself."

"Ah, but your youth and inexperience will prove an asset, I believe, with Prince Louis." Gauzlin insisted.

"How so?"

"Prince Louis is not like his father, bold and fearless. He is much more like his grandfather, Emperor Louis the Pious—a gentle soul who did not relish contest or combat. Prince Louis' previous arms instructor only made the prince more hesitant in demeanor and made his halting speech much worse. As King of Neustria, Prince Louis must inspire confidence in his nobles. If they see him as a weak king, they may ultimately rebel."

Gauzlin stopped walking and lowered his voice when he caught sight of Marius slowly making his way toward them.

"Last fall, Prince Louis' younger brother—young Prince Charles—became king of Aquitaine at the age of only seven. Young Charles lives in Aquitaine under the direction of two administrators who oversee the affairs of that province. This year, the king has set a summer coronation date for Prince Louis, which may be difficult for him."

"You say he has a problem speaking?" Baldwin probed.

"The prince can speak," Gauzlin assured him. "But he does so with a nervous stammer, especially when he is in his father's presence. That is why I counseled you to speak boldly to the king. The king's council hopes if Prince Louis has a companion closer to his own age—one who embodies the qualities the king wishes his son to develop—the prince will become bolder himself. Prince Louis must be ready to take on his role as provincial king of Neustria and—at King Charles' death—high King of Francia."

"How old is Prince Louis? Has he friends?" Baldwin wondered.

"Prince Louis will achieve his tenth year this November. His closest companion is his older sister, by two years, Princess Judith." After some hesitation, Gauzlin continued. "This fall, when Princess Judith achieves her twelfth year, her hand will likely be given in marriage to establish an important alliance with another kingdom. King Charles arranged Prince Louis' own betrothal to the Breton leader Erispoë's daughter just last month in Le Mans. Princess Judith will be next."

"They are both rather young for betrothal," Baldwin remarked.

Gauzlin smiled ruefully. "That is the way with royal children. The king's sons, who are closest in line for the throne, are betrothed when they are very young for political advantage, and they are expected to marry the person chosen for them when they attain their majority at the age of fifteen. Those who are not designated to rule are destined for the church, like Prince Louis' younger brothers, Prince Carlomann and Prince Lothar. Both were sent to abbeys when only four years of age. They have already been tonsured and are being raised by the monks to become abbots. The king's daughters are either married off for political advantage as soon as the law allows at age twelve, or they will be sent to a convent to live life as an abbess. With young Charles now in Aquitaine, Princess Judith is Prince Louis' only friend. The loss of her will devastate him. Hence, your role is not only to teach the prince but to befriend him. It should not be too difficult. He truly is a good and kind child."

"Oh, and Baldwin," he added pointedly as Marius joined them. "I am counting on you to be successful in this assignment. I am the one who recommended you to the king."

CHAPTER II

MARCH and APRIL 856

"Do not doubt yourself, Baldwin." Marius advised when he learned of Baldwin's assignment. "You have been taught by many different mentors who mastered their warcraft and shared it with you. What made you eager to learn? What made you strive to be like them when your body ached, or your strength was spent?"

Baldwin smiled as he remembered. "Each had a way of reducing the most complicated task to mastering a few basic skills and then combining them. They also knew how to make learning those basic skills amusing for me—much like a game."

Marius nodded. "Then, that is your challenge. Find what Prince Louis enjoys doing and make it part of the training. If Prince Louis feels encouraged and he finds your drills amusing, he should progress in the way King Charles desires. You have the power to do much good here, Baldwin. Perhaps God made you for this very moment."

Baldwin contemplated Marius's words as he was fitted by the Mistress of the Wardrobe for palace-blue tunics, leggings, and cloaks, as he selected practice weapons from the armory, and when he wrote a message to his mother. When he announced to the knights in the barracks that he would not be staying with them, their reactions varied. Some were jealous, knowing he would often be in the eye of the king and subject to his benefaction. Others pointed out that such scrutiny would be a negative if he faltered.

"I would not wish to be in your boots," remarked a proud young knight from Aquitaine. "You do not want to be on the wrong side of King Charles' temper, I tell you. Two years ago, the king had Count Gauzbert beheaded for preferring the king's nephew, Pippin, over his rule in Aquitaine. It was so unfair! Others have changed sides in the royal conflicts and lived to tell the tale. Lords are always swearing fealty to one king while making promises to another. It is almost expected. But Gauzbert paid for his choice with his life! No wonder there is so much unrest in Aquitaine."

"You need not worry," another knight assured Baldwin. "King Charles has since promised that a tribunal of nobles will decide the fate of any knight accused of disloyalty to the king. If convicted, the knight will either be allowed to beg forgiveness and remain in the king's service after appropriate punishment, or he will be allowed to leave in peace and serve another kingdom."

"I will believe that when the king swears to it by oath before the assembly," the knight from Aquitaine insisted.

After some heated discussion, most knights expressed contentment with their own assignments, loving the camaraderie, the attention they received from the officers, and their opportunity to rise in the ranks without the pressure of being singled out. Baldwin fell asleep with some natural misgivings, regretting the friendships and experiences that he would be missing with his peers.

In the morning, everyone wished him well as he bade them goodbye and accompanied Marius to the city gate before reporting to Gauzlin at the palace. Gauzlin led Baldwin to the same floor as the throne room. This time, instead of going up the grand staircase they had used the day before, they went by way of the plain, narrow staircase leading up from the side entrance and the kitchens. *This staircase is probably for the servants,* Baldwin surmised.

Gauzlin opened a sturdy oaken door. "John Scotus graciously offered to share his chamber after meeting you. John Scotus tutors Prince Louis as well as Princess Judith in arithmetic, reading, music, philosophy, and languages. You are fortunate to share a room with such a scholar. And the court is fortunate to have the best of the renowned Irish scholars in service here."

Gauzlin paused and glanced earnestly at Baldwin to emphasize his point before continuing. "Coordinate with John Scotus regarding Prince Louis' schedule since John not only tutors in the palace but serves on the king's council. And he is also responsible for overseeing the palace school for the nobles' and officers' children. Sharing a chamber with him will make collaboration much easier, and John Scotus may have insight on how best to teach the prince."

"Where can I find Prince Louis? And when do I begin his instruction?" Feeling daunted by his assignment, Baldwin hoped for some clear direction.

"Prince Louis is usually in the royal family apartments, which lie beyond the throne room on this very floor. All who personally serve the royal family are on this floor, ready to serve at any time, night, or day. As for teaching, I suggest you begin as soon as possible. The king will expect some improvement before Prince Louis' coronation in two months' time. Start by becoming Prince Louis' friend. Friendship is what the young prince needs most to gain confidence."

Baldwin inspected his new quarters with interest. The large and elegantly furnished chamber held two beautifully carved feather beds, several storage chests, a couple of sturdy chairs, and a small writing table. What he found most interesting was an enormous Roman-style bookcase that reached the ceiling and held an impressive collection of books—many of them in Greek. Taking a deep breath, Baldwin left the chamber and went in search of the royal family quarters. *You wanted adventure. Now you have more than you bargained for.* He smiled at his own naivete just a few days earlier.

To Baldwin's relief, the doorkeeper of the royal apartments knew his name and purpose. Baldwin waited while the doorkeeper sought permission to admit him. Having no real plan in mind, he decided to follow Gauzlin's advice and spend as much time as possible with Prince Louis in hopes of building friendship and trust.

The doorkeeper ushered a nervous Baldwin into a vestibule with several doors on either side, knocked on the first door on the left, entered, and announced, "Baldwin Iron Arm, my queen."

He stepped aside and motioned for Baldwin to enter. Following Gauzlin's example of the previous day, Baldwin bowed deeply as he entered the room and remained in place until addressed.

"Come closer, Baldwin," Queen Ermentrude's voice was cultured and kind. Baldwin raised his head and approached. The queen, seated on an exquisite blue brocade lounge, was dressed in a cream silk tunic with an elaborately embroidered blue robe, which did not hide that she was with child. She wore a simple crown atop a silken headdress, partially concealing her chestnut brown hair. Queen Ermentrude's gentle eyes revealed a welcoming smile. At her feet lay a small, black-and-white dog, which rose with wagging tail and bark to greet Baldwin as he approached.

Seated beside her was a young, slender maiden with opalescent skin, wearing a simple golden tiara over rich auburn hair plaited in one long braid hanging almost to her waist. She was a beautiful child on the brink of young womanhood, but the fire in her eyes was less than welcoming. Toward the back of the long room, Baldwin observed several other women quickly glance up and then return to interacting with two small children. *The queen's ladies-in-waiting*, he surmised.

Baldwin's gaze returned to the young girl sitting next to the queen. *This must be Judith, Louis' older sister*, he concluded. Both Ermentrude and her daughter were embroidering golden flowers on white silk tunics.

"You may be seated, Baldwin," the queen gestured to the cushioned bench placed opposite their lounge. "Louis will finish his studies with John Scotus shortly. He is a quick learner. All my children are quick learners," she beamed proudly at Judith. "Tell us of yourself, Baldwin . . . your home and your family," she invited as she resumed embroidering.

For the next half hour Baldwin described what it had been like growing up encountering wolves and bears in the "wilds" of Flanders. Queen Ermentrude seemed genuinely interested in every detail of his account, asking numerous questions to satisfy her curiosity. However, Judith kept her head down, embroidering nonstop as if she were not listening until a door at the back of the room opened and a young boy entered.

14

"Judith, it is y . . . your time with J . . . John Scotus," the young boy stammered hesitantly, glancing warily at Baldwin, who had risen to his feet and bowed at his approach. Prince Louis was slender and rather serious for his age, with the dark brown hair of his mother and the facial features of his father.

Queen Ermentrude made the introduction, "Louis, this is Baldwin Iron Arm, your new companion. He has mastered the use of the sword and halberd, among other things and will be assisting you to master them as well."

"How o ... old are you?" Louis ventured, looking up at Baldwin, who towered over him.

"I have attained my sixteenth year, my prince," Baldwin replied gently. And then, uncertain if he were overstepping his bounds, Baldwin ventured a question of his own. "May I ask, Prince Louis, do you like horses?"

Prince Louis picked up the dog and stroked his black, silky ears. "I ... I like all animals."

"That is definitely something we share, my prince." Baldwin smiled, grateful to have found a way to make the future training enjoyable, as Marius had advised.

From that first meeting, Baldwin's daily routine included presenting himself at the royal apartments and visiting with the queen and her daughter Judith until Louis joined them. Graciously, Queen Ermentrude appeared to genuinely enjoy their interaction. Princess Judith, however, remained aloof. Baldwin saw her smile only when one of her younger sisters came to talk to her or show her something she had learned from the queen's ladies-in-waiting. Then, a radiant smile lit up Judith's face, and she was quick with laughter and encouraging remarks. However, once they were joined by Louis, Judith's guarded manner returned, and to Baldwin's dismay, her beautiful face once again became inscrutable. *Why does she find my presence so distasteful?*

Baldwin turned the palace grounds into a mock battleground, choosing exercises based on Prince Louis' natural ability and the weapons with which the prince needed the most practice. Using

15

Prince Louis' love of animals, Baldwin devised several strength and skill exercises. At times, their play involved "rescuing" the small family dog named Maximus. Baldwin also taught Prince Louis feats of horsemanship. He demonstrated how using the most recent development—stirrups—helped knights remain in the saddle while fighting, allowing them to wield their weapons more forcefully by pushing off against the stirrups.

"Stirrups are great for mounting your horse if you become unseated. But do not rely on them. When you are taller, you must be able to leap astride your horse in full armor without the use of stirrups," Baldwin demonstrated for the prince. "If you become unseated during battle, there will not be time to have someone gather your mount or help you into your stirrups."

In time, they ventured farther afield, discussing defensive tactics as they rode through the narrow cobblestone streets of the village while assessing the vulnerability of the market or the monastery. Occasionally, they rode their horses to the Roman amphitheater outside the walls of Senlis and practiced mock combat as if they were gladiators in the coliseum performing for ten thousand spectators.

Prince Louis' skills increased daily, and he enthusiastically coaxed Princess Judith and her attendant into their war games whenever they encountered them walking about the palace grounds. Baldwin cast Judith as the fair princess whom the brave Prince Louis must rescue from the evil knight, Baldwin. *As long as she does not truly see me as the villain,* Baldwin considered ruefully.

Lest his own skills deteriorate through lack of challenge, Baldwin bid the armorers recruit sparring partners for his personal daily exercise. Every afternoon, Baldwin and Prince Louis went to the armory, not knowing who would try to best Baldwin's "Iron Arm" or even what weapon he would be challenged to use. Prince Louis eagerly joined a growing group of spectators as word spread among the ranks regarding the competitions.

"Are you afraid, g . . . going into c . . . combat?" Prince Louis wondered after Baldwin had bested one especially impressive opponent.

"Not if I prepare properly," Baldwin assured him. "Fear is a funny thing. It feels very much like excitement. If people cheer for my opponent, I tell myself the cheering is for me. And I tell myself whatever fear I feel is actually my eagerness for battle. It takes practice, but a warrior must be mentally strong, especially when his feelings say otherwise."

"Now I know w…why you are called 'Iron Arm!'" Louis cried enthusiastically. "When I am king, you will be my champion!"

"I would be most honored, my prince." Baldwin grinned as he and Louis returned to the palace to dress for the daily feast.

King Charles had many palaces, moving frequently from one to the next to ensure that the royal needs did not overburden the local resources. The king's table was always sumptuous. Wild boar, beef, venison, mutton, goose, fish, chicken, duck, pheasant, cheeses, fruits, and vegetables of all sorts, and a variety of wines were regularly hunted for in the wild or provided by the locals. For their offerings, local nobles, abbots, and bishops were often invited to share the feast with the royal court.

The royal family sat upon a raised platform at the head of the great hall along with Archbishop Hincmar, as ranking cleric, and any honored guests. Behind them hung a banner with the king's colors, while the table featured gold and silver plates and bejeweled goblets.

Baldwin sat with John Scotus and Gauzlin, who often shared their table with visiting dignitaries from Italy, Spain, Africa, and as far away as Constantinople. Humbled, Baldwin listened to the political talk while enjoying the sumptuous creations the royal kitchen produced. Servants offered tempting delicacies and repeatedly scurried to fill any empty cup from pitchers of watered wine, mead, or beer until each man or woman had their fill.

Baldwin's favorite part of the king's feast was the antics of the court jester. The jester in the court of King Charles was a permanent part of the household. Between the serving of the courses, he sang, played upon the lute, harp, or drums, danced, or recited the silly poems he composed. The jester knew a seemingly endless number of riddles and loved to poke fun at the guests.

John Scotus, because of his Irish heritage or because of his vast knowledge, often found himself on the stinging end of the jester's wit. Of course, Baldwin's nickname naturally made him a prime target as well. However, no one—including the king—was safe from the jester's barbs. Everyone left the great hall laughing at themselves as well as others.

❧

Five weeks after Baldwin began working with Prince Louis, Gauzlin stopped him as he arose from the feast. "Hold there, Baldwin, I would have a word with you."

"King Charles is pleased with your progress." Gauzlin clapped Baldwin on the shoulder in friendly encouragement. "The king wishes you to accompany Prince Louis to his coronation in Le Mans at the beginning of May."

"Will Prince Louis be moving to Neustria after the coronation? I understand young Prince Charles removed to Aquitaine directly after his coronation last year." Baldwin wondered.

"He did." Gauzlin continued carefully. "However, Young Charles will return to court in a few days' time. The lords in Aquitaine have rejected young Charles as king and are replacing him with the King's nephew, Pippin, who has escaped imprisonment and rallied his supporters. King Charles does not want the same thing to happen to Prince Louis after his coronation. He wishes to see Prince Louis firmly established in Neustria next month. The king's party will leave for Le Mans following the celebrations of Easter week. Take all your belongings with you."

When Baldwin returned to the room they shared, John Scotus sat at the writing table, sharpened quill in hand. John's gray-streaked, thinning hair was shorter than the usual style, and he preferred to go clean shaven in the Roman manner. John looked up and noticed the concern on Baldwin's face. He meticulously wiped the ink from his quill and laid it on an ink-splotched cloth on the table.

"What is troubling you, Baldwin?"

"The king tasked me with building Prince Louis' confidence and fighting skills. Louis is not much of a fighter, and he still stammers. I fear this journey to Le Mans will reveal I have accomplished nothing."

John Scotus shook his head, "Not so. You have done Prince Louis much good, Baldwin," he asserted. "To be sure, the prince still hesitates when he speaks and probably always will. However, everyone at court has noticed that Prince Louis is a happier young man and speaks out with more confidence since you have been working with him. That will serve him well with the Neustrians."

When Baldwin appeared unconvinced, John continued. "Prince Louis will never be the warrior his father is. But that does not mean he cannot become a great king. Louis has two traits that will help him when he comes to power. He is highly intelligent. And he is good. If he uses those traits to benefit his subjects, he will fare very well as king."

"But can he get through the coronation ceremony without mishap?"

John Scotus nodded. "Louis watched his younger brother go through a coronation last year and will know what to expect. And we will both be there to support him on the day."

"Who will counsel and tutor him when you return with King Charles?" Baldwin asked.

"Joseph, the court notary, will accompany Louis and assume my tutoring duties and King Charles will choose wise advisers for him. You, of course, will remain with him as a companion and military arts instructor. His need of you will only increase after his coronation."

John Scotus sighed deeply before continuing. "Young Charles has been deposed because the nobles in Aquitaine have never accepted King Charles. Some of them believe if they invite the king's brother, Louis the German, to take charge of Aquitaine, he will give them most of the lands King Charles currently holds there."

"Then why reinstate Pippin? Why not wait for Louis the German?"

"Pippin is merely a placeholder for Louis the German, who is busy putting down a Slavic rebellion in his own kingdom. Time will tell whether the nobles in Neustria are as rebellious as those in Aquitaine. But in the end, it will have nothing to do with you, me, nor even Prince Louis. Louis may receive the crown and scepter during the ceremony, but he will have no real power. This is simply King Charles' move to satisfy his lords in Neustria."

"Why would the Neustrians want Prince Louis to be part of an empty ceremony?" Baldwin was confused.

"Ah, that is an excellent question. Some of the lords hope King Charles will appoint them as administrators over Louis, giving them more influence in their province."

"So, they are hoping to use Prince Louis' coronation to gain more power for themselves?"

"Just so." John nodded sadly. "But Louis' coronation also benefits King Charles. By granting his son a provincial regnum, he warns off others who may have seen themselves as pretenders to that throne. King Charles will appoint Erispoë, leader of Brittany, as one of Louis' administrators. The peace negotiations between Francia and Brittany included the betrothal of Prince Louis and Erispoë's daughter—ensuring that Brittany will remain loyal to King Charles. What you are witnessing, young Baldwin, is a game of strategy at its highest level. The players are the king, his brother, and his nobles. One makes a strategic move and waits to see what countermoves the others will make. You and I are merely game pieces. Supporting Prince Louis in Neustria is as important as if you were defending King Charles on the battlefield."

After a short silence, Baldwin ventured to ask a question that had been on his mind for some time. "May I ask about another member of the royal family?"

"Ask away, Baldwin. I will do my best to give satisfaction."

"Princess Judith," Baldwin hesitated before continuing. "From Princess Judith I sense distance . . . even dislike. Have I offended her?"

"Ah, Princess Judith. That would be a natural reaction considering her circumstances." John's expression softened when speaking of Judith. "Princess Judith and Prince Louis have a special bond. Your coming, although good for Prince Louis, has been painful for his sister. Your companionship with Prince Louis has taken precious time away from Princess Judith prior to her brother's departure for Le Mans."

"Is there anything I can do?" Baldwin wondered aloud.

"Nothing for the princess, I'm afraid. You and I can only tend to the tasks at hand and support the prince in his challenges. Neustrian nobles will stop at nothing to increase their power at Louis' expense. You must be vigilant on young Louis' behalf."

Baldwin knew John Scotus was correct. Nothing he could do would ease Judith's situation. The princess was just one small pawn in King Charles's desperate game of survival. He turned his focus to the task before him. He had one month remaining to help Prince Louis prepare for Le Mans. He hoped the coronation would be as uneventful as John Scotus had predicted.

✎

A few days after Easter, the doorkeeper to the royal apartments refused Baldwin admittance, explaining that only the royal family, servants, and the queen's physician were allowed to enter as the queen would soon give birth. Gauzlin also informed Baldwin that his time with young Prince Louis would be suspended for several days because King Charles wished Louis to attend special councils in preparation for his removal to Neustria.

Finding himself at loose ends, Baldwin roamed the palace grounds. He made good friends with the jovial Martin, as well as with the messengers, smiths, carters, and even the grooms. He continued his daily weapons exercises, accompanied the royal huntsmen in their quest for game, and visited with the keepers of the royal hunting dogs. He exchanged occasional greetings with the knights in the barracks, but he was no longer envious of their camaraderie. Instead, Baldwin found himself missing the companionship of his young, royal charge.

After several days, John Scotus informed Baldwin that the queen had been successfully delivered of her child and that they could resume visiting the royal apartments. Baldwin approached

21

the doorkeeper, eager to be admitted. Upon entering, he welcomed the now familiar scene. Ladies-in-waiting oversaw the two younger children playing at the back of the room, and he was greeted by Maximus with wagging tail and joyful bark. However, the queen was not in her usual place. Instead, Judith sat alone on the lounge, quietly embroidering.

Baldwin's discussion with John Scotus had helped him empathize with Judith's reluctance to befriend him. And although they had interacted occasionally during Louis' arms training on the palace grounds, he feared she might keep him standing. Baldwin was, therefore, surprised when Judith graciously invited him to be seated. *She is every bit her mother's daughter,* he decided.

"May I enquire after the health of Queen Ermentrude?" Baldwin ventured following their exchange of pleasantries.

Judith's brow clouded with concern. "The queen fares well. However, my newest sister, Hildegarde, is of delicate health. My mother wishes to remain with her."

Baldwin knew what that meant. Many children did not survive beyond their first year. Hildegarde could be one of those. He expressed his wish that both mother and child would thrive and then steered the conversation into less dangerous waters. When Prince Louis joined them, Baldwin was sorry to see the conversation end–his first real opportunity to know Princess Judith better.

In the coming days, Baldwin discovered that he truly liked Judith. Her poise, her wit and her intelligence were all apparent and admirable. And Judith no longer seemed to resent his presence. *Perhaps, she may someday see me as a mutual friend.*

CHAPTER III

MARCH through MAY 856

Embroidery was not Judith's passion, as it was her mother's. The queen's work adorned altar cloths and priestly vestments in Francia's finest cathedrals. Exquisite in its detail, perfect in its execution, the queen never needed the chalk guide to maintain a straight line. It was as if she were one with her fabric and needle. The result was magnificent.

However, once Judith entered her twelfth year, she and her mother spent several hours each day embroidering clothing for Judith in anticipation of her future marriage. The Mistress of the Wardrobe had made robes and tunics longer than the ones Judith currently wore, stitching up the hems to be let down later as the princess matured. As they finished embellishing each garment, Queen Ermentrude reminded Judith, "You will always have a part of me wherever you go."

As the days passed, Judith began to understand that the intricate embroidery allowed Queen Ermentrude to shut out the world and focus only on the movements of the hand. The queen could block any sorrow she felt in losing her young sons, Lothar and Carlomann, to the church, or the removal of her seven-year-old son, Charles, to Aquitaine, or the imminent loss of her oldest two children. Pain disappeared–if only for a moment–when she focused on just the next stitch. Embroidery was how Ermentrude moved forward. One stitch at a time. One breath at a time.

As her twelfth birthday and a possible arranged marriage drew closer, Judith began to cherish these moments with her mother, along with any time she could spend with her dearest Louis. With only two years separating them in age, Judith and

Louis had been playmates and confidantes from the beginning. *If anyone in this world understands me, it is him.* Judith focused on her embroidery. One stitch at a time. One breath at a time.

The doorkeeper announced that Baldwin Iron Arm requested to meet with Prince Louis. The night before, the king had informed them all that Louis was to have a companion who would train him in military prowess when he was not occupied with his scholarly studies. It was a blow to both Louis and Judith, who loved spending any unclaimed time with each other. For the remainder of the evening, the siblings talked, promising to support each other in whatever their futures might bring.

When the doorkeeper admitted Louis' new companion, Judith barely glanced up. Logically, she knew that Baldwin Iron Arm was not responsible for the changes being thrust on her and her brother. Yet, she kept her head down, refusing to like this large, dark-haired intruder who had been thrust into their lives. She had always thought of herself as Louis' companion. *Accept it with grace,* she reminded herself.

Louis entered the room and approached them. "Judith, it is your t . . . time with J . . . John Scotus," he stammered, looking up warily at the tall young man who stood and bowed at the prince's entrance.

Judith felt a quick, sharp pain in her chest and a tear threatened to betray her as the queen introduced Baldwin to Louis, and they were gone. Carefully laying aside her sewing, Judith made her way to the school room where John Scotus smiled at her approach.

"Good day, Princess. Today, I thought we might continue our discussion on the four divisions of nature," he began. "What do you remember of them?"

"The first division is that which creates and is not created," Judith responded readily. "God creates but is not created. And we can see His very nature in the beauty of His creations."

"Can you give me a syllogism or a fact-based logical argument which supports that statement?" John's questions forced Judith to examine her beliefs and defend them through proofs and logic.

Did she need more evidence? Did she fail to use proper logic? Did she need to reexamine her conclusions?

By the end of their two hours together, Judith's mind felt invigorated. The challenging exercises in reasoning left her hopeful that, if she were to think hard enough, she might be able to make sense of her own life.

Leaving the school room, Judith was at loose ends. Typically, this had been time she could spend with Louis. She played briefly with her two younger sisters, Rotrud and Ermentrud, who, at ages two and four, were full of life and mischief. The noble ladies who served her mother and helped with the royal children shared court gossip, but Judith found herself restless and went to the library for a book of poetry. At mid-morning she met with Queen Ermentrude and Gauzlin, who instructed her regarding her future role in managing a royal household.

"As a queen, you will oversee your seneschal's efficient running of the palace," Gauzlin explained. "You will make decisions in furnishing and decorating the king's palaces. When hosting noble visitors, you must provide for their sleeping accommodations."

"You might also be asked to sit beside the king in the throne room and offer council," Queen Ermentrude added. "When your father is away, I often settle disputes between the nobles."

Judith, who was accomplished in working with numbers, found Gauzlin's review of the accounts most interesting.

"How much money should a queen spend on provisioning the court?" she wanted to know.

"A queen must manage within the boundaries of the king's income," Ermentrude smiled. "That includes purchasing gifts for foreign envoys and annual gifts for nobles and the king's military officers. And on feast and holy days, the queen is expected to provide for the poor and the widows."

"Keep a careful inventory of the king's treasure and guard that treasure within your bedchamber, and you will know how much you can spend," Gauzlin assured her.

When her hour with Gauzlin and the queen ended, Judith sought out Hemma, her personal attendant, and required her presence as she walked the palace grounds, hoping they might encounter Prince Louis and his companion. Hemma placed a fur-lined and hooded mantle around Judith's shoulders and fastened it with a jewel inlaid brooch, before donning her own gray woolen one. She carefully removed Judith's silk slippers, replacing them with sturdier leather boots before they descended the grand staircase and stepped out onto the palace grounds.

As they walked about the still-dormant herb gardens in the brisk but sunny afternoon breeze, Judith realized she knew little about Hemma. For the past four years, Hemma had dressed her, prepared her bath, and kept her clothes clean and in good order. Tall and of medium build, with a quiet and gentle manner, Hemma followed the princess toward the chapel.

"Are you from Senlis, Hemma?" Judith probed

"No, Princess, my family home was south of St. Wandrille."

"How came you to our service?"

Hemma hesitated before answering. "The Bishop of Compiègne referred me to the king's seneschal."

"And what of your family?"

"My father was a knight, a captain in the king's service. The king granted him a *benefice* in the north, and that is where he built our home."

"Any brothers or sisters?"

Again, a hesitation, "I had an older brother, Princess."

They continued past the orchard, where Judith spotted tiny new leaves emerging on the apple, plum, and peach trees. After a brutally frigid winter, any sign of a much-needed spring was reason to rejoice–despite Louis' looming departure. She wondered how Hemma had adjusted to her own separation.

"Do you miss your family terribly?"

"My family, Princess . . . are all dead," Hemma replied softly.

They walked on further in silence. Judith was stunned to hear Hemma had lost her family. She was torn between wanting to know what tragic circumstances had befallen Hemma and fearing that her questions might bring more pain to her attendant. Reaching the chapel, they stepped inside to get out of the chill.

After acknowledging the figure of the crucified Christ, they rested on a pew at the rear of the chapel, the peaceful ambiance giving Judith the courage to venture.

"You need not do so, but if you are able to speak of it, please tell me what happened to your family."

Hemma stared down at her hands, restlessly plucking at the wool of her mantel. Finally, she began. "It was four years ago, this January. A servant came to the house to tell my father he could see smoke on the horizon, coming from the direction of the abbey at St. Wandrille. At first, we thought someone was burning debris or maybe a building had caught fire through carelessness with a candle. But, as the smoke grew in volume, my father realized something was terribly amiss. Our home was on the Seine, and we knew there was always a possibility that Northmen could come down the river. My father told my mother to take me and our maid to the stable and prepare to run and hide if he shouted a warning. It was not long before we heard the shouting. The Northmen were much closer than we had realized.

My mother, our maid, and I ran into the forest, looking for someplace to hide. My mother bid me lie down in a ditch while she and the maid covered me with fallen limbs and dried, frozen brush and told me not to move. I could hear the Danish devils shouting. My mother ran, leading them in the opposite direction from where she had hidden me. I heard her scream and expected the Northmen would discover me at any moment. Eventually, all noise ceased, and it was strangely quiet. I waited as long as I could. Then, I made my way carefully back to what remained of our home. What I found there, I cannot describe. Everything of value had been taken from the house. Food, clothing, treasure. What was left had been smashed. My family, our servants, and even some of our animals had been murdered in the most brutal manner. Any animal which was good for food had been carried off." Hemma's voice broke, and she paused.

"What did you do? How did you survive?"

After a moment, Hemma continued her tale. "I was afraid to go toward St. Wandrille as smoke was still coming from that direction. So, I headed south, where I joined a small group of survivors from other holdings. The next day, some of the monks who had escaped with the relics from St. Wandrille joined our company. We made our way to Rouen and afterward to Beauvais. But in each place, we heard the Northmen were there, burning, looting, ravishing, and murdering. Finally, we found shelter in Compiègne. After a few days, the bishop called me to his office. He asked if I had family I could go to. When I told him I did not, he offered me two choices. He could place me in a convent, or he could write to the king's seneschal and see if they had a position for me in service at the palace. I had no feeling of being called to the church, so I chose the latter. A month later, the bishop told me I would serve the royal family. It has been my honor to serve you since that time, Princess."

Judith impulsively reached for Hemma's hand. "I am so sorry for your terrible loss."

As they began walking back toward the palace, Judith reflected on what Hemma had shared with her. Judith had heard the king and queen speak of Northmen and the danger they were to the kingdom. But this was the first time she really understood the horror and devastation of the vicious attacks. Her life had been sheltered from such brutality. Her father had surely heard many such stories as Hemma's. No wonder he and the other Frankish kings paid enormous ransoms to make the Danes leave. If the king were not in a position to fight, he must pay the ransom. Pay to protect his people.

Nearing the stables, Judith observed Martin talking to a messenger wearing crimson and gold and bearing the banner of Aethelwulf, King of Wessex, with its striking gold wyvern on a crimson background. Judith had first seen that banner at the arrival of Prince Alfred when he had stayed briefly with their court a few years previously. Alfred's father, King Aethelwulf, had sent him alone on pilgrimage to Rome as a child of only five years of age. Then, last year, King Aethelwulf, together with Alfred, stayed with them on their joint pilgrimage to Rome.

When the messenger departed, Judith approached Martin eagerly. "Martin, was that a messenger from the King of Wessex? Is he yet in Rome?"

"Yes, Princess. The King of Wessex will celebrate Holy Week in the holy city."

"Do you know what his message was to the court?"

"Ah, Princess, how would I know? His message was to the court and not to me. That is a question you should be asking your father," he teased affectionately. "But, who knows, we may have English visitors this summer."

As they entered the palace and Hemma dressed Judith for the banquet, Judith reflected on their stroll through the palace grounds. She was disappointed not to have encountered Louis and Baldwin Iron Arm. However, if they had, Hemma would never have shared her tragic story.

Judith would never again see Hemma only as an attendant. *I am glad Louis has found a companion in the tall, dark knight from Flanders. Perhaps I have found one in Hemma as well.*

ॐ

Emerging flowers in the palace gardens and orchard trees heavy with fragrant pink and white blossoms filled Judith with anticipation of new life. Easter was fast approaching, and Judith looked forward to the queen's confinement. It would be an exciting and wondrous event– if all went well.

Judith's walks with Hemma were now a welcome part of her daily routine whenever the weather permitted. She was secretly delighted when they encountered Louis and Baldwin Iron Arm engaged in military training and mock battles. Louis eagerly showed off his new skills. Judith could no longer resent the kind and cheerful Baldwin, especially when she saw his positive influence on her brother. *It is for the best. I am happy that Louis will have a friend in Le Mans.*

Then, young Charles returned unexpectedly after only seven months as King of Aquitaine. He was subdued and did not speak much, in complete opposition to his naturally jovial disposition. Young Charles had always been a jokester. Judith and Louis had often teased their brother, claiming that if he had not been born a prince of Francia, he would have become a prince of jesters. Now, young Charles rarely smiled and spent much of his time with the king's advisers.

"What do they talk about in Council?" Judith asked young Charles and Louis one morning as they broke their fast after morning mass.

Louis and young Charles exchanged glances before young Charles answered. "How to resolve disputes among the nobles and any trouble in the provinces. Father has more problems than you know."

"What, for instance?" Judith prompted them.

"P . . . Pestilence. The p . . . pestilence has taken many lives this year." Louis responded earnestly.

"That is terrible! I had no idea."

"How c . . . could you? It has not reached the p . . . palace."

"And Danes," young Charles chimed in. "Every year brings more attacks. You can thank cousin Pippin for that."

"How so? I thought he was in confinement at St. Medard monastery in Soissons?"

"He escaped. Cousin Pippin is a Dane at heart. When he was King of Aquitaine before me, he brought the Viking, Jarl Oscar, into the country to assist him in his war against father. Jarl Oscar is gone, but Vikings are still looting and burning wherever they choose."

Judith's anger burned hot as she recalled the horrific attack on Hemma's family. "I envy you both. I wish I could use a sword and fight the Danes!"

When her brothers remained silent, Judith asked, "What else do you speak of in Council? Louis told me he is learning from the council how a king uses his advisers. But, what of you, Charles?"

"Oh, I am there mainly to answer questions about the rebel lords in Aquitaine and what their next move is likely to be," young Charles replied. "I never had any real power. I had no chancery and could issue no edicts. I could not even bestow privileges or *benefices*. Father and my administrators decided everything. No wonder the lords of Aquitaine pushed me out. They are hoping for someone who will increase their power and wealth. Louis will find it much the same in Neustria, I fear. A king has no power if he cannot reward his nobles' loyalty with a *benefice* of some kind."

"Was there no one you could turn to?"

"Only the few that accompanied me to Limoges. And they were father's men." Young Charles looked at Louis earnestly. "If your companion is faithful and loyal, keep him close by."

"B . . . Baldwin is f . . . faithful," Louis assured him.

"Then, I envy you, brother. I wish father had found someone like that for me."

Judith regretted the loneliness in young Charles' voice. "It must have been miserable!"

"The worst part of it was having no one I could trust. I am not sorry to be out of it. I only wonder what Father has planned for me next."

"As do we all," Judith agreed.

Easter week was Judith's favorite time of year - a time to reflect on love and forgiveness and on being a better Christian. She also loved the pageantry and beauty of the celebrations. Every day of Holy Week was sacred, commemorating the final week of Jesus' life.

On Palm Sunday, Easter Holy Week began with the bells of every chapel ringing out the glad tidings. Archbishop Hincmar, the royal family, and other nobles gathered outside the city walls. When all were in place, Hincmar, representing Christ and bearing a cross bedecked with flowers, rode his horse through the city gate. He was followed by a massive procession led by the royal family and nobles singing the Hosanna. As they passed, the people of Senlis strewed branches and flowers before the feet of the processionals to represent the palm fronds the Jews had strewn upon Christ's entry into Jerusalem.

When the procession reached the doors of the monastery of St. John the Baptist, the pure sound of young boys' voices from the monastery choir sang out.

> Glory, praise, and honor,
> O Christ, our Savior-King,
> To thee in glad Hosannas
> Inspired children sing.

After mass, Archbishop Hincmar blessed the branches the processionals had brought with them. Then, they wound their way back toward the palace, again with Hincmar bearing the flower-bedecked cross.

Easter Sunday mass was especially solemn, and the Easter feast in the great hall was sumptuous and grand. Instead of his usual hilarious antics, the jester played soothing melodies on the lute and the harp. A choir of young nobles from the palace school entertained the company, and John Scotus favored them all by reciting a poem he had written for the occasion. *If only I could keep this feeling of peace with me,* Judith wished.

Awakened early in the morning to the sound of urgent voices and movement in the royal apartments, Judith suspected that the queen was giving birth. Queen Ermentrude had confined herself to her chamber shortly before Easter in anticipation of the upcoming event. Special prayers had been offered for the queen and her unborn child at mass each day during Holy Week. The queen's midwives had taken turns in constant attendance, and there had been much speculation throughout the palace. Would the queen give birth to a son or a daughter? Would the child be healthy as most of her children had been, or would it be crippled like her son Lothar? And there was always the unspoken concern about the queen's own health.

Judith dressed herself, not waiting to wake Hemma, who slept behind a screen in a far corner of her chamber. Oil lamp in hand, she moved quickly toward her mother's chamber but hesitated when she heard deep moans coming from the other side of the door. Her father's bedchamber remained shut tight. Men did not enter birthing rooms, after all.

Judith had not attended her youngest sister's birth two years earlier. Now, she was drawn to help her mother if she could. She also found herself more than curious. Judith knew she would be expected to give birth when she married. Pushing back the rising panic at the thought, she opened the door.

The chamber was shrouded in darkness except for light from two oil lamps, allowing the midwife to do her work. Judith could see the hunched figure of her mother sitting on a three-legged wooden chair in the middle of the room. The queen wore only her shift, pulled up to reveal her bare legs. The midwife was bending over a metal basin she had placed under the chair.

"Is that you Bertha?" the midwife called without looking up. "Good that you came quickly. This child is impatient. Not long now before the head crowns."

Another cry of anguish escaped the queen's lips, causing Judith to rush to her side. "Mother, how can I help you?"

"Ah, Princess Judith. This is no place for you," the midwife's voice was authoritative. "I have already sent the queen's attendant to bring my assistant."

"But I wish to help," Judith argued passionately. "Is there nothing I can do?"

The pain eased long enough for the queen to speak. "Let her stay, Marie. Let . . . her stay."

"As you wish, my lady," the midwife attempted to calm the queen. "Well then, Princess, you may take this salve and massage it gently on the queen's neck and shoulders. That may ease her pains. And if you recite your prayers softly, that may calm her soul." She handed Judith a small clay pot filled with an aromatic and creamy concoction.

Grateful for something to do, Judith placed her lamp on the floor and immediately went to work. Her mother's cries were intense and came faster and faster, but Judith did her best to keep praying aloud and lightly massaging the queen's shoulders. As she worked, she considered the strange scene she had become part of. The chair upon which her mother sat was unlike any she had seen before, with a large opening cut into its seat, allowing blood and other fluids to flow freely into the basin beneath. This opening also gave access for the midwife to check the progress of the birth.

By the time the queen's attendant returned with the second midwife, the queen's pains were constant. Judith stopped massaging her mother's back. Instead, she held on and grasped the queen's hands when her mother reached up for hers.

"The child . . . is coming," her mother gasped, squeezing Judith's hands even tighter.

And then, with one last agonizing wail, the queen's labor was complete. Judith watched Marie catch the tiny blood-smeared infant girl, holding her up for the queen to see. Then Bertha took a piece of twine and tied it around the cord protruding from the child's belly and snipped it with a pair of shears.

Marie placed the child in a linen-lined basket and began working to wash her and encourage her to breathe. At last, a pitiful, tiny cry rang out, and everyone smiled. Bertha, meanwhile, saw to the queen. She made sure the afterbirth was complete and then allowed the queen's attendant to wash away the blood and perspiration from the queen's body. Ermentrude was then bound with rags to catch any remaining blood and helped into her bed.

Judith had the joyful task of holding her new little sister while the queen was being cared for and the midwives packed up their instruments. She gazed down at the small, swaddled bundle and wondered what the future would bring for the newest member of the royal family. She expected her own marriage would take place within the year. "I fear we will not know each other for long, dear sister," she whispered to the babe.

The child's face was swollen, making it difficult for her to open her eyes, but she appeared beautiful to Judith. Turning to her mother, who was lying back upon her cushions, Judith asked, "Have you chosen a name for her?"

Ermentrude's voice seemed no louder than a whisper. "Hildegarde. The king said if I were to have a girl, he wishes her to be named Hildegarde." The queen smiled peacefully and closed her eyes.

CHAPTER IV

MARCH and APRIL 856

Hincmar, Archbishop of Reims, looked up approvingly at the towering spire, which—when the cathedral was finally completed and the scaffolding removed—would be a lasting symbol of all he hoped to achieve in his life. Hincmar saw many similarities between what he was trying to accomplish with the expansion and renovation of Notre-Dame de Reims and with his work at the court of Charles, King of Francia. Planning and patience had brought the cathedral thus far, just as planning and patience had brought Hincmar to a place where he possessed great influence in King Charles' court.

From early childhood, Hincmar had been destined for a life of religious power. His noble parents sent him as a young child to St. Denis Abbey, where Hincmar was raised by the Church. The renowned Abbot Hilduin mentored Hincmar and took him to serve the court of Emperor Louis the Pious. Hincmar's natural gifts flourished amidst the politics of the emperor's court. And his keen observations taught him how to manipulate people and situations.

Determined to become the power behind King Charles' throne, Hincmar had cultivated a bond with Charles while serving in his father's court. Upon the emperor's death, Hincmar's advice helped King Charles retain the provinces he inherited from his father. All had worked according to plan. King Charles not only named Hincmar the Archbishop of Reims, but he had given him other holdings as well, including Notre-Dame at Compiègne and St. Germer-de-Fly.

The archbishop's breath released little puffs of steam into the early March air as he observed workers on the inside scaffolding reaching up to the majestically vaulted ceilings still under construction. Hincmar had already commissioned artisans skilled in mosaic, tapestry, and sculpture to begin work on future adornments for the cathedral.

"Archbishop, preparations for your journey to Senlis are complete," his manservant approached. "We can depart whenever you are ready."

The archbishop nodded at the news. As much as he enjoyed his occasional visits to oversee the progress of his cathedral, he was eager to return to his place of influence at the royal court. *I am shaping an empire!* His ambitions were as lofty as the vaulted cathedral ceilings of Notre-Dame de Reims.

After three days in the saddle, Hincmar was relieved to arrive in Senlis. Groaning slightly as he dismounted, he accepted the stiffness that came with his half-century of living. Short in stature but still strong in body, Hincmar was grateful he was not of a sickly constitution. However, the silvering of his tonsured hair, as well as his aching joints, reminded him that time was a precious resource.

The archbishop hastened to freshen up before presenting himself at the throne room. Being gone too long from court was always risky. King Charles had other advisers, John Scotus being one such, who could use Hincmar's absence as an opportunity to increase their own influence with the king or to promote their own favored causes. King Charles also had many enemies, and Hincmar was eager to present his latest idea for strengthening the king's tenuous hold on his troubled kingdom.

When the door keeper admitted him to the throne room, King Charles was conferring with both John Scotus, and Gauzlin, the king's seneschal. The king motioned for Hincmar to approach.

"What say you, Archbishop? With you finally present, should we not be able to make up our minds on arrangements for the summer assembly in time for the feast?"

Hincmar wisely went along with King Charles' attempt at humor. "Sire, making up our minds assumes we are still in possession of them. Have I not heard you question more than once if your advisers had lost theirs?"

"Well said, Hincmar," the king laughed. "Now I remember why I keep you close by me. But first, tell us how goes the work on Notre-Dame de Reims?"

"It goes well, Sire." Hincmar was glad he could present a favorable report on the king's substantial investment. "Work has begun on the inside of the structure."

"I am glad to hear it," King Charles smiled. "We need more such happy reports these days."

"What of the young man Gauzlin has found as companion for Prince Louis?" John Scotus proffered. "Is this not cause to rejoice, Sire?"

"Always the optimist, John Scotus," the king laughed. "Now I remember why I keep *you* close by me."

The conversation returned to the business most on the king's mind—the summer assembly. Hincmar was pleased when the king agreed that holding the assembly in June at the Roman fortress at Neaufles would be the most appropriate location to discuss the major problem facing the kingdom—the Danish raiders. With the location and date for the assembly settled, King Charles turned his attention to the business of the assembly.

"Now, as to the presentation of the new laws for the session . . ." the king began.

Every year, new laws agreed upon at an exclusive winter assembly of the king's most trusted nobles were ratified at the large general assembly in summer. King Charles placed immense importance on the drafting and presentation of the laws and relied heavily upon Hincmar's skill in both. Well-drawn up and well-presented laws could mean the difference between nobles who left the assembly satisfied with their king or nobles who were restive and on the brink of rebellion.

When they finished discussing the business of the summer assembly, Hincmar broached another subject. "Sire, have you further considered a possible marriage alliance for Princess Judith?"

King Charles' brow clouded briefly before he responded, "To be sure, Hincmar, I have given much consideration to Princess Judith's future. However, this is not a matter to be resolved quickly. Therefore, we will discuss this on the morrow." He smiled and turned to John Scotus. "My appetite tells me a fine feast awaits us. How do you advise me, John? Shall we eat or talk?"

"My best counsel, Sire," John Scotus replied in mock gravity, "is we listen to your appetite. Let us eat."

"Agreed!" King Charles laughed. "Let us eat!"

୨

The next day, when the council reconvened, King Charles raised the subject of Princess Judith, as promised. "Share with us your thoughts on the matter," the king invited Hincmar.

This was the moment Hincmar had prepared for. This is where he excelled. He must use just the right tone to bring King Charles to the correct conclusion.

"Thank you, Sire," he began. "Last year, following the death of his wife, King Aethelwulf of Wessex and his son Alfred visited your court on their pilgrimage to Rome. At that time, you offered the services of Bishop Markward as a guide to assist the king on his journey. Bishop Markward has written to tell me that the king will depart Rome in the not-too-distant future and should arrive here in midsummer."

"I can confirm that information, Archbishop," Gauzlin jumped in. "I planned to inform the council of the missive I received today from King Aethelwulf to that effect."

Gauzlin turned to King Charles and delivered his report. "King Aethelwulf's messenger arrived shortly before this meeting began, requesting leave to pass through Francia on their return to Wessex. He hopes the king's court can provide accommodations for them. They will be a party of eighty-four, including the king and the young prince, clergy, nobles, warriors, and servants. King

Aethelwulf plans to leave Rome in mid-May and arrive at your court sometime in July."

King Charles acknowledged his seneschal with a nod and then turned back to the archbishop. "Come to your point, Archbishop Hincmar. You would not mention King Aethelwulf in connection with Judith if you were not proposing an alliance. Are you proposing a betrothal between Judith and King Aethelwulf or with Prince Alfred, the son?" the king probed.

"I am proposing neither, Sire." Hincmar protested. "I merely wish to provide you with as many details as possible, so you can arrive at the wisest, most appropriate decision for your kingdom."

"Proceed, then," King Charles settled down upon his throne to listen and consider.

"Thank you, Sire," Hincmar bowed briefly to King Charles before continuing. "This council is all too aware that every year brings more savage attacks on our villages, monasteries, and even on your royal holdings. Only last year, the Danes sacked almost every settlement with anything of value up and down the Loire. The cost to your kingdom in lives and treasure is enormous and growing each year. Should we not seek an alliance that could assist you in ridding Francia of these brutal Northmen?" Hincmar paused to ensure the king was with him.

"Naturally," King Charles replied. "Such an alliance would be most beneficial to all in our realm. But who could really help us stand against the Danes? No one since my grandfather has been able to vanquish them. Not any of my brothers. Not the English."

"True, Sire. But King Aethelwulf has had more success against the Northmen than any other. He has repelled numerous attacks and was victorious in his famous defeat of them at Aclea. Since his youth, King Aethelwulf's success on the battlefield has increased Wessex's holdings and wealth. His experience would make him a valuable ally, whether you face a Danish . . . or a Frankish foe." Hincmar paused for effect.

"I see your logic, Archbishop," John Scotus jumped in. "Joining forces to fight a common enemy provides the essence of a strong military alliance. However, I question whether a union through marriage is necessary to accomplish that goal."

Hincmar knew he must tread lightly. With the recent visit to the court by the widowed King of Wessex, seeds of an improbable plan had begun germinating. The return visit of King Aethelwulf presented an undeniable opportunity—one that could expand King Charles' power and change the course of history. He hoped to lead the king to that same conclusion.

"A marriage alliance is not absolutely necessary to secure a military one," Hincmar admitted. "But it is a wise move, nonetheless. Next to blood ties, marriage ties are strongest."

"Sometimes stronger," the king interjected ruefully.

Hincmar was pleased to have the king's agreement. "But I am here to advise, not to decide. With Princess Judith attaining her full twelve years this fall, I merely ask the question. Have you any better alliance in mind? Perhaps in a year or two, another king will be in search of a royal wife. But would he provide any better assistance with the Vikings or with the unrest in Francia's provinces? And what damage will be done to your kingdom in the interim?"

"What of a betrothal to Prince Alfred?" John Scotus queried. "They are more of an age. King Aethelwulf has passed half a century. A bit long in the tooth as a match for Princess Judith, surely."

Ignoring John Scotus, the archbishop continued. "Prince Alfred will not be old enough to marry for another seven or eight years. And with three older brothers, he will never assume the throne. Sire, your mother, the Empress Judith, was much younger than your father. Surely, your daughter—the great-granddaughter of Emperor Charles the Great and a princess of Francia—should not become anything less than a queen."

"Wessex refuses to have queens," Gauzlin pointed out. "They are the 'wife of the king' only and have no status."

"True," Hincmar admitted carefully. "That is why I do not advise arranging a marriage between King Aethelwulf and Princess Judith unless the King of Wessex agrees to a coronation of Princess Judith as Queen of Wessex . . . and a consecration with the holy chrism as well. The addition of the consecration ceremony would provide Judith with greater status than any other queen before her. Any son she bears to King Aethelwulf, would have greater right to rule than those born to his previous wife. Your grandson could sit on the throne of Wessex."

"Even all kings are not anointed with the holy chrism. How can you persuade King Aethelwulf to go against his kingdom's tradition and agree to such a coronation for a queen?" John Scotus wondered.

Hincmar smiled. "King Aethelwulf also needs allies. His eldest son, Aethelbald, may challenge his father's right to the throne when he returns from pilgrimage. However, a prestigious marriage alliance with Francia might help him retain his kingdom. It would also increase trade and culture between Francia and Wessex. King Aethelwulf would have to be mad to refuse a marriage so profoundly beneficial to his kingdom."

The king arose from his throne. After pacing the room for several minutes, he turned to Gauzlin, "When King Aethelwulf's messenger has rested, send him on his way with this response: King Charles' court will gladly receive Aethelwulf, King of Wessex, at our palace in Verberie this summer. We invite him to remain with us for as long as he desires."

King Charles turned back to Hincmar. "Now then, Archbishop, I suppose we shall see if the King of Wessex is mad or not."

Although Hincmar was pleased with the council's outcome, he wished John Scotus had been more supportive. John Scotus was an accomplished scholar and useful in furthering the king's plans to increase education throughout his realm. But too often John Scotus focused on the needs of the individual when there was an empire to be preserved and strengthened.

Whatever strengthened the kingdom increased the power of the church as well. Rome provided God's acceptance of a king's right to rule with its network of priests, monks, and nuns who could persuade the people to serve their rightful king. In turn, the state granted the church lands and money to build chapels, monasteries, and abbeys—bringing more power to the church.

As Archbishop of Reims, Hincmar corresponded with abbots and abbesses, priests, and bishops throughout the Christian world. Upon leaving the throne room, Hincmar sent messengers to fellow clergy scattered throughout the kingdom of Wessex, requesting information regarding the political situation there. He would be prepared if King Charles needed more convincing when the question of Judith's marriage arose again.

The archbishop also sent messengers to Neustria seeking information on the lords in that province–in particular–Robert the Strong. King Charles had appointed Robert the Strong as administrator over the Duchy of Le Mans three years earlier. Men entrusted with power often believed themselves entitled to accrue more. How would Robert the Strong react when his influence was diminished by the coronation of King Charles' young son, Prince Louis?

By the time Hincmar's messenger to Neustria returned with responses from his contacts in Le Mans, Tours, Anjou, Touraine, and Wessex, Hincmar would be deep in preparation for the most important celebration of the Christian calendar–Easter Holy Week. Hincmar hoped to bring the latest information he had gleaned to the council prior to their departure for Le Mans.

ॐ

Shortly after Easter, Hincmar took his place at the council table where the king waited with young Charles and Prince Louis. The newly appointed advisers for Prince Louis had also joined the council in preparation for Louis' coronation. At King Charles' request Hincmar shared the news he had lately received.

"Vikings have sacked Orléans. The Danes took the townspeople by surprise, and they were unable to mount a defense. The result is what you might expect–widespread destruction."

A discussion ensued as to how the kingdom might defend against the increasing Viking attacks. Council members objected to every proposal. Paying ransom to the Danes was deemed only a temporary fix and forced the king to raise unpopular levies on his nobles. Some feared rebellious lords would commandeer any newly constructed fortifications to use against King Charles himself. Other proposed projects were either too time-consuming to execute or too costly. Hincmar had heard this discussion too many times. *In the end, no logical solution to the problem will be agreed upon, and they will move on to discuss other business,* he predicted.

King Charles' nephew, the rebel King Pippin of Aquitaine, was the next item of concern. Hincmar provided the council with an update on developments in Aquitaine.

"My sources in Aquitaine inform me that the rebel lords already regret expelling young King Charles in favor of the drunken and dissolute Pippin. As expected, they have invited King Louis the German to replace him. However, if Louis the German does not invade soon, the lords of Aquitaine may consider restoring young King Charles to his throne." Hincmar nodded pointedly at a scowling young Charles.

After some discussion, the King moved on to address Prince Louis' coronation in Le Mans. "Louis, Joseph will act as your tutor as well as one of your advisers." The king acknowledged Joseph before continuing. "As a court notary, Joseph will also issue official edicts in your name should we decide that is necessary."

"Th . . . Thank you, Sire," Prince Louis responded. "Will Erispoë b . . . be among my advisers?"

The king's brows furrowed. "Erispoë will have some authority and duties as an administrator, although not as much as he supposes. Consult him on matters of management only—not on matters of politics. Any thoughts from the council?"

Hincmar did not hold back, "As young Louis' future father-in-law, Erispoë's interests lie in Louis' welfare. However, his appointment may have caused problems with Robert the Strong."

"How so?" King Charles demanded.

"The bishops in Neustria say Robert the Strong is unhappy with your removing control of the Duchy of Le Mans from him and giving it to Prince Louis."

"Did Robert think the duchy was a permanent *benefice*? He was appointed caretaker only. Robert the Strong has other holdings which I gave him when he left Louis the German to serve me." The king's irritation was evident.

"Robert the Strong also fears that Erispoë's increased importance in Neustria will diminish his influence in the province," Hincmar admitted.

"Keep an eye on Robert the Strong, Archbishop," the king growled. "He was faithless to my brother, Louis the German. He may yet prove faithless to me. We cannot afford to have Neustria go the way of Aquitaine."

When the council finally adjourned, Hincmar was satisfied that his influence remained the greatest in the court of King Charles. Arranging a politically advantageous marriage for Princess Judith, reinstating young Charles in Aquitaine, and successfully establishing Prince Louis as provincial king in Neustria would all require skillful maneuvering. The archbishop looked forward to the challenge.

CHAPTER V

MAY and JUNE 856

A t the beginning of May, the king's party departed for Le Mans and Louis' coronation. King Charles was determined to see young Louis peacefully established and to remain in Neustria until the summer assembly in Neaufles. The royal entourage consisted of forty mounted nobles, knights, and messengers, followed by as many servants walking behind—each pulling a heavily laden pack horse on a lead. Baldwin and Prince Louis rode side by side for much of the way alongside Mathieu, Louis' newly appointed seneschal. As a minor noble from Tours, Mathieu was well familiar with Neustria, its resources as well as its politics. He shared valuable information with them as they rode, helping Baldwin and Louis pass the long hours in the saddle.

Except for the occasional cloud burst, the weather throughout the journey matched the travelers' high spirits. Nature, as if acknowledging the importance of the regal procession, had put on her most beautiful adornments. Forests, lush in their emerald finery, and crystal streams and rivers were rivaled only by the delicate flowers of cobalt blue and butter yellow.

The company's first stop was at St. Denis, where the king's cousin, Louis, was abbot. Abbot Louis warmly welcomed the royal entourage and proudly walked them through the magnificent cathedral. He reverently related the story of a leper who was healed miraculously by Christ himself after he witnessed a vision of the martyred St. Denis accompanied by a host of angels on the eve of the cathedral's dedication.

As they approached the stately stone tombs where the Merovingian kings lay in rest, King Charles whispered solemnly, "This is where I too shall rest someday."

From St. Denis, they headed southeast to the monastery at Ferrières, the home of one of the king's advisers, Abbot Lupus Servatus. Lupus eagerly showed everyone the new lead roof that the monastery had built through the generous donation of English lead from Aethelwulf, King of Wessex. He also pointedly indicated the parts of the building still in need of renovation.

"The king must stop at as many of his lords' and bishops' holdings as is practical." John Scotus explained to Baldwin and Louis the reason for their stay at Ferrières. "A wise king goes amongst his countrymen, attending to their needs, listening to their concerns, and assessing their loyalty."

Baldwin did not mind the delay. He was excited to be on the road, seeing places of which he had only heard. The accommodations were adequate, even if he and the other knights found themselves sleeping on benches in their hosts' great halls. And Abbey food often rivaled the feasts offered at the king's own table.

As they set out for Orléans, the journey turned somber. A few weeks earlier, Archbishop Hincmar had received report of a devastating Viking attack upon the city, and King Charles, who had sent supplies, wished to see the condition of Orléans for himself.

As they drew closer to the city, Baldwin observed a massive flock of black birds hovering in the branches of a gnarled oak up ahead, diving by twos and threes toward the road. Conversation ceased as the company approached the unsettling scene. What appeared to be a pile of bloody rags lay on the road, strewn about.

The ebony kites scattered at the company's arrival. Baldwin dismounted with the other knights and surveyed the carnage. Merchants, by the look of them, had been set upon by Vikings, their tunics shredded by lethal blows and their fingers severed to quickly relieve them of valuable jewelry. An axe had split open one man's skull, and the ravenous birds feasted on his brains. Off to one side lay the remnants of a smashed cart—its horse missing.

King Charles ordered the servants to bury the bodies while he led a group of knights in an unsuccessful search for survivors or villains.

In beleaguered Orléans, the King's company listened to the residents' account of the vicious Viking raid. The news of the attack on the unfortunate merchants found on the road heightened the townspeople's fear that the Danes were still in the area. Despite the extra provisions King Charles had ordered sent to Orléans, food was sparse, and the accommodations were basic. That night, Baldwin and the other knights slept little, keeping watch for marauders.

By the time the company arrived at Tours, Baldwin and Louis were eagerly anticipating a comfortable rest of several days in the royal palace. Approaching the city, they passed the largest Roman amphitheater that Baldwin had ever seen. Five Roman roads converged at Tours, and a bridge spanning the Loire made Tours a bustling center of commerce and culture. Flat-bottomed boats laden with salt, wine, or exotic imported goods were prepared in Tours for shipment north to Paris. Most would arrive safely. Some would fall prey to the Danes.

At the palace, grooms ran to take charge of the horses while servants transported goods to the various sleeping chambers. The palace chamberlain informed King Charles that several local lords, including Robert the Strong and Archbishop Herardus, would join the company at their afternoon feast.

At age twenty-five, Robert the Strong had accomplished much. After leaving Louis the German's service, and only one year after pledging loyalty to King Charles, he had been made administrator over Maine, Anjou, and Touraine, greatly increasing his influence in Francia. His service for the past three years showed promise in fending off Viking attacks. King Charles hoped to retain this strong and influential lord while ensuring Prince Louis' future as King of Neustria. However, throughout the feast, Robert the Strong appeared aloof. His expression was guarded when the king announced his plan to visit his holding at

Marmoutier Abbey in the morning. That reluctance did not go unnoticed.

When Robert departed, King Charles turned to Hincmar. "Archbishop, you earlier raised the possibility of Robert the Strong's objection to Louis' coronation. What say you now?"

"My concerns still remain, Sire," Hincmar admitted reluctantly.

"Louis' right to rule in Neustria must not be challenged. Robert the Strong must step back!" King Charles snapped. "Tomorrow, I intend to send that clear message. Robert will observe while Louis inspects the abbey and reviews how royal funds are being used there."

❦

On the morrow, a reluctant Robert the Strong and a fawning Archbishop Herardus received King Charles' party at Marmoutier Abbey. John Scotus and Mathieu had prepared Prince Louis to ask pertinent questions regarding their administration of the renowned abbey. Baldwin sensed Robert the Strong's resentment throughout the uncomfortable interview.

"May I show you through the buildings where the royal funds are being used?" Archbishop Herardus eagerly offered at the conclusion of the questioning. And at King Charles' nod, Herardus led the way.

Throughout the tour, John Scotus commented on all things related to St. Martin's most famous abbot, Alcuin. "Sire, your grandfather, Emperor Charles the Great, persuaded the great English scholar Alcuin to help him establish the Palace School in Aachen and begin a system of educating all within his kingdom," John Scotus eagerly pointed out.

"In his later years, Alcuin retired from the court in Aachen and became abbot in Tours," Archbishop Herardus eagerly took up the tale. "He established the famous scriptorium you are about to see which developed the Carolingian form of writing now used throughout many kingdoms."

As they entered the renowned scriptorium, Baldwin saw rows of dedicated monks meticulously copying and illuminating dozens of manuscripts.

"Three years ago, Vikings destroyed our scriptorium, killing one hundred of our brothers here," Archbishop Herardus related solemnly. "We have done our best to rebuild. As you can see, Sire, only a few dozen skilled workers remain. We hope to increase our numbers in future."

At Archbishop Herardus' request, the head scribe stopped the work, allowing the king and his company to observe and ask questions. Before they left the scriptorium, the archbishop presented King Charles with an exquisitely illuminated prayer book bound in intricately carved ivory.

From the scriptorium, the royal party moved into the basilica. Pressing throngs of fervent pilgrims crowded around the tomb housing the hallowed bones of St. Martin. Their fervent passion rendered them oblivious to the danger of being crushed by the size and zeal of the mob. Baldwin felt that the tomb, encased in marble and adorned with gold and jewels, was a fitting resting place for the saint whose miraculous relics had won battles for Frankish kings and even raised the dead.

When they left Marmoutier Abbey, King Charles took leave of an inscrutable Robert the Strong. "We shall see you at the coronation in Le Mans in a few short days, and then again in June at the assembly in Neaufles." The king's voice was firm.

Their stay in Tours had provided the company welcome rest from long days in the saddle. However, the royal company was ready to push on toward Louis' coronation at Le Mans.

༄

The ancient and impressive city walls of Le Mans were a welcome sight for Baldwin. The company had bypassed Angers, although that palace would be one of Prince Louis' three primary residences in Neustria. With the coronation only a few days away, King Charles wished to approve the preparations in Le Mans before the day of the ceremony. After his coronation, Louis' court would move between the palace at Tours, the palace at Angers, and the royal apartments at the abbey of Saint-Pierre de la Couture on the outskirts of Le Mans.

The stately cathedral had been established nearly five-hundred years earlier by St. Julian, who spread Christianity throughout the area surrounding Le Mans. Recently renovated, the cathedral now possessed a large choir with an apse and an ambulatory containing no less than five altars. Baldwin observed that the beauty, grandeur, and history of the cathedral provided a perfect setting for a king's coronation.

Baldwin was becoming increasingly comfortable as part of the elite group surrounding Prince Louis. Although he moved in the background, Baldwin's presence did seem to give Louis courage. John Scotus had been proven correct when he had assured Baldwin of his value to the prince.

On the day of the coronation, a pale and jittery Prince Louis nodded solemnly as Baldwin patiently led him through the mental preparations that he himself used to quell pre-combat fears. Baldwin watched with satisfaction as, not long afterward, Prince Louis took his place in the royal processional with a poise beyond his years. John Scotus and Baldwin walked behind the prince in the procession, which was led by King Charles and Archbishop Hincmar.

As they wound their way through the streets of Le Mans toward the cathedral, Baldwin noted how small the nine-year-old prince appeared, surrounded by his father and other great men of the kingdom. The soon-to-be boy king would have much placed upon his slender shoulders. *Young Louis is not the king I expected to serve when I first came to Senlis. But I will do all within my power to help him become a king worthy of faithful devotion!*

Upon entering the heavy brass doors of the grand cathedral, Baldwin took his place next to John Scotus in front of a pew reserved for those in the procession. At a cue from Archbishop Hincmar, a boys' choir sang, their clear soprano voices ringing out in angelic tones while Prince Louis began his measured walk down the aisle toward his investiture as King of Neustria.

King Charles performed the coronation with the assistance of Archbishop Hincmar. Hincmar read the words of the ritual and received Louis' responses. Louis faltered a bit when he spoke, but he acquitted himself well in spite of that. Then Hincmar handed the weighty crown to King Charles, who put it on Louis' youthful head and presented him with the scepter, which appeared enormous in the young king's grasp. At Hincmar's signal the procession formed again and returned to the royal apartments with King Charles and young King Louis walking side by side leading the way.

Several days later, the royal party moved to the palace built on a rocky promontory in the hilly terrain of Angers. Bordering Brittany, Angers was a stronghold against brutal Viking attacks as well as unruly Bretons. The city lay just south of the confluence of three rivers which combined to form the Maine. The area was known for the richness of its soil teeming with an abundance of plants and wildlife.

On the west, Angers shared a border with Brittany, which King Charles controlled as suzerain. King Charles' inability to completely conquer the Bretons had resulted in their current precarious arrangement. Brittany continued to pay annual tribute to King Charles and recognize him as their high king. But Erispoë referred to himself as "King of the Bretons" and governed Brittany according to the Bretons' local laws and customs. Although Angers' border with Brittany had been troubled in the past, Baldwin hoped that Erispoë would be content with his daughter's betrothal to Louis—as future king of Francia. Erispoë could see a grandson on the throne of Francia one day.

"Tell us, Archbishop, what is your assessment of Louis' investiture?" King Charles addressed Hincmar at their first council in Angers.

Hincmar began carefully. "On the face of it the majority of Neustrian lords and clergy welcome young King Louis. The Bretons are another matter. Erispoë seems gratified by the rise in stature of his future son-in-law. However, I am not certain that his cousin, Salomon, feels the same."

"Salomon has been my *fideles* for four years. Next to Erispoë, he is the most powerful lord among the Bretons. Is he beginning to rethink his oath?"

"Salomon is ambitious, Sire," Hincmar continued. "He is also jealous of Erispoë. Jealousy and ambition lead to trouble."

"What of Robert the Strong?"

"Robert has befriended Salomon and has also contacted the rebel lords in Aquitaine. He observes with interest the Aquitanians' negotiations with your brother, Louis the German. If either Salomon or Robert the Strong sense weakness in your ability to respond to a rebellion, young King Louis could be in trouble." Hincmar warned.

"Sire," John Scotus interjected. "Shall we discuss Aquitaine's ties with Robert the Strong and Salomon during the first session of the summer assembly?"

"It must be done in complete confidentiality," the king cautioned.

Only the king's most trusted lords participated in the first session of the summer assembly, where matters of utmost delicacy were discussed. If nobles discovered they had been the topic of discussion in the first session or felt in danger of losing their *benefices*, the general assembly could devolve into chaos.

"What have we heard lately of Pippin in Aquitaine?" the king inquired.

"Pippin is out, Sire," Hincmar was pleased to announce. "The rebel lords realize that Louis the German is not coming to save their province. They may wish to reinstate young Charles."

"Indeed!" the king exclaimed. "Have the lords of Aquitaine been invited to Neaufles?"

"The rebel lords have not, Sire," Hincmar responded. "However, the clergy will be there."

The king considered briefly before speaking. "Send word to the court in Verberie. Have young Charles meet us in Neaufles for the summer assembly."

"That is wise, Sire," John Scotus concurred. "To exclude young Charles from the coronation and assembly never felt right."

"That decision was made with the purpose of not drawing attention to his ouster as king in Aquitaine," Hincmar reminded the council. "However, if Aquitaine will restore young Charles, his presence at the assembly will be politically advantageous."

King Charles nodded. "Archbishop Hincmar, if the rebel lords are willing, they can present themselves at the assembly, and young Charles will return with them and resume his rightful place as king of Aquitaine. If they accept, the lords will be allowed to retain their holdings without penalty."

"Very generous, Sire," Hincmar nodded. "The lords of Aquitaine will be relieved to hear that."

"And the lesson learned by all at the assembly will be that the lords of Aquitaine only made themselves appear foolish by their petty rebellion," John Scotus smiled.

King Charles next turned to Louis' new seneschal. "Mathieu, have you reviewed Angers' accounts?"

Mathieu responded eagerly, "I have begun doing so, Sire. The accounts for the past six months appear to be in order. The gifts presented to young King Louis at his coronation will help establish his court. However, his expenses will increase, and his coffers will soon need replenishing."

"That is to be expected," the king agreed. He turned to the court notary. "Joseph, send a second summons to attend the summer assembly in Neaufles—this time in both young King Louis' name as well as our own. That should bring tribute to both courts. Include the rebel lords of Aquitaine in the summons."

"It shall be done, Sire," Joseph replied.

As the council adjourned, Hincmar looked forward to the summer assembly as an indication of both strength and weakness within the kingdom. Lords, bishops, and abbots each held their lands at the king's sole discretion and were expected to return a portion of their income in the form of tribute at the annual summer assembly. Those who were miserly in their tributes might find their *benefices* given to another who would be more generous with the king.

At the assembly, one could also observe interactions between provincial leaders. Which lords were natural allies? Who might challenge the authority of the king by refusing to appear and pay tribute? In a few short weeks, Hincmar would have an answer to all those questions.

୨

For the past year, Judith had assisted Queen Ermentrude in planning each removal of the court. However, this time, Judith would take the lead in the court's removal from Senlis to the palace at Verberie, fifteen miles away. Judith eagerly anticipated her assignment. Bringing order to a potentially chaotic event appealed to her logical mind.

Judith was also glad that she could lift some of the burden from her mother, who grew increasingly preoccupied with the delicate health of her newborn. Baby Hildegarde was not thriving, and she cried through much of the night. The midwives suggested using herbs, which they steeped and strained and offered to the little princess on a silver spoon. The court physician proclaimed the fate of the child was now in God's hands. They could only wait and see what transpired.

Judith asked Gauzlin and Martin, Marshal of the Stables, for their help in planning the move. Gauzlin made a list for her of all those who would move with the court to Verberie. They assigned each an allotment of baggage and a mode of transportation based on their station at court and their walking or riding ability. Martin helped her with the number of horses, wagons, and carts necessary and the number of hides or boiled-leather traveling chests needed to protect precious cargo transported by cart. Judith also said a prayer for good weather.

The days before the removal were a bustle of packing and cleaning. Cooks prepared food to be eaten along the way. Those who worked in the great hall carefully wrapped in linen the gold and silver plates and goblets used at the king's table. Gauzlin personally oversaw packing the contents of the king's treasury to transport by wagon. Servants prepared clothing, medicine, favorite books, and even the royal bedding for transport.

"I hope I have not forgotten anything," Judith confided to Hemma as they walked through the palace and its grounds, reviewing the court's final readiness for the move.

"Everything appears in order, Princess," Hemma assured her. "Although, we have not seen much of your brother, young Charles."

"Since my father and Louis' departure, my brother is determined to fill his hours with as much hunting and hawking as possible. After what he experienced in Aquitaine, I am happy to see Charles' playful nature return. But I will make certain that he is ready."

At daybreak, the court, consisting of some two hundred individuals, assembled according to a predetermined order and began the journey that would take most of the day. Trumpeters and knights led the way, announcing the approaching procession and warning those who might be on the road to clear the way. Young Charles and the royal huntsmen and hounds came next. As they moved through the narrow streets of Senlis, villagers leaned out of their windows, hoping to catch a glimpse of the queen or other members of the royal family. Queen Ermentrude rode her horse next to the carts conveying her youngest children and their attendants. Judith and the ladies-in-waiting rode nearby while Hemma and the other attendants walked alongside.

That it had not rained for several days was a blessing. For the long road through the burgeoning forest was not the muddy mire it otherwise might have become. Occasional clouds gathered, but they passed quickly, and a light breeze cooled each traveler's brow.

At midday, they paused to rest and refresh themselves with the food prepared by the royal cooks. The jester, carrying his lute, moved through the company, lifting spirits, and encouraging all. When the procession continued, he led singing competitions to pass the time more enjoyably. By late afternoon, they reached the outer walls of Verberie.

Of the many palaces in Francia, Verberie was Judith's favorite. Commissioned by her great-grandfather, Emperor Charles the Great, the palace was one of the largest and most beautiful in the kingdom. The grounds held massive, terraced gardens. Its park, which extended to the forest, included numerous canals and ponds. In addition to the usual barracks, stables, and dog kennels, the grounds at Verberie contained an elegant church with elements of the classical style that Charles the Great had so much admired.

The palace was also in the classical style, and its two round towers were decorated in bas-relief. Beneath the lead roof were pediments surmounted by colossal statues. The massive outer brass doors led into an interior adorned with marble statues. The floor was inlaid with mosaics and the walls enlivened with colorful frescoes, while the furnishings throughout were inlaid with silver and gold.

The servants who had been sent ahead several days before helped unload carts and unpack saddle bags. The permanent staff at Verberie had prepared the palace to receive the court. And yet, it was still a massive undertaking, as travel weary servants carried enormously heavy chests up flights of stairs and placed them in their appointed rooms. With everyone exhausted, much of the unpacking would wait until morning.

As Judith lay in bed that night, she was grateful that no mishap had occurred during the removal. It was marvelous how the court had moved as one—each playing their own part. *I will have to do this when I have my own household,* Judith thought as she drifted contentedly off to sleep.

❧

Several weeks later, just as everyone was settling in at Verberie, Princess Hildegarde was taken terribly ill. Queen Ermentrude consulted physicians and those knowledgeable in the use of herbs, but to no avail. Little Hildegarde's crying grew more pitiful and weak with each passing hour. The distraught queen lit candles and offered constant prayers in the royal chapel.

However, the little princess wasted away before her mother's eyes.

Judith sat with Hildegarde in her arms, allowing her mother time for a brief rest. The little princess's face had grown pale, with dark blue circles under her eyes—her breathing shallow and sporadic. Gazing down at the tiny child, Judith remembered the night of Hildegarde's birth.

"When I said that we should not know each other for long, I did not mean that you should leave us, dear sister," she whispered tenderly, fearing the inevitable.

In the early hours of the morning, tiny Hildegarde drew her last shuddering breath and was finally at peace. The queen sent a messenger to King Charles in Angers to inform him of her passing. After burying Hildegarde in the family cemetery, Queen Ermentrude kept to her chamber, refusing food, and drinking only a little watered wine. The entire palace mourned.

Judith was relieved when her mother finally emerged from her bedchamber to see young Charles on his way. Young Charles had been summoned to the assembly in Neaufles during the second week of June. He was told to bring all of his belongings.

Judith had seen young Charles tense when he received the summons. What was planned for his future? Was he being sent back to Aquitaine? Or to another province? Young Charles had enjoyed his carefree life for the past few months. If he could choose for himself, Judith knew he would never return to Aquitaine.

However, the royal children's lives mirrored in some ways their recent household move from Senlis to Verberie. The palace servants had each been given individual tasks, which, when combined, had accomplished the removal. The king required his family to move as one—each doing his or her own part to preserve the kingdom of Francia. Regardless of their personal feelings, her brothers Charles and Louis would go wherever they were sent. As would Judith.

❧

Overlooking the banks of the Epte lay Neaufles, a large fortification built after the manner of a Roman Castrum. The fortress was laid out in a rectangle with watchtowers and gates on every side. A clear path ran along the perimeter of the walls, allowing soldiers to move quickly to their defensive positions. The main road inside the fortress led past barracks to the headquarters complex with its great hall and administrative buildings surrounding a large open courtyard.

As the king's party approached the fortress, Hincmar reflected on the crucial business of the morrow. The fortification's rugged setting was perfect for the ideal that King Charles wished his nobles to strive for—a kingdom fortified and united against the Danes.

The first session of the assembly was held early the next morning while the rest of the nobility were just beginning to arrive. The king's trusted council had arrived the night before and found lodging within the barracks or officers' quarters within the fortress. The first session would meet and discuss any sensitive issues and determine the order of presentation of the new laws prior to the general assembly session in the afternoon.

Copies of the new laws decided on in February had been carefully written down and distributed to the morning council who debated the wisdom and timing of presenting each of the laws at the general assembly for a vote. When they moved on to discuss possible rebellion in Neustria and Aquitaine, Hincmar assumed leadership of the council, allowing King Charles to leave the meeting and greet his arriving nobles.

ഏ

"Louis, Baldwin, follow me," King Charles called, stepping out from the council and into the sunlit courtyard where the nobles gathered.

Baldwin marveled as he watched the king move naturally amongst his abbots, bishops, counts, viscounts, and administrators. Wherever he went, nobles crowded to listen to his reasons for taking certain actions throughout the past year. Occasionally, the king would visit with an individual noble, listening to his concerns and allowing him to feel that his opinion was vitally important to the king.

King Charles was a man of many faces. Baldwin had heard of the king's unpredictable rages, especially directed against those who were disloyal. In previous years he had publicly humiliated some unfortunate nobles who challenged his authority by forcing them to wear a saddle in front of the general assembly as the ultimate sign of submission. He had also ordered the execution of Gauzbert of Aquitaine for rebellion. However, in Senlis, King Charles had appeared cultured and intelligent—a lover of art and beauty. On their journey to Le Mans, King Charles had been every inch the commanding leader. Yet he had displayed a genuine air of reverence when he entered holy shrines.

Now, in Neaufles, Baldwin saw the king as patient, perceptive, and even jovial at times. He warmly welcomed the arrival of the prodigal lords of Aquitaine and the recalcitrant Robert the Strong. The king was perfectly willing to use his young children to serve the needs of his realm. However, in Angers, King Charles had shown a deeply tender side for his family when the awful word had been brought of Princess Hildegarde's death. *The king is not an easy man, but I would give my life for him*, Baldwin concluded.

ॐ

The afternoon session of the assembly was held in the great hall, which would be used for the feast afterward. Archbishop Hincmar sat with King Charles, his sons, and his close advisers at the head table. From his position, Hincmar looked down upon the aristocracy of Francia. Each noble had bowed the knee before the king. Now, all eagerly awaited the announcement of the changes proposed in their laws.

King Charles rose to address the assembly. "Once each year, I call you together to join with me in strengthening our kingdom. All Francia, everyone from the meanest peasant to the highest born noble depends upon our resolve, our united efforts to maintain the healthy condition of our realm. But our kingdom is in peril. Our borders, our villages, our abbeys, our rivers are

59

increasingly beset by a brutal enemy. An enemy who does not hesitate to rape and plunder. An enemy who does not hesitate to slaughter the innocent. An enemy whose lust for gold surpasses the very bounds of human decency." Most in the assembly nodded gravely in accordance with the king's remarks.

"This year," King Charles continued, "we meet in a fortress, for that is what we must build if Francia is to survive. In times of peril, our safety and our very lives depend upon the strength of our walls. In like manner, Francia depends upon each one of us to do his duty in defending against a common enemy. Our new laws this year are brought forward for your approval with one objective in mind— the fortifying and protecting of our kingdom against the Vikings!"

The assembly rang with shouts of approval as the king unfolded his vision for a stronger Francia. He spoke at length about the many attacks suffered by the provinces as well as the strategies they had employed in either fighting or appeasing the Northmen. He listened to comments from his nobles and carefully considered Robert the Strong's suggestion that they befriend some of the Danes and use them as mercenaries to fight the others.

At the conclusion of the king's remarks, he ordered copies of the new laws to be distributed amongst the assembly. "These new laws are designed to strengthen our defenses against the Northmen. Read them. Discuss them. Ask me questions about them. We will assemble tomorrow morning so that we may further discuss them, and you may indicate whether or not you support these changes in our laws. Now, we will feast."

Hincmar keenly observed how intently the lords read and discussed the new laws during the feast and afterward in the open air of the courtyard. Nobles freely mingled with each other and the king as he walked amongst them, answering their questions. The morrow's assembly would reveal how persuasive Hincmar's drafting of the laws had been.

The following morning, King Charles addressed the assembly in the open courtyard. "Many of you have supported our efforts to strengthen Francia throughout this past year. We rely upon all of you now to assist our efforts during this coming year. Archbishop Hincmar will introduce our new laws, one by one."

Hincmar was pleased that the morning council had been in complete accord with the laws to be presented. He could see no reason why the vote by the general assembly would be different. One proposed change included expanding the authority of the king's provincial administrators. The administrators already maintained lists of those in each province who were eligible for military service. The proposed change would require that the administrators also maintain physical fortifications within their areas, including assessing peasant labor for bridge and fortification repairs.

The assembly discussion lasted several hours as King Charles answered his lords' concerns upon one matter or another. In the end, each law passed with unanimous vote and the assembly sat down for a final feast.

King Charles remained in the great hall when the feast ended in order to receive tribute, bestow *benefices*, and resolve disputes amongst his nobles. Later, he met privately with the rebel lords of Aquitaine who, as Hincmar had predicted, were eager to be restored to the king's good graces. Each lord swore a new oath of fidelity to the king. As proof of their renewed loyalty, the lords of Aquitaine had brought with them an extremely generous tribute of silver carried on the backs of five sturdy pack horses. The lords and clerics also formally requested that young King Charles be allowed to return with them and resume his regnum in Aquitaine.

Hincmar rejoiced in the outcome. Aquitaine had been a thorn in the side of every Carolingian ruler since Pippin the First had taken the province from the Saracens. Emperor Charles the Great had been forced to conquer and reconquer the province of Aquitaine and yet had forgiven them even though the nobles of Aquitaine's pledges of fidelity had been easily given and just as easily broken. His example of forgiveness had given his grandson, King Charles a model to follow—that of giving second and third chances to errant nobles.

On the following morning, as the assembly dispersed, King Charles met briefly with his inner council, who all agreed that the assembly had accomplished what they had intended. The king's new laws had passed without objection. The king had also strengthened his ties with his aristocracy–including Robert the Strong. Even Aquitaine, with its restoration of young Charles, appeared to be back in the fold.

For the present, unity existed amongst the provinces. For the present, King Charles' *fideles* were loyal. For the present, the king's nobles shared a determination to fight the Danes rather than each other. However, as Archbishop Hincmar mounted his horse and the royal company set out for Verberie, Hincmar feared that– given the challenges facing the king–the tentative unity would not last until the next summer assembly.

CHAPTER VI

JULY and AUGUST 856

The unusually cold, dry winter led to a chilly, damp spring and late summer. The welcome dry heat of July banished the harsh memory of the pestilence that had claimed so many lives in January, February, and March. July also brought the eagerly anticipated arrival of Aethelwulf, King of Wessex, and his son, Prince Alfred, returning from their year-long pilgrimage to Rome. Aethelwulf's messenger arrived a day before the royal party. Queen Ermentrude ordered rooms prepared for the king, his son, and their company, and King Charles summoned the members of his council.

"Sire," Hincmar began when it was his turn to report. "My sources in Wessex confirm that King Aethelwulf's son, Aethelbald, has called upon his thegns to support him as rightful King of Wessex."

"And dethrone his father?" King Charles was outraged.

"Exactly so, Sire. Aethelbald has been liberal with gifts to the lords of Wessex during his father's absence. He has convinced many of them that Aethelwulf, although a great warrior in his day, is past his prime and incapable of ruling Wessex."

"What evidence has he to prove such a charge?"

"Before King Aethelwulf departed on pilgrimage, he granted a tenth of all lands under his control to the church and to some of his thegns, releasing those lands from all taxes."

"Aethelbald, as future heir, might object to his father's divesting himself of so much property. But the nobles should be glad of such an arrangement." King Charles seemed perplexed.

Hincmar nodded. "The lords from Kent and Sussex, who benefited from the king's largesse, were content. However, the envious thegns in Wessex now support Aethelbald as king. Even some clerics have joined Aethelbald's rebellion."

"Who precisely?" John Scotus pressed. "I know the bishops in Wessex. I am astonished to hear that any of them would join in such a disgraceful action."

"Ealhstan, Bishop of Sherborne, for one." Hincmar reluctantly admitted.

John Scotus threw up his hands in disgust. "This is madness! Bishop Ealhstan served King Aethelwulf's father. He also fought with Aethelwulf many years ago, helping him conquer Kent!"

"Ealhstan would not be the first cleric or noble to choose a son's prospects over those of an aging father," Gauzlin interposed. "If King Aethelwulf truly gave one-tenth of his kingdom to his thegns and clerics with no condition, that does not seem wise."

"One of my sources says there was condition upon the gift. Those receiving property were obliged to offer regular prayers on behalf of the king and his ancestors. And at the death of the property holder, all his rights to the land would be transferred to the church."

"So, it was a gift given only to certain of his nobles," John Scotus considered carefully. "And during his father's absence, Aethelbald generously bestowed gifts on those who had been overlooked."

"Surely, that is not the extent of Aethelbald's evidence against his father's fitness to rule?" the king pressed.

"There is more," Hincmar agreed. "Aethelwulf took lavish gifts with him to Rome. Gifts an emperor such as Charles the Great might have offered the pope."

"Nobles and kings are expected to bring gifts to the pope when they go on pilgrimage," Gauzlin commented. "Which is probably why so few of them make the journey–unless it is for the purpose of dying and being buried in Rome," he added ironically.

"Here is the list of some of the gifts he gave the pope. Judge for yourself if these gifts are not excessive for a king of Aethelwulf's stature." Hincmar read from one of the parchments he had brought with him into the council. "A golden crown weighing four pounds, golden goblets, a sword inlaid with gold, silver bowls, silver candleholders worked with gold, purple-dyed silk tunics embossed with golden keys and gold-interwoven veils."

"Extremely generous. But surely not excessive to the point of madness," King Charles asserted.

"There is more," Hincmar continued. "He brought bags of gold to give to the pope, the clergy, and the nobility in Rome. And he also brought bags of silver to distribute amongst the people of Rome. There is still more. He paid for the reconstruction of the Saxon quarter in Rome which was destroyed by fire several years back. Finally, while in Rome, King Aethelwulf pledged that Wessex would send an enormous tribute to the pope each year, even after Aethelwulf's death."

John Scotus shook his head. "King Aethelwulf is an extremely pious man, and he may have more wealth to distribute than we had supposed. But, to deprive his kingdom and heirs of lands, taxes, treasure, and his own presence when his kingdom is increasingly threatened by Vikings . . ."

"Especially in light of the treasure he previously sent with his son, Alfred, when he went on pilgrimage but two years earlier." Gauzlin's tone was thoughtful.

"King Aethelwulf appeared sound when he stayed with us on his way to Rome last year. Archbishop Hincmar, in light of his precarious political position, do you still see the King of Wessex as a good match for Judith?" King Charles voiced his concern.

Reluctant to abandon his carefully conceived plan, Hincmar took his time answering. "Sire, John Scotus correctly points out that King Aethelwulf is extremely pious. However, piety does not make a madman of him. King Aethelwulf is a powerful warrior, and I would not wager against him should his son oppose him. And, even if he were to lose Wessex, he will yet retain Kent, Surrey, East Anglia, and Sussex. Judge for yourself when he arrives. If you deem him a valuable ally, then an alliance may also strengthen his position when he returns to Wessex."

Hincmar's reasoning won the day. King Charles agreed to wait and see what Aethelwulf's visit would reveal about his state of mind. If Aethelwulf appeared strong and in full possession of his faculties, Hincmar would advise King Charles to move forward with their plans for Judith.

৩

Judith had rejoiced at her father's return from the coronation and summer assembly. With the departure of Louis and Baldwin Iron Arm, the reinstatement of young Charles, and the death of Hildegarde, the past several months had felt increasingly empty. Judith had spent much of her free time in the palace library.

Knowing this, her father had presented her with a gift from the scriptorium in Tours—a small prayer book, beautifully bound in ivory with gold inlay. The intricately illuminated pages captured Judith's imagination. Embellished in rich reds, blues, and gold, each illuminated letter was a work of art. Carefully tracing the letters with her finger, Judith wondered at the patience and skill involved in creating such a work.

She was eager to resume her lessons with John Scotus. Without hesitation, John Scotus told her about the journey to Le Mans, the coronation, and the summer assembly. That led to a discussion about the politics and intrigues affecting both Louis and young Charles.

"I will pray for them," Judith promised as they concluded their lesson. *Will politics be part of my future as well?* Judith could not help but wonder.

৩

"Our guests are arriving!" Judith heard the distant clarion of the royal trumpets announcing the approach of the King of Wessex as she and Hemma walked through the gardens with

Maximus. Quickly returning to the palace, Judith joined her parents to receive King Aethelwulf, Prince Alfred, and Bishop Swithun of Winchester—Aethelwulf's spiritual adviser. King Aethelwulf and his son were much as Judith had remembered them. Alfred's hair was darker, and he had grown over the past year. The last vestiges of black had given way to silver in King Aethelwulf's hair and beard, but he still had the same kind eyes that Judith remembered.

"Our court is honored by your visit," King Charles welcomed the king of Wessex. We look forward to hearing your impressions of Rome."

"This pilgrimage was the fulfillment of a life-long dream," King Aethelwulf smiled. "Your kind hospitality, King Charles, helped make that possible. I was honored to see the place where your grandfather, Charles the Great, was consecrated Emperor by the Bishop of Rome."

"That is a place I hope to visit myself someday," King Charles admitted. "Let us speak more of Rome at the feast."

Judith had directed the preparations for the feast welcoming their royal visitors. She requested an additional table added to the dais to accommodate King Aethelwulf, Prince Alfred, and Bishop Swithun. Behind Aethelwulf's table hung a banner with the colors of Wessex.

Judith had earlier reviewed the list sent ahead by the King of Wessex and had assigned seating at the feast based on the rank and seniority of the king's party. Even with additional tables, Judith found it challenging to find just the right place for each noble of Wessex without displacing Francia's own courtiers.

At Judith's direction, the kitchens had baked extra breads and pastries for several days prior to the visitors' arrival. In honor of their guests, the king's butler had reduced the amount of water he normally mixed with the wine to be served at the feast. For future feasts, the cooks of Wessex would work with those of King Charles' court, showing off dishes they had learned to prepare while in Rome as well as dishes from their native Britannia. But this first feast together was a chance for King Charles' cooks to display their prowess. Servers brought forward course after course of delicacies—each course announced with a trumpet flourish. The court jester, with the help of a boys' choir and other musicians, entertained throughout.

On the following morning, Alfred entered the schoolroom where John Scotus tutored Judith. "My father sent me to join you," his manner was tentative.

"Of course, please sit down, Prince Alfred," John Scotus gently invited, sensing the young boy's discomfort. "Will you tell us about Rome? Rome is a very great city, is it not?"

"Rome is very large and also very dirty!" Alfred spoke with youthful honesty. "And the monuments are always crowded."

As Judith listened to Alfred recount in fine detail the dozens of churches and abandoned monuments he and his father had visited during their year in Rome, she was amazed at his powers of observation as well as his memory.

"What are your impressions of the pope?" John Scotus asked.

"It was not the same pope I met three years ago," was Alfred's reply. "On my first visit, Pope Leo blessed me and anointed me with holy chrism. He said that made him my spiritual father."

John Scotus nodded. "Ah, yes. It sounds as if he performed the sacrament of confirmation."

"And he gave me a sword and made me a Roman Consul!" Alfred pronounced proudly.

"Did he now? Impressive!" John Scotus smiled.

"But Pope Leo died last year. By the time we arrived in Rome, it was Pope Benedict. We brought gifts for Pope Leo. My father gave them to Pope Benedict instead."

When John Scotus left to meet with the king's council, Judith invited Alfred to go with her to the palace library. They browsed through the impressive collection of books, including Emperor Charles the Great's favorite tome, *The City of God* by Augustine. As Alfred reverently turned the pages in one especially beautifully illustrated volume, Judith realized that the young prince shared her fascination with illuminated letters. She opened one of her favorite books of poetry.

"Do you want to hear a poem?" Judith offered. When Alfred nodded, they enjoyed an hour together, looking at the illustrations and speaking about the meaning of the poetry she read aloud.

From that day on, whenever Alfred was not riding to hunt with his father and Judith was not otherwise engaged, the royal children enjoyed each other's company. Alfred seemed a combination of her two younger brothers. Like young Charles, Alfred loved pursuing manly sports with his father. And, like Louis, he was very interested in pursuits of the mind.

Judith enjoyed reading aloud to Alfred and discussing with him the complexities of the world. For a child in his eighth year, Alfred showed remarkable understanding. King Aethelwulf planned to resume their journey by the middle of August, hoping to cross the channel separating Francia from the island of Britannia before unsettled weather made the crossing more difficult.

As July drew to a close, Judith was already regretting Alfred's approaching departure.

࿇

Shortly before midnight, Archbishop Hincmar hurried through the shadows along the torch-lit palace corridors toward the council room. *Has Louis the German finally invaded Aquitaine?* he wondered. *Something serious must have happened for the king to call a council at this hour!* Hincmar was surprised to see the King of Wessex and his chief military officer, as well as Charles' own military advisers, in attendance. He quickly took a place at the table as the meeting had already begun.

"Archbishop Hincmar," King Charles acknowledged him. "Good to have you join us. King Aethelwulf and I were deep in conversation when a messenger from our fortification at Pitres arrived with urgent tidings. A fleet of more than one hundred Danish longboats attacked them, but the fortress is holding. The fleet has moved on down the Seine. The Danes may be planning to rebuild their former encampment at Jeufosse. If they succeed, they will once again use Jeufosse as a base from which to attack

Paris, St. Denis, and all the settlements along the river—if not further inland. King Aethelwulf has graciously offered to advise us on how best to address this threat. He defeated a larger Viking force at Aclea and has had considerable experience in facing the Danes." King Charles surveyed the council. "Ask him whatever questions you may have. And listen well. I value his advice."

King Aethelwulf nodded in acknowledgment. "I can offer what little we learned of the Danes by fighting them at Aclea. Five years ago, they came with more than 350 long boats up the Thames, ravaging Canterbury and London. The King of Mercia and his army were forced to flee. That gave us time to gather our forces. Rowing south, they crossed our border and came down the river into Surrey. Our ten thousand sturdy men met their ten thousand at Aclea and gave them battle. At the end of the day, our men stood firm against them. Less than a thousand Danes remained to escape to their homeland. Vikings have not attacked us in force since that time."

"What weapons did you use against them?"

"Bows, spears, and swords," Aethelwulf replied. "Very few of them wear armor. The bows have a great effect if you can get beyond their shields. You cannot allow them time to form a shield wall. Once they rush upon you, they fight like demons, wielding their swords, axes, and spears with great energy. But their greatest weapon is fear. They use several tactics to create fear amongst their enemies. They decorate their shields and ships with ghastly pagan figures. They travel silently by night in order to attack early in the morning or on a holy day. Perhaps their most effective tactic is to display mutilated corpses to strike fear in the hearts of their enemies. Many militias have run from such sights. But our victory at Aclea proved that a disciplined army—one that stands and does not run—can defeat them."

"What sort of defense can we mount?"

King Aethelwulf shook his head sadly. "It is too late to speak of defense. In the future, I advise you to build and fortify more bridges over your rivers. Francia is an inviting target because of your many navigable rivers and prosperous cathedrals. But you can build bridges low enough to stop a longboat from passing under while allowing your flat-bottomed barges to travel unimpeded. Now is the time to attack! Ride with as much haste as possible to intercept them. Send your messengers to every province and assemble whatever forces you can. If these longboats carry thirty Vikings each, you will need a force of more than three thousand to outnumber them. If they are the longboats that carry fifty men, you will need more than five thousand. The more men you muster, the more quickly you can drive them out."

"By the time we gather an army, they will have plundered, destroyed, and departed."

"True," King Aethelwulf admitted. "But you may surprise them. That is key. If they know you are coming, they will dig trenches and build ramparts to defend themselves against your mounted knights. Then, your only recourse will be to besiege them. If they are taken by surprise, however, your mounted knights will prove more than a match for them, as they have not yet mastered fighting from horseback."

When King Aethelwulf finished addressing the questions from the council, he turned to King Charles, "I have given my best advice. But I am desirous of giving more. King Charles, if you will allow it, I and my warriors will fight alongside you as you face this common enemy."

After a moment of silence, King Charles replied solemnly, "King Aethelwulf, I admire your greatness of spirit. It would be an honor to have such a valiant warrior by my side." He turned to the council. "Our assembly this summer prepared us for just such a time as this." His eyes fell upon Hincmar, "Send word to the provinces to muster in defense of Francia. We will meet to plan our attack at the fortification near Auvers. Gather your courage, all of you! We depart within the hour!"

৯৫

Baldwin eagerly answered the call to arms. He and young King Louis set out to meet the summons as soon as the word arrived, taking with them the one hundred knights under Louis' immediate command garrisoned at the palace in Angers. Erispoë, as Louis' administrator, sent word to each of the landholders and nobles in Neustria to muster all capable men who could shoot a bow or fight from horseback to join them at Auvers in defense of Francia.

The Roman fortification near Auvers was laid out in the same pattern as the one in Neaufles and lay on a hill overlooking the Oise. Although quite large, the open space within the walls was filling quickly by the time Louis and Baldwin led their company of knights inside its massive gates. Banners from the provinces provided gathering places as each man sought to join others of his own province. Louis moved his mount to an open space for his knights to plant Neustria's banner. Then, Louis, Baldwin, and the captain of Louis' guard made their way to the headquarters building.

Louis motioned for Baldwin to accompany him inside the great hall. "Warfare is y . . . your specialty, Baldwin," he insisted. "I w . . . want you with me!"

They entered the great hall where dozens of nobles and a few abbots milled about in battle dress. On the dais, Baldwin observed with interest King Charles, his military adviser, and Archbishop Hincmar conversing with a large, silver-haired warrior. Several messengers stood off to one side, awaiting instructions.

"The K . . . King of Wessex is here," Louis answered Baldwin's unspoken question.

When Louis joined the other kings on the dais, Baldwin noticed Robert the Strong in close conversation with Salomon, Erispoë's ambitious cousin. Shortly, Erispoë entered with his military advisers and moved to join the kings on the dais. Conversation ceased when King Charles stepped forward to speak.

"My lords, I am gratified to see how quickly you answered my call to arms. Here with me is Erispoë, leader of the Bretons, who has brought with him one hundred of his finest knights, whose superior horsemanship is most welcome in our hour of need. We are also graced with the presence of King Aethelwulf of Wessex, a legendary warrior who has fought and won great victories against the Vikings. Their support is much appreciated and shall long be remembered." Charles nodded toward Aethelwulf and Erispoë.

"The Danes are made up of two groups led by Bjorn Ironside and Sigtrygg. They began their attack at Pitres and are moving south along the Seine—ransacking and ravaging at will. They may be headed to Jeufosse. We will camp here tonight to allow time for more of our forces to gather. On the morrow we will cross the Seine at Paris and move north to camp at the monastery at Argenteuil. On the following day, we will move north along the Seine until we encounter the Danes. At first report of the enemy, assume the order of battle. Archers first, followed by knights with their lances. Typically, only their leaders wear chain mail. If you see two separate groups gathering around warriors in armor, drive a wedge between them. If we divide them, they will be easier to defeat. Few Danes are mounted. Our greatest strength lies in our horsemanship and our unity. If we remain united, we will utterly defeat them!"

After answering questions from his lords, King Charles asked King Aethelwulf and Erispoë to address the assembly. More questions emerged as each king related his experience in fighting the Northmen. Finally, the meeting adjourned, and each leader went to inform his men of the plan for the morrow.

The forces of Aquitaine had not arrived by the time the army departed Auvers. King Charles posted messengers on all major roads to direct any latecomers to their new destination. The march from Auvers to their encampment at the monastery in Argenteuil was long, hot, and muggy. August had brought with it no cooling breeze to provide respite from the relentless sun. *We are in ill condition to fight if we meet the Danes now*, Baldwin considered as they neared their stopping place for the night.

Moving north along the Seine from Argenteuil, word came that the Danes were sacking the monastery at Évreux. King Charles ordered the army to move inland, hoping to intercept the enemy. As they drew nearer to Évreux, the tell-tale black smoke of a ransacked village rose on the horizon.

King Charles' army assumed battle order, spreading out across the meadow more than one hundred men wide and twenty men deep. Each province's banner was carried by a horseman riding beside its commander or king. Several rows of archers strode before each commander. Knights riding with lances at the ready followed closely behind.

Several scouts rode ahead of the army, looking for signs of the enemy. Their report spread quickly throughout the ranks. Vikings were spotted just beyond the line of willows in the distance, headed in their direction. Some Danes were on horseback, but most were afoot, leading pack horses laden with what appeared to be treasure taken from Évreux. King Charles ordered the archers to fire their arrows upon first sight of Vikings and then move aside for the knights' charge.

"Where d . . . did the D . . . Danes get so many horses?" Louis' question was on every man's mind. Baldwin had never heard of Vikings traveling by horse or fighting from horseback. He thought they traveled only by longboat or by walking. If the Danes were becoming accomplished riders, the entire nature of the conflict would change, and Francia's advantage would be lost. The army moved steadily but cautiously forward.

Emerging from the shelter of the trees, the Danes were taken by surprise. Those who rode horses dismounted, allowing their horses to wander off as they took up their weapons and shields. In those brief moments of surprise, however, King Charles' archers had fired several deadly volleys before moving aside for the knights, who charged with a blood-chilling feral roar.

Baldwin saw one Viking struck in the mouth with an arrow. A shaft cut down another Dane as he turned toward his fallen comrade, and a third was taken before he could raise his shield. Excitement coursing through his veins, Baldwin urged his mount forward, cutting a path for Louis by nearly decapitating one Viking and cutting off the arm of another who ran screaming toward the vulnerable young king. The Dane's brightly colored wooden shield fell to the earth, still grasped in his dismembered fist. Panicked horses wheeled about, adding to the chaos.

The Danes, still behind the grove of trees, had little time to prepare for battle. Dismounting, they raised their shields and fought like madmen with spears and swords. But the lightning momentum of Erispoë's charging knights, followed by King Charles' and King Aethelwulf's men, overwhelmed them before they could form a shield wall. The knights were upon them, their swords and lances inflicting lethal damage upon the enemy archers. The slaughter of Vikings was great that day, and the air soon filled with the metallic smell of spilled blood.

King Charles' army had won a great victory—killing more than twelve hundred Vikings while losing only a handful of the men of Francia, with another score wounded. King Charles ordered his scouts to search the area for signs of other bands of Danes while the knights began digging a massive grave before the stench of death in the sweltering sun grew oppressive.

The scouts returned with word that the Danes had fled northeast on horseback, headed toward the Seine. King Charles called a meeting of his commanders and gave them their assignments. King Louis' company would gather the abandoned horses and take them, with any wounded, to Évreux. They would assess the damage to the monastery, provide whatever assistance they could to those in the area, and return any recovered stolen property. When their task at Évreux was complete, the company would join the others at Jeufosse.

As they carried out their assignment, Baldwin rejoiced that his young king had survived his first battle unscathed. With Baldwin striking down all enemies before him, Louis may not have wielded his sword in combat. But he had also not run away. Older and more seasoned warriors sometimes turned tail and ran when faced with such a brutal enemy. King Louis had ridden into the heat of battle and had proved himself a worthy leader of men.

～

After burying the dead, the army moved east toward the Seine. They camped for the night on the steeply sloping hillside near the small settlement of Jeufosse overlooking two islands in the river. Fossa Givaldi, as it was commonly known, was the larger of the two islands and protected by thick forest, allowing archers to shoot at anyone approaching while providing cover from returning fire. The longboats, which were pulled up along the banks of the larger island, and the horses, which could be seen on the smaller, indicated the Danes' encampment.

Archbishop Hincmar knew this place well. Four years earlier he had accompanied King Charles when the king and his brother Lothar had pursued Godfrid the Dane and forced him to take refuge on Fossa Givaldi. The Danes had settled on the island for the winter–building their fortifications on the larger island and keeping stolen animals on the smaller. By Christmas time, King Charles' lords had refused to stay any longer at Jeufosse. The siege fell apart, and Godfrid remained in possession of Fossa Givaldi.

Hincmar hoped they would not be facing a similar standoff. After two days, young King Louis' men, as well as a group of knights from Aquitaine, arrived as reinforcements. Then, a messenger from Pitres arrived saying twenty-five longboats, believed to have been led by Sigtrygg, had retreated up the Seine toward the coast. The fortification at Pitres had sent a wagon with the planks and cords necessary to assemble a manganeau should it be required for a siege. It would arrive in a day or two. The kings and their advisers met in council.

"Sigtrygg is gone," King Charles began. "What do we know of Bjorn Ironside?"

King Aethelwulf was first to respond. "He is Lodbrok's son and will not be easily deterred from raiding. He means to wait you out."

"Then, perhaps we should strike a bargain with Bjorn and pay him to leave the area." Erispoë proposed.

Aethelwulf was skeptical. "If you pay him, he will leave for this season only and will return in spring to collect even more treasure."

"Unfortunately," Hincmar observed, "a siege requires an army willing to stay for months if not years. The Danes can survive the winter with all the horses they have taken which can be used for food. Our soldiers, however, will have to rely on what they can hunt and what supplies we send them. In the past, the lords have been unwilling to pay such a price."

"Then they will pay a much dearer price next year in blood and treasure," was Aethelwulf's opinion.

King Charles decided to wait for the arrival of the manganeau. If they could put it to good use, perhaps Bjorn would be content just to escape with his life. In the meantime, they would see where the war machine could be best set up and gather appropriate stones for projectiles. Three days later, they tested their newly assembled manganeau. At seventeen-feet tall, the manganeau required a team of men to draw the cord and release the lever, sending its stones hurling toward the Dane's island fortification.

Stones rained down upon the banks of Fossa Givaldi, damaging several of the Vikings' boats. Quickly, the Danes dragged their longships further onto the island, out of reach of the war machine. Occasionally, stones reached the main part of the island. However, the dense forest made it impossible to tell if the manganeau was inflicting damage.

After a week of firing stones at Fossa Givaldi with no apparent result, King Charles called a halt. He sent a messenger in a boat midway between the shore and the island waving a white flag as a request to parlay. Almost an hour later, a single longboat, also displaying a white flag, made its way to meet the messenger from Francia. The king's messenger returned disheartened. Bjorn Ironside had rejected King Charles' offer to allow the Danes to depart in peace. Without payment of copious amounts of silver, he would winter on the island and continue his raiding in spring.

The final council of kings decided to leave a contingent of knights to continue firing the manganeau and ensure the Danes did not leave the island throughout the fall. In winter, if Bjorn still had not departed, the knights would be free to return home. In spring, King Charles would address the problem of Bjorn Ironside.

It was not a perfect solution. However, Hincmar was content. King Aethelwulf had planned to be on his journey home by now, and yet he had remained to help Francia. Aethelwulf had proven a valuable ally and had delivered King Charles his first real victory against the Danes. Throughout the entire campaign, he had demonstrated strength and superior judgment. Hincmar felt certain that the King of Wessex would know exactly how to reclaim his kingdom from a rebellious son. He hoped King

Charles would not miss this opportunity to unite the two kingdoms in a more permanent way.

As they turned their horses toward Verberie, Hincmar was pleased to overhear King Charles say to King Aethelwulf, "We have worked well together against a common foe, Aethelwulf. Perhaps we should consider a more formal alliance."

CHAPTER VII

SEPTEMBER to OCTOBER 1, 856

Archbishop Hincmar sat at his writing table, staring down at the untouched parchment before him. He was a prolific writer, spending hours each day expressing himself through philosophical treatises, historical or religious notation, and personal correspondence. Writing came easily to him. He loved the way the rhythm of his hand, moving the quill between ink and paper, was an extension of his mind, an expression of his soul.

The task before him daunted and excited him. Here was a challenge worthy of his talents. His efforts had the potential to change the future and ensure his place in history. Hincmar was creating something no one had done before. A king might place a crown upon the head of his queen, granting her the right to rule alongside him. Yet, no queen in history had ever been anointed by the church with the holy chrism. A queen honored by such a sacred rite would be elevated above any other queen. Her right to rule would be acknowledged by Heaven itself. Hincmar's task was to write the first consecration ceremony for a queen.

The day after returning from battling the Danes, King Aethelwulf, Bishop Swithun, and Aethelwulf's other advisers had been invited to join King Charles and his advisers in the council room. Hincmar had shared with them the reports he had received from his fellow bishops in Wessex concerning Aethelbald's rebellion. Afterward, King Charles came directly to the point.

"Your help, King Aethelwulf, with our immediate crisis was of great value to us. We wish to return the favor," the king began.

"Would a formal alliance with Francia strengthen your position if your son, Aethelbald, challenges your right to rule?"

King Aethelwulf took his time answering. "It might prove helpful. Who would not wish to be allied with the great court of King Charles of Francia? However, a military alliance is hardly practical for either of us. With the channel between us, we could not respond in a timely manner to each other's external or internal threats."

"Agreed," King Charles nodded. "You know my own challenges in defending my kingdom from my brother, Louis the German. I propose that we send a message to our overly ambitious relatives that by trying to displace one of us, they would create an enemy in the other. A strong alliance warns others to be cautious in their dealings with a king."

"That might be true in the case of Francia. The reputation of your court and that of the emperors, your father and grandfather, are revered amongst our people," King Aethelwulf acknowledged. "However, how would an alliance with Wessex help your own status?"

"What other king on the island of Britannia is stronger or holds more land than King Aethelwulf?" King Charles countered. "Your deeds are legendary. Any country would be honored to ally themselves with the great warrior King Aethelwulf."

"If not a military alliance, what sort of alliance do you propose?" King Aethelwulf wondered.

King Charles took a deep breath before proceeding. "King Aethelwulf, I am offering you the most personal, the strongest alliance possible. I am offering you my daughter, Judith, as your new Queen of Wessex."

Silence filled the throne room. King Charles had clearly put Wessex in a precarious position. To refuse such an offer might be considered an insult to Francia and King Charles.

King Aethelwulf's spiritual adviser, Bishop Swithun, broke the silence. "King Charles, Wessex does not have queens. We do not allow our kings' wives to sit upon a throne or assist as Francia does."

"I am aware of that difference, Bishop," King Charles acknowledged. "However, Judith will not only be a queen but also consecrated by the church when she marries."

"The first queen to have been so anointed," Hincmar pointed out eagerly. "The granddaughter and great-granddaughter of emperors cannot receive any less honor!"

The offer had been made. King Aethelwulf requested time to consult his advisers, which King Charles freely granted. When they came together on the following morning, King Aethelwulf addressed King Charles' council.

"You have done Wessex great honor by offering us a marriage alliance with Princess Judith," he began solemnly. "Wessex has not been used to having queens in the same sense your kingdom has. However, my counselors agree that Wessex will benefit in both stature and trade from such an alliance. King Charles, we will be honored to be the first kingdom to have a queen who has been consecrated and anointed by the church. Your daughter will be treated with the greatest honor and respect."

"Your assurances are most welcome," King Charles smiled. "We will make arrangements for the ceremony."

The marriage would take place at the beginning of October when Judith achieved her full twelve years, satisfying Frankish law and custom. Hincmar knew that the king of Wessex had conceded a great deal in agreeing to Judith's being consecrated and crowned his queen. Not only was he breaking his kingdom's tradition in order to form an advantageous alliance, but this second marriage would assuredly cause concern within his own household.

No pattern for anointing queens with holy chrism existed. Hincmar must create a masterpiece, confirming in everyone's mind that God had bestowed upon Judith and her future children the "right to rule." Hincmar looked to the consecration rites of kings and emperors for guidance.

Judith's consecration ceremony would be rich with biblical references. Hincmar would pronounce blessings of fertility and power upon the head of the young queen. And he would lay the responsibility for ruling in righteousness upon her shoulders. *God has placed it in the hands of his bishops to consecrate and anoint kings. Now, God is entrusting me with anointing queens, as well!* Hincmar took up his quill and began to write.

❧

King Charles' court reacted immediately to the news of Judith's betrothal. The court notary sent invitations to the leaders of the provinces for the ceremony to be held on October 1st at Verberie. Gauzlin instructed the closest palaces at Senlis and Compiègne, as well as surrounding monasteries, to prepare to accommodate traveling wedding guests. With no precedent as to clothing appropriate for the rite of a queen's anointing, Queen Ermentrude consulted with Archbishop Hincmar and the Mistress of the Wardrobe, who immediately put her assistants to work creating garments suitable for Judith's consecration, coronation, and wedding feast.

On the morning following the agreement reached between King Charles and King Aethelwulf, Ermentrude summoned Judith into her bed chamber. The queen dismissed her attendant, and they were alone. Ermentrude pushed back a decorative screen next to the head of her bed, revealing a door with a warded lock. Removing a gold chain from around her neck, she used the key hanging on it to unlock the door. Judith knew instantly what she was looking at—the king's treasure room. Ermentrude stood aside and motioned for her to enter.

The enormity of the treasure her parents possessed was breathtaking. Chest after chest filled with silver or gold lined the walls. The contents of each chest were carefully inventoried on a page of parchment attached by a leather strap. Even more astonishing were the shelves of precious artifacts and jewels. One shelf held a dozen crowns that she had never seen her mother or father wear. Each of her parents wore one crown for holy days and special feasts and a lighter, simpler crown for their everyday duties. She, herself, had two tiaras—simple gold circlets, really—which she could choose from as the occasion required.

Ermentrude selected three dazzling crowns and an ivory box and carried them into her bed chamber. She motioned for Judith to join her in sitting on the bed. "What do you remember hearing of your grandmother?" the queen asked.

"Empress Judith?" At the queen's nod, Judith continued hesitantly. "I know she died the year before I was born. I have also heard that she was chosen by my grandfather from all the young maidens in his kingdom for her beauty and purity. I know she was gifted in music. And I also know that I am named for her."

Ermentrude smiled. "All of that is true. Your grandfather, Louis, was much older than Judith—with several grown sons—when they married. Emperor Louis was kind to Judith, but his sons were not. If your grandmother had not sacrificed to protect your father, Charles, from his brothers, he would not be alive today. Empress Judith was very wise and very strong. She did whatever was required to serve her husband, her children, and her kingdom. Judith's example is one I have tried to follow and one I hope you will follow as well."

When Judith nodded, Ermentrude continued. "These three crowns belonged to your grandmother. And they will soon be yours."

Judith handled the exquisite crowns wonderingly. The most elaborate of the three was made from golden plaques covered with jewels set on raised panels. Diamonds, emeralds, rubies, sapphires, topaz, and pearls were among the more than one hundred jewels adorning the crown. The golden filigree was also mesmerizing.

As Judith returned the crown to her mother, Ermentrude spoke gently, "This is the crown your grandmother used when she was crowned Empress of the Holy Roman Empire. You may use it when you are anointed a queen."

Ermentrude opened the ivory box and displayed a collection of rings for Judith to look through. "These rings belong to me. You may choose your favorite of my rings as well."

Judith selected a simple gold ring with a sparkling emerald stone surrounded by the tiniest, most delicate of seed pearls.

"You have made an excellent choice," Ermentrude smiled. "Emerald is the gem of kings and queens. Your father gave me permission to give you these things upon your marriage."

"Am I to be married soon?" Judith whispered.

"We have spoken frequently of that possibility. Now, it seems, the time has come. Remember your grandmother . . ." Ermentrude's voice caught with emotion, "and move forward with strength and courage."

"Who am I to marry?"

"You are betrothed to King Aethelwulf."

"I am to go to Wessex, then?"

"As soon as you are married. In October."

Judith's eyes filled with tears.

Ermentrude took her daughter in her arms. "I would never have agreed to this marriage if I thought King Aethelwulf would be cruel to you. He is a good and pious man, like your grandfather, Louis."

Neither mother nor daughter was able to speak further. They clung to each other in silence, their emotions washing over them.

∾

Judith sought solitude in the palace library. Despite the training and preparation of the last year, the prospect of marriage had never seemed real to her. And she had always imagined that her husband would be closer to her age—like Baldwin Iron Arm—not older than her father. She was being asked to leave her family and everything she had come to love. *Please, God, help me through this!*

"Is it true? Are you really going to be my new mother?" Alfred approached quickly.

"It does sound strange," Judith admitted.

"But you are younger than most of my brothers!" Alfred considered for a moment. "You will come with us to Wessex."

"That is true." *I hope your brothers do not treat me how my uncles treated my grandmother.*

"Good! I will teach you everything about our kingdom. For once, I shall know more about something than you do," he proclaimed.

Judith smiled hesitantly. "You will be my only friend in Wessex, Alfred."

"No matter what happens, I will always be your friend!"

"I shall hold you to that promise, Alfred of Wessex!" In spite of her best efforts, Judith's voice trembled with emotion. "Now let us read something that will cheer our hearts."

∾

Two weeks before the wedding, as the royal family left their private chapel following morning mass, the priest, Father Paulus, requested Judith remain behind. "For instruction," he added. Curious, Judith resumed her place on the pew and turned her attention to the priest.

"Princess Judith," Father Paulus began. "With your marriage approaching, the king and queen have requested that I instruct you in the laws of the church regarding the marriage bed."

Judith felt the blood rush to her face. Intimacy between husband and wife was something she had been aware of for a few years, but she did not like to think about. Judith knew she must endure having someone touch her body in ways she might not like if she was ever to bear children. But the thought terrified her.

"Princess Judith," Father Paulus continued. "As you know, there are many ways to commit sin, and you are used to making confession. Once you enter the marriage bed, there are many new ways in which you might sin. As Eve was tempted by the serpent, you will be tempted. If your actions are governed by reason and righteousness, you will not be led astray by the tempter."

Judith's mind reeled as the priest listed all that was proscribed by the church within the bounds of marital intimacy. For the most part, she had no idea what the priest was even talking about.

At the end of the seemingly endless instruction, Father Paulus asked, "Have you any questions, Princess?" When Judith shook her head, he handed her a rolled-up parchment. "Here is a penitential list to help you avoid the sins we have discussed today. Study it. If you violate any of God's laws, you must confess and do penance. This is for the salvation of your soul! If you remember that sexual intimacy between husband and wife is only for the procreation of children, you will do well," he added.

Released at last, Judith hurried to her bedchamber where a startled Hemma was repairing a seam on one of Judith's gowns.

"Is anything amiss, Princess?" Hemma asked, seeing the look on Judith's face.

Judith hesitated. Then, needing someone to confide in, she held out the parchment for Hemma to see. Hemma untied the ribbon holding the parchment and unrolled it.

"This is very complicated," she observed after a moment or two. "How does one ever avoid sin?"

Judith took back the parchment, and they studied it together. Hemma was right. Among other things, the parchment included a list of days when sexual intimacy was not allowed. The list was so complicated it seemed impossible to find a time when intimacy was allowed. *Maybe that is a good thing,* Judith considered. In its daunting complexity, the list eventually seemed humorous to the girls, who giggled as they discovered each new prohibition.

"Listen to this, Princess," Hemma cried. "You cannot have sexual contact on your wedding night—or for three days after, for the truly religious—because the marriage rite is sacred."

"Nor on Sundays," Judith noted. "If you conceive a child on a Sunday, it may be lame or deformed in some way." Judith briefly considered her lame younger brother, Lothar.

"No holy days, or Holy Week for that matter," Hemma chimed in.

"Banned for three days each during Advent, Lent, and Pentecost" was Judith's contribution.

"Wednesdays and Fridays are out, as they are for fasting and penance," Hemma discovered.

"Nor during a woman's monthly flow. Else a child conceived then might be born possessed of a demon!" Judith had yet to experience this "flow" for herself, although she knew it would happen eventually.

"The list goes on and on. What days are left?" Hemma laughed.

"Are men informed of these rules as well?" Judith wondered aloud. Secretly, she also wondered if she would ever be able to look at King Aethelwulf again without blushing.

∽

The last week of September was a blur. Judith received her final lessons from John Scotus, who encouraged her to continue learning throughout her life. Archbishop Hincmar reviewed with Judith the order of the coronation ceremony and explained what was expected of her. She had fittings every day for her ceremonial gowns. Judith chose the crown with which her grandmother was crowned empress for her own coronation and her mother's ring to be used in her wedding ceremony.

She also helped select the few retainers who would accompany her to live in Wessex. Hemma asked questions regarding which of her personal effects she wished to take with her to Wessex. Queen Ermentrude and Gauzlin seemed determined to stuff all their knowledge about palace management into her mind before she departed. She was kept so busy that Judith regrettably had little time to spend with young Charles, Louis, and Baldwin Iron Arm when they arrived for the wedding.

Despite being physically and emotionally exhausted, Judith did not sleep well on the night before her marriage to King Aethelwulf. She was already awake when Hemma came to dress her for morning mass. Judith spent some of the morning playing with her younger sisters, not knowing when she would spend time with them again.

Then, it was time to prepare for the ceremony. As symbol of Judith's purity, Hemma dressed her in a plain, white linen shift for her anointing. Her hair flowed freely as symbol of her virginity. During the ceremony, she would be clothed in queenly robes. For now, Judith covered her simple linen shift with a deep blue cloak lined with ermine for the procession to the church within the palace grounds.

Abbot Lupus Servatus would lead the procession bearing Judith's royal robes. Next to him, Bishop Swithun would carry Empress Judith's crown on an embroidered silken cushion, its jewels breathtaking in their radiance. Her parents would walk arm-in-arm before her. Louis, young Charles, John Scotus, Gauzlin, and other nobles of her father's court would follow behind. The procession would wind past knights and servants and lesser nobles who would not have a place within the church.

At noon, Judith descended the stairs and joined her parents, waiting to begin the procession. Her nervous stomach had prevented her from breaking her fast. Every instinct within her wished to turn and run. She remembered her mother's advice. *Follow the example of Empress Judith. Accept it with grace.*

Judith stepped out into the foggy morning, shivering at the early fall chill in the air. Forcing her feet to move, she prayed for strength as she walked with the procession toward the chapel where Archbishop Hincmar and King Aethelwulf waited.

◦

Baldwin and Louis joined young Charles at Compiègne several days before Judith's wedding to Aethelwulf. The brothers' personal retinues had grown large enough to require their staying at a place other than Verberie since the palace already held the courts of Francia and Wessex. The palace at Compiègne, about two hours' ride, was most convenient to the ceremony. Young Charles greeted Louis warmly and immediately made plans for hunting in the well-stocked Compiègne forest.

As they dined that night upon the pheasant and venison they had procured, it was apparent to Baldwin that young Charles was no happier in Aquitaine than he had been before. Nothing had changed. The rebel lords of Aquitaine were biding their time, still hoping to receive Louis the German as their ruler.

Louis did not complain about his situation in Neustria, but he was not happy with the marriage King Charles had arranged for Judith.

"Judith has got the w . . . worst of it," he growled angrily. "Marrying a m . . . man old enough to be our g . . . grandfather!"

"What can she do? What can any of us do?" young Charles sounded resigned. "We are the king's children. He does with us as he pleases."

"I w . . . wish I could do something! I am angry with Father. Judith deserves b . . . better. W . . . We all do."

The following morning, they rode to Verberie to visit Judith and report to the king. Baldwin watched the princess greet each brother affectionately. He was pleased when she gave him a welcoming smile as well. But Judith seemed distracted. She had little time for visiting as her schedule was completely full.

After paying respects to Queen Ermentrude, the young kings met in council with King Charles, who received their reports of their provinces. Following the afternoon feast, Gauzlin instructed them as to the part each would play in the wedding processional and the coronation before they rode back to Compiègne.

❧

Early on the morning of October 1st, Louis, Baldwin, and young Charles set out for Verberie. Despite a thick and rising fog, they arrived in good time to join the afternoon wedding processional. Baldwin felt honored to be among the court nobles included at the rear of the procession.

He caught his breath as Princess Judith descended the sweeping staircase at Verberie, looking pale but regal. Her loose auburn hair flowed freely in brilliant contrast to the royal blue of her cape with its black and white ermine lining. Judith took her place behind her parents, wearing their ceremonial robes of purple, and the wedding processional began.

Along the path to the chapel, nobles, knights, and servants bowed or curtsied as the procession passed. Many called out blessings upon the king, queen, princess, or royal family. On the steps of the church, Abbot Lupus Servatus and Bishop Swithun led the company in prayers for the sacred rites about to take place within and for the health of the future Queen Judith.

Lupus and Judith stepped back to allow the company to follow Bishop Swithun into the church. Each took his or her place, row by row as they entered, standing until all were in place. Baldwin noticed six thrones on the dais at the head of the church, surrounding the intricately carved altar where Archbishop Hincmar waited. King Charles and Queen Ermentrude took their places before two thrones on the left of the altar, while Louis and young Charles took their places before the two thrones behind them. On the right side of the altar, King Aethelwulf stood before one throne. The other throne remained empty.

With the first dulcet tones from the choir, Princess Judith entered, preceded by Abbot Lupus carrying her ceremonial robes. When Judith stood before the empty throne next to King Aethelwulf, Hincmar bid the congregation be seated.

The Mistress of the Wardrobe removed Judith's cape, revealing her simple, linen shift, and Judith knelt on a cushioned footstool facing the congregation. Bishop Swithun brought forward the sacred horn holding the holy chrism. Pouring the sacred chrism oil onto a silver spoon, Archbishop Hincmar dipped his fingers in the chrism and anointed Judith's hands, her face, and her breast, pronouncing blessings of purity, righteousness, or fertility with each anointing.

At the conclusion of the anointing, the Mistress of the Wardrobe stepped forward, placed a golden tunic over Judith's linen shift and King Aethelwulf stood next to Judith before the altar. Taking from Archbishop Hincmar the emerald ring that Judith had chosen for the ceremony, King Aethelwulf repeated after Hincmar the words, "Receive this ring as a sign of faith and love and unity." He then placed the ring on the third finger of Judith's right hand.

Solemnly, Archbishop Hincmar proclaimed, "No man may put asunder what God has joined." Quietly, Judith voiced her agreement. Then, King Aethelwulf and Judith knelt upon footstools facing the altar while Hincmar pronounced his blessing upon the marriage.

"Oh Lord, pour out thy blessings upon thy servant and thy handmaiden. May their marriage be a spiritual union, in love, through Christ. Bless their marriage bed with the blessings bestowed upon the holy patriarchs. Bless their union with the blessings of the breast and the womb. Open the doors of Heaven, Oh Lord. And visit them with peace and the fullness and riches of the earth. Bless them with a posterity worthy to rule and to inherit the eternal paradise. The Creator and the Redeemer and our Lord Jesus Christ who reigns and lives with the Father and the Holy Spirit, who are one God. Amen."

Next King Aethelwulf arose from his footstool and assisted Judith to take her place upon her throne. Receiving Empress Judith's crown from Bishop Swithun, Aethelwulf placed the crown on Judith's head and repeated after Hincmar.

"May the Lord crown you with a spiritual crown of glory and honor, that your good works may shine forth as glittering gold and gleaming jewels. And make you partaker of an everlasting kingdom, through Jesus Christ, our Lord to whom is all honor and glory. Amen."

The Mistress of the Wardrobe next clothed Judith in the purple robe of royalty, and Hincmar pronounced his blessing on Judith—the first anointed Queen of Wessex.

As the choir sang one last hymn, King Charles and Queen Ermentrude led the company, row-by-row in the order they had arrived, back to the palace for the marriage feast. Judith entered the processional on the arm of Aethelwulf, King of Wessex, with Prince Alfred walking behind his father alongside Louis and young Charles.

Baldwin bowed deeply as Judith passed his pew. His heart was touched by the image of the pure, young girl accepting with grace what life and her father had chosen for her. *The Kingdom of Wessex has been richly blessed today by their ruler's choice.* Baldwin was certain of it.

༅

Queen Judith and King Aethelwulf's marriage feast was one of richness and splendor, celebrating the alliance of two renowned kingdoms. The cooks of Francia and Wessex provided sixteen courses of their kingdoms' most exquisite delicacies. Queen Ermentrude had imposed no restraint on the use of the most expensive ingredients, including spices such as cinnamon and saffron. She had also made generous provision for feeding the local commoners and servants so that all could rejoice in the celebration.

The climax of the feast occurred when a trumpet fanfare announced the most fanciful dish of all—the swan and the peacock. Carried in on enormous platters, the delicate white swan symbolized Judith, while King Aethelwulf was represented by the preening peacock. As part of the drama, the peacock was borne upon the shoulders of strong Wessex warriors, while the swan arrived on the sturdy shoulders of knights of Francia.

Tumblers and fire dancers, musicians, and the court jester all performed between wedding speeches and the serving of new courses. Throughout the feast, King Aethelwulf and Queen Judith received congratulations and gifts from their wedding guests.

Judith noticed many of the nobles were eager to speak with King Aethelwulf, the legendary warrior, having heard of his victories at Aclea in Mercia, Wales, and Kent. They were also keenly aware of the assistance he had provided King Charles at Fossa Givaldi. Abbot Lupus made his way to the King of Wessex's table. He came not only to congratulate the couple but to invite them to stay at his monastery near Quentovic on their return to Wessex.

After more than four hours of feasting and entertainment, Queen Ermentrude rose and beckoned Judith to accompany her. They went to Judith's chamber, where Hemma washed Judith's body with aromatic soaps. Then she massaged her skin with soothing oils, dressed her in a golden sleeping robe, and combed her hair. Satisfied with their efforts, the queen and Hemma led Judith to the chamber of King Aethelwulf.

Judith's stomach churned. *Lord, please help me survive this night,* she silently prayed.

The doorkeeper smiled when he saw them and ushered them into King Aethelwulf's chamber. Several oil lamps lit the room, and a glowing fire burned brightly in the hearth. Hemma turned down the bed.

"From now on, you will share King Aethelwulf's bed. He will expect to see you here when he has finished speaking with your father," Ermentrude instructed gently. "King Aethelwulf is a good and kind man. You are his queen now, consecrated and anointed. The sacred blessing you received today promised that you will give birth to kings. Hold to that promise. It will see you through."

When her mother and Hemma left her alone, Judith shivered nervously. She waited for what seemed like hours, bone weary and yet afraid to sleep. At last, the chamber door opened, and King Aethelwulf entered, followed by his attendant, who helped the king remove his clothes and don a robe. Then, the servant hurried out of the room carrying the king's soiled clothing. King Aethelwulf sat on the bed next to Judith's huddled form. It occurred to Judith that this was the first time she had ever been alone with King Aethelwulf. They had never even had a conversation other than to exchange greetings. *Has he read the list Father Paulus gave me?* Judith shivered.

King Aethelwulf cleared his throat. "Sit up, Judith. I have no intention of talking to a lump in my bed."

Judith complied but could not stop herself from shaking.

"I must apologize," Aethelwulf spoke after some hesitation.

"F . . . For what?" Judith asked warily.

"For the situation you now find yourself in. It is, after all, partly of my choosing."

"I do not comprehend, King Aethelwulf," Judith admitted.

Aethelwulf smiled. "Then, I shall do my best to explain, child. When your father proposed the alliance between our kingdoms, I was tempted because I feared what awaited me at home. I have allowed you to become part of my problems with my son, Aethelbald. He wishes to take my kingdom from me, and an alliance with Francia may make him hesitate to move against me. However, my conscience tells me I have much to repent of."

Judith did not dare ask for elaboration and waited for Aethelwulf to continue.

"You see, Judith, I am aging. My problem is not that I need an heir. The problem is that I have too many heirs, and the eldest is impatient for me to die. Here is what I am guilty of. I am guilty of deceiving your father, who wishes you to bear me a son when I have no intention of siring more children. I am guilty of trapping you in a marriage where you will have no chance of bearing children and may even come under condemnation if people believe you are barren. And I am guilty of deceiving my son, Aethelbald, into believing that he might be displaced by any child we would have together. I despise deception, and yet I am thrice guilty of it."

Judith was beginning to understand. She remembered Father Paulus had said that sexual intimacy was only allowed for the purpose of creating children. *Maybe he has read the list!* "I think you are saying, King Aethelwulf, that you do not wish me to bear children for you."

Aethelwulf nodded in relief. "That is correct. The last thing I want is another son to contend for my kingdom when I am gone. I only have one daughter, and she is married. Perhaps you will allow me to treat you as a daughter, my young queen. I will give you all honors due the first anointed Queen of Wessex and more. I have made generous provision for you in the bride's gift. You now own land in Wiltshire and estates in Kent and Sussex. And you shall have your own throne next to my throne. That is the least penance I can do for all of my deceptions."

Judith's heart rejoiced, the cares and responsibilities of the past weeks gone. *Mother said Aethelwulf is kind and honorable. Perhaps Wessex will not be such a bad place to live.*

"Now, Judith lay your head on my shoulder, and I will put my arm around you to keep you warm. You shall sleep safely all the night. But do not become accustomed to sleeping this way. You will have your own bed chamber once we arrive in Wessex."

Relieved, Judith did as she was bidden. King Aethelwulf's body was warm. His shoulder was broad, and she quickly slipped into a deep and peaceful sleep.

PART II

JUDITH OF WESSEX

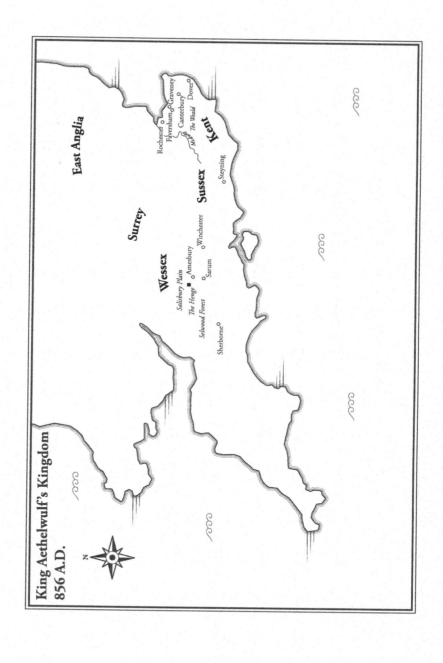

King Aethelwulf's Kingdom
856 A.D.

East Anglia

Surrey

Wessex

Sussex

Kent

Rochester o
Faversham o Graveney
Canterbury o
Dover o
The Weald
Medway
o Steyning

Winchester
o Amesbury
Salisbury Plain
The Henge
o Sarum
Selwood Forest
Sherborne o

N

CHAPTER VIII

OCTOBER and NOVEMBER 856

"What is bothering you, Hemma?" Judith asked as she and her melancholy companion walked one last time through Verberie's stately grounds.

"It is the language. I will not understand the people of Wessex, my lady," Hemma admitted nervously.

"I will help you," Judith quickly assured her. "John Scotus taught me the English vernacular. I will translate for you until you learn it yourself."

They stopped at the church, where the priests offered a prayer for Judith's safe journey on the morrow. Next, they visited the Mistress of the Wardrobe, who presented Judith with an intricately embroidered golden girdle she had saved for such a time.

At the stables, Judith teased Martin. "It is not too late to change your mind and come to Wessex. Someone must care for the more than twenty horses you are sending with me."

Martin laughed. "Queen Judith, is it not enough that I am sending my four best grooms with you? If you had less baggage and a smaller dowry, you would not need so many horses."

"I shall miss you, Martin," Judith squeezed his hand. "My first memory on horseback is perching on a saddle in front of you." Martin had taught her to ride side-saddle, his strong arm helping her balance as a groom led her mount around the palace grounds.

Martin's voice sounded gruff. "Be safe, Queen Judith. Wessex is a long journey on horseback. Keep your seat, and do not drift off to sleep."

When she had finished saying her bittersweet goodbyes, Judith remarked, "I shall miss them all, Hemma! I am very grateful that you are coming with me!"

Judith's entourage would be small. Father Electus would act as Judith's spiritual adviser, Bertrand as her seneschal, and Hemma as her attendant and companion. They would also bring two servants, two messengers, and four grooms to assist with the horses.

As Judith and Hemma were not allowed to guide their own mounts, the royal company would move only as quickly as the groom leading the queen's horse could walk. The soft-spoken and humble Bishop Swithun had also insisted on walking the entire pilgrimage. So, Father Electus, inspired by Swithun's pious example, joined him on foot.

Aethelwulf's itinerary provided sufficient opportunities for rest and refreshment, moving from one abbey or grand estate to the next as they journeyed west. King Aethelwulf planned to travel twenty miles each day and reach the coast in one week. As the journey progressed, Judith understood the king better each day. Aethelwulf was a man full of contradictions. He appeared strong and invincible. Yet, he revealed a softer side during their nightly talks.

"Everyone thinks of me as a great warrior," he confided one night. "I have fought many battles from my youth in defense of family, friend, or kingdom. However, my heart was never in it."

Judith was intrigued. "What did your heart desire?"

Aethelwulf was thoughtful. "I was drawn to the church. But if God and my father wanted me to be a king, I knew I must accept it."

"Is that why you wanted to make the pilgrimage to Rome?"

"Many years earlier, I was inspired by the stories of King Ceolwulf and King Ine's pilgrimages. I vowed to go to Rome myself. When I became high king, I thought I could fulfill that vow and began preparations. But I was needed in Wessex."

"Why did you not go when you sent Alfred three years ago?"

"I wished to. But my wife was dying. And I felt that my older sons were not ready to defend my kingdom should the Danes attack."

"But why send Alfred on his own? He was so young."

"For several reasons, Judith. Alfred, as youngest son, will probably never rule in Wessex. Many kings who have 'extra' heirs force the youngest sons into the church to ensure a peaceful succession."

"My father did that with two of my younger brothers. They were both tonsured at age four."

"I did not wish to do that to Alfred. I hoped that if Alfred went to Rome, he would know for himself if he desired a life in the church. There were also other reasons."

"Tell me, please."

"I wished him to offer prayers for his dying mother . . . and for my soul as well. I am often troubled by the blood I have shed in battle." Aethelwulf paused before continuing. "Perhaps I also hoped that sending Alfred in my place might satisfy my own vow. But when he returned, his account of Rome made me long even more to make the journey."

"And last year, you finally fulfilled your vow," Judith smiled.

"The time seemed right. I made Aethelbald subking of Wessex and Aethelberht subking of Kent, Surrey, and Sussex. I charged them with leading and defending my kingdom for the year I would be gone. But I did not anticipate that Aethelbald would try to displace me during my absence." Aethelwulf's voice betrayed his sorrow.

How could Aethelbald be so cruel? Judith wondered at such selfishness.

§

Quentovic teemed with the constant activity of ships arriving laden with goods from Britannia, and travelers usually found ships waiting to transport them between the continent and the island. However, in unsettled weather, travelers could be stranded in Quentovic for weeks. Too calm, and the ships' sails had no wind to propel them forward. With too strong a wind, lives and precious cargo were endangered.

As abbot of the monastery at St. Josse, less than three miles from Quentovic, Lupus Servatus hosted many nobles and clergy on pilgrimage from Britannia to Rome. When Aethelwulf's party rode through the large double gates of the monastery, Lupus Servatus welcomed them warmly.

"I am grateful for this opportunity to repay your kindness, King Aethelwulf. Several years ago, I wrote to you about our need for a new roof at the abbey in Ferrières. Your gracious gift of providing the lead for our roof was a great boon to us!"

Aethelwulf smiled. "I was happy to assist. We look forward to staying at St. Josse."

"Perhaps you would like some refreshment. Please follow me." Lupus led them to a spacious building on the right of the gate. "Our guest house has a large storeroom for your baggage. I suggest your servants store all but your most essential personal items here. Then, when you receive word that the winds are in your favor, you can be ready to leave in good time."

"Wise counsel, Abbot," Aethelwulf agreed.

Lupus showed them the royal chamber and led them into the common room, where servants waited with trays of rich cheese and meats, baskets of crusty aromatic bread, and pitchers of wine. "We have a well-stocked larder and wine cellar here for your use. We have bedchambers for your nobles and stalls for your horses here as well."

"Your attention to our needs is much appreciated, Abbot Lupus," Judith smiled.

"It is my pleasure," Lupus assured them. "And should you so desire, I will be happy to assist you on the morrow in finding the best ships to carry you across the channel."

In the morning, Aethelwulf, Alfred, and a few of the king's men accompanied Abbot Lupus to Quentovic. When they returned at midday, Alfred was eager to share what they had discovered.

"Judith," he cried excitedly. "We secured ten ships for our voyage!"

"The servants will take most of our baggage to Quentovic this afternoon to be loaded on the ships, and some of our warriors will remain there to guard them," Aethelwulf contributed. "Then, when the wind is right, we can be on our way."

"How long does the crossing take?" Judith asked.

Aethelwulf answered, "With the wind in our favor, only a few hours."

"That is if everything goes as planned," Alfred jumped in. "Sailors at the port told us that one ship last week had to turn back when it took on water. By the time they returned to port, the horses on board were standing in water up to their bellies!"

"That is rather alarming," Judith laughed. "I hope that will not be our fate!"

"Neither Alfred nor I have encountered any such problem on our previous crossings," Aethelwulf reassured.

"But, in Dover, we had to wait eight days for the wind to change on our way to Rome," Alfred reminded his father. And then I felt ill while upon the water."

"You were ill?" Judith was concerned.

"I was . . . but not father. Many people become ill while making the crossing. You will see."

"I am definitely not looking forward to seeing that!" Judith assured Alfred.

Two days later, servants awakened the royal company to announce that the wind was changing. While it was yet dark the company was on the road to Quentovic.

The sun was still but a promise on the horizon as Judith took in the intriguing, briny smell of the ocean. As they made their way through Quentovic, Aethelwulf pointed out warehouse upon warehouse. Some belonged to abbeys, lords, merchants, or the king. At an enormous warehouse owned by King Charles, servants loaded ox-drawn wagons to transport goods to the king's various palaces.

Six of the ten ships they had hired would carry the horses, with men enough to control them. The other ships would carry the remainder of the company and their baggage. King

Aethelwulf 's party would travel on the second ship, following the one carrying the royal mounts.

Waiting for their turn to board, Alfred pointed out to Judith a thin white line on the horizon.

"That line is a ridge of chalky cliffs above Dover. They form the eastern edge of the weald."

"What is the weald?" Judith inquired.

Alfred was eager to share his knowledge. "The weald is a great forest running west from the white cliffs more than one hundred miles through Kent, Sussex, and Surrey. Almost all the iron in our kingdom comes from the rocky ridges in the weald. And its forests in Sussex are famous for hunting wild cattle and boar."

"Sounds like an interesting place."

"Not for most travelers," Alfred insisted. "Too many brigands. But they do not dare attack the king or his men."

Judith and Hemma settled on cushions set for the royal family under a silken shade canopy. As they set sail, Judith's heart ached for the family and friends she was leaving behind. *Will I see any of them again?*

With the rise and fall of the waves, Judith felt the tightness in the belly and light-headed discomfort caused by the undulating motion. Some of their company, including Aethelwulf, showed no signs of distress and moved about the ship unaffected. Others spent the entire crossing prostrate on the deck or hung over the ship's side, relieving themselves of the contents of their stomachs. Judith was grateful that she was not among the worst afflicted. The four-hour voyage already seemed much, much longer than it was.

As the ship neared the shore and the chalky cliffs loomed large, Judith noticed matching stone towers upon the heights, with a fortification adjacent to the eastern tower.

"Those towers are lighthouses built by the Romans," Alfred explained. "And we use the fortification to watch for Vikings."

Eagerly, they left the ship to find their horses and baggage already waiting for them. Judith, Hemma, and Alfred walked about, regaining their "land legs" while King Aethelwulf consulted his thegns.

"We will depart for Canterbury Abbey, where we will sleep tonight," Aethelwulf informed them. "The remainder of our company will follow shortly."

The king's party mounted their horses and moved northwest on a well-paved road. "This is the best road in Britannia," Alfred informed Judith. "Watling Street leads all the way to London. Do not expect all the roads to be this good." Pausing for reflection, he added, "This is also part of the Via Francigena pilgrim's road that runs from Canterbury all the way to Rome. When we arrive in Canterbury, I shall have completed the pilgrimage twice."

"You are blessed, indeed, Alfred," Judith remarked. "Most people never make the pilgrimage once in their life. Since women are not encouraged to do so, I doubt I shall ever see the holy city."

They arrived at the abbey, located just outside the Canterbury city walls, while it was yet light. Archbishop Ceolnoth, an aged man with trembling hands, greeted them and led them to their accommodations for the night, where the monks provided them with a simple supper.

Archbishop Ceolnoth listened intently to Bishop Swithun's account of Judith's anointing. He also eagerly questioned Aethelwulf and Swithun about their sojourn in Rome. However, he became solemn when Aethelwulf asked Ceolnoth about recent events in Wessex.

"Sire, your son, King Aethelbald, has persuaded many of the ealdormen and thegns of Wessex to support him as king. That is not the case in Kent. Canterbury has supported you for twenty years. I will not change loyalty now," Ceolnoth was calm and determined.

Aethelwulf's brow furrowed. "Your loyalty means much to me, Archbishop. What of my second son, King Aethelberht? Does he follow his brother?"

"Aethelberht would never betray you, father!" Alfred insisted hotly.

Ceolnoth's hand quivered as he raised his cup to his lips. "I agree, Prince Alfred. They are two very different sort of men."

Aethelwulf nodded his acceptance. "It appears I have some work to do."

When Aethelwulf and Judith retired to their bed chamber, Judith expressed her concern. "What will you do about Aethelbald? Will you fight him for your kingdom?"

"It will not come to that," Aethelwulf assured her. "I have killed many men in battle who were trying to take my kingdom. But I will not shed the blood of my son. Nor do I wish to shed the blood of the men of Wessex."

On the following morning, the king's entourage celebrated mass in Canterbury's stately cathedral. While Aethelwulf remained in the city to meet with Canterbury's leaders, Archbishop Ceolnoth offered to give Judith and Alfred a tour of the abbey and its grounds.

"Do you know, Queen Judith," he began. "Canterbury Cathedral as well as our own abbey were founded by St. Augustine, who brought Christianity to Britannia almost 250 years ago. Ours is the oldest diocese. The second oldest is in Rochester, which I am sure you will also visit."

"My father plans to stop at the royal estate in Faversham for a day or two. Then we are on to Rochester," Alfred confirmed.

Archbishop Ceolnoth showed them the three churches in the abbey and the grave of St. Augustine in the largest church of Saints Peter and Paul. The cloister, chapter house, and other monastic buildings were all very interesting. But Judith was troubled after inspecting the scriptorium where a lonely pair of monks painstakingly copied two manuscripts.

"I was surprised to see only two scribes at the abbey. Does Rochester have a larger scriptorium?" she asked as they set out from Canterbury on the following morning.

"Sadly, no," Aethelwulf admitted. "It was not always so. Education has sharply declined in the last decades. Few of our priests can read Latin. And many of my thegns do not read at all. That is why I employ Felix of Francia as my personal secretary."

"But Britannia produced Alcuin, who spread education throughout Charles the Great's empire," Judith protested. "His scriptorium at Marmoutier Abbey is legendary!"

Aethelwulf shook his head sadly. "Everything you say is true, Judith. My father, King Egberht, fled Wessex for his life when he was young and thought to be a challenger for the kingship. Your great-grandfather, Emperor Charles the Great, allowed him to remain at his court during the thirteen years he was in exile. My father benefitted from Alcuin's teaching during his stay."

"I did not know that."

"While he was there, my father learned the importance of education. It is shameful that now, even the priest's school in Canterbury has but a handful of students. I pray that someday Wessex will have a king who will be able to rekindle the love of learning in every heart."

Judith noticed Alfred hanging his head, unusually silent.

They left the paved road and followed a wide, beaten path north, pausing to appreciate the ruins of an enormous Roman amphitheater set upon a rise where the amber and gold trees in the valley and on the gently sloping hills appeared to catch fire. Ahead, Judith saw the thatch-roofed timber buildings and church making up the settlement of Faversham. The path followed a crystal stream running along the vale.

"This place has many natural springs, creeks, and streams," Aethelwulf informed her.

"A canal also runs through here, bringing boats from Faversham to the ocean," Alfred chimed in. "And on the other side of the estuary is the Isle of Sheppey, where the Danes overwintered while we were in Rome."

"Are Vikings still there?" Judith wondered anxiously.

"I think not," Aethelwulf assured. "However, I will inquire as to the current state of Sheppey while we are here."

Entering Faversham, Judith noted vestiges of Roman architecture interspersed with Saxon thatch-roofed construction. Even the church appeared to be of Saxon timber built upon a Roman foundation. Oxen-drawn wagons loaded with goods from flat boats traveled up the marshy swale. From Faversham, the heavy-laden wagons made their ponderous way toward the paved road of Watling Street and London.

On the west side of Faversham, amidst a grouping of golden-leafed oaks, a path led to a large rectangular two-level timber structure flanked by a variety of outbuildings.

"There it is!" Alfred cried enthusiastically. "Our estate at Faversham."

Judith was eager to see a royal Kentish estate. All she had known were grand palaces planned and executed with the extravagant taste of Emperor Charles the Great. *Faversham is certainly not Verberie!* Judith smiled at the comparison.

Instead of a reception area, the royal manor opened directly into its enormous great hall with a grand fireplace. Chambers of varying use flanked either side of the hall. While the great hall itself could be divided by screens to create more rooms or to hide entrances. An embroidered screen behind the king's table—set upon a raised dais—led directly through a door into the royal bedchamber.

Aethelwulf met with his estate steward as Judith and Hemma eagerly followed Alfred through the manor, discovering more private bedchambers, a kitchen, storage rooms, a latrine, and a small chapel. A staircase led to additional space for storage and more bedchambers. Outside, they inspected stables, animal pens, beehives, a vegetable garden, a laundry, and a forge.

Aethelwulf joined them in the courtyard and pointed out a distant grove. "On the other side of that grove is former Archbishop Wulfred's estate, Graveney. Wulfred was Archbishop Ceolnoth's predecessor, and his estate lies near the canal. After Wulfred's death, Kent came under Wessex's rule, and the estate became part of our royal domain. Graveney is now yours, Judith, as part of your bride gift. You will find that it brings a good income."

Judith was speechless. Her father owned many properties, but she had never held land in her own right. She was glad that her mother had insisted she bring Bernard, who would act as her personal seneschal. Already, work awaited him in the management of Graveney.

The following morning, Aethelwulf, Judith, and Alfred rode over to Graveney with Bernard and Aethelwulf's steward for an inspection. The estate was almost as big as that of the royal estate at Faversham, although not as well maintained. Breathless with excitement, Judith had Bernard make note of tapestries, screens, and furnishings needing repair or replacement. While Bernard consulted with Graveney's servants, Judith and Alfred explored the estate's special treasure trove. Archbishop Wulfred had maintained an extensive library of manuscripts and bound books in Greek, Latin, and even a few in the English vernacular. *This is all mine!* Judith thought wonderingly. She would have gladly settled permanently at Graveney. But they were leaving for Rochester in the morning. Choosing two books, she rode back to the royal estate, thrilled with her bride gift.

❦

"The men of Canterbury and Faversham assure me of Aethelberht's loyalty. But I must see him, hear his voice, and look into his eyes before going on to Winchester. I do not believe Aethelberht will prove false . . . but I was wrong about his brother," Aethelwulf explained as they followed the wide and rapidly flowing river Medway leading to Rochester.

Arriving at the monastery in Rochester late in the afternoon, Alfred cried out with joy to see King Aethelberht and Prince Aethelred awaiting their arrival. Judith witnessed the tender reunion and embrace of father and sons. As they retired to the monastery, she observed her new family closely. Wistfully, she noted that Prince Aethelred was about the same age as her brother, Louis. King Aethelberht, perhaps ten years his elder, shared not only similar facial features with his father but his quiet strength and regal presence as well.

When they finished speaking of the pilgrimage, Rome, and events at King Charles' court, Aethelberht turned to less happy matters. "Father, you know of my elder brother's opposition to your kingship in Wessex. However, I have not deserted you. I rule only under your high kingship."

"Which of my ealdormen support Aethelbald? Has the rebellion spread to Winchester?" King Aethelwulf pressed.

"I am not certain. I believe Aethelbald has only the support of the thegns and ealdormen west of Selwood Forest. I can only promise that I will not take Aethelbald's part against you. And I wish to accompany you to Winchester to demonstrate my support to any thegn or ealdorman who may doubt it!"

"I feel the same, father!" Prince Aethelred assured the king, whose eyes grew moist at his sons' expressions of faithfulness.

Judith's respect for the brothers increased as each pledged loyalty to their father. King Aethelwulf and his three sons had united to confront a rebellious prodigal. They would depart for Winchester the following morning.

৯

The journey from Rochester to Winchester took nearly a week, their progress slowed by rain and rough roads. Alfred, thrilled at being reunited with his brother, visited with Aethelred while the two kings rode ahead, discussing the kingdom's concerns. Bishop Swithun and Father Electus had developed a brotherly bond as they had walked the entire way from Verberie and were deep in conversation. Not feeling part of any of these groups, Judith held back with Hemma, missing the camaraderie she had enjoyed with Louis and his companion, Baldwin Iron Arm.

Winchester was one of the largest and most prosperous towns during the Roman occupation of Britannia. The town had retained its Roman walls as well as the orderly layout of its town center and streets. At the heart of the town lay the minster and the palace. The stately minster was under the direction of Bishop Swithun. The building, dedicated to St. Peter and St. Paul, also held the tomb of Aethelwulf's father, King Egberht.

Next to the minster stood the royal residence at Winchester. Smaller than the palaces in Francia, and with fewer bedchambers, it provided less opportunity for privacy. Judith was, therefore, not surprised to find that her private chamber was much smaller than what she had been used to. With her bed, books, a couple of traveling chests, and a small table, there was just enough room for a mattress and privacy screen for Hemma. However, Judith was content. *I have all I truly need.*

After meeting with his advisers, King Aethelwulf sent a messenger to Sherborne requesting that Aethelbald meet him at the hilltop fortress at Sarum during the first week of November. From Sarum, the court would move to the royal estate at nearby Amesbury for Advent and the Christmas season.

King Egberht, Aethelwulf's father, had loved Sarum and often stayed there. Only one day's ride from Winchester, the journey required fording the Avon River south of the fortress. Aethelwulf chose Sarum as a meeting place, hoping that its history would remind Aethelbald of his duty to his family. Within a few days, the messenger returned with an answer from Sherborne. Aethelbald would arrive at Sarum on November 7th.

The royal party heading west toward the fortress at Sarum was small. Aethelwulf chose to bring only Judith, his sons, Bishop Swithun, and their personal attendants. The rest of the court would proceed directly to Amesbury to prepare the palace for the king's arrival. The mood was somber amongst the king's companions.

To make the journey faster, rope hand grips were attached to Judith and Hemma's side saddles. Holding the grips steadied them through the forest and while fording the river as they were led by grooms who were mounted rather than on foot. Judith longed to control her own mount. *I could do this if they would but give me the reins!* she thought.

Sarum was a fortified settlement set on a rather steep hill. The walls, built of Roman brick and stone, were surrounded by earthen works dug to create a deep, defensive trench protecting against enemy assault. Within the walls were a minster, barracks, shops, and cottage dwellings. At the center of the settlement rose a second hill upon which the Roman palace fort stood, protected by an inner wall.

Once past the outer walls of the settlement, the company made their way up the steep incline leading through the inner walls to the brick hillfort palace, where they were received with warm food and drink. Over their meal, the discussion turned to the looming confrontation with Aethelbald.

"I shall first attempt to meet with him alone," King Aethelwulf began. "I wish to allow Aethelbald the opportunity to withdraw his opposition to my kingship."

"A private meeting is your best hope, father," Aethelberht agreed. "Aethelbald will not withdraw in front of an audience. His pride has taken him too far. He cannot appear weak before his supporters after what he said about you during your absence."

"What is your plan should he refuse to meet with you in private?" Bishop Swithun questioned.

"That depends on his demands. If Aethelbald is not willing to honor me as his father, perhaps he is willing to spare the kingdom needless bloodshed." King Aethelbald looked into the faces of his sons. "I have no wish to fight Aethelbald."

"It will serve us all better if Aethelbald does not know that," Aethelberht advised.

"True," Aethelwulf agreed. "I can only hope he does not wish to fight me."

જ

King Aethelbald arrived at Sarum two days later. Refusing to meet with his father privately, he boldly entered the palace's great hall accompanied by more than twenty nobles with holdings ranging from Selwood Forest to the western borders of Wessex. Aethelbald was tall and muscular, with a face that might be handsome, but for his arrogant demeanor and the calculating look in his eye. When Aethelbald's glance rested on Judith, his upper lip curled in a definite sneer. *He has weighed me in the balance and found me wanting,* Judith concluded.

Aethelbald faced his father and brothers without any form of greeting. "You requested that I come. What is it you desire?"

King Aethelwulf replied calmly. "The question should be, 'What is it you desire, my son?'"

"I desire . . . we all desire for you to no longer pretend to the kingship of Wessex, which you abandoned more than one year ago," Aethelbald declared coldly.

"You would take my kingdom from me?" Aethelwulf stared down at his son.

His piercing gaze fell upon his former close advisers and friends–Bishop Ealhstan of Sherborne and Eanwulf, ealdorman of Somerset, and in turn upon each of his other thegns and ealdormen. "*You* would take my kingdom from me?" he repeated. Ealhstan and Eanwulf each dropped their gaze. "Well, I do not intend to relinquish my kingdom," Aethelwulf spoke with grim purpose.

"Is it war you propose, then?" Aethelbald shifted uneasily as King Aethelwulf took his time in answering.

Finally, Aethelwulf broke the silence. "No. War is not what I have in mind. I propose in mid-December to call upon the Witan–the ealdormen and thegns, the bishops, and archbishops throughout all the shires of Wessex. We will assemble at the great henge near Amesbury. Each will make his arguments before the Witenagemot. Rather than declare war, we will allow the council of Witan to decide who is rightful king in Wessex."

Aethelbald's face waxed pale, the possibility of losing power affecting him deeply. "I must confer with my advisers," he growled.

'Of course," Aethelwulf replied. "The decision to go to war is never to be made lightly. Many lives hang in the balance."

After some time in discussion outside the great hall, King Aethelbald and his followers returned. Aethelbald's jaw was clenched, and his eyes steeled with determination.

"Call your Witenagemot," he growled. "Next month the Witan of Wessex will decide whom they choose as their king. But, if the decision goes against you, you shall never set foot in Wessex again. Do I have your word?"

King Aethelwulf gazed solemnly at his rebellious son for some time before answering.

"You have my word," he agreed.

CHAPTER IX

NOVEMBER and DECEMBER 856

Aethelwulf's decision to call a Witenagemot had not been made lightly. The exclusive group of counselors known as the Witan advised the king on the formation of secular laws, regulated ecclesiastical matters, and even levied taxes for public services. The Witan also had the power to make and enforce treaties and mete out justice in both criminal and civil cases. In matters of holdings, they could confiscate the estates of traitors and approve charters transferring properties from public or "folk" land to private or "book" land. Finally, when a royal controversy arose, the Witan could depose one king in favor of a new ruler.

Only the king could call for an assembly of the Witan, and the Witenagemot was held wherever the king was in residence. With the royal family at Amesbury for the Christmas season, King Aethelwulf called for the assembly to take place at the great stone henge not far distant. The surrounding plain provided ample space for setting up tents and canopies. And the ancient henge would add solemnity to the process of choosing a king.

Judith was fascinated by the wild surroundings of Amesbury, with its grassy plains, barrows, and hillside lynchets—very different from the heavy forests of her native land. The city was set in a valley and was a convenient fording place for the Avon River on the road to London. Vestiges of past settlements were everywhere, from the ruins of a large hill fortress overlooking the river to the Roman roads and remnants of Roman buildings and graveyards still in evidence.

As the days grew shorter and the nights colder, Judith found it curious that the weather did not hinder the plans for holding an outdoor assembly. She was assured that—if it were to storm—the Witenagemot could remove to the royal estate at Amesbury. However, the king and his nobles were accustomed to camping on the downs and in the forests in all seasons and for various purposes, especially in pursuit of their favorite pastime—the hunt.

Although there was not an abundance of trees in the area, Amesbury was rife with quail and hares. However, Alfred longed to go hunting for bigger game in Selwood Forest. His persistent enthusiasm eventually persuaded Judith to join the party setting up a hunting camp on the eastern side of the forest in late November.

Judith and Hemma wrapped themselves in furs for warmth and remained on cushions under a canopy, watching for the return of the hunters. Judith used the time to enrich Hemma's vocabulary in the English vernacular and even teach her some of the embroidering she had learned from her mother. Felix, King Aethelwulf's Frankish secretary, had become a good friend to Judith and Hemma and remained behind to assist them with their studies of English.

"Hemma," Felix began with a twinkle in his eye. "Do you know what is tonight?"

Hemma looked confused. "Is it not the 29th of November?"

"That it is," Felix agreed. "But it is also St. Andrew's Eve. German legend has it that on St. Andrew's Eve, a young woman may discover something about the man she will marry."

"What, for instance?" Hemma was drawn in.

"Well, you may only choose one thing that you wish to know. On this night, if a young woman recites a poem to St. Andrew just before going to sleep, her dreams will reveal the face of her future husband."

"What if she doesn't dream?" Judith joined in the fun.

"Then she must wait until the next year. Perhaps that is why there are other methods of discovery as well," Felix assured them.

"Tell us more," both young women begged.

"Of course!" Felix laughed. "A girl can pour the white of an egg through the hole of a key into cold water. Whatever shape the egg white forms represents the tools her future husband will work with. Or she can go out into the darkness and select a piece from the wood pile without looking. The length and girth of the stick will determine if her future husband will be tall and slender or short and broad."

"Might a young man attempt similar things to discover his future wife?" Hemma wondered.

"He might. And married people may also discover something about their futures. It is said if you make a small heap of flour on a table before going to bed, you will die in the next year if the heap collapses during the night."

"I don't think I want to know that!" Judith grimaced.

Felix agreed, "Sometimes it is better not to know our future."

Aethelwulf, his three sons, and their party of nobles returned jovial and triumphant, with everything from young stags to a squirrel, which Alfred proudly displayed. Judith saw value in the king's spending time hunting with his followers. It provided an opportunity to discuss things outside of formal councils and strengthened the bonds between king and thegn. Later, as she retired to her tent for the night, Judith spotted Hemma returning from the wood pile with a long, sturdy stick in her hand, which she laid gently upon the fire.

As mid-December approached, the king's closest advisers arrived to discuss the possible outcomes of the fast-approaching Witenagemot. Aethelwulf sought to ease Judith's concern over the ensuing conflict.

"If the worst happens and the Witan decide against me, I will still be high king in the eastern realm and rule with Aethelberht as king under me."

"You would accept banishment from Wessex?" Judith asked softly.

"If that is the decision of the Witan, I must."

Aethelwulf chose to camp at the stone henge the day before the assembly to mingle with his Witan and assess their loyalty. King Aethelwulf's servants had already set up camp with the banner of Wessex floating above the king's tent amidst the many other tents surrounding the great stone circle. Large and discernible from a distance, the henge was impressive.

"Who built this place, and how?" Judith asked Alfred.

"No one knows," Alfred answered eagerly. "But it is perfect for assemblies. The blue stone pillars ring out when you strike them as the signal for everyone to gather."

Judith retired to her tent, eager for respite from the icy breeze that had nipped at her nose and cheeks on their ride from Amesbury. She and Hemma watched from the door of her tent as King Aethelwulf and his sons made their way into other camps, mingling with the nobles of Wessex.

With few trees in the area, King Aethelwulf had ordered wagons full of logs brought in to sustain the Witan's many fires already burning brightly. And the Witan had brought provisions of food and ale for three days. The odor of burnt wood and meat roasting on the spit permeated the air as servants turned freshly snared quail and rabbits over the glowing embers.

As darkness fell, the oil lamps lighting the tents from within would have seemed festive had the somber purpose of the assembly not cast a gloomy pall over Judith's spirits. *Our fate is in the hands of those who gather here. Please, God, let them choose right.*

Shortly before mid-day on December 15th Judith heard the clanging of the blue stone summoning the Witan. She found King Aethelwulf outside her tent waiting to escort her to the henge. As they approached the stone circle, Judith was glad to see she was not the only woman attending the assembly of fifty or more persons, as here and there appeared an abbess or the wife of a nobleman.

The stone henge was even more impressive from the inside of the circle. Pairs of standing stones, topped by massive lintels, towered over the attendees. Judith guessed the tallest pair of standing stones to be four times taller than the king. An inner half circle with several somewhat smaller pairs of stones encased a central stone lying recumbent, dressed with an altar cloth, and bedecked with wine and bread for the eucharist. Bishop Swithun, Father Electus, and a few other clergy members stood ready at the center of the henge to administer the mass.

Members of the Witan entered, found place within the henge, and sat upon stools or cushions they carried from their tents. A few chose to stand and lean against the pillars, leaving access to the inner circle. Raised eyebrows and whispers followed King Aethelwulf as he guided Judith to one of two thrones placed at the center of the henge while he took his seat upon the other. Aethelbald arrived not long after. Two of his thegns carried a throne for him, which they also placed within the inner circle near the altar.

At Aethelwulf's nod, Bishop Swithun addressed the Witenagemot. "Kings and queen, princes and nobles, bishops and clergy, we are all gathered here at this solemn place and time of judgment. This place and our judgment will be sanctified by our reliance upon the judgment and mercy of Christ, He who sacrificed all for us. We begin this assembly with celebrating that sacrifice by administering the holy mass."

Bishop Swithun read a scripture from the first book of Samuel in which Israel desired a king who would judge righteously and lead them in battle. He next read St. Matthew's warning that man would be judged by whatever judgment he himself meted out. And finally, he read from St. Paul's admonition to the Romans that man should make peace with his brother.

The homily, which followed Swithun's readings, touched on the themes in the three scriptures he had read. He concluded by entreating each man or woman to follow the advice found within holy writ.

"When ancient Israel desired a righteous and powerful king, God listened, and Samuel the prophet anointed Saul. This assembly must choose which king will rule Wessex. Members of the Witan! Search your souls and judge righteously for the good of Wessex and the good of your own souls. Members of the Witan! We must choose a king who will lead in righteousness and brotherhood. If we do that, God will be with us, and we shall have peace!"

As an olive branch to those who had deserted King Aethelwulf in favor of his son, Bishop Swithun invited Archbishop Ealhstan of Sherborne to recite the prayers over the bread and wine of the holy eucharist. When the host was distributed, Swithun called upon the assembly to greet each other with the kiss of peace. The men in the assembly arose and exchanged the greeting with those nearest them. Bishop Swithun then pronounced his blessing upon the assembly and invited King Aethelbald to stand and make his arguments before the Witenagemot.

King Aethelbald stood before the altar stone. He gazed left and right, engaging everyone except his father. Judith shivered when his cold, piercing glance passed over her. "Honored and wise members of the Witan," he began. "Bishop Swithun most appropriately shared with us the story of King Saul—a king who began his reign chosen by God. Saul led his people in battle and did much good among them. But as Saul aged, his heart and mind turned from serving the people to serving his own purposes. When God chose another king for Israel, Saul refused to step aside."

This time Aethelbald's accusing stare sought out his father's eyes. When Aethelwulf refused to look away, Aethelbald turned back to face the assembly. His face was flushed. His eyes steel.

"I cannot deny that King Aethelwulf served this people well . . . in the beginning. I fought beside him at Aclea, where we routed a massive horde of Danes. But of late, his first thought is what is best for himself and not what is best for Wessex. Is it because he atones for some secret sin? Or is it because he is aged and knows that his days are numbered? I cannot see into his heart, but I can tell you that his actions are not those of a wise king!"

Aethelbald paused briefly while members of the assembly whispered amongst themselves. He walked the path leading out from the inner circle as he sought to connect with each member of the assembly.

"Ask yourselves, was it wise for King Aethelwulf to dispose of one-tenth of his lands to benefit only a select few within his kingdom and without consulting his Witan? I say no! To absolve his sins, he demanded prayers be offered on behalf of his soul as contingent upon the gift. Was it wise for him to leave his kingdom and make a pilgrimage to Rome, allowing the Danes to overwinter on the Isle of Sheppey from whence they could launch their murderous raids on Britannia? I say no! Again, his pilgrimage was done solely for the king's personal benefit. Ask yourselves, was it wise for Aethelwulf to take a young Frankish wife when he already had heirs aplenty? I say no! He did so solely to satisfy his own lusts. Once again, he did not consult this assembly, and he did not act for the good of Wessex!"

Aethelbald, having reached the end of the outer circle, turned, and started back down the path toward the altar.

"The question then arises, what is the remedy for a kingdom that is not well served by its king? We need look no further than our own history. Wessex was faced with that very question exactly one hundred years ago in 756 in the days of King Sigeberht. When King Sigeberht consistently put his own interests above those of his kingdom, the members of his Witan wisely removed him from the kingship and replaced him with King Cynewulf. Wessex was better for that decision. We can also look to the example of biblical Israel as noted by Bishop Swithun. Saul, in his old age, put his own welfare above that of Israel. So, God replaced him with young King David. Aethelwulf, like Sigeberht and like Saul, has lost his way. And, for more than one year, he left his kingdom in pursuit of his own selfish interests!"

Aethelbald, once again reaching the center circle, stood before his throne to make his final plea.

"Members of the Witan, Aethelwulf is not the only king in Wessex. I was appointed king before my father abandoned his position. During my father's absence, I have been the guardian of Wessex. Aethelwulf's supporters would have you believe that I am trying to supplant him as king. But is it not the other way around? Is it not he who seeks to displace me? Two of my father's closest advisers—Archbishop Ealhstan of Sherborne and Ealdorman Eanwulf of Somerset—have taken my part. I entreat you to use that righteous judgment, which Bishop Swithun mentioned in his homily, to join them in supporting me as rightful King of Wessex!"

At the conclusion of Aethelbald's remarks, Judith knew that inevitable comparisons would be drawn between father and son. Aethelbald represented youth and strength—the future of Wessex. Would Aethelwulf be seen as the foolish old man his son accused him of being? *I pray that Aethelwulf's gentleness and goodness do not make him appear weak!* Judith held her breath as Aethelwulf rose to present his arguments.

"Members of the Witan and honored guests, I stand before you to answer the charge that I have forsaken my duty to Wessex in deference to my own interests. This charge is based on three points: my decimation of land charters of 854, my pilgrimage in 855, and my marriage to Judith of Francia in 856. I will address each of these points in order."

All eyes were on King Aethelwulf. His voice was confident and strong, his bearing regal.

"I begin by quoting from the third book of the prophet Malachi. This scripture weighed heavily upon my thoughts and influenced my actions in 854. Malachi writes, "Will a man rob God? Yet ye have robbed me. But ye say, wherein have we robbed thee? In tithes and offerings. Ye are accursed with a curse, for ye have robbed me, even this whole nation. Bring ye all the tithes into the storehouse, that there may be meat in mine house, and prove me now herewith, saith the Lord of hosts, if I will not open you the windows of heaven, and pour you out a blessing, that there shall not be room enough to receive it. And I will rebuke the devourer for your sakes, and he shall not destroy the fruits of your ground; neither shall your vine cast her fruit before its time in the field, saith the Lord of hosts. And all nations shall call you blessed; for ye shall be a delightsome land, saith the Lord of hosts."

Aethelwulf paused to allow the assembly to contemplate the meaning of the scripture. "I conferred with my council on how I might observe this commandment of tithes and offerings. Bishop Swithun assured me that the charters I issued would be an acceptable offering on behalf of myself as well as our entire kingdom. One that would bring God's blessings upon the people of Wessex and protect my kingdom from the ravages of the devourer—whether it be drought, pestilence, or Dane. I dedicated a tenth of the land under my control to God with the hope that all nations would call us a blessed and delightsome land, as the scripture promises. Not all my advisers agreed with my decision."

Aethelwulf's gaze rested on Archbishop Ealhstan and Ealdorman Eanwulf as he continued. "The second charge against me is that of deserting my kingdom in time of need. Bede, the venerable monk who devoted his life to recording the history of our island kingdoms, believed that kings have a responsibility to spread Christianity amongst their people through example and not by force. Many of you know that I have long desired to go on pilgrimage to Rome. I desired to bring offerings to the Holy Bishop of Rome as token of my Christian faith and as a representative of our Christian kingdom. But I would never have gone if my kingdom had been threatened by an enemy. At the battle of Aclea, I led my son and my warriors in our God-given victory over the largest invasion force the Danes have ever sent against any kingdom on our island. For four years, I waited to see if the Danes would return. They dared not. Last year, my sons were old enough to assume temporary stewardship of my kingdom. It was also to be a trial for them to see how they would serve the people. Aethelbald claims it was irresponsible of me to allow him to rule Wessex for one year during my pilgrimage. And yet, he claims it would not be irresponsible for me to allow him to continue ruling my kingdom upon my return. Such conflicting claims expose Aethelbald's own lack of wisdom. And wisdom is an essential part of ruling with righteous judgment."

Judith noticed Aethelbald shift uneasily on his throne. He gazed at a random point on the horizon, his jaw clenched.

"The last charge is most easily dismissed. I was not able to seek counsel from this assembly when Charles, King of Francia, unexpectedly offered a marriage alliance designed to benefit both our kingdoms. No one can deny that strengthening ties with the court of King Charles will bring our kingdom great opportunities. We will see increased trade with Francia. We will learn much from Frankish education and schools. We will exchange art and culture.

And we will share ideas for building better defenses against the Vikings. All of this strengthens our kingdom and directly benefits Wessex. This benefit was my sole intent when I married Queen Judith."

King Aethelwulf's voice echoed majestically against the stones as he made his final plea. "Most honorable members of the Witan, I have been guided by your wisdom for nearly twenty years. You have been my loyal followers. You have been my friends. You know my heart. My desire always has been, and ever will be, to serve and prosper our kingdom through the grace of God. I know your heart as well. You also have acted for the benefit of our kingdom. You have always chosen wisdom over folly, faithfulness over treachery, and peace over disharmony. Together, we have accomplished great things in the past. Stand with me now and we will yet do great things in the future for Wessex!"

King Aethelwulf took his throne as Bishop Swithun stood before the assembly and broke the silence. "This is a day we will all remember," he began. "A day of solemn decision. The kings will now withdraw and allow the assembly to deliberate. If any questions arise for either party during those deliberations, a messenger will bring that question to the appropriate king and return to the assembly with the king's response. We will stay until we reach a decision, at which time the sounding of the stone will summon all to return. My admonishment for those who will be casting their vote comes in the form of a verse composed by that venerable monk, Bede."

> *Before the journey awaiting us all*
> *No man is so wise that he need not recall*
> *That judgment is given when his soul shall depart*
> *Was it good or evil that dwelt in his heart?*

The royal family returned to King Aethelwulf's tent where refreshments awaited. Aethelwulf paced and had no appetite. Aethelberht left to try reasoning with his brother Aethelbald. Alfred and Aethelred were uncharacteristically quiet, and Judith was uncertain what to say. After several hours, Aethelberht returned.

"While I was visiting Aethelbald, a messenger arrived with a question from the Witan," he reported. "They asked if Aethelbald would accept a division of Wessex."

"What was his response?" Aethelwulf wanted to know.

"He was not pleased. He would not be satisfied with half a kingdom if he thought the Witan would give him all. But I reasoned with him, and he eventually agreed that half a kingdom is better than none. He will accept the division only if he retains the western portion of Wessex with Sherborne as capital. He proposed Selwood Forest as boundary. I came to warn you that the assembly may ask the same question of you."

As Aethelberht finished speaking, a messenger from the Witan arrived. The assembly asked if King Aethelwulf would accept dividing Wessex, allowing King Aethelbald to retain the western half? Or would King Aethelwulf insist on ruling the whole? Aethelwulf asked the messenger to wait outside while he discussed his options with his family.

"You might hold out for the entire kingdom. It is your right, and you may have enough votes to carry the day," Aethelberht mentioned hesitantly.

"Do you think your brother will accept the decision of the assembly if it goes against him? Would he agree to rule as a subking again under your father?" Judith wondered.

"I fear not," Aethelberht admitted. "I love my brother, but his pride makes it impossible for him to compromise. It took a great deal of persuasion on my part just to get him to consider the division. And he only agreed because our father would be left with what Aethelbald deems the lesser part of the kingdom."

"I should have taught Aethelbald that pride is a weakness and not a strength," King Aethelwulf sighed deeply. "I do not intend to shed the blood of Wessex. Summon the messenger."

When the messenger entered the king's tent, King Aethelwulf addressed him. "You may tell the Witan that I will not press my rights to the western portion of Wessex. For the benefit of my kingdom and for the sake of peace, I will accept the proposed division. However, I insist upon retaining my title as King of Wessex for the remainder of my life."

Not long after the messenger left, the blue stone pillars of the henge rang out. "It is done," Aethelwulf announced. "We shall hear the decision of the Witan."

As the royal family rode back to Amesbury, Judith felt that a heavy burden had been lifted from their shoulders. The kingdom of Wessex was divided, but it was also at peace. King Aethelwulf had agreed to remain east of Selwood Forest while King Aethelbald would reign in the west. Aethelwulf mourned the loss of his son more than the loss of half his kingdom. However, the decision also brought with it the hope that there would be no war between father and son.

♥

Judith now looked forward eagerly to Christmas. Not only was it the celebration of Christ's birth, but it was also a time to reflect on the blessings of the old, dying year and look forward to the new year, which was ushered in on Christmas Day. At the beginning of Advent, the servants had decked the estate with holly, ivy, mistletoe, and boxwood boughs brought from Surrey. The greenery would continue to decorate the halls until Candlemas on the second of February.

Wessex and Francia both shared the tradition of lighting the Yule log as a central piece in the Vigil of the Nativity on Christmas Eve. Because Amesbury was not directly adjacent to the forest, King Aethelwulf had brought in a supply of logs from Selwood Forest. Throughout the month, the most perfect and majestic logs were set aside to be used on Christmas Eve.

Before sunset, the royal family went out with their closest retainers to the enormous woodshed behind the palace. Together, they selected the best log from those set aside for their size and symmetry. King Aethelwulf, himself, bore the log into the great hall and set it in the newly swept hearth. As father, he offered a wish for the health and prosperity of his family and his kingdom throughout the coming year. Alfred, as the youngest, poured wine upon the log. And Aethelberht, as the eldest son present, had the privilege of striking the tinder and lighting the Yule log flame.

Judith, along with her Frankish retinue, cried," Joy, joy, joy! Christmas brings all good things. May God shower joy upon us all!"

Once lit, the fire would burn all twelve days of Christmas, replenished with the choicest logs from the pile. If a house allowed their Yule fire to die, they could not ask for a light from another's Yule log. Nor could they give another some of their own light during the season without bringing evil upon their own house for the coming year. The servants kept vigil over the fire as carefully as the shepherds of Bethlehem had kept watch over their sheep.

Hundreds of flickering candles created a peaceful reverence for those entering the church for the Vigil of the Nativity shortly before midnight as they watched for the birth of the Savior. They heard with reverence Bishop Swithun's announcement, "This day you shall know that the Lord will come, and in the morning, you shall see His glory. Tomorrow, the iniquity of the earth shall be canceled, and over us shall reign the Savior of the world!"

Christmas Day marked the beginning of the new year and the end of the Nativity Fasting period that began in November. To the delight of all, the hunt during the week before Christmas had proven successful. Two kitchen servants carried a boar's head upon a silver platter around the great hall with much spectacle. The Christmas feast bordered on gluttony. Every sort of fish and fowl, game, and farmyard meat was offered. Judith had ordered a wide array of cheeses and pastries, nuts, apples, and even oranges and lemons had been brought from Italy at great expense.

Despite the free-flowing wine and joviality, Judith deeply missed her family in Francia. She had received a message from her mother the week before. Amidst the expressions of love and concern for her health and happiness, Queen Ermentrude had also shared tidings that next summer would bring another addition to the royal family. This was welcome news, indeed. The queen had never stopped mourning the loss of little Hildegarde. *Mother needs another babe to fill her arms with love.*

To Judith's delight, a missive also arrived from her brother Louis in Le Mans. In March, Louis planned to visit his future father-in-law, Erispoë, at his palace in Brittany. He was curious to meet his betrothed for the first time. But for now, he and Baldwin Iron Arm were looking forward to spending Christmas with young Charles and their parents at the palace in Compiègne.

The year 856 had turned all of their lives upside down. Briefly, Judith wished she could see what the next few years would bring. Then, she recalled Felix's words during the hunt. *Sometimes, it is better not to know our future.*

CHAPTER X

SPRING 857

Archbishop Hincmar prepared meticulously for the royal conference between King Charles and his nephew, King Lothar II of Lotharingia. King Lothar disliked traveling outside the borders of his own kingdom. So, Lothar's willingness to travel to King Charles' palace in St. Quentin indicated that Lothar wanted something. If rumor proved true, he wanted Charles' support in ridding himself of his unwanted queen, Theutberga.

Shortly before his death, King Lothar's father had forced his son to marry Theutberga, daughter of Count Boso and sister of Hubert who controlled several alpine passes leading to Italy. The alliance had been intended to keep the passes open. However, Lothar II was already deeply in love with his beautiful concubine, Waldrada, and wished to marry her. His forced marriage to Theutberga had never been consummated, and Hincmar suspected that Lothar hoped to level a charge of "barrenness" at Theutberga as grounds for an annulment.

On his part, King Charles urgently needed an alliance against his brother, Louis the German's aggression. Recently, Louis the German had tried to get Lothar's support for an invasion of

Aquitaine. If successful, this conference could eliminate that possibility.

Hincmar was grateful that St. Quentin was but a long day's ride from the court at Quierzy, as the king's party would travel in the persistent March rain and mud. St. Quentin was where the young Roman missionary named Quentin had been martyred in the late third century. His tomb was a major place of pilgrimage and the site of many miracles. Passing the monastery, Hincmar noted that, even in the chilly, drizzling rain, pilgrims lined up in front of the chapel door, eagerly awaiting their turn to plead for their own miracle before the saint's holy relics.

When King Lothar arrived on the following afternoon, King Charles embraced his nephew with familial affection. "Welcome, Lothar. I look forward to our conference. We have much to discuss."

Fair haired, of medium height and slender build, Lothar returned Charles' warm greeting. "I agree uncle. We have much to discuss that will benefit us both."

"In his final years, your father and I made a custom of meeting annually to renew our bonds of kinship and determine how we could best support each other. Perhaps, we should continue that tradition," King Charles smiled.

Lothar exchanged glances with his two advisers, Archbishop Gunther of Cologne and Gunther's nephew, Bishop Theutgaud of Trier.

"It is an interesting idea, uncle," Lothar replied guardedly.

"Good! Then we shall discuss it more tomorrow." King Charles put his arm around his nephew's shoulder. "Right now, I think you may be interested in joining us at the feast. In addition to our local favorites, my cooks have prepared some of the dishes King Aethelwulf's cooks shared with us last summer upon their return from Rome."

During the feast, Hincmar, who sat next to the Lotharingian bishops, discovered that Theutgaud was the brother of Lothar's concubine, Waldrada, and Gunther was Waldrada's uncle. Indulging freely in the abundant wine, Gunther let slip that

Lothar had abandoned his fruitless quest for an annulment and found grounds for seeking a divorce from Queen Theutberga.

"I cannot say more at present," Gunther slurred ponderously when Hincmar pressed for details. "All will be revealed in due time."

Hincmar was intrigued. Grounds for divorce were more serious than grounds for an annulment. And proving them could be ugly, indeed! *Lothar may be asking for trouble,* Hincmar thought as he left the great hall.

The meeting of the two kings on the following morning began with the most pressing concerns for both kingdoms—the Vikings.

Lothar explained, "My father allowed the Danes to build forts and set up permanent encampments along the coast of Frisia, hoping to control trade routes through Dorestad. For many years now the Danes have traded with the Frisians, co-existing with them. But their presence does not stop other Danes from raiding whenever or wherever they wish. Now, the Danes are increasingly encroaching upon my kingdom's territory."

"Our problems with the Danes are, perhaps, even more severe than your own," Charles sympathized. "We have been unable to rid ourselves of those led by Bjorn Ironside, who settled at Fossa Givaldi last August. Their raids, as well as their trading with the locals, have provided them with horses. Now that the Danes are more mobile, they attack farther and farther inland. A few days after Christmas, they burned parts of Paris and sacked Tours as well. They will likely continue to attack until they are paid off or driven out. The situation has been made even worse by some lords in Aquitaine, Brittany, and Neustria, who have paid other Danes to pillage our own countrymen!"

"What are you doing to stop it?" Lothar was keenly interested.

"The Danes are drawn by the gold and silver adornments in our cathedrals and abbeys. We are reinforcing the walls around those buildings. We will fortify the villages as well. Eventually, we hope to follow King Aethelwulf's suggestion and build fortified bridges as an impediment to their longboats."

"That seems sound advice," Archbishop Theutgaud commented.

"It is," Charles continued. "But building fortifications requires time, money, and labor. As long as we must contend with Louis the German's forces seeking to invade our kingdom, we cannot bring our full force against the Danes."

"My brother Louis, Emperor of Italy, has set his greedy eyes on parts of my kingdom as well." Lothar smiled ruefully. "It seems that we both have a 'Louis' problem."

Hincmar interjected. "Might I observe that the problems concerning you both are the very reason for having an annual conference such as this? Joining forces, you could support each other against your brothers and also work together to drive the Vikings from your kingdoms."

"How, exactly?" Theutgaud questioned.

King Charles provided the answer. "If one of us were beset by Danes taking permanent hold in one of our cities, we could call upon the other to help us rid that city of the invaders."

"It is something to consider," Lothar was cautious.

"At an annual conference, you could also share ideas on how to make your kingdoms less inviting to such raids." Hincmar proposed. "As you have seen in Frisia, many Danes establish permanent strongholds through trade and cooperation with the local farmers and tradesmen. The new law King Charles is considering would make selling or trading with the Danes a crime punishable by death."

"What other ideas are you considering?" Lothar seemed genuinely interested.

The conference discussed a variety of strategies against the Northmen. Then, they moved on to other points of mutual interest. The two kings agreed that rogue nobles, playing one kingdom against the other, had weakened both. Maintaining peace and stability within a kingdom was difficult in the best of circumstances. To be beset on every side by Vikings, greedy brothers, and rebel nobles from within made the task nigh impossible.

Finally, King Lothar brought up his most pressing challenge. "As you are aware, Uncle, shortly before my father's death he arranged my marriage to Theutberga, sister of Hubert. Alas, Queen Theutberga has proven to be barren. I have a son, Hugh, who should be my rightful and legitimate heir. But, without an annulment or divorce, I cannot marry his mother, Waldrada, and make him my successor. I have pled my case for annulment unsuccessfully before Pope Leo. I will now move forward and seek a divorce decree from the new pope."

"Have you grounds sufficient for divorce?" King Charles inquired.

King Lothar exchanged looks with Archbishop Gunther, who replied. "We have more than sufficient grounds. It has been brought to our attention that Queen Theutberga participated in an incestuous relationship with her brother Hubert prior to the marriage and may have even continued that relationship afterward."

The silence in the room was palpable. *So, this is how they will seek a bill of divorcement!* Hincmar was grateful that he and King Charles had already discussed not being pulled into the controversy.

Finally, King Charles broke the silence. "That is a serious charge, Lothar. You have evidence to place before a tribunal?"

"We have witnesses prepared to testify against the queen," Theutgaud confirmed. "We will bring the matter before a synod court in Aachen this summer."

"I dislike sullying Queen Theutberga's name in such a public forum," Lothar asserted. "But I cannot continue to have her as my queen! And she refuses to agree to an annulment or retire quietly to a nunnery. I hope to have your support in the matter, Uncle."

King Charles' response had been carefully crafted. "You are in a difficult situation, Lothar. However, my opinion means nothing, as matters of annulment and divorce are solely for the church to decide. The new pope is the one you must win over. Proceed cautiously with any trial you may convene. Make a record of all hearings and preserve all evidence if you wish to persuade

Pope Benedict. I repeat . . . use caution! This is not a light matter you are undertaking."

"I know," Lothar agreed grimly. "But it must be done!"

At the conclusion of the conference, King Charles and King Lothar pledged to punish any rogue nobles who sought to set kingdom against kingdom. They also agreed to present a united front against attacks from their brothers. In the end, King Charles masterfully sympathized with his nephew's marital plights without actually agreeing to support him. Uncle and nephew would meet again in one year at King Charles' palace in Quierzy.

Having attended many such royal conferences, Hincmar was not naïve enough to expect the pledges given that day would last. He hoped, however, that the efforts to shore up relationships with the ruler on King Charles' northeast border would provide Francia with at least one border free from conflict.

The duchy of Brittany was unique in Francia. Settled by Celts from Devon, Cornwall, and Wales, the Bretons had retained their Celtic language and customs. Breton warriors were the finest horsemen in Francia. They had won the battle at Jengland against King Charles' superior numbers because of their mastery of fighting from horseback.

After the battle, King Charles had officially granted the Neustrian counties of Rennes, Nantes, and pays de Retz to Erispoë as leader of the Bretons. The king had also given Erispoë honorary kingly regalia, including a crown and royal seal. In turn, Erispoë had pledged loyalty to Charles and had agreed to pay tribute to him as suzerain. Louis' betrothal to Erispoë's daughter, Abria, was also designed to shore up King Charles' relations with the Bretons.

Erispoë's itinerant court most often remained at Vannes, an important coastal city and trading port on the bay of Morbihan. While Erispoë called himself "King of the Bretons," others in the area saw themselves as potential rivals for his power. One of those rivals was Erispoë's cousin, Salomon.

Second only to Erispoë in power and influence, Salomon guarded with a jealous eye the one-third of Brittany, which King Charles had promised him when he pledged loyalty in 852. However, part of his holdings included land previously granted to Erispoë, initiating conflict between the cousins. Furthermore, the betrothal of Louis and Abria left Salomon feeling threatened as his cousin Erispoë rose in importance.

Baldwin noticed the growing friendship between Salomon and Robert the Strong as they spent considerable time conversing at the assembly in Neaufles. Robert had also received visits from Salomon while young King Louis' court was in residence at Tours. Now, Louis' journey to Erispoë's court at Vannes would take them through Nantes, where they planned to stop for the night with Salomon. Baldwin wondered if Robert the Strong would be in attendance.

For two days, Louis' entourage followed the Loire in its southwesterly flow toward the ocean, passing forests, well-cultivated fields, meadows, orchards, and heath. As they approached Nantes, patchwork farms gave way to large vineyards, which were gradually overtaking tin and iron mining as a foundation of the Nantes economy.

Salomon's estate was large, with well-established farmland, vineyards, and orchards. Upon their arrival, Salomon and his wife, Wenbrit, came out to greet King Louis. They were joined by their other guests—Pascweten, Count of Vannes; Deacon Felix, a member of Erispoë's court; Almarcus, Salomon's *fidelis;* and Robert the Strong. Salomon received Louis' party politely, but all too often for Baldwin's liking, he exchanged meaningful looks with Robert the Strong as if they shared a secret form of communication.

At the feast held in honor of King Louis, wine and conversation flowed freely. Salomon's wife, Wenbrit, smiled at Louis. "You go to Vannes to meet your betrothed, Abria, for the first time?"

"That is so, m . . . madam," Louis replied solemnly.

"Abria is a sweet young thing," Wenbrit observed. "She is three years your senior and taller than you. But then, King Louis,

I am sure that when you marry—in perhaps five years—you shall be the taller." She nodded at a young woman several places to her right at the table. Our daughter is shortly to marry Count Pascweten. She will enjoy living on the coast where Count Pascweten has extensive holdings near Vannes. Deacon Felix, who is also passing through on his way to Vannes, has been invited to assist with their marriage ceremony."

After a brief awkward silence, Wenbrit added, "Since you are both going to Vannes, perhaps Deacon Felix will guide you for the remainder of your journey?"

"Of course, King Louis. If you permit me, I shall be glad to accompany you and point out areas of interest in Brittany along our way." Deacon Felix jumped in enthusiastically.

"Tell us, King Louis," Robert the Strong took up the conversation. "Do you travel to Vannes only to meet your betrothed, or have you some royal business there?"

Robert's question seemed a casual one, but Baldwin sensed everyone listening intently for the response. Louis appeared unaware of the heightened tension in the room.

"A . . . actually, I am going for t . . . two reasons. First, Erispoë, as my administrator, invited me to come. And s . . . second, I have never been to Brittany and wanted to see it for m . . . myself. If Erispoë has b . . . business to discuss with me, he neglected to m . . . mention it."

The answer of an innocent boy. Baldwin sighed with relief at the company's laughter. He suspected Louis' response would not completely satisfy Salomon and his guests, but at least he had not said anything that might put him in danger. Baldwin was glad they would resume their journey on the morrow.

That night, Baldwin saw Louis safely to his bedchamber and then retraced his steps to the great hall, where he and others of the young king's entourage would sleep. He descended the stairs carefully as it was dark, and the manor house was poorly lit. He wished he had thought to ask for an oil lamp. Baldwin followed the sound of voices, thinking they would lead him to the great hall, but stopped short when he recognized the voices of Salomon and Robert the Strong coming from an antechamber off the great hall. He turned to go in the other direction upon discovering his error. But when he heard mention of King Louis, he stayed to listen.

"I cannot agree with you there, Salomon," Robert the Strong was saying. "Louis is a young fool, but I do not think he stopped here to spy on us. He is not capable of strategy or treachery."

Salomon was not convinced. "How can we be certain? Why take this road to Vannes? He should have taken the northern road from Le Mans. Why leave from Angers?"

Robert sought to calm his host. "Perhaps he prefers Angers to Le Mans?"

"Perhaps he heard we would be meeting here and wished to see for himself!" Salomon retorted.

"Then he is either braver or stupider than I supposed, putting himself in so vulnerable a situation. In any case, your wife was excellent at allaying any suspicions. She provided a perfectly reasonable explanation for Deacon Felix's presence," Robert commented.

"Wenbrit is clever," Salomon agreed. "I shall convey your admiration. A pity that Deacon Felix will not be joining us tomorrow. His closeness to Erispoë gives him a unique perspective."

"I agree." Robert paused before adding, "Let us hope Louis leaves before the others arrive. Else, he might truly begin to suspect that we are convening a council."

Salomon's voice was like ice. "This council means everything to both of us. This child king has deprived you of most of your holdings. And I know my cousin. Erispoë will use a marriage alliance with King Charles to relieve me of the rest of my *benefices*. Two people stand between us and our desire to rule our own provinces. I will rid myself of my cousin. But it will be up to you to rid yourself of your own impediment!"

"Agreed," was Robert's grim answer.

Not daring to breathe, Baldwin shrank back into the shadows as Robert and Salomon exited the room and moved toward the stairs. With the light from their oil lamps and the dim light from the wall sconces, they might have seen him if they turned his way. They did not.

Once the two men were out of sight, Baldwin moved silently to the great hall, considering what he had just learned. Whatever plot was being hatched between Robert and Salomon was still in the planning stage, and Louis' party had stumbled onto it unawares. It might prove dangerous to mention what he had heard to Louis. These men were looking for any sign that Louis was suspicious of their activities. And Louis had not yet learned to hide his emotions well. The presence of Deacon Felix was also troublesome. *If Deacon Felix, one of Erispoë's close advisers, is capable of treachery, who else at Erispoë's court might report to Salomon?*

Baldwin breathed much easier the next morning once the royal party, joined by Deacon Felix, set out again on their road to Vannes. The road took a northwesterly turn as they left the banks of the Loire. Gradually, the terrain began to change as well. Rich, fertile land with forests teeming with roe, beaver, boar, and fox was replaced by salty marshland, used for grazing sheep and home to wading birds. Eventually, they left the marshland behind as they drew near Vannes.

Vannes lay on a small inlet of the bay of Morbihan, a natural harbor providing protection from the ocean for ships on three sides. The city's Roman walls were a testament to its centuries-long importance as a trading center. With a scarcity of arable land, fishing and salt production were vital to the surrounding area.

Louis' reception at Erispoë's court was vastly different from the one he had received from Salomon. Erispoë seemed genuinely pleased to have Louis accept his invitation. He introduced his family, which included his wife, Marmohec; his son, Conan; and his daughter, Abria. Baldwin cringed when Louis stammered, and Abria raised a haughty eyebrow.

"I d . . . do not think Abria l . . . likes me. B . . . but I do not m . . . much like her, either." Louis confided later to a sympathetic Baldwin.

Thankfully, Louis was determined to enjoy himself. The feasts were a spectacle, with Erispoë flaunting his full royal regalia. His cooks produced many dishes unknown to Baldwin, who had never eaten lobster, shark, porpoise, or sea turtle. The cooks also prepared the largest, most delicious escargot brought by boat from Quimper in the north of Brittany. Between the many courses, talented musicians and dancers performed traditional songs in the Breton language.

Erispoë took great pride in displaying the wonders of his province to his future son-in-law. As they sailed to visit some of the many islands located in the Bay of Morbihan, sea turtles, porpoises, and dolphins often swam alongside their boats while enormous sharks basked in the warmer waters on the lee side of the islands.

ر

On their final day at Erispoë's court, Erispoë took them to a place where row upon row of enormous rock structures and single-standing stones rose up like an army of a thousand silent giants. Erected by an unrecorded people, the relics had a sobering effect on everyone. *A reminder of how short our journey is upon this earth,* Baldwin considered.

Ever eager for new experiences, Louis quickly accepted Baldwin's suggestion of returning to Neustria by way of the northern road leading to Le Mans. Erispoë was delighted.

"You must stay at my estate in Talensac," he urged. "I will send a rider to have the house prepared. The adjoining forest is superb for hunting. The finest in Brittany. You may remain there several days if you like to hunt."

Louis was gratified by Erispoë's generosity. "Thank you. We shall be g . . . glad of both sport and accommodations."

Erispoë beamed with pride. "Talensac is full of history. Two centuries ago, Judicael, the king of all the Bretons, had his estate there. I always stay in Talensac every time I travel to Le Mans."

Baldwin was relieved to know they would be traveling far from the southern road leading through Salomon's holdings.

During their visit to Vannes, he had looked for a chance to warn Erispoë. However, Deacon Felix had always been in attendance. Baldwin hoped, when he finally shared his concerns about Salomon and Robert the Strong with Louis' council, that they would find a way to guard against what was certain to be future treachery.

CHAPTER XI

SUMMER and FALL 857

The summer of 857 began with a joyful event. Queen Ermentrude safely gave birth to a baby girl, whom they named Gisela in honor of King Charles' elder sister. That both mother and child were healthy was a joyful respite in what would prove a challenging summer.

A messenger informed Archbishop Hincmar that, in response to King Charles' and Lothar's conference in March, Louis the German had met in July with Lothar's brother, Emperor Louis of Italy. The two agreed to uphold each other's interests against Charles and Lothar. *Lothar was right. Both kings do have a Louis problem!* Hincmar inwardly grumbled.

More pressing was the re-emergence of Pippin and his followers in Aquitaine. Pippin was conspiring with Robert the Strong and several Neustrian nobles, enabling the Danes to attack Poitiers and other places in both Neustria and Aquitaine. The rebels hoped the resulting chaos would rid their provinces of the child kings. Combined with the raids from the Danes who had overwintered at Fossa Givaldi, the summer of 857 found the whole of Aquitaine and Neustria on fire.

Trouble was also brewing in Brittany. Erispoë had learned of the conspiracy against him led by his cousin, Salomon. The cousins' confrontations increased in intensity throughout the summer and into the fall. Hincmar watched carefully to see which of the two firebrands would prevail. Francia's Neustrian policy was built upon appeasing Erispoë. However, if Salomon were to wrest the province from Erispoë, all of Hincmar's careful planning would be for naught.

After discussing the troubled provinces at the first council meeting in October, King Charles brought up a different concern. "Archbishop Hincmar, as you are well aware, our nephew, King Lothar, is officially seeking a divorce from his wife, Theutberga. There are new tales being spread about the queen. Is there any truth to them?"

Hincmar measured his words carefully. "I have been reluctant to speak of the sordid rumors spread about Queen Theutberga, Sire. The accusation changes and grows as it spreads and now includes an accusation of rape leveled against Theutberga's brother Hubert and an accusation of abortion against Theutberga herself. The scandal is now at a fever pitch and has even reached across the channel to inflame the kingdoms of Britannia. I do not see any possibility of a happy resolution for either King Lothar or Queen Theutberga."

"Is there any truth to the matter? What do your sources tell you?" John Scotus pressed.

"Theutberga is innocent but politically naïve. She has some support within Lothar's court. But openly supporting the queen is proving dangerous for her supporters," Hincmar admitted sadly.

"My brothers used the same vile tactics against my mother," King Charles growled. "She cleared her name at the end, but the false reports had already damaged her family and her reputation!"

"It seems your nephew Lothar is cut from the same cloth as his father and will stop at nothing to remove an obstacle in his path," Gauzlin observed.

"Why do people reject logic and truth without fully examining all the arguments? They willingly believe any lie that is told loudly enough and often enough!" John Scotus complained.

"People believe whatever they wish to be true," Gauzlin commented wryly.

"Can we help Theutberga without ending our alliance with my nephew?" Charles asked.

Hincmar took a deep breath. "It is wise for you to maintain the appearance of being neutral, Sire. Francia needs the alliances you have built with Brittany, Wessex, and now with Lotharingia. You cannot fight on all fronts at the same time and survive. My advice is to wait and see how this develops. However, if Queen Theutberga were to seek asylum in your court, I think you could provide that . . . if we handle the matter with discretion.

King Charles nodded. "Archbishop, send word privately to Queen Theutberga that she will find sanctuary here should it become necessary. I can do no more at present. Now, we must talk of the Danes. They have raided Paris twice this year without any resistance. What is being done to prevent a third attack?" The council finally turned, as it always did, to the Viking problem.

᪻

For Judith, the year since her marriage to King Aethelwulf had been one of growth. Her body was beginning to mature and change. Grateful that the Mistress of the Wardrobe had planned for such circumstance, Judith had Hemma lengthen the sleeves and hems on her robes. She was now thirteen years old and had seen many new places and met new people. And her life had settled into somewhat of a routine.

Judith spent most mornings in the throne room next to Aethelwulf and Aethelberht, listening to complaints or petitions from local peasants or lords. At first, she listened more than she spoke, afraid to say something foolish. However, as King Aethelwulf and King Aethelberht encouraged her to ask questions of petitioners, she began to distinguish people's needs from their desires and learn when to apply justice as well as mercy.

Aethelwulf did not stay more than one or two months in any place, wishing to address the concerns of the thegns throughout his kingdom. When the court removed to Faversham, Judith spent her time in daily visits to Graveney where she blissfully oversaw the renovations she had ordered and delved deeper into her treasured library.

Judith was even becoming accustomed to sleeping in a tent, something she had not done before her marriage. When the king and his sons rode out for the hunt, Judith and Hemma often rode with them. Waking up to the musical chirping of birds and the musky scent of a cheerfully burning open fire was something she delighted in.

Autumn's brilliant amber and scarlet leaves adorning the oaks and elms reminded Judith that Advent would soon be upon them. King Aethelwulf expressed his desire to spend Christmas in Sussex at his palace at Steyning. Aethelwulf had traditionally celebrated Christmas either at Winchester or at Amesbury. However, the memories of the previous December's Witenagemot and the treacherous conduct of Aethelbald were still too fresh. He would celebrate Christmas this year in Sussex.

Fall also brought a nip in the air and rain that lasted for days at a time. On one cold, rainy day, Alfred sought out Judith, who was reading by the fire in the palace library.

"What makes you laugh so?" Alfred demanded.

"Solve me this riddle, Alfred." Judith began reading aloud, "Although I am tiny, I laugh with many voices at twilight. While sitting at home in the gathering dark, I bewitch thousands. What am I?"

Alfred puzzled for a moment before crying out, "A bird! Is it a nightingale?"

"You guessed correctly," Judith congratulated him.

"Read another," Alfred coaxed.

"Alright," Judith agreed. "But listen carefully, for this one is longer. 'My life is a battle against wind and water as I seek a place below earth and wave. With no kingdom of my own, stillness gives me strength. Mud and stones hold me fast so I cannot be broken. What am I?'"

This riddle took Alfred a bit longer, but finally he arrived at an answer. "Is it an anchor?"

"It is," Judith smiled. "You are too good at guessing these. You read the next one to me, and I will try to solve it."

Excitement vanished from Alfred's eyes, replaced by wariness. Judith had seen that look before but had never pushed to find out what was behind it. This time was different. Alfred and Aethelred were like the younger brothers she had left behind in Francia. If something was bothering Alfred, she wished to know.

"Alfred, tell me what is troubling you," Judith probed gently. "I am happy to read to you whenever you like. But you have never yet read to me."

"I do not like to read aloud," Alfred insisted.

Judith suspected the problem was bigger than Alfred was admitting. "Is it because you do not like to read? Or is it because you cannot read?" she wondered aloud.

Alfred's flushed face and bowed head provided the answer.

"This is your secret, then," Judith whispered gently. "And it shall remain between the two of us. I know you love books and are very quick to learn. Would you like me to help you learn to read?"

Alfred nodded, bravely fighting back the tears. Judith put her arm around Alfred's shoulders and gave him an encouraging squeeze.

"It must have been painful for you to visit our schoolroom in Francia while trying to keep your secret. Why were you not taught to read before now?"

"My mother became ill when I was but four years old," Alfred explained. "My father sent me on pilgrimage, and I was traveling for more than a year to Rome and back. When I returned, my mother had died, and no one thought about books. The next year, I went on pilgrimage with my father. My father does not know that I have never learned to read. I have been too ashamed to tell anyone."

Judith's heart ached when she thought of the burden Alfred had carried. "We will apply ourselves to your education from now on. You have an amazing memory. It will not take long for you to master Latin, and then we can study reading the English vernacular. That is something I need more practice with myself. I am eager to begin."

Judith's infectious enthusiasm brought a smile to Alfred's face. "I am eager to begin, as well."

୨

It was young King Charles' passion for hunting that took Louis and Baldwin back to Talensac. Upon Louis' return from Vannes, Baldwin reported on what he had overheard at Salomon's estate. Louis' council insisted that the young king confine himself to Le Mans for the time being. The palace at Angers was too close to Salomon's power base for safety, and for Louis to stay near Robert the Strong in the palace at Tours would be like inviting a lion to supper with a lamb.

Joseph also sent word to Erispoë, warning him to be careful in his dealings with his cousin Salomon and with his adviser, Deacon Felix.

As summer progressed, Salomon seemed intent on provoking Erispoë to some sort of action in hopes of justifying violence against him. Here and there, a building belonging to Erispoë mysteriously caught fire. Brigands captured goods shipped by Erispoë as if the thieves had foreknowledge of when and where to attack.

And the Danes who were known confederates of Salomon, struck Erispoë's holdings further inland, bypassing more accessible lands owned by Salomon or his son-in-law, Pascweten. Throughout the summer and into the fall, Erispoë was so busy putting out fires he had no opportunity to come to Le Mans and fulfill his duties as Louis' administrator.

The summer had proved difficult for young King Charles as well. The Danes ravaged city after city in Aquitaine. They entered the royal palace at Poitiers, which young Charles had escaped just moments before, helped by his "favorite knight," Odo, son of Count Hardouin. In mid-October, young Charles journeyed to Le Mans for a few weeks' respite before returning to ravaged

Aquitaine. He shared with Louis the story of his narrow escape from Poitiers.

"The Danes did not take much from the palace. I think they were hoping to take me for ransom instead. Father pays thousands of pounds for hostages," young Charles remarked thoughtfully.

"T . . . true!" Louis agreed.

"What did you think of your betrothed?"

"Not m . . . much," Louis admitted. "Too haughty for me. Erispoë was n . . . nice, though."

Young Charles laughed. "Too bad you are not marrying the father. I am not looking forward to Father's choice of a bride for me. I am sure I will not like whoever it is."

"Neither of you should waste time worrying about future brides," Baldwin laughingly pointed out. "You will not reach adulthood for the next five or six years at least."

A messenger arrived, informing Louis that Erispoë would arrive in a day or two to conduct business in Le Mans and resume his administrative duties. He requested that any documents needing his approval be ready and that Mathieu, Louis' seneschal, be available to review the young king's financial affairs.

This was the first visit from Erispoë for nearly six months. Although Louis's second administrator, the Bishop of Séez, had been available, Louis had grown to like Erispoë and looked forward to his visits. Young Charles was also eager to meet the flamboyant Breton.

"Will he wear his kingly robes and carry his scepter?" young Charles asked excitedly.

"N . . . Not likely," Louis smiled at the thought. "He only wears them in his own c . . . court."

To Baldwin's dismay, Erispoë arrived with Deacon Felix as part of his retinue. He wondered what had convinced Erispoë to travel in the midst of his province's woes. The answer, when it came, did nothing to allay Baldwin's concerns.

"It is good to feast with you again, King Louis. And it is a pleasure to meet young King Charles as well," Erispoë toasted the royal brothers. "I would not have made the journey if my *fidelis*, Deacon Felix, had not encouraged me to do so."

So, he came at Deacon Felix's urging. He must not have believed Joseph's warning, Baldwin silently lamented.

"Fortunately, we have experienced a lull of late in the attacks that have so beset our province," Deacon Felix interjected.

"I am glad t . . . to hear the attacks have stopped," Louis sounded genuinely relieved.

Erispoë agreed. "I am not certain why the attacks stopped. Perhaps Salomon has troubles of his own. Whatever the reason, Deacon Felix rightly pointed out that this was my chance to come to Le Mans, if only for a few days."

Erispoë remained in Le Mans for a week, sitting in council with both Louis and young Charles and giving sound advice regarding managing a household as well as a kingdom. In the evenings he shared with the young kings the history of Brittany.

He told of Judicael, King of the Bretons, who, being summoned to the Frankish court in 635, reluctantly presented King Dagobert with elaborate gifts. But Judicael's pride forced him to refuse to eat at table with the Frankish king. Erispoë explained that many of the early Breton rulers' residences were guarded by hedges, ditches, and marshes as protection against the Franks.

"We have been at odds, the Franks and the Bretons, for centuries," he noted. "It is time for our people to become allies. Your marriage to Abria may accomplish this—an end to centuries of strife between two peoples. I only wish we Bretons could stop fighting amongst ourselves."

"My father would say the same thing about his relations," young Charles commented. "I have never been to Brittany. Tell me what it is like."

At his invitation, Erispoë gave a glowing description of the rich farmlands, the cliffs and stone monuments of the coast, the islands, and the marshes with their wildlife. "We also have forests with excellent hunting. I always stop at my residence at Talensac on the way to and from Le Mans, where the hunting is unsurpassed!"

"Sounds wonderful!" young Charles exclaimed. "I wish we were there now. Le Mans is not especially known for its hunting."

"You are most welcome to come with me when I depart tomorrow. If we push our horses a bit, we can be in Talensac in three days. You can hunt for a few days, after which you can return to Le Mans, and I will return to Vannes."

Erispoë's invitation took them all by surprise. Deacon Felix especially seemed taken off guard. "But, my lord, did you not wish to be in Vannes by Martinmas?" he queried.

"I have sufficient time to do both, I wager." Erispoë smiled expectantly at Louis and Charles. "What do you say, young kings? Will you go hunting at Talensac?"

"I wish to go! What do you say, Louis?" young Charles turned eagerly to his brother.

Baldwin's concern intensified. Protecting the young kings would prove an even bigger challenge when removed from the confines of Le Mans. However, he knew young Charles' enthusiasm for sport could prove very persuasive.

Seeing the excitement on his younger brother's face, Louis smiled at Erispoë. "We w . . . will go with you, Erispoë."

"Excellent!" Erispoë clapped Louis on the shoulder. "I always rise before the sun and go directly to chapel. Then we shall be on the road. We must use the daylight while we have it."

"I shall send messengers ahead to make the necessary preparation," Deacon Felix assured them.

ও

Baldwin was grateful that the journey to Talensac was uneventful. Pushing themselves, they arrived at Talensac late on the third day, just as the sun was setting. Erispoë's Talensac estate was surrounded by ditches and hedges as an effective defense instead of building a high wall.

From their earlier stay in Talensac, Baldwin remembered the large residence with its enormous great hall, sufficient to house the knights accompanying all three leaders. Most importantly to young Charles, the adjacent forest provided ample game to feed the party of eager hunters.

Young Charles was not disappointed, especially when he dispatched a monstrous wild boar on the first day of the hunt which fell on November 1st. "This old fellow must have been the sire of all the boars in these woods by the size of him," he pronounced triumphantly. "I am eager to get a taste of him."

At the feast that evening, Deacon Felix offered special thanks in honor of All Saint's Day as well as thanks for the success of their hunt and the bounty provided by nature. To young Charles' gratification, the boar's meat was admired above all the other dishes served for its richness and flavor. As they prepared to retire for the night, Baldwin overheard Deacon Felix quietly tell Erispoë that the church in Talensac had recently been robbed of a sacred relic during a raid.

"If you desire to visit the church, my lord, we could go to mass early tomorrow while it is yet dark and be back in time for the hunt," Deacon Felix proposed.

"A good plan, Deacon," Erispoë nodded. "You know I have trouble sleeping. Better to do something useful rather than lie sleepless in the dark. We will return before the others waken."

Baldwin retired for the night, but he could not silence his uneasiness. *God grant that my suspicions of Deacon Felix are groundless!*

An urgent cry awakened the household before dawn. Erispoë had been murdered. The only witness was the young stable groom whom Erispoë had taken with him to hold the mounts while he and Deacon Felix were inside the church. The groom had returned alone, frightened nearly witless, to spread the word to the household. He was questioned by Erispoë's captain of the guard.

"My lord took me up behind him and we rode to the village, where he and Deacon Felix went into the church while I gave the horses some water. After some time, Deacon Felix came out of the church, followed by Lord Erispoë."

The young groom's face was ashen, and he paused before continuing his harrowing tale. "Two men with swords drawn approached my lord. When my lord saw them, he shouted, 'Felix, it is Salomon, run!' And then he ran back into the church. The men pursued my lord, and I heard shouting and a terrible scream. Deacon Felix fled from the church. He took his horse's lead from my hand, telling me to flee as well."

What did you do then, boy?" the captain probed when the groom started shaking.

"I did not know what to do. I heard someone yell, 'He is dead!' Then I heard more screaming, and I saw my lord's cousin Salomon running from the church. He spied me holding my lord's mount. I feared Salomon would kill me, but my limbs would not move. Salomon claimed that a man named Almarcus had killed my lord Erispoë by the altar of the church and that he had avenged my lord by killing Almarcus. He told me to ride quickly and tell everyone what had happened." At this, the groom burst into tears. "My lord Erispoë is dead."

All Baldwin's instincts told him to get Louis and young Charles out of Brittany as quickly as possible. Without delay, Baldwin conferred with the young kings' guards and organized the royal party's immediate departure. As they passed by the church in Talensac, they heard the high-pitched keening of women in mourning and saw the devastation on the villagers' faces.

Along the road to Rennes, where they would shelter for the night, Baldwin took stock of all that had happened. This was the culmination of Salomon's plan to rule Brittany, which Baldwin had overheard in Nantes six months earlier.

There was no longer any question in Baldwin's mind as to the part Deacon Felix had played in the conspiracy. Deacon Felix had encouraged Erispoë to leave Vannes, lulled into security by the break in hostilities. And Deacon Felix, well aware of Erispoë's difficulty in sleeping, knew precisely when to arrange for the assassins to attack their victim when he was most vulnerable.

Baldwin suspected that Brittany's inner power struggles and the ensuing chaos would also bring trouble to Francia. Louis' betrothal with Abria and its accompanying alliance would be dissolved. Would Salomon demand total independence for Brittany? Or would he form an alliance with Aquitaine and Louis the German to fight against King Charles? Either choice could bring disaster.

Baldwin spent a sleepless night in Rennes, helping guard the two young kings resting in a monastery on the road to Le Mans. The question keeping him awake was that of the second part of the conspiracy. Now that Salomon had removed his impediment, what did Robert the Strong intend for Louis?

CHAPTER XII

DECEMBER 857 through JANUARY 858

The vast forest of the weald, bounded on north and south by chalky downs, was spread across parts of Sussex, Kent, Surrey, and Wessex, and provided sanctuary for hermits, brigands, and a variety of wildlife. From the moment Alfred pointed out the eastern edge of the weald on their crossing of the channel, Judith was fascinated by such an immense expanse of woodland stretching like a great sleeping dragon for more than 120 miles sparked her imagination. Although their travels over the past year had taken her around the outer parts of the weald, she both desired and feared to explore its inner depths.

King Aethelwulf's court took up residence at Steyning in early December, not far from St. Leonard's Forest, marking the southern border of the Weald. Alfred and Aethelred, who went out with the huntsmen several times each week, were unusually impatient to go on an extended hunting trip before Christmas.

"Why so eager, boys?" Judith queried.

"You will see," Alfred answered cryptically.

"We have a plan . . ." Aethelred began to elaborate. But after receiving a fist in the shoulder from Alfred, he thought better of it. "It is meant to be a surprise."

"You can come on the hunt with us if you like. That part is not meant to be kept secret." Alfred clarified. "We plan to go deep into the weald after wild boar."

Tenting on a misty gray December day did not really appeal to Judith. However, the allure of exploring the forest that had captured her imagination was almost impossible to resist.

"If it is not raining, I will consider it," she laughed.

Before dawn, on a gray misty morning, the hunting party set out for St. Leonard's Forest, north of Steyning, with King Aethelwulf, King Aethelberht, and the lead huntsman riding ahead, followed by the young princes and several nobles. Judith and Hemma rode behind. Judith had requested that they be allowed to guide their own horses, and Aethelwulf had not objected. The dogs and their handlers came next, with the servants and supply wagons bringing up the rear. After an hour or two, they approached a thick line of trees stretching both left and right as far as the eye could see. From that point on, they followed the lead huntsman and Aethelwulf, two abreast on a path that entered the weald.

Judith shivered as the light from the cloud-shrouded sun grew even dimmer, hindered by the myriad of mostly bare branches stretching high their bony arms. As their horses plodded through layers of aromatic, molding leaves, Judith tried not to think about the stories King Aethelwulf and his sons had told the night before of dragons deep in the middle of St. Leonard's Forest, along with the wild boars, wild bulls, and even wild horses. They caught sight of a roe, but this time, the hunters were not looking for deer, hoping to encounter something more thrilling.

The path ended abruptly, but they continued on for another hour until they arrived at a small glade with a brook. Here the servants began setting up camp while the hunters formed a circle to discuss their plan of attack.

Feasting all autumn long on fallen acorns, the wild boars of Sussex were known for their succulent and tasty flesh. One Sussex boar made a good Christmas feast. Two would make the feast exceptional. So, everyone was astonished when Alfred and Aethelred insisted that they needed to bag at least three boars by the end of the hunting trip.

"I am not sure it can be done in one trip," Aethelwulf tried to lower their expectations. "Boars are crafty animals. Once one of their own is taken, the others will be more difficult to obtain."

Aethelberht also seemed perplexed. "What would we do with so much flesh?"

"We would give it to the poor, of course," Alfred volunteered.

Aethelred agreed. "It is Christmas, after all."

"But Aethelred and I get the head of the third," Alfred hastened to add.

"Yes, we get the head," echoed Aethelred.

That raised several eyebrows. But in the end, the hunters agreed to try for three Christmas boars. They split into four groups. The first two groups would give the other two groups time to get in position. Then, they would use the dogs to sniff out the wild boars. The receivers would wait for the game to be driven toward them.

Mounting his horse, Alfred had some parting advice for Judith and Hemma. "If you see a dragon, do not touch it. Their fangs are poisonous, you know," he cautioned.

To Judith and Hemma's delight, Felix, King Aethelwulf's Frankish secretary, stayed behind to keep them company, promising to protect them from all lizards—poisonous or otherwise. While the servants pitched the tents, the three of them pulled stools up next to the fire to take the chill from the December air.

"Did you know that Steyning is sometimes referred to as 'St. Cuthman's port?'" Felix asked.

Sensing a good story coming, Judith encouraged Felix to continue. "I know the church in Steyning is dedicated to St. Cuthman. Can you tell us more about the saint?"

"Yes, who is St. Cuthman?" Hemma wished to know.

Pleased that he had piqued their interest, Felix proceeded. "Two hundred years ago, a young shepherd named Cuthman lived with his father and crippled mother. Every day, Cuthman cared for his sheep, guiding them to pasture while his father cared for his mother. When his father died, the job of caring for his mother fell to Cuthman. What could he do? He was forced to choose between caring for his sheep or caring for his mother!" Felix paused for full effect.

"He cannot have deserted his mother!" Hemma insisted.

Felix smiled. "You are right, Hemma. They ate some of the sheep and sold the rest. But when the money ran out, Cuthman looked for another way to care for his mother. Relying upon God, he built a one-wheeled cart to transport her, attached a rope to the handles of the cart, and placed it over his shoulders as they headed east, begging from village to village. Then, one day, the rope broke."

"Oh, that is terrible! The poor boy!" both Judith and Hemma cried together.

"Indeed," Felix agreed. "Cuthman was nowhere near a village. Blessedly, he was near a copse of willows. Gathering the slender willow stems, he used the withies to weave his own rope, which he prayed would allow him to continue transporting his mother. The withies held! In gratitude, Cuthman promised God he would build a church wherever his makeshift rope failed."

"The rope broke at Steyning?" Hemma anticipated.

"At Steyning," Felix confirmed. "Cuthman knew that was the place God wanted him to build a church. He prayed, 'Father Almighty, you have brought my wanderings to an end; now enable me to do this work. For if I rely on myself, it will be of no avail. Make up for my lack of skill and help me complete this work."

"And that is the church at Steyning," Judith concluded.

"That is not the end of the story," Felix insisted. "The villagers, inspired by Cuthman's devotion, assisted him in building a hut for his mother as well as the church. One day, during the church's construction, Cuthman had problems placing the roof beam. A mysterious stranger appeared and showed him how to do it and how to complete the church. Cuthman thanked the stranger and asked his name. The stranger replied, 'I am He in whose name you build this church.'"

Time passed quickly as Felix, always a fount of knowledge, related other miracles associated with St. Cuthman. He also shared with them local legends regarding the poisonous dragons said to inhabit St. Leonard's Forest. Judith observed with interest Hemma's eyes light up whenever Felix spoke. *Is it the stories, or does Hemma have feelings for Felix?* she wondered.

Miraculously, the hunters returned victorious with three boars an hour before sunset. They had spread out, forming a large circle deep into the weald. The dogs quickly caught the scent and led the drivers to a cluster of wild boars. Boars did not often gather in large herds, but these had been brought together by an especially good supply of acorns, which had not been depleted by squirrels. At the dogs' approach, the boars scattered, running directly toward the hunters who waited to receive them. The animals were taken and bled out in the forest. So, all that remained was for the servants to pack them in salt and transport them in the supply wagon back to Steyning.

"We could have taken four or even five boars if we had wanted," Alfred informed Judith. "But we left some, so there will be plenty to hunt next time."

⁓

Christmas day dawned crisp and clear. A special Christmas mass was followed by a feast in which two of the boars' heads were celebrated. Ever since the hunt, Judith had wondered how the young princes would use the third boar's head. Whatever their plan, it obviously demanded some preparation and time. Alfred, who had made good progress in learning to read, spent the entire week before Christmas out of doors with Aethelred instead of joining Judith in the library. At the end of each day, the princes came inside, tousled and dirty, increasing Judith's curiosity. They promised to reveal all at the feast.

The Christmas feast was even more bountiful than the one they had shared in Amesbury the previous year. After everyone had eaten their fill, Aethelred and Alfred stood before the company.

"Kings and Queen," Alfred began, bowing to the royal table. "Thegns, Clerics, Ealdormen, and Ladies," he addressed the remainder of the hall. "You are all invited to a new sort of entertainment to be offered in the courtyard."

Aethelred took up the narrative. "Since we first heard tell of it, Prince Alfred and I have taken great interest in a competition practiced in some parts of Wales and Kent. The competition

157

consists of two sides vying over something which can be carried or thrown. Adam, one of our groomsmen, comes from a village in Wales where such a competition has become part of their Christmas Day celebrations. Adam helped us prepare this entertainment for your enjoyment."

"The two sides will be the groomsmen with Prince Aethelred as leader," Alfred contributed, "and the huntsmen with me as leader."

"What is it you are vying for?" King Aethelberht smiled knowingly.

"The winning side will carry off a boar's head," Aethelred announced grandly.

"I do not approve!" King Aethelwulf called out. When the young princes appeared deflated, he grinned and added, "I think the prize should be made more interesting. I will include a keg of the finest cider to be enjoyed by the winning side!"

The great hall roared with laughter, and everyone donned their winter cloaks and followed the princes outside to watch the competition. Servants brought benches from the great hall for guests to sit upon while enjoying the entertainment. In the middle of the courtyard was a rectangular space marked by stakes on its four corners, with a line of rope laid across the ground on either end of the rectangle. Two groups of young men lined up facing each other in the middle of the field. The huntsmen wore red linen tunics, while the groomsmen were dressed in brown.

King Aethelberht was explained the rules and began the competition. "Each side will defend one side of the line. A side that carries the boar's head across the opponent's line will earn a mark upon a post. When a mark is achieved, the process will begin again. The first side to achieve three marks will be declared victor."

He raised the brined and toughened boar's head for all to see. Then, using both hands, he tossed it straight up in the air and quickly backed away as chaos ensued. First one, and then the other side controlled the head, tossing it to one another while trying to keep it out of reach of the other side.

The groomsmen and the huntsmen took the competition quite seriously, as did Alfred and Aethelred. Upon several occasions Judith feared the young princes would be run upon by the older, larger men. It soon became obvious, however, that no one wished to injure a member of the royal family and took extra care when one of the princes was nearby.

When each side had achieved two marks, excitement reached a fever pitch, knowing that the next mark would decide the victor. Victory was finally declared when a burly huntsman took Alfred—holding the boar's head—upon his shoulders and barreled over the groomsmen's line. Aethelred objected heatedly, yelling that the boar's head was not properly won since Alfred should have run it across the line with his own legs.

King Aethelwulf stepped in to resolve the matter. With the wisdom of Solomon, he proclaimed the entertainment such a success that both sides would receive a keg of cider for their efforts. As to the boar's head, he called for a servant to bring him a silver coin minted with his mark. Aethelwulf had Alfred choose which side of the coin he wished to wager the boar's head upon. After marking the coin with a knife, Aethelwulf threw it into the air. It fell to the earth with the marked side showing. Huzzahs erupted, for the huntsmen had won the boar's head!

Later, as Hemma helped her prepare for bed, Judith remarked on the princes' entertainment. "The competition was entertaining, but why did they attach such secrecy to the boar's head?"

"And why would they want such a nasty thing after it has rolled in the mud?" Hemma added.

Judith considered for a moment and laughed, "That may be something only comprehensible to young men."

࿐

During Christmas week, Hincmar visited Reims to see the progress on the renovation of his cathedral. He pondered the serious threats facing Francia on his return trip, hoping to present them at the king's first council after Christmas. The council lacked Gauzlin, who had recently been promoted to Archchancellor, had not yet returned from his visit to the king's cousin, Abbot Louis, in St. Denis. Hincmar shared his thoughts with the remainder of the council.

"Sire, I have a list of the five major threats currently or potentially facing your kingdom. The list includes Vikings, Salomon in Brittany, the rebellious lords of Aquitaine, Robert the Strong in Neustria, and Louis the German.

"That sounds correct, archbishop," King Charles allowed. "However, none of these problems, with the exception of Salomon, are of recent origin."

"True, Sire," Hincmar continued. "And you have dealt with problems such as these since the beginning of your reign. My concern is how we might counter these threats if all attack simultaneously."

"Is that likely?" John Scotus asked sharply.

Hincmar nodded. "I think it is not only likely, but probable. Sources in both Aquitaine and Brittany confirm that Robert the Strong and Salomon are cooperating to bring chaos to both provinces. They expect Robert the Strong to try and wrest Neustria from King Louis this year."

"It would be a good strategy on his part," John Scotus admitted.

Hincmar nodded. "If Robert the Strong pushes the lords of Aquitaine to rebel at the same time as the kingdom is under attack from Vikings, Brittany is in chaos, and Neustria is in revolt, he might overwhelm whatever resources remain to the king."

"Especially if Louis the German crosses the borders into Aquitaine at the same time," John Scotus contributed.

"At that point we have a convergence of all five threats without the ability to respond to them at the same time," King Charles summed it up.

"That is precisely my concern, Sire," Hincmar confirmed. "We must plan a course of action."

"Where do you suggest we begin?" the king prompted.

Hincmar was ready with his response. "Sire, I suggest we start by driving a wedge between any lords of Neustria who are leaning toward supporting Robert . . ."

The council was interrupted by a messenger, who reported that Paris had once again been sacked by Vikings camped at Fossa Givaldi. This time, however, the Danes had taken two noble hostages—Abbot Louis of St. Denis and the king's archchancellor, Gauzlin. Bjorn Ironside, the Viking leader, was demanding an enormous ransom of gold and silver, or the two men would be brutally executed.

After a brief stunned silence, King Charles spoke, "We must raise the money for the ransom. St. Denis must pay what it can, and I will contribute, but the majority must come from Francia's nobles and clerics."

"Aquitaine and Neustria will not like paying more money to the Danes," Hincmar observed. "It could push more of them to side with Robert the Strong."

"Archbishop Hincmar's warning has suddenly become more urgent," John Scotus observed.

King Charles nodded grimly. "Your suggestions, Archbishop?"

Hincmar obliged. "Robert has his following in Neustria, but I can make a list of Neustrian nobles who may remain loyal to you and young King Louis if we strengthen those ties."

"Do so at once. And make a list for Aquitaine as well. The sooner we begin working with those nobles the better," the king replied. "What about the Danes?"

"Sire, we must consider making allies of some Danes as a counter to our own rebels. Robert the Strong and Salomon have already established allies with some of the Vikings. King Lothar might agree to help us drive out any Danes who ally themselves with the rebels."

"I shall ask Lothar," King Charles agreed. "But first, we must address our most immediate concern—freeing Abbot Louis and Gauzlin from Bjorn Ironside."

Hincmar was unconvinced. "Increasing assessments at this time of unrest is dangerous."

"It is a risk I must take." King Charles insisted. "Now, how shall we counter Louis the German?"

"Sire, you must solidify your alliance with King Lothar at your meeting in March," John Scotus observed. "But you must tread lightly when it comes to his treatment of Queen Theutberga."

"Lothar's treatment of his queen is reprehensible! Salomon's murder of his cousin is appalling! And the Danes are nothing but vicious monsters! But I must parlay with them all to achieve peace for Francia. That is the ugly reality of kingship," King Charles admitted sadly.

The year 858 had begun with another terrible attack on Paris and the taking for ransom of two of the king's men. Hincmar feared this was only a shadow of what was to come.

CHAPTER XIII

JANUARY through FEBRUARY 858

Following Erispoë's murder in November and their subsequent flight from Brittany, Baldwin's senses told him it was only a matter of time before Robert the Strong would strike against Louis. What troubled Baldwin was that he had no idea what form the attack would take. Who amongst the young king's court would prove loyal or traitor?

Disturbed by what had occurred in Talensac, both Louis and young Charles had ridden in silence for most of the way back to Le Mans. For three days, Baldwin had ridden guard at the front of the company while the rest of the young kings' retinues formed a circle around the two boys.

Young Charles finally spoke aloud what everyone had been thinking, "Being king is a dangerous business. Lots of people wish to kill you and take your place."

That plaintive remark haunted Baldwin. He was gratified when shortly before Christmas King Charles sent Count Hardouin, one of his Neustrian administrators, with a message commending Baldwin for his role in protecting the young kings and bestowing upon Baldwin the title of Count of Flanders with additional holdings in Ghent. Even Queen Judith in Wessex wrote a special message thanking Baldwin for his actions on behalf of her brothers. However, all the congratulations had not dispelled Baldwin's feeling of unease.

Christmas had come and gone, and still no sign that Robert was ready to make his move. Several days after Christmas, news reached Le Mans that Paris had been sacked again and that Abbot Louis and Gauzlin had been taken for ransom. Baldwin feared this was the opening that Robert the Strong had been awaiting. When word came that the nobles would be taxed to pay the Abbot's ransom, tensions in Neustria rose, increasing Robert the Strong's influence.

ֆ

"Normally, I have at least one or two l . . . lords each day with p . . . petitions," Louis complained to Baldwin as he surveyed his empty throne room.

King Louis spent his mornings with an administrator weighing his nobles' requests and resolving their disputes. Requests requiring higher approval were sent to King Charles for review. With no petitions coming in, Louis had too much time on his hands. As Baldwin and Louis started back to the royal apartments, a messenger arrived from Louis' palace chamberlain at Tours.

"This is m . . . my p . . . province!" Louis fumed. "He is trying to usurp my p . . . province."

"What has happened?" Baldwin pressed urgently.

"R . . . Robert the Strong is using my p . . . palace at Tours to decide p . . . petitions from the local l . . . lords."

King Louis' council deliberated endlessly, but Joseph and Mathieu found no solution that would not endanger the young king. The council sent word to King Charles at Compiègne requesting help with Tours. Before they could receive an answer, Robert the Strong made his move. Emboldened by his success with the nobles in Tours, Robert moved to hold court in the palace at Angers. It was only a matter of time before he set his eyes on Le Mans as well.

To Baldwin's relief, Mathieu suggested King Louis remove to Count Hardouin's estate in northeastern Neustria until King Charles could send knights to restore Louis to his rightful place. The council vowed to prevent anyone from discovering Louis' absence for as long as possible to make it more difficult to track the young king's movements. Baldwin and Louis would travel alone, and the king would forgo his kingly attire to avoid detection. If Robert moved on Le Mans or discovered their place of refuge, Baldwin would conduct Louis safely to Compiègne.

Baldwin and Louis began their four-day journey northeast from Le Mans under the cloak of pre-dawn darkness. Louis had grown several inches in the past year and was no longer a child's height. To casual observers they met along the road, the young men appeared to be two unremarkable knights. Baldwin did all the speaking, fearing that Louis' stammer might give them away.

Count Hardouin's manor house lay in a remote setting amongst vineyards, orchards, and green rolling pastures. Even in the midst of winter, the bucolic countryside was a welcome contrast to the rising political tensions threatening to boil over in Le Mans. Count Hardouin and his wife, Warimburg, greeted them warmly on their arrival.

"Welcome, King Louis and Count Baldwin," the countess's voice was soft and gentle.

Count Hardouin added, "You will find sanctuary here. This house will always be loyal to King Charles and his family."

"Thank you," Louis replied. "I hope that we w . . . will not inconvenience you for long. I do not think R . . . Robert the Strong can win in the end against m . . . my father!"

Louis and Baldwin were given adjoining rooms with windows looking out onto extensive now-dormant gardens. Baldwin was grateful that his new title provided him with sleeping quarters in close proximity to King Louis. It was comforting to know that he could be at the young king's side within seconds should they need to leave in the middle of the night.

At the evening meal, Count Hardouin introduced his son Odo and his daughter Ansgard to King Louis and Baldwin. Odo, who was of an age with Baldwin, mentioned his service in Aquitaine with young King Charles.

Baldwin remembered hearing of Odo's quick actions when the Danes had attacked the palace at Poitiers. "Young King Charles told us of your valor in rescuing him from the Danes," Baldwin remarked. "He called you his favorite knight."

Odo smiled. "I am sorry I was elsewhere in service when he was in danger at Talensac! Well done, Count Baldwin!"

"It is what we have sworn to do," Baldwin acknowledged. "I cannot understand those who so easily break the vows they have taken."

"My feelings exactly," Odo agreed.

Glancing at Louis, who had yet to speak a word, Baldwin noticed the young king's gaze fixated upon Odo's younger sister. Ansgard was indeed beautiful and had the same gentle manner as her mother. With hair the color of a golden sunrise and eyes the palest blue, set in a lightly browned complexion, the young girl was stunning. Obviously, Louis thought so as well. Throughout the meal, Louis barely spoke, so Baldwin did his best to fill in any noticeable lapses in conversation.

Later, Baldwin pressed Louis a little. "You did not speak much tonight, my king."

Louis' face reddened, and he shook his head.

"If you like Ansgard, speak with her. Come to know her better," Baldwin encouraged.

"S . . . She will not like the w . . . way that I s . . . speak," Louis worried.

"Ah, that is what concerns you," Baldwin nodded solemnly. "I do not know Ansgard's character. But if she is like her mother at all, and I think she may be, you wrong her if you believe she cannot look past your hesitant speaking."

"I have n . . . never seen anyone like her. She is b . . . beautiful," Louis whispered.

"She is that," Baldwin agreed. "She also seems very kind. And she looks to be about your age. Do you not wish to know if you have ideas in common? You will never know unless you try. Let her see what is good about you. Perhaps she will return your regard."

"It is useless anyway," Louis moaned. "F . . . Father would never allow such a m . . . match. What p . . . political advantage would he g . . . gain by allowing me to m . . . marry the daughter of one of his loyal followers?"

"Then it does not matter if she is impressed with you or not," Baldwin reasoned. "Think of her as if she were Judith, your sister. Just be yourself."

"I will t . . . try," Louis agreed.

On the following day, Baldwin was pleased to see Louis approach Ansgard as she read a book by the fire in the great room. Louis, like his older sister Judith, was an enthusiastic reader. Louis was probably correct in believing that a betrothal to a young woman with no beneficial political ties was unlikely. But it was good to see Louis befriend someone his own age.

Count Hardouin broke up the tableau when he and Odo suggested they ride out on his property and do some hunting. Louis' eyes were bright, and his face reflected his pleasure when he arose from his conversation with Ansgard. She, in turn, smiled at Louis as he left the room with her father and brother.

The group rode east toward a distant grouping of elms. They moved slowly so Count Hardouin could point out different features of his holding.

"This estate is smaller than the one we have in Burgundy, where we cultivate grapes and produce wine. The climate in Burgundy has been good to us this year. I will send you some of our best wine, King Louis when you return to Le Mans."

"W . . . Why do you choose to live in N . . . Neustria instead of B . . . Burgundy?" Louis questioned.

"Five years ago, your father asked me to return to my childhood home here and act as an administrator for him. Of course, I wished to serve my king. My family returns to Burgundy from time to time as business requires."

On the other side of the elms, Hardouin pointed out a small path leading into the forest. "I brought you both here to show you the most discrete way out of Neustria, should the need arise.

Follow this hunting path east through the forest and it will lead you to the Seine and a good fording place. I pray you will not need this path and that order will soon be restored in Neustria. But the path is a good one–should you need it."

On the following day, Odo set out to return to Aquitaine and young King Charles' service. He promised to journey by way of Le Mans and send word as to what he discovered there. So, Louis and Baldwin settled in to wait for word from Odo.

Ansgard's presence made Louis' confinement much more tolerable. Ansgard proved to be as gentle and kind as her mother. If she found Louis' stammer upsetting, she did not reveal it, and Louis seemed happier than Baldwin had ever known him to be. *Louis will be loath to return to Le Mans when the time comes.*

Nearly two weeks later, a messenger from Odo arrived bearing ill tidings for King Louis. King Charles had not yet sent an army to put down the rebellion in Neustria. Robert the Strong had taken control of Le Mans and had men searching for Louis, suspecting he was still in Neustria. Since a captive Louis would give Robert the upper hand in any negotiations with King Charles, his agents were searching all the estates of the king's loyal supporters for evidence of the young king. The messenger reported passing some of those agents earlier in the day as they traveled in the direction of Count Hardouin's holding.

Neustria was no longer safe for King Louis. Within minutes of hearing the messenger's report, Baldwin packed their horses with enough food for several days and Louis took reluctant leave of Ansgard. Promising to delay any searchers who might arrive at his door, Count Hardouin wished them a safe journey as they turned their mounts toward the forest path that would lead them to the Seine.

%

"Why such a fuss over a bean?" Aethelred demanded as Judith enlisted the young princes' help in a kitchen project.

"In Francia, this bean is not just any bean. The whiteness and the shape of the fava bean represent the infant Christ wrapped in swaddling clothes. In fact, this humble bean is powerful enough to create a king, even if only for a night.

Judith, Alfred, and Aethelred were overseeing the cook's preparation of the small king cakes on the Eve of Epiphany. Judith shared with the young princes an Epiphany tradition in many households in Francia. The cook would hide a bean in one of the cakes prior to baking. Whoever discovered the bean in their cake would become King of the Epiphany Feast.

"What does the king get to do?" Alfred wondered.

"The King of the Feast will wear a crown and royal robes and sit at the head table," Judith replied.

"Like Father," Alfred concluded.

"Exactly," Judith confirmed. "And the King of the Feast can command the court fool to perform whatever he pleases for the remainder of the feast."

"What if a woman finds the bean?" Aethelred wanted to know.

"If a woman finds the bean, she chooses which man will be king," Judith informed him. "The King of the Feast may also select a woman to be his queen and sit beside him at table."

"What if a real king is already at the table?" Alfred pressed. "Who is the ruler?"

"The real king, of course," Judith laughed. "Selecting a King of the Feast is merely an amusing way to celebrate the eve of Epiphany when the three kings came in search of baby Jesus."

"I hope I find the bean," Alfred's excitement was infectious. "I should love to command the fool!"

"It may very well be you, Alfred," Judith smiled. "No one knows who will be king until the bean is discovered."

"One thing is certain," Aethelred contributed. "We shall have three kings at our table for Epiphany. Father, Aethelberht, and whoever is King of the Feast."

"That is a brilliant observation, Aethelred! I shall make use of it," Judith congratulated him.

Aethelwulf had given Judith complete freedom to order the Epiphany Feast as she desired. When the kings' cakes were finished baking, she went in search of the king. At Judith's explanation of the king cake tradition, Aethelwulf laughed.

"Aethelberht and I shall observe with great interest who joins us as one of the three kings tonight."

After the first course of the Epiphany Feast, Judith arose and addressed the guests.

"My lords and ladies, we welcome you on this Eve of Epiphany. The night when we honor the three kings who set out in search of the infant Christ Child led by a star within the heavens. We have two kings already seated at this table. However, this is the night honoring the three kings."

She clapped her hands, and servants brought forth the king cakes.

"You are each being served a king cake. A white fava bean, representing the holy baby, has been baked into one of these cakes. Whichever lord finds the bean in his cake will take his place in the empty seat at the end of the king's table as King of the Epiphany Feast. He will have the right to order when the courses are served and will command the fool to provide our entertainment. If a woman finds the bean, she may choose which man will be our third king for the evening. Please eat your cake carefully so as not to swallow the bean whole. When the King of the Feast has taken his place at the table, he will order our next course. I hope you enjoy this tradition of Francia."

Excited chatter filled the great hall as the guests carefully searched their cakes for a bean. Judith quickly discovered that the bean was not within her own cake and began to fear that someone had swallowed the bean when no one stepped forward to claim the honor. Then she noticed Hemma, sitting with bowed head and scarlet face. Although Hemma typically ate with the servants, she had been included in this special Frankish feast at a table not far from Judith.

Crossing over to Hemma, Judith whispered, "Hemma, did you find the bean?"

Not daring to look up, Hemma opened her closed fist to reveal the white bean. It was an awkward moment, but Judith kept

170

her composure. "Think, Hemma," she whispered. "Whom do you wish to name King of the Feast?"

The answer was slow in coming, but finally, Hemma whispered back, "Felix."

With that, Judith took the bean and raised it above her head. "Hemma has found the bean and has selected Felix to rule the feast. Come forward, King Felix, and be seated," Judith bade.

Felix, laughing at the circumstance, good-naturedly arose from his bench and ascended the platform where he was dressed in a crown and robe. Felix, coming from Francia, knew precisely how the King of the Feast should conduct himself. King Felix insisted that Hemma's chair be moved next to his own at the end of the table as his queen, and the feast proceeded with fun and merriment.

๛

The week following Epiphany, Alfred and Aethelred approached Judith as she left the throne room. "Judith, on Epiphany, you shared with us a Frankish tradition. We think you will like our tradition of the wassail," Alfred pronounced.

"Wassail? Is it not a greeting, meaning 'good health?'" Judith asked.

"Oh, it is much more than a greeting," Aethelred assured her. "At least in Sussex."

Judith responded, "Why did we not see this wassail tradition last January?"

Aethelred explained. "Last year, we were in Amesbury. Wassail is a peasant celebration in Somerset, Kent, and Sussex."

"Must I prepare something for the celebration?"

"Not really," Alfred assured her. "The servants will prepare everything. We just need to convince Father and Aethelberht to join us, and it will be perfect."

On the morning of January 17th, Judith awoke to servants greeting each other with "Wassail!" Throughout the day, even the royal family used the greeting. In the afternoon, Alfred and Aethelred told Judith and Hemma what to expect that evening.

"Wassail is not just good wishes of health for people," Alfred began. "It is a wish of good health for crops and, in some places, for animals as well."

"Here in Sussex, they wassail the orchard trees, hoping they will give an abundance of fruit during the year," Aethelred added.

"Father says it is a harmless pagan ceremony, left over from before Britannia was Christian," Alfred continued. "He and Aethelberht have promised to join us."

At sunset, the royal family found torch-bearing servants and local villagers waiting in the palace courtyard. Alfred and Aethelred gave each member of the family a small bowl which they carried into the orchard. When they reached the apple trees, several strong men filled each bowl from heavy kegs of cider.

"Take a sip," Alfred urged Judith.

Judith tasted the sweetness of apples and herbs. At King Aethelberht's nod, the head gardener stepped forward and chanted a blessing upon the tree.

"We greet thee, blessed apple tree,
and bid thee blossom, and bear caps full,
baskets full, and barrels full of fruit!"

His recital was followed by the company shouting, "Huzzah, Huzzah, Huzzah."

Then, each took turns pouring a few drops of their cider on the roots of the tree. They repeated the ceremony, moving from tree to tree with small variations in the chant to reflect the variety of fruit being blessed. Judith found the chanting amidst the torch light oddly stirring, as if she had become one with the people and the trees. When they had blessed the last tree in the orchard, the royal party headed back to the palace for apple cider and apple cake.

Enjoying the festivities, Judith was unaware at first of King Aethelwulf's distress. When she noticed him removed from the company, his face was ashen, and he appeared to be in pain. She approached the king in alarm.

"I need to get to my bed," Aethelwulf spoke softly as he doubled over.

Judith called Aethelberht and Bishop Swithun, who helped the king to his room. She had never seen the king suffer any sort of illness. His face, so pale and full of agony, disturbed her deeply. Judith, Aethelred, and Alfred waited nervously for Aethelberht's report.

"I am not sure what is the matter," Aethelberht's eyes showed the depth of his concern. "At first, Father said he was sick. I thought he would feel some relief when he emptied his stomach, but he complained his chest hurt as if a rock were crushing him. His physician is with him. If he cannot drink herbs, they will have to bleed him to relieve the pressure in his chest."

Aethelwulf's physician eventually joined them. "I put a little poppy juice in his mouth. He is sleeping at present. We will see how he is in the morning."

When Judith arose after a restless night, the news was not reassuring. Aethelwulf was very weak. His physician had given him more poppy juice to keep him comfortable, but his breathing had grown shallow. Bishop Swithun and Father Electus administered the holy rites.

Shortly before noon, each of the royal family entered King Aethelwulf's room alone to say a final goodbye. Judith entered Aethelwulf's chamber and leaned over his bed to stroke first his face and then his hand. The king's breath, barely perceptible, reminded Judith of a farrier's rasp scraping against hoof.

So many memories played like shadows in the sunlight dancing through her mind. Aethelwulf's gentleness on their wedding night, his consideration of her every need, his strength when facing the Witenagemot, his devotion to God, and his ability to laugh at himself and others. This great man and great king had placed others' needs before his own. An invincible warrior, yet a kind and gentle father to his sons. *How fitting is your name! Rest in God's peace, Noble Wolf!*

☙

King Aethelwulf was buried in St. Cuthman's church at Steyning. King Aethelbald had arrived from Wessex with a few of his thegns to pay homage to the former king and to discuss with King Aethelberht what would be done with the kingdom.

Several months earlier, King Aethelwulf had ordered his final testament be written. He had made generous provision for the Church, his retainers, and Judith. He had also made provision to avoid conflict between his sons over the disposition of his land and property. King Aethelwulf had designated Aethelberht sole king of Kent, Essex, Somerset, and Sussex. He further bestowed upon Aethelberht his personal estates in Kent to be passed down to Aethelberht's heirs.

Aethelbald was furious when he discovered that his father had not provided for him in his will. Rather than leave his holdings to his eldest son, Aethelwulf had left his estates in Wessex to Aethelberht, Aethelred, and Alfred jointly. Through this unique arrangement, control of the land, and the kingship, would pass to the next oldest brother upon the death of each, until only one brother remained to inherit all of Wessex. Judith suspected that Aethelbald would seek to contest the will.

During the week that King Aethelbald remained at Steyning, he spent much of his time in earnest discussion with Aethelberht. Devastated by their loss, Alfred and Aethelred stayed by Judith's side.

"What is it that Aethelbald and Aethelberht are discussing?" Alfred wondered.

"Aethelbald is trying to convince Aethelberht to split up part of Kent and Sussex and give them to us instead of having us be in line to inherit father's part of Wessex," Aethelred opined sadly.

"Can he do that? Can he thwart the terms of the testament?" Judith spoke angrily.

"I do not know," Aethelred shrugged. "But he will try."

❧

With the death of Aethelwulf, Judith retained Felix as her private secretary. The first assignment she gave Felix was to send word to King Charles, informing him of the death of King Aethelwulf and requesting that he send an escort for her return to Francia. Next, Judith consulted Bertrand, her seneschal, regarding preparing to sell the land King Aethelwulf had given her upon their marriage. She would especially regret losing her manor house at Graveney. She had loved owning and restoring that historic estate. But Judith knew she must be ready to move whenever her father sent for her. In the meantime, she would do what she could to comfort Alfred and Aethelred at the loss of their father.

Throughout King Aethelbald's stay, Judith had sensed a gradual change in his attitude toward her. From their first meeting at Sarum he had looked upon her with disdain, seeking fault in her every word or action. Now, his gaze seemed shrewder, as if he were trying to discern how she, like all the other people within his circle, could be used to his own advantage.

On his final night in Steyning, King Aethelbald attempted to engage her in conversation. "Tell me, Queen Judith," he began, "what are your plans? How long will you remain in Britannia?"

"You need not fear that I will remain much longer, King Aethelbald," Judith replied curtly. "I have written to my father requesting an escort back to Francia."

"Judith can remain as long as she desires!" Alfred cried passionately.

"I did not intend to imply that Judith is not welcome here, Alfred," Aethelbald protested. "I am only interested in her future well-being. What do you intend to do once you return to Francia, Judith? You are very young, after all. You are not more than thirteen years of age."

"That is correct, King Aethelbald. But my father will ensure my well-being."

Aethelbald nodded his understanding and then turned to converse with Aethelberht.

175

My father will probably arrange another marriage for me as soon as he receives my missive. Judith admitted to herself. She took no joy in that prospect.

❧

On the final day of February, following morning mass in the family chapel, King Charles drew Hincmar aside. "Archbishop, I wish you to meet me in the church on the palace grounds in one hour. I have something of importance to discuss with you outside of these walls."

"Of course, Sire," Hincmar hastily agreed.

The king nodded and hurried to join Queen Ermentrude and his family for the breaking of their fast, leaving Hincmar pondering. The king's request was highly unusual. What could possibly be of such moment that King Charles wished to ensure absolute privacy?

One hour later the archbishop approached the church as requested. King Charles sat in the empty chapel with his head bowed. The king's personal attendant stood at the door, ready to deny others admittance. He nodded at Hincmar as the archbishop entered and sat next to the king. The king was holding two parchment scrolls. After several minutes, he raised his head and turned toward Hincmar.

"I have received two missives from Wessex," King Charles spoke softly so as not to be overheard by his servant. "The first is from Judith requesting an escort for her return home following the death of King Aethelwulf. And the second is from King Aethelbald, offering to continue the marriage alliance between our two kingdoms."

"He seeks to marry Judith?" Hincmar sought clarification.

"He does," the king confirmed. "This is not a question I can bring before the council. Nor can I discuss this with Queen Ermentrude."

"I understand, Sire," Hincmar nodded. "Now that King Louis has returned and is part of your council, such a delicate matter regarding Judith could inflame family passions."

"Precisely! You know the issues involved. Advise me, Hincmar, I do not know how to respond."

Hincmar tried to suppress his growing excitement at the news King Charles had shared. The plan to expand Charles' influence in Wessex was still viable with this offer from King Aethelbald.

"The greatest objection to a marriage between Judith and King Aethelbald is that of consanguinity. It is not unheard of for a widow to marry her stepson, but if such a marriage is objected to on the grounds that it violates the Church's laws of consanguinity, the pope could annul the marriage."

"Who would be allowed to raise such an objection?" Charles wished to know.

"Anyone might object. But unless her guardian objects, the pope would not be inclined to act."

"I cannot sanction the marriage publicly without risking a rift in my family," Charles asserted.

"Sire, you need not sanction the marriage. You need only not oppose it," Hincmar assured.

King Charles shook his head sadly. "I despise such deception, but I see no choice in the matter. With Francia in turmoil I do not have the resources to send as an escort for Judith. Neither do I have another potential marriage for her at present."

"Marriage with King Aethelbald not only preserves your initial alliance with Wessex but improves upon it." Hincmar pointed out.

"How so?" the king questioned.

"The impediment to the plan was always the threat of King Aethelbald himself," Hincmar explained. "That impediment is now removed. Any son born of this union will ascend the throne of Wessex without opposition. And Aethelbald is young—no more than 24 years of age, surely. There will be plenty of time for him to produce that son before he dies."

King Charles handed the two scrolls to Hincmar. "You are right, as usual, Archbishop. Marriage to Aethelbald is the best I can do for Judith in our current circumstances. I trust that I can rely upon you to carefully craft the replies to these two missives."

"Of course, Sire," Hincmar nodded his agreement.

CHAPTER XIV

MARCH through AUGUST 858

At the beginning of March, King Charles instructed Louis to accompany him to Quierzy for his annual conference with King Lothar. Baldwin prepared to join the king's company as well. However, several days before they were to depart, King Charles called Baldwin to his throne room.

"Count Baldwin," King Charles greeted him warmly. "I need you for a special assignment."

"Of course, Sire," Baldwin responded. "How may I be of service?"

"Abbot Louis and Archchancellor Gauzlin's ransom is ready to be paid. The Danes abandoned their island hold at Fossa Givaldi and moved south to set up a stronghold downriver of Paris at Oissel. I need a capable and trustworthy knight to deliver the ransom to Bjorn Ironside at Oissel and bring the hostages home. I believe you are that man."

Baldwin, caught off guard by King Charles' faith in his ability to handle such a perilous situation, could see no other option but to graciously accept.

When Louis learned of Baldwin's errand, he was less than pleased. "I would rather go with you and confront Vikings than go with my father and meet with my cousin Lothar," he complained.

Baldwin was not sorry to miss the conference in Quierzy. The latest report was that Theutberga had been ordered by a court of Lothar's laymen and nobles to undergo Trial by Ordeal—in this case, by boiling water.

Theutberga had the right to appoint a champion. But if her champion failed to retrieve the stone from the cauldron of boiling water with his bare hand unscathed, Queen Theutberga would be subject to whatever penalty the law would impose, including death.

When King Charles' entourage set out for the conference at Quierzy, Baldwin pointed his mount in the direction of Oissel. The danger lay not only in their destination—a Viking stronghold—but also in its proximity to territory held by the rebel lords of Aquitaine and Neustria. Baldwin had selected two strong knights and three grooms for his party. The group must appear as unremarkable as possible, for they were leading pack horses and carts laden with enough gold and silver to purchase a small kingdom.

∾

Rising seemingly overnight from the surrounding landscape, Oissel had been built upon the backs of slaves taken in Viking raids over the past year. With earthen ramparts twelve feet high, topped by wooden stakes and a deep trench dug around the ramparts for additional security, the stronghold also bordered on the Seine—providing easy access to the river. Rivaling some of the largest Roman fortifications, Baldwin estimated the stronghold at Oissel could accommodate up to ten thousand Danes and their longships.

After observing Oissel from a protected position on a nearby forested rise, Baldwin approached the only gate into the stronghold alone. If he did not return on the morrow, Baldwin told his group to make their way back to the court at Compiègne. He attached a white cloth to the end of his sword and, holding it aloft, rode slowly toward the stronghold, leaving the knights and grooms to guard the ransom.

The approach to the stronghold seemed endless as Baldwin imagined unseen eyes watching his every move. When he reached the gate without an arrow or spear embedded in his chest, Baldwin breathed a bit easier. Two grizzled Vikings, wearing boiled-leather jerkins and armed with swords, guarded the gate. *Please, God, this works!* Baldwin prayed.

"Sheath your sword," one of the guards barked gruffly.

When Baldwin complied, the guard continued, "What business have you here?"

Baldwin replied with as much bravado as he could muster, "I am Count Baldwin Iron Arm, with a message from King Charles. I am here to speak with Bjorn Ironside regarding ransoming the captives, Abbot Louis of St. Denis and Archchancellor Gauzlin."

The guard motioned to Baldwin. "Dismount and follow me."

Baldwin followed him inside the gate which closed behind them with a distinct report, leaving the other guard on the outside. The guard motioned to another Dane to watch Baldwin while he went in search of Bjorn Ironside. Baldwin took the opportunity to assess Oissel's defensive capabilities.

The stronghold teemed with activity that indicated the Danes were planning to stay for a good long while. The perimeter of the ramparts was lined with row upon row of makeshift tents. But in the center of the stronghold, filthy, emaciated slaves were building timber longhouses and huts. Tragically, the ransom would only purchase freedom for the abbot and the archchancellor.

When the guard returned, he led Baldwin to one of the largest tents nearest the middle of the stronghold and gestured for him to enter. Baldwin was surprised by the sumptuous comfort of the tent's furnishings, with feather beds, embroidered coverlets, an inlaid table, and silver chalices. He suspected the items had been stolen in numerous raids within Francia. A tall, broad-shouldered Dane, with blonde hair and beard stood to one side observing Baldwin. The man wore chainmail, indicating he was more than an ordinary Viking warrior.

"So, you are Count Baldwin Iron Arm," the Dane sounded amused. "I am Bjorn Ironside, leader of half of the men here at Oissel. King Charles sent you?"

"That is correct," Baldwin affirmed. "He gave me this missive for you." Baldwin removed a parchment scroll from under his chain mail and extended it to Bjorn.

181

Bjorn did not reach for the parchment. "Read it," he demanded. "Or tell me what it says."

He does not read our writing, Baldwin realized. Carefully, he unrolled the parchment and began to read. "To Bjorn, leader of the Danes, from King Charles, ruler of Francia. With great sacrifice from our people, we have raised the ransom of 688 pounds of gold and 3,250 pounds of silver. We now request that in exchange for that ransom, you release to our representative the two captives, Abbot Louis and Archchancellor Gauzlin as promised."

"Hah! I knew he would raise the money. When do we make the exchange?" Bjorn asked impatiently.

Baldwin held up a hand to halt his enthusiasm. "That is not the entire message. May I continue?"

At Bjorn's nod, Baldwin read on, "Know this, that after your many years of raids, the coffers of every church in Francia are now empty. Should you continue to raid our houses of worship, you will find no treasure within. However, if you come to me at my court in Verberie next month and pledge to leave Francia and never return, I will give you 500 pounds of silver from my own treasury. If you accept this offer, Count Baldwin Iron Arm shall grant you safe passage to our court at the appointed time. Any further raids will result only in the murder of innocent people with no material gain to yourselves. Signed, Charles, King of the Franks."

"An interesting offer," Bjorn mused.

Baldwin watched Bjorn carefully consider his options. Bjorn was shrewd. If Francia was becoming a dry well, perhaps it was time for him to move on to relieve other kingdoms of their excess wealth. An additional 500 pounds of silver, which need not be divided amongst other Vikings, was appealing.

"May I see the hostages?" Baldwin interrupted Bjorn's musings.

Bjorn smiled agreeably. "You shall not only see them, Baldwin Iron Arm, you shall share their tent this night while I discuss King Charles' proposal with my men."

Baldwin knew he could not linger at Oissel without risking the knights and grooms returning to Compiègne with the ransom. "King Charles expects me to depart with the hostages in the morning," he stressed.

"King Charles will have his answer and we shall make the exchange on the morrow," Bjorn promised. He ordered the guard standing outside to take Baldwin to the captives' tent.

Abbot Louis and Archchancellor Gauzlin were brought to tears when they learned that their months of confinement would soon end. Thin, weakened, and depressed, they nevertheless wished to hear whatever news Baldwin could tell them of St. Denis, Paris, and Francia. They talked well into the night, Abbot Louis and Gauzlin relating their experiences during the raid on St. Denis and their move from Fossa Givaldi to Oissel.

In the morning, Baldwin returned to Bjorn's tent to discuss the exchange. Bjorn held out his hand. "Give me your sword, Baldwin Iron Arm."

Baldwin complied. Bjorn held the sword aloft admiringly and tested its sharpness with the tip of his finger. "My men would kill to have such a sword," he remarked. "Frankish swords are far superior to those of the Danes. Perhaps we should capture your blacksmiths rather than your church relics," he laughed. "My men would also kill to have armor like yours rather than the leather jerkins worn by most. That is how I got my chain mail. I took it from a dead knight."

Baldwin felt his hackles rise as Bjorn laughed and returned his sword without a second glance. "No matter. I like you, Count Baldwin Iron Arm. I will promise you safe passage out of Oissel, and you will promise me safe passage when I come to the court of King Charles at Verberie. Tell the king I accept his offer. Now, let us arrange the exchange."

When he reached the forest, Baldwin was relieved to find his men still there. Quickly, they packed up the horses and carts and made their way to the gate of the stronghold. Their approach was observed by dozens of Vikings who had climbed upon the ramparts to watch the exchange. Bjorn inspected the gold and silver in the saddle packs and carts to the cheers of the Danes.

Relieved of its heavy burden, the carts were used to transport Abbot Louis to St. Denis and Gauzlin back to King Charles' court.

As Baldwin returned to Compiègne, he contemplated what would happen the following month when the court moved to Verberie. Bjorn would arrive to pledge his departure from Francia and receive his reward of silver. However, only part of the men at Oissel were his. If half of those currently in the stronghold departed, King Charles had no assurance that the remaining Danes would leave Francia in peace.

Crystal May sunlight streaming through her bedchamber window reflected the peace Judith felt in awakening at Graveney. This feeling was something she had hitherto never experienced. The right to order one's own life. To choose to rise and embrace whatever challenges the day would bring. Or to choose to lie in bed the entire day and do nothing at all. Even after several months, the freedom still felt new to her. She stretched her arms wide as she lay on her bed, savoring the exhilarating feeling. *This is bliss.*

Following six weeks of mourning at Steyning, Judith had begun preparing to sell her estate at Graveney. If the message she had sent to her father had not already reached him, it would shortly. So, she had come to Graveney to oversee the renovations which had been undertaken months earlier.

King Aethelberht, who was ready to move his court, offered to have the royal household accompany her, for which Judith was thankful. She was not yet ready to say goodbye to Aethelwulf's sons, who had become like brothers to her. King Aethelberht's court would spend the next two months at their royal estate at Faversham. And so, they would be neighbors—a good transition for the inevitable moment when she must part with Alfred, Aethelred, and Aethelberht.

Judith rose, calling for Hemma to help her dress. She had begun sorting through the books in the library. How many could she read before her departure, and how many would she be able to take with her to Francia? She was busy sorting the books into piles when a servant admitted a Frankish messenger. Judith sighed, sensing her time remaining in Graveney would be cut short.

"Have you a message for me?" Judith asked the messenger.

"I do, Queen Judith," the messenger assured her, removing two scrolls from his bag. Judith saw other scrolls yet within the bag before the messenger closed it. "I see you have several other missives remaining," she pointed out.

"Yes, Queen Judith. I was not sure where to find you. And as I was also given missives for King Aethelbald and several of the clergy, I went to Wessex first. I carry replies for Archbishop Hincmar and for King Charles from those in Sherborne. I will remain here until you are ready to write a response as well."

Judith felt uneasy. *What business do my father and Hincmar have with Aethelbald?* She motioned for the servant to step forward. "Provide this messenger with refreshment and lodging." To the messenger she added, "I should have a response for you on the morrow."

Judith set the scroll aside, continuing her sorting. She was not in a hurry to find out how soon she would be leaving. The news could wait until her task was complete. When the last book had been carefully examined and placed in its proper pile, Judith sat down to read the missives.

Running her thumb beneath the wax on the scroll bearing her brother Louis' seal first, Judith unrolled the parchment to read with consternation that Louis had been pushed out of Le Mans by Robert the Strong. And once again, she had the intrepid Baldwin Iron Arm to thank for safeguarding her brother—this time on their flight from Neustria. Many forces threatened her father's kingdom. Judith wondered what she would be returning to.

The next missive bore the seal of her father. But when she opened it, she recognized the writing of Archbishop Hincmar. The message was short and to the point. Judith would not return to Francia. She was to remain in Wessex and marry King Aethelbald, who had requested the alliance. Judith reread the missive a second and then a third time. A hollow feeling formed in her belly, and a cold chill ran up her spine.

When Hemma entered the library sometime later, Judith sat frozen in the same position, unwilling or unable to move. "Are you well, my Queen?" Hemma asked tentatively. Then, noticing what Judith was holding, she asked, "Have you received ill tidings from Francia?"

Judith handed the scroll to Hemma. "I am asked to do what I cannot imagine doing."

Hemma gave a little moan as she finished reading the parchment. "Oh, I am sorry for you, Queen Judith," the tone in her voice indicating that she understood Judith's dilemma. "Perhaps Father Electus can comfort you."

"I fear I shall need more than that," Judith admitted. "I wish I had John Scotus here to advise me. Or a council like my father has to advise him in times of trouble."

"Can you not assemble your own council?" Hemma suggested.

Judith paused to consider. "I do have Father Electus and Bertrand."

"And Felix as well," Hemma reminded her. "He is also one of your retainers now."

"That is true," Judith sounded a bit hopeful. "It will be up to you, Hemma, to assemble this council. I feel overwhelmed and a bit nauseous."

"You need not move at all. I will bring your council to you." Hemma quickly left the room.

Within the hour the queen's council had assembled in the library. When each had read the troubling missive for himself, Judith asked the questions running persistently through her mind.

"Why is King Aethelbald eager for this alliance? And what, if anything, can I do to prevent this marriage from taking place?"

Bertrand was the first to speak. "I do not presume to know what is in King Aethelbald's mind. However, as your husband he would assume control over all your considerable property. This could be an attempt to regain some of the property he felt should have been his own."

"King Aethelbald was very displeased to learn that King Aethelwulf had put both Aethelred and Alfred in his will as heirs to Wessex, if their older brothers precede them in death," Felix pointed out. "He may contest that portion of the testament if his claim to the throne is strengthened by an alliance with the court of King Charles."

Father Electus agreed. "And any son you bear Aethelred would have a stronger claim to the throne of Wessex than either of the two princes. Perhaps you are not aware of the power your consecration as Queen of Wessex brings with it."

Judith knew that her consecration was unique. But she had not considered that her consecration might be used as a political tool to disinherit both Aethelred and Alfred.

She shivered. "What of my second question?" Can anything be done to prevent this marriage?"

Father Electus responded quickly. "Queen Judith, in the eyes of the church, a marriage between you and your stepson is not allowed on the grounds of consanguinity."

"Father Electus," Judith addressed her spiritual adviser, "I recognize the handwriting on this missive as that of Archbishop Hincmar. The archbishop must see a way around that objection, or he would not have written this missive for my father."

"It is true that someone must raise the objection for the church to act," Father Electus admitted.

"Can I raise such an objection?" Judith asked hopefully.

"I am afraid not," Father Electus replied sadly. "Although rare, a few such marriages have been sanctioned by previous popes. Your objection might be briefly considered. But, unless King Charles or King Aethelbald object, the pope will see no impediment to the marriage."

"The queen's objection might be used to delay the marriage," Bertrand offered. "Perhaps something would arise in the meantime to make the alliance no longer desirable to either king."

Felix offered a suggestion. "As a delay, the queen's best argument may be to insist that the laws of Wessex require that a widow wait a year after her husband's passing before marrying again."

"However, King Aethelbald is the final arbiter of the law in Wessex," Bertrand pointed out. "Who dares object if he decides to suspend the law in his own circumstance?"

"Is there nothing I can do?" Judith pleaded.

Father Electus had another suggestion. "You could inform King Aethelbald that you have written to King Charles asking him to reconsider his consent on the grounds of consanguinity. Tell him that you await your father's ultimate decision. At least you will have the several months it takes for the messenger to ride to Francia and return with a response."

"Will it anger King Aethelbald if I appear to despise his offer?" Judith wondered.

"That is certainly something you will have to weigh when you consider how to act," Felix admitted. "My experience is that King Aethelbald is neither patient nor understanding."

Judith pondered the counsel she had been given. "Each of you has given me much to consider. It seems I have but two choices. The first is to accept my fate and marry Aethelbald. The second is to delay, appeal to my father, and hope something will arise to prevent the marriage, while risking Aethelbald's displeasure. I do not know what my decision will be. I will delay sending my reply with the messenger for as long as possible. If another idea occurs to any of you within the next few days, we can discuss the idea as a council."

After several days of mulling over her choices, Judith finally made her decision. She would resist the marriage with whatever means she had. First, she would send word to King Aethelbald informing him that she was asking her father to reconsider the alliance based on the laws of the church. Her father's messenger would take her missive to Aethelbald's court at Sherborne before he returned to Francia, adding a few precious weeks to the process.

If her father refused to withdraw his permission, Judith would delay the wedding day for as long as possible, arguing the laws of Wessex regarding widowhood and remarriage.

Judith had Felix carefully craft a letter to King Aethelbald as well as a response to her father's missive. When the messenger was safely on his way, Judith rode to the royal estate at Faversham. King Aethelberht's court had planned to move to Winchester upon Judith's own departure. They had delayed their move in hopes of seeing her on her way. Now everything had changed. *Please do not let them judge me, whatever happens in the future with Aethelbald!*

⁓

Following Bjorn's appearance at Verberie, he took his 3,000 men and 62 longships and departed for more profitable kingdoms to pillage. With the number of Danes drastically reduced, King Charles' council decided that a siege of the stronghold at Oissel was in order. King Charles began his siege of the remaining Vikings at Oissel in July.

Hincmar was optimistic about their chances. Past sieges had failed when the lords refused to maintain sieges over winter. This time, they began the siege earlier in the year, and the army had received support from unexpected areas. Pippin, recently ousted again as King of Aquitaine, decided to join his forces with those of King Charles. When young Charles—reinstated as king— brought his men from Aquitaine to join the siege, Pippin and his followers accompanied him. Pippin placed his hands between those of King Charles and swore allegiance, finally acknowledging young Charles as the rightful King of Aquitaine. In turn, King Charles bestowed on Pippin several counties and monasteries as *benefices.*

The arrival of King Lothar and his men in August provided the greatest boost to the siege forces. King Lothar had been forced to restore Queen Theutberga to his palace in Aachen after her champion had miraculously endured the Ordeal of boiling water, thus establishing the queen's innocence. Perhaps King Lothar's decision to join the siege reflected his desire to be as far from Queen Theutberga as possible. No matter what the reason, King Charles welcomed his nephew's support.

In June, while plans for the upcoming siege were still being laid, King Charles received two missives from Wessex. In the first message, Judith begged her father to reconsider the proposed marriage based on the laws of consanguinity.

In the second missive, King Aethelbald spoke of his pleasure in the proposed alliance between the two kingdoms. However, a postscript–obviously added after he had learned of Judith's objections–expressed his concern. Could Aethelbald rely on King Charles' decision, or would Judith have the final say in the matter? Aethelbald acknowledged that this marriage was an alliance of state and not of personal preference. But he assured King Charles that Judith would continue to be given the respect she had been accustomed to at King Aethelwulf's court.

"What do you make of these missives?" King Charles asked Hincmar. "Apparently, Judith does not wish to marry King Aethelbald."

Hincmar was careful in his response. "Judith expressed her concerns over consanguinity. However, unless you object, the pope will not do so."

"That was certainly true with Pope Benedict. But what do we know of Pope Nicholas? Since Pope Benedict's death in April, we have learned little of the new pope." Charles observed.

"True," Hincmar acknowledged. "However, Pope Nicholas will tread lightly at first. He will wait to see your own reaction to the marriage before acting."

"What of Judith's personal feelings about marrying King Aethelbald? Do we have reason to suspect a problem there?" King Charles wondered.

"None that are stated within the missive," Hincmar pointed out. "Perhaps Queen Judith should be reminded that royal marriages are for the good of the kingdom and not for personal pleasure."

King Charles nodded. "Once more, I leave it in your capable hands to craft the appropriate responses, archbishop. I have a siege to implement!"

"I understand, Sire," Hincmar assured him. "This matter shall not trouble you again.

CHAPTER XV

SEPTEMBER through DECEMBER 858

K ing Charles became seriously ill, and that changed everything. What had begun as a promising siege at Oissel with tents as far as the eye could see started to unravel like a worn and threadbare tapestry. With King Charles confined to his tent, every day more lords found reason to return to their provinces. Eventually, King Lothar also abandoned his uncle's siege and returned with his men to Lotharingia. Without Charles' charismatic leadership and determination, the king's followers simply vanished from the conflict. *This siege has become like the previous ones,* Baldwin mourned. *A lost opportunity. A spectacular waste of time.*

Baldwin, who had gained rare insights into the inner workings of the Danes' stronghold, had been an invaluable resource early on in the siege. However, once King Charles became ill, no one was interested in what was going on inside the stronghold. All the attention was given to what was going on inside the king's tent.

King Charles' illness had started with a cough and soreness when swallowing. His appetite had declined and within a week he experienced pain in his chest and difficulty breathing. The king's physician worked tirelessly to restore the king's humours. But the purging, herbal poultices, and bleeding were to no avail. The king was alive but greatly weakened. His body would need time to recover–time he could ill afford.

Then, in late September, messengers brought word that Louis the German had at last invaded Francia and was marching toward Aquitaine. Nobles allied with Robert the Strong had traveled to Louis the German's court and pleaded with him to relieve them of the "tyrannical reign" of King Charles. They promised that Charles' former confidant, Archbishop Wenilo of Sens, who had crowned Charles King of Francia in 848, now stood ready to receive–and crown–Louis the German.

Report of Louis the German's invasion ended the siege of Oissel. King Charles emerged from his tent, gaunt and overcome by frequent bouts of violent coughing. The number of followers remaining with him was small. As they turned their horses toward the palace at Verberie, Baldwin wondered if Charles could muster enough knights to survive the long-anticipated battle with his brother.

လ

Hemma packed the last of Judith's possessions to be transported to Sherborne. All the objections Judith had raised to a marriage with King Aethelbald had merely pushed the wedding back to autumn. It was nearly two years since she had been crowned Queen of Wessex by King Aethelwulf. Now, she would marry his son. Judith had decided not to sell her estate at Graveney. Knowing that she owned it brought her comfort, even if Aethelbald would not allow her to return. Graveney had been her refuge, the first place where she felt truly free.

King Aethelbald sent several thegns to escort Judith to Sherborne. The company must depart Graveney no later than the end of September, for the wedding would take place in mid-October. Judith was grateful that King Aethelberht and the young princes would join her entourage when she reached Rochester.

Aethelberht had been guarded, and the young princes were surprised when she had first shared with them the possibility of her marriage to Aethelbald.

"How can you be our sister if you were our mother?" Alfred had demanded.

"It is confusing for me, as well," Judith admitted ruefully.

"You do not wish to marry Aethelbald, do you?" Aethelred remarked perceptively.

"No, I do not," was Judith's emphatic reply. "I am doing all within my power to object. However, royal marriages are for the benefit of kingdoms and may even be against the will of those involved."

"No one had better try to make me marry someone against my will," Alfred declared hotly.

"I hope they do not, Alfred. I truly hope they do not," Judith whispered.

When the two young princes were out of earshot, Judith spoke earnestly with Aethelberht. "I fear Aethelbald may use this marriage to block Aethelred and Alfred from inheriting Wessex."

Aethelberht nodded his understanding. "I hope that is not Aethelbald's purpose in proposing this marriage. My father's will sought to curb Aethelbald's greed by providing each of my brothers the "right to rule" in succession—including Alfred. If I have the opportunity, I will reunite my father's kingdom and care for my younger brothers as my father would have done. Trust me."

With her mind at rest concerning the two princes, Judith had returned to Graveney to continue her own battle. With her council's help she had countered every assertion by her father and Aethelbald with her own objections. However, in the end, others had decided her future.

෨

It was odd, the feeling of retracing her path from nearly two years earlier. The road to Rochester was the same. Aethelberht and Aethelred, joined by Alfred, waited for her at the place where she had first met them as the new bride of King Aethelwulf. It was not until they traveled deep into Selwood Forest that the feeling of sameness left her, replaced by dread of the unknown. They were now entering land forbidden to Judith and King Aethelwulf after the decision of the Witenagemot.

Alfred's enthusiasm for life made the journey tolerable. He eagerly pointed out animals and points of interest along their way. His interest in reading was as great as ever and he was continuing his studies with a priest who was teaching him to write in Latin.

"I wish I had learned earlier. But now that I have begun, I shall never cease," he promised.

"I believe you, Alfred," Judith smiled. "You are very intelligent and very determined. Someday, you will be one of the most learned men on the island of Britannia!"

Beyond the western border of Selwood Forest lay Sherborne, the seat of King Aethelbald's power. The grand cathedral and the nearby imposing royal palace rose above the heart of the city with its streets radiating out from the center. Judith was greeted by the palace steward, who explained that King Aethelbald was out hunting. He would see them at the evening feast. Meanwhile, servants unpacked the horses and conducted the royal travelers to their chambers.

Similar to Frankish palaces, Sherborne Palace opened into a large entry with a grand staircase leading up to the sleeping chambers. Everything, from the palace's mosaic floors to its Purbeck marble columns, displayed a regal grandeur. *I see why Aethelbald wanted Sherborne!*

King Aethelberht and the young princes were given rooms in one wing of the palace while the steward showed Judith and Hemma to King Aethelbald's private apartments. The keeper of the door to the king's apartments stepped aside, allowing them to enter. Smaller but similar to Senlis, the apartments featured a sitting room on the left and a passageway leading to several chamber doors. Judith was given the first chamber on the right. The steward informed her that the king's chamber was the last door on the left.

Two small windows in Judith's bedchamber allowed light into the room and provided a view of the outer world. The bed was large, and the stone fireplace was already lit. As servants brought in chest upon chest of her belongings, Judith decided the room was not as large as she had first believed. However, Hemma quickly found a place for everything, including a privacy screen and a small bed for herself.

After unpacking Judith's clothing, Hemma helped her dress for the feast. Not wishing to encounter Aethelbald alone, Judith waited until she heard him return from the hunt and move down the passage to his chamber. Then she went in search of Aethelberht and the young princes.

The three royal brothers were conversing at the foot of the grand staircase. Judith, who had worn her simple golden tiara rather than one of her more ostentatious crowns, was surprised that all three brothers were dressed formally, with Aethelberht wearing a ceremonial crown.

"Aethelbald revels in the ceremony of the royal court and expects others to do so as well," Aethelberht explained somewhat sheepishly.

Moments later King Aethelbald appeared for the feast, proud, handsome, and wearing his own elaborate crown.

"Welcome Queen Judith," King Aethelbald's tone held no warmth. "You have decided to grace us with your presence at last. With the wedding in three days, we were beginning to wonder." Judith could think of nothing appropriate to say and felt her face flush with embarrassment.

"And welcome, brothers. Thank you for bringing me my reluctant bride," Aethelbald laughed. "The hunting today was superb! You must hunt with me tomorrow."

As they turned to enter the great hall, Aethelbald offered Judith his arm and remarked, "You must wear a crown more appropriate to your position as Queen of Wessex. My father was not one for ceremony, but it is expected at Sherborne. You do own a proper crown, do you not?"

"I have several," Judith acknowledged.

"Then it is understood," Aethelbald cautioned her as he led the way into the feast.

The great hall at Sherborne was richly decorated with tapestries and mosaics reflecting King Aethelbald's elaborate taste, and the servants presented each course with fanfare and ostentation. Personal attendants stood behind the king's chair throughout the feast, quick to respond to his every demand with a fawning obeisance.

Seated next to King Aethelbald at the high table, Judith was grateful that he did not engage her in conversation. Aethelbald seemed content to display her for his court—another acquisition. He drank heavily, visited with his brothers, singled out several of his thegns for attention, interacted with the court fool, and flirted with two of the serving maids. Later that night, Hemma reported encountering a serving maid in the passageway, having just left the king's bedchamber.

≈

The morning of the wedding dawned bright and clear in sharp contrast to Judith's emotions. Hemma dressed Judith in silken robes elaborately embroidered in gold and silver. Judith wore the pearl and sapphire necklace, earrings, and bracelets that King Aethelbald had given her to use for the day.

"A far cry from the simple white tunic you wore at your first wedding," Hemma remarked as she put the finishing touches to Judith's dazzling wedding attire.

Built of the distinctive yellowish stone from Somerset, Sherborne Cathedral sat upon the foundation of a former Roman palazzo complete with mosaic tile floors. The wedding procession began in the late afternoon. The aged Bishop Eahlstan, who had been Archbishop of Sherborne for more than forty years, came to the palace to lead the royal procession to the cathedral. Judith and King Aethelberht were next, with Aethelred and Alfred following closely behind. Other than those in her immediate circle, Judith spotted no familiar face amongst the throngs of townspeople, and royal retainers gathered to watch the queen's arrival.

Holding tightly to Aethelberht's arm as they stepped through the massive oaken cathedral doors, Judith paused in the entryway. King Aethelbald waited at the end of the nave to lead her to the chancel. She could see one of her grandmother's crowns lying on the altar.

"God give me strength," Judith breathed softly.

"Are you alright, Judith?" Aethelberht whispered back.

Not knowing how to respond, Judith watched silently while her entourage took their places within the cathedral. The ceremony was thankfully short. King Aethelbald had instructed Archbishop Eahlstan that they would not be celebrating mass. Before Judith barely had time to realize it, they had repeated their vows, and Judith felt the cold weight of Aethelbald's ring encircle her finger. The marriage had been accomplished.

King Aethelbald motioned for Judith to sit on the throne nearest the altar. With trembling hands, Archbishop Eahlstan removed the glittering crown from the altar and handed it to Aethelbald, who stood behind Judith. King Aethelbald raised the crown high above Judith's head for all to see.

"Judith, Regina," King Aethelbald pronounced while lowering the crown upon Judith's head. "By my sovereign power and authority, I declare you to be Queen of Wessex." Then, raising Judith by the hand, he led the procession from the cathedral back to the palace.

The wedding feast rivaled any Judith had experienced in the abundance of food and wine offered. Judith's nerves, which had not allowed her to do more than peck at her food, were even more on edge when Aethelbald began noticing her lack of appetite.

"Not to your liking?" he remarked after servants removed Judith's third course barely touched.

King Aethelbald's sneering displeasure reached the far end of the table. "Perhaps Queen Judith finds the food in Wessex inferior to that of Francia."

He grabbed the arm of the serving maid, presenting a platter of roast pheasant. "Inform the cooks that the queen is displeased with the first three courses. If the remaining courses do not please her, there will be the devil to pay!" Then, watching the maid rush off to the kitchen, Aethelbald drained his cup and laughed.

"I do not dislike the food, King Aethelbald. I am only feeling unwell," she remonstrated.

"She speaks!" Aethelbald roared. "What a relief. I thought, perhaps, I had married a mute."

Aethelberht tried to calm his brother, but no amount of reasoning had any effect on the King of Wessex, who grew louder and more aggressive with each new course and every cup of wine.

Judith rose from the table and started for the door. "I shall retire for the evening."

King Aethelbald called after her, "Eager, are you? No fear. I will join you presently."

Judith hurried to her bedchamber, where Hemma tended the fire.

"I know not what to do, Hemma," Judith cried, throwing herself on her bed. "I cannot abide his very looks. If he touches me this night, I shall die!"

Hemma's face filled with concern. Then I shall not allow him to touch you!" she declared.

"There is nothing you can do. There is nothing I can do," Judith moaned.

"The church's penitential list forbids intimacy for up to one week following the marriage," Hemma reminded her.

"King Aethelbald cares nothing for that. He is king, and his will is law." Then Judith whispered, "I feel ill."

Hemma's expression was steel. "Then that is what I shall tell King Aethelbald should he come to your door. I will not let him in. I will tell him you are ill."

"I pray it works," Judith covered her face with a pillow.

"It will," Hemma assured her. "But I do not know for how long."

The plan worked. When King Aethelbald tried Judith's chamber door, Hemma was waiting with her excuse. Aethelbald was not pleased, but he also needed assistance to his chamber, having indulged too freely in his cups.

Judith remained in her chamber for the next two days, preserving the pretense. She regretted the necessity for the deception, but she desperately needed time to adjust to her new circumstances. She especially regretted the departure of Aethelberht, Aethelred, and Alfred without the chance to say goodbye. Hemma saw them riding east with their entourage on the third morning following the wedding.

That night, King Aethelbald did not continue to his chamber when Hemma tried turning him away at Judith's door. Instead, he roughly pushed her aside, forcing himself into the room. Seeing Judith standing before the fire, Aethelbald turned to Hemma and snarled, "Leave us!"

When Hemma looked at Judith for direction, Aethelbald added, "I can take your servant from you, Judith. I can take everything from you."

Judith quickly nodded, and Hemma left reluctantly. Steeling herself, Judith stared at the small twigs in the hearth being broken down and overcome by the intense white flames. She sensed Aethelbald's approach but did not turn to face him. His smoldering rage was palpable.

"You have done your best to humiliate me for the past three days before my brothers, before my thegns, and before my household."

"That was not my intent." Judith's voice sounded hollow.

"I find that hard to believe," Aethelbald snorted.

"Nevertheless, it is the truth." She turned to face Aethelbald's anger. "Why did you force this marriage? How could you want to marry your father's widow?"

"Do you truly not know? You may be young, but you cannot be that naive. I have no wish to plow my father's fields, but you are the first queen to ever have been consecrated by the church. What did that consecration promise? Blessings of the breast and of the womb? Not much sign of either of those blessings in you, is there?"

Judith blushed to hear her slender body so ruthlessly examined and dismissed.

Moving to stand menacingly over Judith, Aethelbald continued to spew his venom. "Any child you bear to a king of Wessex will have the right to rule superior to that of my brothers. Aethelwulf's age may have kept him from getting you with child. I shall not have that problem."

"How can you speak so of your father? You were a terrible son. Your rebellion against him was inexcusable! He was a good king—a pious man—a man of the church!"

"What care I for the church? It was my father's 'spiritual adviser', Bishop Swithun, who convinced him to give away much of my inheritance before they left on pilgrimage together. And then, my fool of a father gave away even more to the church while he was in Rome. When he married you, he gave you lands that should have been mine. If I had not stepped in and claimed half of Wessex, there would have been nothing remaining. Bishop Swithun started my father's craziness. I want nothing to do with the church!"

"You dare blaspheme?" Judith demanded.

"You dare lecture me?" Aethelbald countered. Grabbing her arm, he pushed her in the direction of the bed. "You are nothing! Nothing but a pawn—a weak one at that. First, you were used by your father, who wished to gain political influence. Then, you were used by my father to counter my political moves. Now, Judith, you are *my* pawn to use for *my* political purposes. Let me make that perfectly clear. Unless you are on your deathbed," he threw her down upon the bed, "you will attend every feast, sit each day in my throne room, and obey my every whim!"

"You are loathsome," Judith cried. "There is nothing . . ."

King Aethelbald's hand closed around her throat, stopping further utterance.

"You do not yet understand." Aethelbald put his knee on her stomach, his hand still clutching her throat. "But you will. You only exist to do *my bidding*!"

Judith's arm ached, and she could barely breathe. She had no protection against Aethelbald's words, which came at her like daggers in the dark.

"If you are an exceptionally good girl, Queen Judith, I may allow you to keep your retainers. I may even wait for you to grow those breasts before trying that womb of yours. Submit and make your life easier. Try my patience, and you will wish you could trade places with that serving girl of yours."

When he saw that Judith had ceased resisting, Aethelbald slowly released his hold upon her throat, withdrew from her bed, and headed for the door.

"I will provide you with a list of what is expected of you," he tossed back at her. "When I am ready to get an heir, you will be the first to know."

ço

With the treaty of Verdun in 843, King Charles had received his portion of the kingdom held by his father, Emperor Louis the Pious, who was heir to the empire of his father, Charles the Great. From that day on, Archbishop Hincmar had done all within his power to help King Charles retain his kingdom. Now, he wondered if those fifteen years of hard work and strategy would be for naught. With all the wars and political gamesmanship, King Charles had never been so close to losing everything. The simultaneous attack by all of Francia's enemies had finally occurred. Hincmar feared this latest gambit might be King Charles' last.

Not long after King Charles returned from the unsuccessful siege, ill and weakened, Hincmar received word that Louis the German's invasion had progressed further than previously known. Louis the German's army had crossed the Rhine and moved deep into Francia, reaching the royal villa at Pantheon unimpeded. From there, he pushed on to Sens and eventually reached Orléans, where he met with rebel lords from Brittany, Neustria, and Aquitaine, who eagerly offered their pledges of loyalty. Emboldened, Louis the German had moved on and was attempting to take all of King Charles' kingdom.

By November, King Charles–still recuperating from his illness–had mustered what forces he could to repel his brother's invasion. When Louis the German, with his growing army, moved toward Brienne, King Charles moved to counter him. On the 9th of November, Charles sent his brother an offering of peace, which Louis the German completely rejected. Three days later, the armies lined up across from each other at Brienne. Louis the German's overwhelming numbers forced King Charles to withdraw and take refuge in loyal Burgundy, leaving hundreds of followers behind to be slaughtered by Louis the German.

Louis the German then moved north to Reims, where he tried to pressure Archbishop Hincmar into betraying Charles by consecrating him as the new King of Francia. Hincmar had delayed giving Louis the German an answer. Louis the German needed acceptance from King Charles' bishops. Without their support, he could take but never hold Charles' kingdom. Louis the German invited King Charles' bishops to gather at Reims on November 25th for the purpose of sanctioning his coronation.

Earlier in the year, a synod had been planned for November 15th at Quierzy to discuss ecclesiastical matters. Now, Hincmar saw the synod as an opportunity to save his life's work as well as his king. If he could convince a majority of bishops to stand firm against Louis the German, the entire invasion might begin to crumble. If not, Hincmar might be forced to submit to Louis the German's rule when the king arrived at Reims.

Hincmar was disgusted by the aged Archbishop Wenilo, who had come to Quierzy as an emissary for Louis the German to encourage the bishops' attendance in Reims on the 25th. *The crafty old fox! He knows this synod is where the real battle is to be fought.*

Wenilo would address the bishops, but Hincmar would speak directly afterward–the most important speech of his life. Hincmar mingled with the crowd, greeting his fellow clerics who had gathered from all over Francia. Many bishops looked to him for guidance, trusting his judgment. Would they follow his lead today?

When the time came, Archbishop Wenilo arose to address the synod. His hoary head bowed, and his voice quavered as he read from his prepared remarks. "Honored members of the synod," he began. "I come today as an emissary of King Louis the German, the oldest living son of Emperor Louis the Pious and grandson of Emperor Charles the Great. Louis the German has not invaded our kingdom. He has come by invitation from myself and the lords of Aquitaine."

Wenilo peered up from beneath white, bushy brows to engage his listeners briefly before continuing to read. "For the past several years, King Charles has allowed the Danes to attack our kingdom unchecked. His only response is to pay large ransoms and then tax the lords and the church accordingly. Each one of you emptied your coffers this past year to pay for King Charles' mistakes. We cannot allow this to continue."

Again, Wenilo paused to see what effect his words were having. "King Louis the German has proven he can fight the Danes without impoverishing his lords or his bishops. Everywhere King Louis the German has gone in our kingdom, lords have come to pledge themselves. I also have pledged myself to him. More than a decade ago, it was I who placed the crown upon King Charles' head. Now, I ask you to join me in removing that crown. Let us give it to a king who can truly bring us security and prosperity. Join me in Reims on the 25th of this month. We will coronate the elder brother, for the younger no longer deserves the crown of Francia."

Archbishop Wenilo raised his head. His piercing glance seemed to bore directly into the minds of the bishops before he resumed his seat. The whispers filling the room ceased as Archbishop Hincmar rose to speak. He used no notes, knowing that he must speak from his heart if he wished to have any chance of winning the hearts of the bishops.

"I speak today, not as an agent of an earthly king. I, like most of you, have spent my life serving a Heavenly King. That is my first and true allegiance. That is also what unites us as bishops of the church. However, I have also served Charles, King of Francia, whom Archbishop Wenilo requests that we remove as sovereign. I know King Charles' heart. He is a man of God who is faithful to his oaths and his followers. Think of your individual relationships with him. When King Charles promises you something, does he not move Heaven and Earth to fulfill his promise? Are you willing to trade such a king for one who is known for *not* keeping promises?"

Hincmar looked around the gathering. Seeing several bishops nodding in agreement, he continued. "King Charles places his loyal subjects' welfare above all else. Archbishop Wenilo would have you depose the king for ransoming Abbot Louis of St Denis. I ask you, who would you rather have as king should you be captured by the Danes? A king who will forget about you, preferring to save his coin in desperate times? Or a king who will unite the kingdom in seeking your release? A human life, on one hand, weighed against money on the other. Which is more important to God? Which is more important to you?"

Archbishop Wenilo appeared uncomfortable with the direction of Hincmar's argument. Hincmar singled him out again and pointed in his direction. "Archbishop Wenilo would have you believe that all these vicious raids will cease if you choose King Louis the German as your ruler. This claim could not be further from the truth. Louis the German's seat of power—with his lords and bishops—is far removed from Francia and its concerns. If his kingdom has fewer troubles with the Danes, it is not because he is better at fighting them. It is because Louis the German has repeatedly broken faith with his brother Charles. How many lives, cathedrals, and monasteries might have been spared had King Louis the German not attacked King Charles, but had supported him while he was fighting the Danes? Choose Louis the German, and when the Vikings attack, he will merely shrug his shoulders and say nothing can be done for our small part of his kingdom."

Hincmar paused long enough for all eyes to turn toward a restless Archbishop Wenilo. "Ask yourselves, how many lives would have been spared if the King's faithless lords and bishops had not withheld their support in our time of greatest need? And how often have sieges failed because of lack of support from the king's own lords and clerics? We must look to our *own* houses before laying the entire blame for the Viking attacks to King Charles' charge."

Hincmar had them now. He could sense it. It was time to conclude. "My brothers, God would want us to remain faithful to a king who has always been faithful to us. Strength lies in unity. Let us, as one body, refuse to attend Louis the German's conference in Reims and thus deprive him of our support. As honest and loyal subjects of a Heavenly King, we must not betray our oaths to a faithful king in favor of false promises made by a faithless invader!"

When Archbishop Hincmar finished speaking, the synod allowed time for the bishops to consult amongst themselves. Several bishops made their way to Hincmar, expressing their approval of his words. The archbishop could detect no such visible support for Wenilo. When the synod reconvened, the bishops unanimously agreed to withhold support from Louis the German until all military conflicts were resolved. Archbishop Hincmar was asked to draft a careful response to King Louis the German declining his invitation to convene at Reims.

The synod concluded. Hincmar had done his best for his king. And he had rallied the bishops to do the same. The rest would be up to King Charles to take back the kingdom which was being stolen from him.

CHAPTER XVI

859

King Charles' army was on the move. Reinforced by knights from the provinces of Burgundy and Septimania and the remaining loyal lords in Aquitaine and Neustria, the king's army had grown substantially. The unspoken question lingered in the air. Would the army be large enough to drive the invaders from Francia? Or would all be forced to bow the knee to Louis the German? As they pushed north toward Louis the German's camp at Laon, the order was given to prepare for battle.

Baldwin always spent the night before battle preparing himself physically, mentally, and spiritually. After checking his armor, he saw to his mount. Running his hand carefully along its smooth brown hide calmed Baldwin's nerves while he looked for any problems needing his attention. He inspected his saddle and stirrups and, finally, his sword and lance, looking for any knicks or stress fractures and carefully honing the cutting edges.

Normally, Louis would be by Baldwin's side, mirroring his battle preparations, but the young king was otherwise occupied with his brother's "favorite knight," Count Odo. After moving his family to their estate in Burgundy, Count Hardouin had become ill and had died before Christmas, leaving Odo to care for his mother and his sister, Ansgard. Since King Charles' army had taken refuge in Burgundy, Louis had visited Ansgard at Count Odo's estate as often as possible. As the army prepared to move north, Louis went with Odo to inform Ansgard of their imminent departure.

Baldwin chose not to wait for their return before finishing his own preparations. Prepared physically, Baldwin transitioned to mental readiness. Using his newly sharpened sword, he closed his eyes and imagined himself defending Louis from a variety of attacks. He practiced his movements with precision, hoping that they would prove second nature to him in the heat of battle.

Finally, his spiritual preparation, Baldwin knew, would take some time. No man wanted to go into battle with a burdened conscience, and the lines for confessional were lengthy. After visiting with the priest, Baldwin took advantage of a rare opportunity to sit in the solitude of the chapel. His thoughts were interrupted when King Charles entered and sat on the pew in front of him. Baldwin arose, wishing to give the king the solitude he himself had briefly enjoyed.

"You need not leave, Count Baldwin Iron Arm," King Charles assured him. "We are both seeking the same peace, are we not?"

"Yes, Sire," Baldwin resumed his seat.

"It was a good day when I chose you to be a companion for Louis. You have served us both well."

"Thank you, Sire."

Moments later, the king spoke again.

"If I defeat my brother, Louis the German, it will only be because the King of Kings sees fit to restore me to my kingdom. He, alone, can give us the power to scatter our enemies. It will take a miracle of Heaven. Will you pray for that miracle, Count Baldwin?"

"With all my soul, Sire," Baldwin promised.

After sitting quietly for several minutes, King Charles left Baldwin alone in the chapel.

❧

January 15th dawned clear and cold. Tension amongst King Charles' forces ran high. This would be a day of decision. For the previous ten days, Louis the German's forces had moved unimpeded toward Burgundy. Now Francia's loyal men were moving to intercept them. King Charles began the morning with mass and a rousing speech to encourage his knights, promising them that if God were on their side they would prevail.

Baldwin and young King Louis rode ahead of the loyal Neustrians along with their banner bearer. The banner would act as a rallying point for Louis' followers should his forces become scattered during battle. Baldwin expected to encounter a multitude of attacks, as the banner was also a target for those wishing to capture or kill his young king.

At midday, in a field south of Jouy, the two armies met. And for the first time, Baldwin felt confident that King Charles could carry the day. At Brienne, Charles' forces—vastly outnumbered—were left no option but retreat. Now, it looked like the numbers might be in King Charles' favor. *How did Louis the German lose so many followers?* Baldwin wondered.

Then, the miracle that King Charles had asked Baldwin to pray for began to unfold. As King Charles gave the order to assume battle formation, the forces of Louis the German began retreating. King Charles' forces advanced cautiously, lest the retreat be a trap, allowing hidden forces belonging to Louis the German to surround King Charles' army.

The retreating forces moved north, back toward Laon. Then, after several hours, Louis the German's army began moving east, his numbers shrinking with each mile traveled. Baldwin shook his head, astounded by what he was witnessing.

For several days, King Charles doggedly pursued his brother until what was left of Louis the German's men had been pushed to the banks of the Rhine. With their backs against the massive river, Louis the German sent a messenger bearing a white flag and suing for peace. King Charles, humbled by the bloodless victory with which he had been blessed, allowed Louis the German's forces to return home unimpeded.

News of King Charles' miraculous defeat of Louis the German spread like lightning throughout Francia, affirming the people's belief that God was with their king. Cheering throngs greeted the king's forces in every village on their return trip to Compiègne. Before disbanding his army, King Charles gave due credit to God for the miracle they had witnessed and allowed his men to return to their home provinces.

The royal court celebrations continued for weeks. John Scotus composed a poem lauding Charles and his miraculous, bloodless victory. Baldwin rejoiced to have been part of such a campaign, but his thoughts turned to King Charles' next move. How would the king deal with the traitors who had almost stolen his kingdom?

ം

As sheltered as her life had been, cruelty had seemed a foreign concept–elusive and difficult to envision. Now Judith understood it all too well. Life as Aethelbald's queen was a daily battle for survival. The "list" he provided her became her focus and her reality. Any deviation from the list brought swift punishment for herself or a member of her inner circle.

Her routine did not differ greatly from what she was used to in King Aethelwulf's court. Judith spent her mornings in King Aethelbald's throne room. However, she was not allowed to ask questions or give opinions. Instead, she was expected to sit quietly and listen to King Aethelbald dispense judgment aligned with his prejudices.

Judith's "council" tried their best to support her, but there was little they could do. She sent Bertrand to Graveney to manage what he could from there, hoping to shield some property from Aethelbald's notice. Felix became skilled at writing messages that could pass the king's inspection of Judith's correspondence. And Father Electus listened to her confessions, helping her work through her feelings of anger and loss.

"Believe in miracles, Queen Judith," he encouraged. "God has sustained you thus far. Trust Him to bring you safely through this trial as well."

Thankfully, Aethelbald was an avid hunter, providing Judith with some freedom in the early afternoon until it was time to dress for the most difficult part of her day–the feast. The knot that formed in her stomach before each meal made Judith wonder if she would ever again enjoy food. Each day, Judith was expected to be waiting for King Aethelbald in the sitting room of the king's apartments before the feast. Sometimes, Aethelbald was prompt in arriving and escorting her to the great hall. On other days, she might wait for some time before the king arrived, often followed by a pretty serving maid.

At the high table, Judith was under Aethelbald's constant scrutiny. He criticized the robes she wore, the way her hair was dressed, her intellect, how much she ate of each course, how often she spoke, which words she used, and whether she smiled or laughed at the appropriate times and in the appropriate manner. *Is there no pleasing him?* Judith wondered.

King Aethelbald drank cup after cup of undiluted wine throughout his meals. As his drinking progressed, his comments grew louder and more negative. However, Judith was forced to wait until the king wished to leave the feast before rising from her chair. Taking his arm, Judith accompanied the king back to the royal apartments, often supporting him as he navigated with difficulty the steep staircase. Thankfully, Aethelbald's attendant was always ready to assist the king to his bedchamber. Judith had no desire to do that office for him.

☙

Six months after her marriage to King Aethelbald, Father Electus informed Judith of an upcoming visit from Bishop Swithun.

"This is good news! It has been such a long time since we have seen Swithun," Judith replied.

"I pray it is good news," Father Electus responded cautiously.

"What do you mean?"

"Bishop Swithun says that King Aethelbald has ordered him to come. I am not sure why."

"In that case, I fear the reason for the summons is not a happy one," Judith acknowledged.

Bishop Swithun arrived two weeks later and sought to pay his respects to Queen Judith almost immediately. Judith received him in the sitting room of the royal apartments.

"I have learned that some property I own is in jeopardy," Bishop Swithun began. "King Aethelbald wishes me to turn over the land King Aethelwulf granted me at Farnham."

"This is the first I have heard of the matter," Judith admitted.

"Queen Judith is there any influence you can use on my behalf?" the bishop pleaded.

Judith's heart ached, but she could do nothing for this kind and saintly man who had been Aethelwulf's closest adviser and friend. Any effort she made would only make things worse for both of them.

"Bishop Swithun you were King Aethelwulf's truest friend. If I could help you, I would do so gladly. However, my speaking on your behalf would not be well received. I cannot help you."

Bishop Swithun shook his head sadly. "I understand, Queen Judith. I will do nothing to make your own situation more complicated. Is there something I can do to assist you?"

With tears welling, Judith whispered. "Pray for me, Bishop Swithun. Pray for me."

Two days later, Bishop Swithun signed over his property at Farnham to King Aethelbald. The scene in the throne room had been painful. Aethelbald reminded Swithun of the part he had played in King Aethelwulf's disposing of ten percent of his property. Aethelbald claimed that it was only justice for Bishop Swithun to rid himself of part of his own land. Aethelbald said it would do the bishop's soul good. Bishop Swithun bowed his head as the charter granting King Aethelbald use of the bishop's property was drawn up. Judith signed as a witness.

❦

Archbishop Hincmar rejoiced in the miraculous reversal of his king's fortunes. Somehow, King Charles had been made stronger by surviving all the challenges of the previous year. The rebel lords of Aquitaine had come to offer new pledges of loyalty to the king. And Archbishop Wenilo had gone into hiding, fearing the king's retribution. In February, King Charles and King Lothar signed a treaty creating a united front against any future aggression by Louis the German. Throughout Charles' kingdom a feeling of renewal was spreading. Robert the Strong and Salomon remained the only exceptions to Francia's new-found unity.

At the end of May, bishops from both King Charles and King Lothar's kingdoms held a synod at Metz and convened an episcopal court to judge King Louis the German's actions. After first considering excommunication, they drew up instead a list of penances to be imposed as a condition for Louis the German to avoid ecclesiastical punishment. Hincmar was appointed to lead an official delegation tasked with delivering the court's verdict to Louis the German's palace at Worms.

Louis the German had been a thorn in King Charles' side since the day of Charles' birth, repeatedly threatening his kingdom and his very life. On the six-day journey from Metz to Worms, Hincmar envisioned Louis the German's reaction when he presented the penances demanded by the episcopal court. *I hope he sweats when he realizes how close he is to being excommunicated,* he mused.

On June 4, Hincmar's delegation was ushered into the ornately furnished throne room at Louis the German's palace at Worms. The king was attended by his bishops, including Abbot Grimald of St. Gallen—his principal adviser.

Abbot Grimald smiled warmly, intercepting the delegation at the back of the room. "Archbishop Hincmar, your reputation is one to be admired. I have long desired to meet with you in person. Having read with interest several of your treatises, I am certain we have many ideas in common."

Hincmar smiled inwardly at the abbot's attempt to disarm him. "Abbot Grimald, we are not here on pleasant business. The episcopal court of Metz has given us a charge that must be fulfilled."

"Of course, of course," Abbot Grimald assured Hincmar. "What is your message?"

"That is something we must present to King Louis himself," Hincmar insisted.

"What is your message?" Louis the German demanded from across the room.

"King Louis, may we approach the throne?" Hincmar requested.

"Approach!" came the reply. "That is close enough," the king called as they drew within six feet. "Deliver your message."

Hincmar withdrew the scroll he had brought, listing the penances demanded by the synod at Metz. He offered it to Abbot Grimald, who handed it to the king.

Louis the German broke the seal and unrolled the parchment. Silence reigned as the fifty-three-year-old king perused the document. He took his time—reading very carefully, his furrowed brow revealing his displeasure. Finally, he looked up only to be met by cold determination in the faces of the ecclesiastical delegates.

"What do you want from me?" the king demanded.

"Precisely what the synod has determined, Your Majesty," Hincmar replied. "Bishops from Francia and Lotharingia have found you guilty of disturbing the peace and of conduct unbecoming a Christian king. The synod considers your crimes worthy of excommunication. They offer you a means of removing your guilt through penance for your crimes."

"I cannot give you an answer today," Louis the German growled. "I will discuss these demands with my bishops and give my reply tomorrow."

"Understood," Hincmar nodded. "We will return tomorrow."

When the delegation returned to the palace the next day they were met by Abbot Grimald and the Bishop of Minden.

"Ah, Archbishop and my fellow clerics, how good it is to see you again," Abbot Grimald gushed.

Hincmar's response was terse. "You have the king's response for us?"

Grimald smiled. "We appreciate your patience, and we hope to appeal to your mercy as well."

"What are you saying, abbot?" Hincmar was cautious.

The Bishop of Minden explained. "The synod at Metz was too angry with King Louis. He has hurt none of you personally. Why force our king to submit to penance? Why not forgive him instead?"

"Our king is a godly man," Grimald took up the plea. "As requested, he will meet with King Charles and King Lothar, and he will beg forgiveness for entering King Charles' kingdom. He would never have entered Francia except at the invitation of your own nobles and clerics."

"Then the king has agreed to two of the four points demanded by the synod," Hincmar observed. "What of the other points—to establish a lasting peace with his brother and nephew and to break off all ties with the rebel lords in King Charles' kingdom?"

Abbot Grimald looked at his companion before answering. "Are the first two demands not enough? Surely, you would not push the king farther than he is able to go!"

Archbishop Hincmar's expression was steel. "No, that is not enough! The king must yield to all of the council's demands if he wishes to make amends. If King Louis maintains ties with Francia's rebels, he is no man of peace and must pay the price."

"The king will meet the third demand and sign a treaty of peace with his brother and nephew," the Bishop of Minden admitted reluctantly.

Abbot Grimald looked uncomfortable. "He may sign a treaty. But as to your final demand—breaking off ties with those who supported him in Francia—I am uncertain. The king values those relationships."

"We are not here to negotiate, Abbot Grimald. The king must comply with all of the synod's requests or bear the consequences." Hincmar stood firm.

Abbot Grimald shook his head sadly, "This will wound the king."

"This will better the king," Hincmar countered. "For once, he can play the peacemaker."

The sacrament of penance was one of the seven holy sacraments of the church. And the king could not be forgiven without accomplishing the penance determined by the synod. After a day of resistance, Louis the German eventually accepted the terms of his forgiveness.

As the delegation journeyed home, Hincmar reflected on the importance of their mission. Louis the German's aggression was finally contained. Was Francia at last secure? Or would Robert the Strong, Salomon, and the Danes succeed where Louis the German had failed?

CHAPTER XVII

860

In January, Lothar's queen, Theutberga, faced a synod court of King Lothar's bishops led by Waldrada's uncle, Bishop Gunther. Held as a prisoner within the palace at Aachen, Theutberga had previously smuggled a message out to Pope Nicholas saying that she feared she would be forced to confess by the council.

"I throw myself upon the mercy of this council," Theutberga pleaded before the synod.

Bishop Gunther called out, "We cannot aid you unless you first tell us what is troubling you. Be honest and confess! Let no hope of gain nor fear of penalty—even death—lead you to declare what is untrue."

Softly, Theutberga whispered, "Bishop Gunther is the one who knows the particulars. Honored council, it is through him that what must be known must be told."

Bishop Gunther then proceeded to reveal the lurid details, accusing Hubert of the incestuous rape of his sister, Theutberga. Queen Theutberga accepted Gunther's testimony but denied that she had conceived Hubert's child by witchcraft and had aborted the child. The synod declared for her a lifetime penance of confinement in a convent. However, much to King Lothar's frustration, without the weightier charges of witchcraft and abortion, the council did not approve a divorce. The king immediately appealed to the pope.

News of Queen Theutberga's conviction spread like a great wave bursting forth from Lotharingia. It poured across Francia, crossed the channel, and covered Wessex in the spring. People throughout several kingdoms had followed the controversy surrounding the marriage of Lothar and Theutberga for four years. Now, many of those who had taken the queen's part while she maintained her innocence switched sides in the wake of her forced confession.

Judith was not one of them. Judith's uncles had falsely imprisoned her grandmother Judith. Somehow, her grandmother had fought and won against her enemies. Now Judith herself was part of that unfortunate history that viewed women as mere pawns. Judith did not judge Theutberga, as she was also a prisoner in her own room, forced to say or do whatever was required of her.

⁊

Judith noticed Hemma's behavior had been odd of late. Usually meticulous about her appearance, particularly when they were to meet with Felix, Hemma had begun to let her hair go unwashed and her clothes appear crumpled. Her normally friendly manner had become withdrawn. When Judith observed Hemma reach down and touch the ash in the hearth and then touch her forehead and cheek, she confronted Hemma.

"Hemma, why would you do such a thing?" Judith asked.

"What?" Hemma replied distractedly.

"The ash. Why would you purposefully put ash upon your face?" Judith wanted to know.

Hemma hung her head guiltily. It took some coaxing, but Judith finally got her answer.

"I did not wish to trouble you, Queen Judith," Hemma hesitated. "I hoped to handle the situation myself."

"What situation?" Judith prompted.

"The king . . . his eyes have fallen upon me. When he encounters me alone, he touches me and says things that make me afraid." Hemma gulped before continuing. "I hoped to make myself disgusting to him so he will turn his interest elsewhere."

"Oh Hemma, I am so sorry!" Judith put her arms around her attendant, who had become so much more than that to her. "I will put a stop to this!"

"How, my lady? He will punish you. It is better that I suffer than you," Hemma insisted.

Judith had raged within over King Lothar's treatment of Queen Theutberga. Now, from that anger, she took strength.

"I do not know how Hemma. But I will draw a line protecting you which King Aethelbald will dare not cross!" she promised.

King Aethelberht arrived with Aethelred and Alfred for a rare visit. Judith was excited to see them again. It had been six months since their last journey to Sherborne. She hoped to spend time with Alfred, talking about the books he had read since their last visit. Their visit also provided Judith an opportunity to confront Aethelbald while his brothers' presence might temper his anger. The best time for such a confrontation would be in the sitting room prior to descending for the feast.

At age fifteen, Judith was now taller than average height and still quite slender. She would never be the buxom beauty that King Aethelbald favored. However, Judith knew if she were to forbid Aethelbald access to Hemma, he might turn to her—whether he found her attractive or not. Protecting Hemma was worth the risk.

"King Aethelbald, I must speak with you about an urgent matter," Judith addressed the king as he entered the sitting room.

"What could be more urgent than satisfying my appetite?" Aethelbald countered.

"It is your appetite that concerns me." Judith persisted. "My attendant says you have been touching her and making her feel afraid."

King Aethelbald laughed. "Oh, that. She is but a serving girl."

"Nevertheless, it must stop! You are not to touch nor even speak to Hemma."

"Hemma, is that her name? I will speak to whomever I please!" Aethelbald declared hotly.

"If you persist, I will let your brothers know of your reprehensible behavior. I will let the entire kingdom know of it!"

"Are you jealous?" Aethelbald sneered. "You need not be. Your turn will come."

"I am not jealous! I am disgusted by you!" Judith put as much scorn into her voice as possible.

King Aethelbald raised his hand as if to strike Judith but changed his mind. His tone was measured and menacing.

"It has been some time since I have had need to punish you, my queen. I am sorry to see that you have forgotten who rules in Wessex."

He grabbed her wrist, drawing her to him and applying pressure until she was forced to cry out. "Your presence is not wanted at the feast tonight. I will make your excuses to my brothers. I must consider your disobedience and what will be your punishment. You may keep your serving girl if she is that important to you. But there will be a price. You will not want to challenge me again."

Watching Aethelbald leave the room, Judith was relieved that she was not required to attend the feast. She had no interest in food at present and wished to share her news with Hemma as soon as possible. Her small victory over Aethelbald's cruelty was exhilarating. *I have won a battle. But at what price?*

Within hours, she had her answer.

Judith's time spent in the throne room the following morning was at first more tolerable with Aethelberht's presence. After listening to the usual complaints and petitions, a final order of business was brought forward. Osmund, One of Aethelbald's closest thegns was party to the transaction. Aethelbald asked Osmund to step forward.

"I understand that you desire to have a charter granted for the following property."

"Yes, Sire," Osmund smiled knowingly.

King Aethelbald read the description of a holding at Teffont in Wiltshire, which Judith recognized as part of the bride's gift given to her by Aethelwulf upon their marriage. When he finished reading the proposed charter, Aethelbald looked pointedly at Judith and asked, "Are there any objections?"

This, then, is the price he demands to protect Hemma. If I object, he may take Graveney!

Judith shook her head to indicate that she had no objection. Judith, along with an unsuspecting King Aethelberht, witnessed the charter.

๛

The meeting of the three kings - Charles, Louis the German, and Lothar, took place on June first in Lothar's fortress at Koblenz on the banks of the Rhine. Baldwin and Louis were part of the company attending King Charles. Increasingly, Baldwin was included in meetings, not as young King Louis' companion but as the loyal Count of Flanders.

The kings planned to negotiate and sign their treaty in the renovated Roman fortress atop the hill at Koblenz, rising above the confluence of the Rhine and Moselle rivers. Oath taking would be done before a synod in the Liebfrauenkirche below in the village. In this setting, Louis the German could finally satisfy the demands Hincmar's delegation had presented almost one year earlier. Baldwin was eager to see if Louis the German would keep his promise.

Peace in Francia would rely heavily upon this day's work. With young Charles reinstated in Aquitaine, it remained only for young King Louis to regain his kingdom in Neustria. However, as long as Robert the Strong could receive aid or influence from Louis the German, King Charles hesitated to reinstate his son.

Louis the German and his bishops crossed the bridge from Andernach to Koblenz in the early morning drizzle and made their way to the fortress where King Charles and King Lothar waited. After initial pleasantries, the kings got down to business. When Louis the German still resisted on some points, Charles and Lothar presented a united front and insisted that all elements of the penance be fulfilled.

"What I wish to see come of this meeting is a mutual acknowledgment of our relationship as a family and our duty as Christian kings to maintain that relationship." King Charles asserted.

Louis the German hastened to assure him. "Then you shall have what you desire, brother. I now wish to behave toward you as a brother rightly should."

"I am glad to hear that, uncle," King Lothar commented. "It seems we are close to agreeing upon a treaty."

"Only one point remains," Charles pointed out. "Your promise to break off ties with all the rebel lords within my kingdom."

"I am ready to promise that . . . upon one condition," Louis the German responded.

"No conditions," King Charles was adamant.

"Hear me out," Louis the German pleaded. "I only want your word that you will be merciful and restore those who came over to me to their former positions and *benefices*."

"Those who are willing to pledge loyalty and live peaceably in Francia will be given back any holdings that were rightly theirs prior to my kingship." King Charles paused for emphasis before continuing. "I will grant this upon the condition that *you*, my brother, also do the same for any lords who may have holdings within your kingdom and supported me in our conflict."

Louis the German shifted uneasily in his chair but eventually nodded.

"Furthermore, I reserve my right to determine whether I will restore any rebel lord to positions I have personally granted them. Several lords have yet to submit to our rule. When the time comes that they wish to be reconciled to us, we will deal with them as seems us good."

Louis the German wanted more assurances for Robert the Strong. However, both Charles and Lothar stood firm. In the end, the three kings signed a treaty of peace and cooperation.

Afterward, they met in the chapel of the Liebfrauenkirche to pledge brotherhood with each other. The synod then absolved King Louis the German but charged him to honor the vows he had taken.

Following the conference, King Charles' council discussed what had occurred. Time would tell if the synod had forced Louis the German to permanently change his behavior. However, Baldwin was hopeful.

King Charles concluded his council by stating his next objective. "I am determined to see Robert the Strong submit and Louis reinstated as King of Neustria before the end of the year!"

৵

He had recently begun touching her as if he were punishing her for stopping him from touching Hemma. His touching was accompanied by sneering comments disparaging her appearance and her body. Each afternoon grew increasingly tortuous as she endured his attentions alone in the sitting room, waiting for him to escort her to the feast.

With the onset of summer, King Aethelbald planned to travel to Kent to visit his brothers at Faversham. Judith suspected that the real purpose of his journey was to inspect her property at Graveney with a mind to use it as leverage to gain her compliance. Although Judith regretted not seeing Aethelberht and the young princes, she was looking forward to several blessed weeks' respite from Aethelbald. *If only he would never return!*

In Aethelbald's absence, Judith and Hemma walked daily in the gardens, drinking in the healing warmth of the bright June sunshine. On the day before Aethelbald's expected return, Judith's thoughts turned toward Graveney. *I defied Aethelbald once in defense of Hemma. I shall fight him again if he tries to take Graveney from me!*

A messenger rode full bore toward the courtyard and jumped from his mount, moving toward the palace entrance with great haste. Sensing something amiss, Judith and Hemma hurried back to the palace. The king's chamberlain, who was in close conversation with the messenger, looked their way when he saw Judith and Hemma enter.

"Queen Judith, we have distressing news." He paused as if gauging how Judith would react to what he would say. "My Queen, I am terribly sorry to inform you that King Aethelbald, on his way home through Selwood Forest, was thrown from his horse and suffered serious injury."

"Will he be alright?" Judith asked hollowly.

"His physician was with him and is doing all that can be done. They are bringing him home to Sherborne."

"When will he arrive?"

"Later tonight."

"Will he live?"

"I know not."

Amidst her turmoil of emotions, Judith called for Father Electus. It was a sin to wish ill upon another person, and yet she had hoped Aethelbald would never return. Judith prayed to banish the dark thoughts cycling continuously through her mind. Her immediate reaction had been to take joy in the idea that she might be free of her tormentor, thoughts unworthy of a Christian. She needed God's forgiveness, and she needed Father Electus' help to sort everything out.

Aethelbald's body arrived at the palace that night. Something had spooked his horse on their journey through Selwood. When he forced the mount forward, it reared. Aethelbald was thrown and hit the side of his head on a tree. Unable to revive the king, his servants had made a bed for him in the baggage cart and continued on slowly, hoping he would live through the night. He had not survived the journey.

※

Ten days later, King Aethelberht arrived in Sherborne with the young princes. Because of the summer heat, Aethelbald's body had already been placed in a tomb within Sherborne Cathedral. However, a second mass was said for Aethelbald's soul upon the arrival of his brothers.

Afterward, all three brothers agreed to reunite King Aethelwulf's former holdings under one kingdom. They also agreed to carry out their father's wish that each brother would have the right of succession should an older brother die first. Shortly thereafter, Bishop Swithun formally crowned King Aethelberht the King of Wessex.

King Aethelberht vowed to rule wisely and contain the lawlessness that had begun creeping in during King Aethelbald's short reign. And although King Aethelberht offered to allow her to remain at Sherborne for as long as she wished, Judith prepared to leave as quickly as possible. Too many unpleasant memories lingered there.

Judith packed away her grandmother's crowns. As beautiful as they were, in her mind they had become a symbol of servitude rather than of honor. Judith resolved never again to be forced to wear a queen's crown. She knew where she wanted to go, and now there was nothing stopping her.

Upon arriving at Graveney, Judith wrote to her mother and her brothers. The only word she sent her father was a terse notice of King Aethelbald's death. She did not ask her father to provide for her return. Every moment at Graveney was like a drop of liquid gold touching, healing her soul, helping her realize she no longer needed to fear waking up each morning.

Just before her sixteenth birthday, Judith received answers to the missives she had sent. Her mother spoke of domestic things— of her sadness at the departure for the convent of both Judith's younger sisters. Rotrud and Ermentrud, at ages six and eight, had been designated for a life of service in the church.

Louis' missive shared with Judith his fear that King Charles would not allow him to marry Ansgard of Burgundy when he achieved his adulthood in little more than one year. Louis also said that King Charles planned to take the monastery of St. Martin of Tours away from Robert the Strong and bestow it upon him prior to reinstating Louis as King of Neustria in November.

King Charles' missive, which she read last, troubled Judith the most. It had an air about it of being rushed and distracted. Instead of pressing her to return to Francia, her father simply wanted to know if King Aethelberht had yet taken a queen.

Alarmed, Judith did not reply to her father's missive. Quickly, she called her council together and asked each to be ready to depart for Francia within the month. Bertrand would make immediate provision to sell Judith's remaining properties—including her beloved Graveney. Felix would send a missive informing King Aethelberht of Judith's planned departure. And Hemma would help Judith sort her belongings. She would need to leave much behind since her entourage would probably be small.

Two weeks later, King Aethelberht, Aethelred, and Alfred arrived at their royal estate in Faversham with a contingency of men, extra carts, and pack horses to put at Judith's disposal. King Aethelberht had come prepared to provide Judith with a royal escort to Francia. The brothers spent part of each day of Judith's final two weeks visiting with her and sharing memories. On their final visit, Judith shared a moment alone with Alfred.

"Follow the example of your father, Alfred," Judith advised. "He was a strong king, yet so good and so kind."

Alfred nodded in agreement.

Judith picked up the ivory-bound prayer book King Charles had given her years before on his return from the monastery of St. Martin of Tours. "I know you love illuminations as much as I do. Will you keep this book to remember me?"

Alfred's hands traced the beautifully illuminated letters on the first page. "Do you remember my promise before you came to Wessex? We shall always remain friends—no matter what happens," he reminded her.

Judith turned to look one last time upon Graveney—a place from which she had drawn strength. Through the grace of God, she was returning home a very different person from the naïve young girl who had first crossed the channel. The peace she had found at Graveney had given her the steel to face her father and fight for a life of her own choosing.

PART III

JUDITH OF FLANDERS

CHAPTER XVIII

NOVEMBER 860 through NOVEMBER 861

For Baldwin, the period from Louis' reinstatement as King of Neustria in mid-November leading up to Christmas and the new year was filled with unexpected turns, including a change in Louis' attitude. The young king was becoming his own man and chafed at his father's insistence on an administrator for his last year before adulthood.

Two weeks after Louis settled in at the palace in Tours, a messenger arrived with news that Queen Judith would arrive in a day or two. Louis shouted for joy. He sent a missive to young Charles in Aquitaine inviting him to celebrate Christmas in Tours and help him welcome their sister home. The last time the siblings had been together was four years earlier at Judith's wedding to King Aethelwulf.

Nothing prepared Baldwin for the changes that had taken place in Judith over the past four years, nor his feelings upon seeing her again. The child he had once admired as intelligent and graceful was now an elegant, slender young woman whose presence seemed to lighten each room she entered. It was more than her appearance. Something about Judith caused Baldwin's skin to prickle with excitement whenever she drew near—a marvelous and, at the same time, extremely uncomfortable feeling.

On their first day together, Judith wanted to know the details of all that had happened with Erispoë, Robert the Strong's rebellion, and Louis the German's invasion. Baldwin found himself increasingly drawn into their conversation, especially when Louis exaggerated Baldwin's feats of bravery. He blushed when Judith pressed him for particulars on his dealings with Bjorn Ironside and the ransom of Abbott Louis and Gauzlin. The three talked well into the night, removing to their separate chambers only a few hours before dawn.

On the next day, Judith insisted that Louis tell her of his first meeting with Ansgard. As Judith drew him out, Louis spoke of his progressing feelings for Ansgard and his fear of being forced into another politically motivated betrothal.

"F . . . Father will never approve a marriage to Ansgard," he complained bitterly. "He sees n . . . no b . . . benefit to a marriage strictly for love."

After some reflection, Louis turned his attention to Judith. "What of you? You are a y . . . young widow. F . . . Father will be looking for another husband f . . . for you."

Judith shuddered involuntarily. "I pray he does not."

"It must have been difficult for you," Baldwin interjected. "Losing two husbands."

Judith nodded. "King Aethelwulf was kind and noble. He was like a father to me."

"And K . . . King Aethelbald?" Louis prompted.

Judith's brow clouded as she hesitantly replied, "I would rather not speak of Aethelbald."

The mood cooled abruptly, and Judith, pleading weariness, excused herself to lie down until it was time for the feast. Louis and Baldwin looked at each other. *Whatever happened with Aethelbald has wounded Judith deeply*, Baldwin concluded.

When young King Charles arrived with Ansgard's brother, Count Odo of Burgundy, he persuaded Judith to remain two more weeks and celebrate Christmas with them.

"I would not be in a hurry to confront father," young Charles warned. "Louis says you don't wish to marry again. You know, father. He will have his own ideas on that subject. Louis and I live in terror of what sort of marriages he has planned for us," he laughed.

"If you do not w . . . wish to m . . . marry, what would you wish to do?" Louis wondered.

"I would purchase a small estate somewhere far away from all political maneuvering and live out my days in peace." Judith remarked wistfully.

"Does such a place exist?" Count Odo asked.

Baldwin spoke spontaneously. "Flanders is such a place."

"Is it really?" Judith's eyes sparkled. "It sounds heavenly. Why did you ever leave?"

Baldwin felt his face grow warm as he had just been imagining Judith in Flanders. He needed to watch his tongue before someone discovered his growing feelings for the young queen—an attraction that grew stronger every day. He now sympathized with Louis' plight—a desire for a marriage that could never take place.

Louis' Christmas Day feast was replete with singers, a group of Moorish fire dancers, as well as tumblers—all interspersed with humor and poems provided by Louis' jester. When the servers brought in platters of boar's meat, Judith amused everyone by telling of the contest over the boar's head arranged by Alfred and Aethelred. Shortly after Christmas, young Charles and Count Odo returned to Aquitaine. Then, it was time for Judith's departure. Louis provided an escort to replace King Aethelberht's men and horses, which Judith had sent back upon her arrival in Tours.

"I wish you were coming with me to Senlis, Louis," Judith hugged her brother goodbye.

"Neustria is still in d . . . danger. I c . . . cannot leave except at f . . . father's request."

"Then, I will visit you both as often as circumstances allow," Judith promised with a smile. Baldwin was delighted to be included in that promise.

౿

Judith regretted having to leave Tours. The banter and camaraderie between her brothers and their companions had pushed back the shadows of Aethelbald, which daily haunted her.

Judith's feelings for Count Baldwin Iron Arm had also changed over the years. How wrong she had been at the beginning to resent his influence on Louis! His body might be as strong as iron, but his eyes revealed a gentleness that touched her heart deeply. If King Aethelbald had been such a man, Judith might have felt differently about kings–and marriage.

As Judith's party drew close to Senlis, memories and emotion threatened to overwhelm her. Senlis was where she had been trained by her mother and Gauzlin to be a queen. From the palace at Senlis, she had organized the royal household's move to the palace at Verberie, where she was consecrated and married to King Aethelwulf. Four years ago, Judith was an obedient child doing her best to satisfy the demands of her kingdom and the wishes of her father. Judith was no longer that person. *What will my parents make of the woman I have become?*

The villagers of Senlis leaned out of their windows and stood in their doorways, watching Judith's royal procession make its way along the narrow streets leading to the palace grounds. The guards at the palace gates waved Judith's entourage through, and they were greeted by Martin, the Marshal of the Stables.

"Welcome back, Queen Judith," Martin beamed at her. Noting that she now controlled her own mount, he added approvingly. "I see your riding has improved."

Judith laughed. "I have practiced since I last saw you, Martin."

Queen Ermentrude, who was waiting to greet Judith as she entered the palace, seemed startled at first that the young girl she had bid goodbye to four years previously had now surpassed her in height. Quickly recovering, Ermentrude embraced her daughter.

"The king is in council, or he would be here to greet you," Ermentrude explained. "There has been yet another attack on Paris."

"Never mind, mother," Judith assured her. "You are the one I most wished to see."

Arm in arm, the two queens ascended the stairs and entered the sitting room in the royal apartments. Memories of embroidering with her mother and of lessons with John Scotus belonged to a different time. Everything felt so foreign and yet so familiar. Her sisters, Rotrud and Ermentrud, no longer played in the background, supervised by her mother's ladies-in-waiting. However, she now had a three-year-old sister, Gisela, whom she was eager to meet.

Judith spent the hours until the feast getting to know Gisela and visiting with her mother. Life had not changed much for Ermentrude. The queen spent each day meeting the needs of her husband first and her kingdom next. Her own needs and the needs of her children would come after all else was seen to. *This is not a life I would take joy in,* Judith concluded.

Shortly before the family was to descend to the great hall, King Charles appeared—distracted and harried as usual. He greeted Judith without affection, "We will talk more tomorrow."

Then, he offered his arm to Queen Ermentrude. Judith and Archbishop Hincmar followed behind as they went into the feast.

୨୦

Judith watched through the window of the sitting room as enormous snowflakes drifted lazily down from a ponderous, brooding sky. At first, peaceful and lovely to look at, the snow soon fell faster and faster with punishing speed until it seemed the heavens were determined to smother every living thing with overwhelming white. Hemma entered the room to tell Judith that King Charles wished to see her immediately in his throne room.

John Scotus and Gauzlin greeted Judith warmly as she approached the council table. However, Archbishop Hincmar did not look up, and her father's face appeared troubled as she took the seat he indicated.

"Judith," King Charles began, "you left Wessex without our providing escort for you. And, instead of sending word upon your arrival in Francia, you remained for a month with Louis at Tours. Explain your actions."

Here was the reckoning Judith had been anticipating. She was prepared with her answer. "If my actions have brought you distress, I am sorry. With all else that has caused you concern, I

233

thought to relieve you of the burden of transporting me and my entourage back to Francia. King Aethelberht offered to supply the escort. I accepted."

"That was my decision to make. Not yours," King Charles asserted.

"As a queen—a dowager queen—I thought I could make arrangements for my own return," Judith countered.

"Then, you were wrong!" King Charles was adamant. "As your father, any rights your husband had over your movements revert to me. What if I had wished for you to remain in Wessex until I arranged another marriage for you?"

Judith knew what she was about to say would make matters worse. "That is precisely what I feared and precisely why I did not seek your assistance."

The silence was palpable. John Scotus and Gauzlin looked down at their hands. Only Archbishop Hincmar looked directly at King Charles, whose face had flushed with anger. Charles' voice was measured.

"What is it you are saying, Judith?"

"That I have decided not to marry again."

"I decide what is best for you!" King Charles stood, his voice increasing in pitch and intensity.

"Not in this. If I ever marry again, it will be of my own choosing." Judith stood to confront her father. She had faced down King Aethelbald for Hemma's sake. Now, she would face down King Charles for her own.

"I have enough rebels outside my household. I will not tolerate a rebel within!" King Charles roared.

Judith had never seen such fury in her father's face. Speaking in a softer tone, she sought to calm the waters. "I am sorry, Father. I do not mean to rebel. But I cannot obey you in this one thing."

Archbishop Hincmar intervened. "Sire, perhaps Queen Judith should retire to her chamber while the council discusses what is to be done in this situation."

Hincmar had provided a way out of the escalating confrontation, and King Charles took it. Judith left the throne room, knowing she had advocates in both John Scotus and Gauzlin, who would temper any wrath that might otherwise be directed her way. Of course, her father would punish her. He, like every king, needed to maintain absolute authority over his subjects. Yet, her father had been merciful to many of his *fideles* who had broken their oaths and betrayed him. She hoped he would be equally merciful to his own daughter.

Several hours later, Judith was again summoned to the throne room. This time, no smiles greeted her. Members of the council stood near the throne where King Charles was seated. The king addressed Judith directly.

"Judith, are you determined to work your own will and defy me in decisions regarding your future?" he asked.

"If you ask whether I refuse to marry again at your command, the answer must be yes," Judith replied steadily.

At King Charles' nod Archbishop Hincmar read from a scroll the council's determination. "Judith, Regina, you will be confined in the palace at Senlis until such time as you submit to the rightful will of King Charles in all things—including marriage. You will be accorded all deference as a queen during your confinement. However, you will not be allowed to leave the palace for the term of your confinement."

Leaving the throne room, Judith went directly to her chamber and retrieved her grandmother's crowns. She sought out Queen Ermentrude.

"Mother, I wish to return these crowns to you," she held out the bundle she carried.

Ermentrude's brow furrowed with concern. "Judith, you were anointed a queen. Even I have not had that honor. That anointing cannot be undone."

"I understand," Judith acknowledged. "Will you hold them for me in safekeeping?"

"Of course." Queen Ermentrude looked relieved. She bid Judith follow her into her bedchamber, where she opened the door to her treasure room. Taking the bundle from Judith, she removed each crown and lovingly set it on the shelf. "The crowns will be here when you want them."

The sound of her mother's turning the key in the lock on the treasure room door lifted a weight from Judith's shoulders. No amount of confinement would make her wear a queen's crown again. Of that she was certain.

One month later, when King Charles' court moved on to Verberie, Judith was left behind. And Senlis—Judith's childhood home—had become her prison.

৵

King Louis' reinstatement in Neustria had only been partially successful. King Charles had secured Tours and the surrounding area for him, including St. Martin's Abbey. But Robert the Strong still controlled Angers and would retain the support of many Neustrian lords unless King Louis could win them over by demonstrating leadership in fighting the Danes. The time was right to make another attempt at dislodging the Vikings from Oissel. King Charles wanted Louis and Baldwin Iron Arm to be part of what he hoped would be a successful campaign.

Throughout spring and early summer, King Charles raised a levy of 5,000 pieces of silver as well as livestock and grain to pay the infamous Northman, Weland, to besiege the other Danes at Oissel. Weland camped with his 200 ships on the lower Seine while he coordinated with young King Louis and his men. Baldwin, having personal knowledge of the inner workings of the stronghold, spent hours consulting and strategizing with Weland and his advisers. He described for the Northmen the layout of the stronghold, within and without—its relationship to the forest and roads, as well as its strengths and weaknesses. He also described what King Charles' forces had previously attempted during the siege of 858, analyzing what had worked and what had not.

Weland expressed his gratitude for Baldwin's assistance. "The valuable information you have provided may save many of my men. If you are ever in need, Baldwin Iron Arm, be assured I will offer what help I may."

Baldwin received Weland's offer with composure. However, he hoped Weland and his men would leave Francia following the siege, as the Dane had promised, or Baldwin feared he would be in a position of having to fight him.

Setting Dane against Dane proved to be an expensive but successful strategy. Weland countered every trick the Danes at Oissel employed to circumvent the siege. Time after time they blocked those at Oissel from renewing their supplies until, at last, the stronghold was threatened with starvation. By fall, the Vikings at Oissel were ready to pay Weland 6,000 pounds in gold and silver to be allowed to leave with their ships and sail down the Seine to the sea.

Robert the Strong, seeing young King Louis' influence increase with his success against the Danes and his own power diminish, decided at last to reconcile with King Charles. In a spirit of generosity, King Charles forgave Robert's years of treachery and allowed him to retain control of Angers. With Aquitaine and Neustria, both returned to the fold, only Salomon remained in open rebellion against the king.

ço

Returning from their summer-long campaign, an old, unread missive from Judith awaited Louis. By the look on Louis' face, the news was troubling.

"What is amiss?" Baldwin grew impatient.

"It is J . . . Judith. She is c . . . confined at Senlis by order of my f . . . father until she agrees to marry at his command."

"What will you do?" Baldwin wanted to know.

"I must v . . . visit her there. But I answer to my administrator Adalard until I achieve my m . . . majority in N . . . November."

"And then?"

"I will v . . . visit her often. I w . . . will not abandon her!" Louis declared passionately.

"A good plan," Baldwin agreed. Inwardly, he too was anxious to see how Judith was faring.

❧

In the many years Hincmar had served King Charles, they had not always agreed. However, the king had always been brought to reason before bringing dishonor to him or his kingdom. Now, to Hincmar, King Charles seemed no better than his older brother Louis the German. *He will prove himself as big a fool,* Hincmar grumbled silently.

In an eerie similitude of what had happened between Louis the German and the rebel Lords of Aquitaine, King Charles received a delegation of lords from the neighboring kingdom of his nephew, Charles of Provence–King Lothar's younger brother. The lords of Provence appealed to King Charles to come and set their kingdom right.

Their first complaint was that Charles of Provence was sickly. His epilepsy grew steadily worse, interfering with his governance. The severity of his illness had also prevented the young king from marrying or siring an heir. The lords feared that Louis the German or King Lothar might invade and claim their kingdom if Charles of Provence should die unexpectedly. They claimed that Provence preferred King Charles over any alternative.

In spite of Hincmar's admonition to proceed cautiously, King Charles chose to do as the lords of Provence requested. He assembled a small force of 300 men, sufficient for a venture he had been assured would offer no resistance. He had also taken Queen Ermentrude with him, expecting that they would be crowned king and queen of Provence before Christmas.

Hincmar was unhappy about embarking on this fool's errand. Nor did he like traveling in the middle of winter. The entire venture was ill-conceived, ill-timed, and ill-planned. Hincmar could foresee nothing but humiliation at the end of it.

Almost immediately, as the royal party made their way through Burgundy, problems arose. In their haste to depart for Provence, insufficient provision had been made to feed Charles' small army. As a result, King Charles' men began foraging for themselves, even plundering their own countrymen in Burgundy in order to eat. By the time the force reached Mâcon, King Charles recognized the need to disband.

Hincmar was relieved to have the misguided venture come to an abrupt end. Alerted to the invading force on his borders, Charles of Provence had lost all trust in his uncle. And the loyal Burgundians were not pleased with the raiding done by King Charles' men. King Charles ordered his entourage to make their way to the royal villa at Ponthion.

Not long after arriving at Ponthion, King Charles received a delegation from King Lothar and Louis the German who united in demanding that he cease his ambitions regarding Provence. Hincmar's fears had been justified. King Charles had merely succeeded in making himself appear hypocritical for his own outrage at Louis the German's earlier invasion of Francia.

Queen Ermentrude encouraged King Charles to winter at Senlis, hoping to spend time with Judith. However, the king had other ideas. King Charles chose to celebrate the holy day at Ponthion in spite of the queen's concern that Judith would be alone at Christmas.

CHAPTER XIX

DECEMBER 861 through JANUARY 862

Throughout the fall as Neustria enjoyed increasing peace, Louis and Baldwin made several visits to Judith at Senlis. The three enjoyed happy hours reminiscing as well as discussing life and their futures. When it was time for them to leave, Judith missed Louis' companionship as well as Baldwin's steadiness and endearing sense of humor. However, she had been given something to look forward to. Louis' promise to stay for at least one month during the Christmas season had lifted Judith's spirits during her lonely months of confinement. Young Charles had also promised to visit for several weeks during the new year.

With the sale of her properties in Britannia, Judith, at age seventeen, was a wealthy woman and dreamed of purchasing a small estate for herself and her staff. She was grateful for her council and hoped they would not grow weary of her solitary life. Her prison had been their prison. She would not blame them if they chose to seek employment elsewhere. Judith eagerly planned to make Christmas a special time for her retainers as well as for Louis and Baldwin.

A servant brought word that King Louis and Count Baldwin Iron Arm had ridden into the palace courtyard. Judith checked her reflection in the glass one last time before descending the staircase, pinching her cheeks to bring a little color to her face. She acknowledged wryly that she was not primping for her brother's sake, but to impress Count Baldwin. With that embarrassing thought, Judith hurried to greet her visitors.

She waited at the foot of the stairs somewhat impatiently. By order of the king, Judith could not leave the palace without close attendance by two guards. When, at last, the palace doors opened to admit Louis and Baldwin, Judith quickly embraced her brother.

"Louis," she chided. "Will you never stop growing? How can I call you my little brother when you are taller than me?"

Louis laughed. "Baldwin says he thinks I w . . . will be as tall as F . . . Father."

"And you are your own man, now," Judith pointed out. "Are you enjoying your majority?"

"I w . . . would, but for B . . . Baldwin," Louis replied with a gleam in his eye. "He is w . . . worse than an administrator! He will not let me d . . . do anything stupid."

Baldwin laughed at that. "How do you know, King Louis? You have not tried to do anything stupid for at least a day or two."

Judith turned her attention to her brother's companion, trying her best to keep from him the fact that he set her heart racing, and smiled.

"Count Baldwin, I am forever in your debt. Your shielding Louis from his own folly has allowed him to reach his majority!" She laughed cheerfully as, arm in arm, Judith and Louis climbed the stairs with Baldwin by their side.

Baldwin climbed the grand staircase, reminded of his youth and inexperience when he first entered King Charles' service. He could never have imagined the friendship he would have with Louis and the experiences they would share. Nor could he have imagined falling in love with the king's daughter.

The next ten days flew by. The celebration of Christmas Week was intimate and joyful. Everyone, including the servants, was involved in the festivities. Louis and Baldwin practiced swordsmanship in the courtyard and went hunting to provide fresh meat for the table. But most days were spent simply in lively conversation, which brought them all closer together. The three agreed to drop their titles when addressing each other—at least while in private.

Louis enjoyed books as much as Judith. When they entered the library, they made it a challenge to see who could find something that might catch the interest of Baldwin, who was not an avid reader. Judith discovered a book of riddles that reminded her of Alfred, whom she dearly missed.

Baldwin quickly sensed Judith's change in mood. "Is the book of Wessex?"

"Not really. Why do you ask?"

"You become very quiet when something reminds you of Wessex."

"That is right," Louis chimed in. "You n . . . never speak much of W . . . Wessex. You speak sometimes of Aethelwulf, yet n . . . never of Aethelbald. W . . . Was he a good k . . . king? Was he a g . . . good husband?"

Judith was angry with herself for the tears that threatened to flow. It was as if Aethelbald was always in the back of her mind, waiting to steal her joy. The wound was deep, but she managed a brief response.

"If he had been a good husband, Louis, would I be willing to be imprisoned for a year—perhaps for the rest of my life—to avoid another such marriage?"

Neither Louis nor Baldwin could offer an appropriate response.

Soon after Christmas, young Charles arrived with Count Odo of Burgundy, bringing with them distressing news. "Shortly before we reached Senlis, we heard that Weland's son, instead of leaving the country after the siege at Oissel, made his way further inland. He and his band have now taken over the monastery Saint-Maur-des-Fossés."

Count Odo nodded. "The abbey is less than ten miles from our estate!"

"Odo must relocate his sister, Ansgard, who is there with only family retainers for protection." Young Charles turned to Louis.

"We continued on to Senlis to see if you and Baldwin would accompany us."

Louis did not hesitate. "Of c . . . course w . . . we will!" He looked to Judith.

"You must go," Judith replied softly, trying to hide her disappointment.

Baldwin understood Judith's reaction. Louis had promised her a month-long visit. Her faith in that promise had kept her going through long months of isolation. Now, less than two weeks later they would be leaving.

"Could we bring Ansgard here for safety?" Baldwin suggested.

"Why n . . . not?" Louis agreed. "I w . . . want Ansgard to meet Judith."

No one, especially Judith, raised an objection.

"If we push ourselves, we can be there in a hard day's riding, pack up Ansgard, and be ready to return within a day." Count Odo figured.

"Allowing two days for return, we should be gone four—no more than five days at the most," Baldwin assured Judith.

Judith responded quickly. "I will order the cook to prepare food for your journey. And Martin will furnish you with fresh mounts. I will pray for your success."

❧

During her brothers' absence, Judith reflected on the nature of her confinement and its similarity to the sieges her father had mounted against the Danes. If the purpose were to starve her of companionship and use that stifling isolation to force her submission, the king had come close to achieving his goal. Only visits from Louis and Baldwin had allowed her to survive longer than expected.

When Judith's cousin Lothar had been forced to take Queen Theutberga back as his queen, he had confined her to her rooms in the palace at Aachen. Theutberga had recently escaped her confinement and had been given refuge in King Charles' kingdom. *How ironic it is that my father has rescued his nephew's wife from the same isolation he is now imposing on me.*

Snowstorms, illness, broken carts, lame horses, thieves, and pillaging Vikings. In spite of her prayers, each disastrous possibility had occupied space in Judith's mind and disturbed her sleep for the past four days. She could not bear the thought of any of the group being injured. Her mind would not rest until all returned safely.

In the midst of her worry, Judith was surprised when Baldwin entered the sitting room unaccompanied. Judith and Hemma were seated on the lounge, embroidering as she and her mother had done years before. At Baldwin's disheveled appearance, Judith laid aside her sewing and rose to meet him.

"Baldwin, is everything all right?"

"All is well. I only wanted to put your mind at rest as soon as possible," he admitted. "Ansgard and the others are safe. They should arrive late tomorrow afternoon."

"You are exhausted. Have you ridden all day?"

"I started riding last night."

"Have you taken any refreshment?" Judith's voice was full of concern.

"Not yet today," Baldwin admitted.

Hemma rose quickly. "I will see to it, my lady."

"Thank you, Hemma," Judith replied. She turned to Baldwin. "Please sit down, Baldwin. You should not have exerted yourself so on my behalf."

"I could not do otherwise," Baldwin was too exhausted to pretend.

Judith caught her breath. "I am not sure that I understand."

"I could not have slept knowing you would be worried about the outcome of our venture. I thought that I might as well be riding as tossing and turning."

"Your kindness and your concern for my feelings are not what I am used to." Judith walked toward the window, looking out over the torch-lit courtyard. She sensed him follow her, although he said nothing, patiently waiting for any further explanation she would give. Something about Baldwin made Judith feel safe. She could confide in him, and he would not judge her. She could tell him what she had been unable to tell any other soul.

"In the back of my mind, I hear him sneering at me, telling me every day for nearly two years that I am ugly. I hear him say over and over again that I am worthless, nothing but a king's pawn–his pawn–to be used at the whim of the king."

The pain in Judith's voice was palpable, and Baldwin knew immediately that it was King Aethelbald of whom she spoke. It was not Baldwin's right to say something. Baldwin knew it was not his right. And yet, those whose right it had been–and was–had neither comforted nor reassured this beautiful young queen of her own worth. *God give me wisdom,* he prayed.

When Baldwin spoke, he shared with Judith his memories of her from the first time he had seen her in this very room. Baldwin spoke of her regal poise and elegance at her wedding to King Aethelwulf, her kindness, her intelligence, and her courage–all qualities he had admired in her. He finished by telling Judith how all of this, combined with her breathtaking beauty, had made him wish to be near her and caused him to feel empty when they were apart.

Judith's back was still turned toward Baldwin, making it easier for him to share the thoughts he had never dared speak aloud. Baldwin needed to know how she felt about what he had said. He gently took her by the shoulders and turned her to face him.

Tears poured down Judith's cheeks. "No one has ever seen me that way before." Her voice broke. Instinctively, she reached out to Baldwin. He took her in his arms, resting his chin on top of her head, and allowed her to shed tears that had been building for many years.

Hemma was alarmed at the picture they presented when she returned with Baldwin's food. But Baldwin sought to reassure her.

"I think she has had much to weep over for a long time. Is this not so?" When Hemma nodded, Baldwin added, "Can you give us just a few more moments of privacy?"

Hemma looked to Judith, who confirmed the request with a nod.

Once more alone, Baldwin spoke again. "Judith, the man whose evil thoughts you carry in your mind was alone in his lunacy. I want you to replace his cruel words with the words that I have just spoken. When I leave—and I know that I must—remember there is one who would hold you, protect you, and treasure you as you deserve, if only he were allowed."

"Do you speak the truth, Count Baldwin Iron Arm?" Judith asked, not daring to lift her head from his chest.

"With all my soul!" was Baldwin's answer.

"Then do not leave me," Judith whispered. "For I feel the same. I am miserable without you."

"Judith," Baldwin's lips caressed her hair. "If I were a king, or you were less than royalty, I would never let you go."

⚬

Baldwin was not sure if the previous night's revelations had made things better or worse for Judith and him. He retired to the bed he had slept in when he had shared a chamber with John Scotus so long ago. But sleep did not come until early morning. All night, he wrestled with his conscience.

Senlis was where Baldwin had pledged himself to serve his king and protect the king's family with his life. He had fulfilled that promise by protecting both Louis and young Charles on several occasions. Now, the very vow he had taken demanded an impossible choice. Either he would continue to serve the king, or he would choose to protect Judith, a member of the king's family, from the king himself. Whatever his decision, Baldwin would become what he had always despised—an oath breaker.

By early morning, Baldwin knew what he must do. He would speak with Judith about the risks involved in any plan to free her from her father's control. But he would not make the decision for her. The choice to act or not would be hers.

Baldwin and Judith met in the library at noon, where Judith, shy but hopeful, waited to discover whether the feelings Baldwin

247

had professed for her the previous evening had not been imagined. Baldwin hastened to reassure her. For several hours they discussed their possible choices of action and their risks before finally settling on an elopement. They discussed how they would tell Judith's brothers.

൧

When the rescue party arrived, Judith immediately saw why Louis was so smitten with the beautiful and intelligent Ansgard. As they conversed, Judith saw Ansgard's real affection for Louis, which made Judith like Ansgard even more. When the conversation lulled, Judith surprised everyone with the decision she and Baldwin had reached earlier.

"I have decided to marry again, after all," she announced.

"Then F . . . Father will have his w . . . way." Louis was obviously disappointed.

"Not if I marry someone of my own choosing," Judith smiled.

"Who?" young Charles demanded. "Who do you even know well enough to marry?"

All eyes turned simultaneously to Baldwin as the realization set in, and Baldwin winked at Judith, who smiled back at him.

"Would such a marriage even be legal without Father's consent?" young Charles asked.

"Excellent question, Charles. Consent is a legal requirement, and we have consulted Father Electus. Louis has achieved his majority. As my brother, in the absence of my father, he can provide that consent," Judith assured them.

Baldwin offered his hand to Judith, who stood with him before Louis. "King Louis, I am not of royal birth. But if you permit me to wed your sister Judith, I will honor her, protect her, and do all within my power to bring her joy for the remainder of her life."

Stunned, Louis could only shake his head and laugh. "I believe you m . . . mean that, Baldwin. No one c . . . could protect Judith b . . . better!" Then, Louis pronounced quite seriously,

248

"Count Baldwin Iron Arm and Judith, I g . . . grant you b . . . both my consent to marry."

And everyone began chattering excitedly.

"When will you marry?" Ansgard asked.

"It must take place soon while King Charles is away. This is an extremely dangerous venture," Baldwin reminded everyone. "We cannot allow any error in planning or execution."

"I will have to escape the palace first, or Father will have the marriage annulled and Baldwin imprisoned, or worse," Judith added.

"You will need to find a priest who will not be too afraid of King Charles to perform the marriage," Odo pointed out. "That may mean going to another kingdom."

They began discussing the advantages of seeking refuge in Lotharingia, Provence, or even Italy. When the candles burned low, the company agreed to continue strategizing on the morrow. After two days, they had developed a workable plan providing for the method of Judith's escape, possible choices of where the marriage would take place, and a plan to protect Judith's retainers from King Charles' certain wrath.

Judith refused to leave either Hemma or Felix behind, fearing that they would be blamed for aiding the elopement. She also argued that they would prove helpful along the way. Provision was also made for the rest of Judith's council. Count Odo would retain Bertrand as a steward to assist with the management of his estates. And Louis would see to it that Father Electus was given a position in the renowned monastery of St. Martin of Tours.

Judith had Hemma summon her council to the king's throne room. Judith requested that Felix bring his ink and parchment. The council was surprised to find Count Baldwin was also in attendance. However, Judith's announcement of their betrothal brought congratulations as well as concern for the couple's safety. Each council member understood Judith and Baldwin's risk in attempting an escape from the palace. And each agreed to do their own part in the venture. Everyone left the throne room prepared to leave Senlis in a two days' time.

Felix remained to draw up Louis' formal consent for the marriage. When he put the final flourish on the parchment, Felix hesitated before handing over the document.

"Queen Judith, I would like to ask your permission to draw up another document such as this."

Judith was confused. "Do Count Baldwin and I need an additional consent, Felix?"

"No. The consent I am seeking is your own. I ask for your consent to marry Hemma."

"I did not know my consent was required," Judith was genuinely surprised. "Hemma is of age and has no father or brother to object. Is she not free to consent for herself?"

Felix hastened to explain. "Perhaps, but Hemma does not see it that way. She will never marry without your formal consent."

Hemma had served Judith for nearly ten years, and they had a powerful bond. However, Judith had been so concerned with her own needs that she had been unaware of Hemma's.

"Draw up whatever is necessary, Felix, and I will sign it. And have Bertrand calculate what Hemma's wages have been for the past ten years. She shall have two-fold that amount as dowry."

Once begun, it seemed nearly everyone was eager to announce a betrothal. That night, as they discussed their plans for Judith's escape from Senlis, Louis had his own declaration.

"C . . . Count Odo has given consent for Ansgard and me to m . . . marry," he beamed.

"Father will never allow it," young Charles warned. "He will be furious."

"King Charles will already be furious with Louis once he discovers that he has consented to Judith's marriage," Ansgard pointed out gently.

"This is our only chance," Louis insisted fiercely. "And I plan to t . . . take it." He took Ansgard's hand.

"How will you avoid King Charles' punishment?" Baldwin asked with concern.

"I have my own p . . . plan," Louis assured him.

I pray God it is not a stupid one, Baldwin fretted silently.

"I refuse to be left out! When I return to Aquitaine, I shall marry as well," young Charles pronounced grandly.

Judith was the first to raise the obvious objection. "Be serious, Charles. You are not yet fifteen. The marriage would not be legal."

Young Charles insisted. "This is also my only chance to choose my marriage partner. If I do not act quickly, Father will choose for me. Besides, he will be so distracted by both of your marriages, he will not have time to object to mine until after I reach my majority."

If the risks had not been so real, Judith would have laughed at what she and Baldwin had started. It seemed Count Odo was the only person in the room who was not planning a wedding.

❧

Spirits ran high on the morning of Judith's escape. Young Charles was first to depart Senlis, taking Count Odo, Ansgard, and Bertrand with him. The party took four pack horses loaded with Judith's belongings and provisions, three extra mounts and both of Judith's grooms on horseback. They planned to leave the grooms, pack horses, and extra mounts at the coliseum outside of town. Then young Charles' party would travel southwest until they reached Tours, where they would await Louis' arrival.

At midday, Louis and Father Electus took their leave. Felix, wearing Baldwin's armor and riding Baldwin's mount, rode next to King Louis, convincing the guards that Count Baldwin had also departed. Once at the coliseum, Felix would don peasant clothes, ride one of the grooms' horses, and lead the other back into Senlis for the final part of the plan. Judith's grooms would remain behind to guard the horses and baggage.

It was near torture for Judith, not knowing what—if any—complications her supporters were facing. Her future depended on the outcome of today's plan. Baldwin had been hidden in the schoolroom all morning dressed as a servant while Hemma kept watch to ensure no one came upon him unawares.

251

They planned to wait until Judith ate her evening meal and retired to the royal family apartments. At that time, on a winter's day, darkness was falling, and the few royal servants remaining in the palace would be settling into their own nightly routines, expecting Queen Judith's attendant to see to her needs.

Only the guards at the doors would prove a hindrance. Baldwin could have easily overpowered one or more of the guards. But the aim was to have Judith's escape remain completely unknown for as long as possible. They could not accomplish that if Baldwin were forced to fight their way out of the palace.

Before Judith and Hemma went down to the great hall, Baldwin took Judith in his arms to calm her nerves as well as his own. He suspected Judith felt that familiar feeling he had before going into battle–the unsettling knowledge that your life depended upon your ability to think clearly and make good decisions unclouded by emotion or fear.

Judith relaxed against Baldwin's chest, enjoying the warmth of his body seeping into hers. A thought occurred to her. Tilting her head to look up into Baldwin's face, she teased, "It is a very strange thing, Count Baldwin, to have been twice married but never yet kissed."

Baldwin laughed. "Is that a royal request, Queen Judith? Or is it merely an observation?"

"A request, if you please," Judith smiled. Baldwin willingly complied.

When the meal was finished, and they returned to the royal apartments, Hemma helped Judith don peasant clothes while they waited for a change of the guard. Then, Hemma let the new guard know that Queen Judith's trunk, filled with old clothing, was ready to be taken to the chapel for distribution to the poor. Baldwin held the trunk upon his shoulders, keeping his head bowed so as not to draw attention to himself.

The guard motioned for Baldwin to lay the trunk down. After looking through its contents and discovering it was only clothing, the guard allowed Baldwin to shoulder his burden again. The suspicious guard paid no attention to Hemma and the other "serving girl," who followed along behind the trunk to see to its proper disposition.

Their next challenge was to exit the palace itself. The main entrance was too well-guarded. However, next to the door of his former bedchamber, Baldwin remembered the narrow servants' staircase leading to the palace side entrance near the kitchen. The ruse of the clothing distribution worked even better at the servants' door. When Hemma informed the guard at the side entrance that they were taking the trunk to the chapel, the guard merely stepped aside, not even bothering to inspect the contents.

They could not use the same ploy going through the gates leading from the palace grounds into the village of Senlis, so Baldwin carried the trunk through the snow-packed courtyard as far as the stables, looking for a place of concealment.

The torch-lit courtyard was rich with shadows, providing good cover. Baldwin kept watch while Hemma and Judith dressed in peasant boy outfits they pulled from the trunk and covered their plaited hair with peasant caps. As they turned toward the gate, a familiar voice pierced the darkness, causing Judith to catch her breath.

"What is it you are about there?" Martin's gruff voice called out. "Who are you and what are you doing near the king's stables?" He approached rapidly, torch in hand—his boots crunching sharply in the ice-crusted snow.

Baldwin, Judith, and Hemma stood frozen in place. Judith prayed that Martin would not look too closely into their faces. But when he lifted his torch, Judith saw immediate recognition in his eyes. Martin paused as if deciding a course of action. Then, he lowered his torch and demanded they follow him to the gate leading into the village.

"Guard!" Martin cried with authority. "I have finished with the services of these stable lads. Send them on their way and do not allow them inside the gates again!"

As the guard opened the gate to let them pass through, Judith looked back at Martin, hoping her expression portrayed her deep feelings of gratitude. Martin, in return, allowed a twitch of a smile to reach his eyes before Judith, Baldwin, and Hemma were pushed roughly through the palace gate and it closed behind them.

They entered the street leading to Senlis' main gate. As they made their way quickly down the dark, cobble-stoned way, Felix stepped out of the shadows, leading two horses. Felix had been present when Judith and Hemma had learned to guide their own mounts while riding sidesaddle. He had convinced Baldwin that the two young women would be able to ride astraddle as well. Their ability to do so meant the difference between a smooth exit from the city and being questioned by suspicious guards.

Baldwin and Felix boosted the young women into their saddles and followed at a distance on foot. With great relief, Baldwin watched as Judith and Hemma successfully guided their mounts past the unsuspecting guards, through the gate, and into the darkness beyond. Then, Baldwin and Felix placed their arms across each other's shoulders, weaving their way toward the gate as if they had spent too much time in the tavern.

Judith's heart rejoiced when she saw Baldwin and Felix walking up the road from Senlis. They had done it! Except for the heart-stopping moment when Martin had recognized them, everything had gone as planned. Baldwin leaped up behind her and turned their horse toward the coliseum, with Hemma and Felix following closely behind.

"How was it?" Baldwin asked. "Can you continue riding astride for a while?"

"In some ways, it is easier than riding sidesaddle," Judith assured him.

"Good." Baldwin was relieved.

Judith and Hemma's disguises would serve them well on this journey. Anyone watching for an escaped queen might overlook a group of men and their baggage. The grooms, mounts, and pack horses waiting for them at the coliseum were well-rested and ready to go. Baldwin planned to travel through the night, getting as far as possible from Senlis before the palace would raise the alarm over Judith's absence. They eagerly turned their horses north toward Flanders.

CHAPTER XX

JANUARY through FEBRUARY 862

Traveling only at night, the journey to Flanders took twice as long as Baldwin had taken when he and Marius had set out for Senlis five years earlier. It could not be helped. Every day increased the chance that they would encounter knights on the road searching for them. As they camped by day, hidden within the extensive forests, Baldwin shared with them details of his life as a boy in Flanders including hunting deer, wild boar, and even bears. Some of the largest bears were able to take down a horse with one blow and hunting them had been more for the protection of livestock than for their meat.

A harsh breeze cut like a knife through Judith's woolen mittens, making it difficult for her to grip her horse's mane as the party of six turned west toward Bruges, where they would leave the road and head south to Baldwin's estate. Baldwin had doubts about going home. Their rushed plans for the elopement had left them no time to send a message ahead. They were simply moving forward on instinct—on faith. Baldwin knew his mother would take them in, but she could only conceal them for a day or two at most. After a brief rest they would need to seek refuge elsewhere.

Normally, as the sun's rays started to peek above the horizon, they would pitch their tents. However, Baldwin pushed on. Having finally left the Roman road at Bruges, they were only a few miles from their destination. Baldwin knew the way perfectly through the dense forest separating his mother's estate from Bruges, but he worried the others might have difficulty following him as steadily falling snow obscured what little light the early dawn provided. He paused until they were all together.

"Keep your eyes on the person directly in front of you," he cautioned. "I will lead you slowly through the forest. If you feel yourself falling behind, call out and we will regroup."

Judith rode behind Baldwin with Hemma and Felix in their wake. She had become accustomed to tenting while in Wessex. However, the knowledge that they would be resting in beds at the end of their journey made the last few miles seem infinitely longer.

A rustling in the frozen brush ahead warned Baldwin of someone or something quickly approaching, and he drew his sword. A great bellowing roar caused the hair to rise on Judith's arms and nearly lose control of her mount, which tried desperately to run in the opposite direction. The rest of the party was in confusion, their horses also wheeling in terror. If they had not been linked together by a sturdy rope, the pack horses would have broken away from the grooms.

Hearing the spine-chilling roar, Baldwin instinctively dropped his sword and grabbed his lance. Quickly, he moved forward to protect Judith and thrust his lance out in front of him as a massive charging bear towering above him, attempted to knock him from his horse. With all his strength Baldwin drove the razor-sharp lance home, pinning the monster to a tree, where it died almost instantly.

Shaken, Judith dismounted, shivering both with cold and fear. Baldwin retrieved his sword and turned to pull his lance from the enormous, impaled beast. Even in the dim light, Judith could see the huge proportions of the bear. Fully extended, the animal was more than nine feet long, with paws as large as a human head. Its claws—perfectly designed for tearing—were longer than Judith's fingers.

Securing their mounts, the grooms removed the head and pelt from the massive creature, wrapped them in a tent cloth, and tied it to one of their saddles. Baldwin cleaned the blood from his lance which was bent from the force with which the bear had been skewered. Judith shuddered, thinking of what might have happened if Baldwin's instincts had not been so quick or his thrust so powerful. They rode the last couple of miles in silence, each deep within their own thoughts.

♀

Marius, alerted by the barking of hunting dogs, left his cottage, and entered the yard to see who or what was threatening their peace.

"Marius!" Baldwin hailed him. "Have you no welcome for Baldwin after five years?"

The two men embraced, and Marius proudly observed, "You have earned quite a reputation for yourself, Count Baldwin! Everyone speaks highly of your service."

"Alas, Marius, that is at an end," Baldwin remarked sadly as he helped Judith from her horse.

"What have you done?" the concern evident in Marius' voice.

"Let us first see to the horses and then I will tell both you and Mother at the same time."

Marius roused the grooms and servants who helped the men unload the pack horses. When they came to the bloody cloth containing the remains of the bear, Marius shook his head.

"This monster has been terrorizing the farms around Bruges ever since you left. We have tried many times to lay traps for him. Now you return, and he is dispatched the first night. I call that a successful hunt."

"Not for him," Baldwin laughed. "He was hunting us!"

When the servants had carried all the baggage into the house and helped Judith's grooms lead the mounts toward the stables, Baldwin led the party through the front door. Countess Guinhilde, eager to greet her son, was already in the great room instructing one housemaid to build up the fire and another to find refreshment for the group.

Baldwin rushed to embrace his mother. Then, turning back to Judith, he removed her cap. The dancing flames from the fire illuminated the auburn highlights in her long braid. Taking Judith by the hand, Baldwin led her to stand before the countess. "Mother, this is Judith, dowager Queen of Wessex, her companion, Hemma, and her secretary, Felix." He indicated each in turn.

As they warmed themselves by the fire, Baldwin and Judith explained to Marius and Countess Guinhilde the serious trouble they were facing.

"Where will you go from here?" Marius wanted to know.

"I considered going further north to Frisia to see if we could find refuge among the Danes," Baldwin admitted. "Some of them are not as bad as others."

"I prefer not to go there," Judith insisted. "Hemma's family was murdered by Danes. I cannot ask this of her if there is an alternative. We also talked about going to my cousin Lothar in Aachen or my cousin Emperor Louis in Italy. Or even to my uncle Louis the German."

Marius shook his head sadly. "Your choices are all filled with uncertainty."

"That is true. We would merely be pawns for Louis the German. He would hand us over to my father as soon as it became politically advantageous," Judith admitted.

"What of your cousin, King Lothar?" Guinhilde asked.

"Presently, he is at odds with my father over his marriage to Queen Theutberga and would likely welcome an opportunity to spite him. But if circumstances were to change, I am not sure what he would do."

"King Lothar wishes to marry his concubine, Waldrada. Would he not sympathize with your desire to marry whom you please?" Guinhilde wondered.

"King Lothar may be our best hope, but I hate seeking refuge from one who has abused his queen so terribly," Baldwin fumed.

"My son, none of us are completely good or bad. We are all flawed." Guinhilde gently reminded him.

Eventually, Baldwin was convinced to head southeast toward Lotharingia. They were at risk no matter where they chose to go.

However, King Lothar was used to defying convention. If he granted them refuge, he might not easily yield to King Charles' intimidation.

As Guinhilde led Judith and Hemma to the bedchamber they would share, she whispered reassuringly, "Trust in God, Judith. He has seen you thus far on a dangerous path. I pray He will protect you and my son and bring you back within these walls someday."

Two days later, the party of six resumed their journey. They would be another ten days on the road to Lotharingia—riding at night and hiding during the day. Baldwin and Judith hoped there would be some peace at the end of it.

સ

It was finally finished! All that remained was the furnishing. The elation Archbishop Hincmar felt upon receiving word that the workers had removed the final piece of scaffolding from the cathedral at Reims quickly dispelled any resentment Hincmar still carried over King Charles' foolhardy attempt to acquire Provence before Christmas. The king shared his archbishop's excitement that the six-year renovation was finally complete. King Charles and Queen Ermentrude stopped in Reims on their way to Soissons, where the king would hold his winter assembly.

As they walked the length of the towering cathedral, admiring the new transepts and baptistry, Hincmar enjoyed harmony once again with his king. Charles and Ermentrude both had a connoisseur's eye for beauty and religious art. They discussed the placement of each commissioned sculpture or tapestry to best inspire awe in all who entered the cathedral at its dedication in the fall. Kings had been crowned within these walls. Hincmar hoped emperors would be crowned here in the future.

The warm glow of satisfaction upon completion of the cathedral was not to last. Upon arriving at Soissons, King Charles received devastating news. Judith had eloped with Count Baldwin Iron Arm. Her escape from Senlis had been well planned and executed, and the couple were now in hiding. Young King Louis had granted formal permission for his sister's marriage and had assisted the couple in their flight.

In addition, Louis and young Charles had followed their sister's rebellious footsteps and had also married without the king's permission. Louis had fled with his bride to Brittany, where he joined Salomon's rebel forces in their fight against the reinstated Robert the Strong. Young Charles, although underage, had returned to Aquitaine and had wed the widow of Count Humbert.

The rage King Charles felt at the rebellion of his three oldest children threatened to consume him. He was also deeply wounded by Count Baldwin's faithlessness.

King Charles sought out Hincmar as soon as he arrived at Soissons. "My soul is deeply troubled by Count Baldwin's treachery. I believed I had finally found an honest and loyal man, one who would keep his oath. I was deceived. Baldwin Iron Arm must be found and punished as a traitor!"

"As a traitor, he could be blinded or even executed," Hincmar remarked hesitantly.

King Charles' expression was stone. "This wound is personal."

"I understand, Sire. Within a few weeks, I can assemble a tribunal of bishops and lords who will sit in judgment of Baldwin and Judith."

"That is too long to wait. I can strip Count Baldwin of his lands and title immediately," the king pointed out.

"True, but your judgment will have more impact if it is also accompanied by condemnation from your nobles and excommunication by the church," Hincmar suggested.

"Is excommunication in order here?" King Charles wondered.

"I believe so, Sire. Pope Gregory II, in the year 721, said that any man who stole away a widow and married her—and anyone who supported him—should be declared anathema."

"Assemble those you think best for the tribunal to be held two weeks from today. Also, send word to every leader in Francia and all neighboring kingdoms–including the Danes. Warn them of our severe displeasure if they offer refuge in any way to Baldwin or Judith."

"I will do so, Sire!" Hincmar agreed with the king's command. Baldwin and Judith must be made an example of, or the powerful political tool of marriage alliances between kingdoms could become a thing of the past. If a bloodline were diluted through non-royal marriages, an heir's right to rule might also be questioned. *This insidious thinking must not be allowed to spread any further!*

Two weeks later, the tribunal reached the foregone conclusion urged upon them by both King Charles and Archbishop Hincmar. They stripped Count Baldwin of his holdings in both Flanders and Ghent. They also excommunicated both Baldwin and Judith from the sacraments of the church. King Charles planned further punishments for Baldwin and Judith as his soldiers scoured the kingdom searching for them.

"What of King Louis and young King Charles' marriages?" Hincmar asked following the judgement of the tribunal. "Do you intend to allow those to stand?"

"No!" the king assured his archbishop. "However, they will have to wait. Several lords at the tribunal reported that Weland and his son have broken their promise to overwinter peacefully here. Weland's men have gone upriver toward the abbey at Meaux. They are destroying bridges, cutting off our ability to cross the rivers and intercept them. I will muster what men I can to build bridges up and down the seine, the Marne, and the Oise and fortify them with knights."

Neither the king nor the archbishop mentioned the obvious. In past such campaigns, Louis and Count Baldwin Iron Arm had provided stalwart support against the Danes. They would both be sorely missed.

৯

During his final years, Emperor Charles the Great had commissioned the construction of a palace complex designed to rival the opulence of Constantinople and the Byzantine Empire.

Set in Aachen, surrounded by thick forests teeming with game and blessed with natural hot springs, the palace complex became the crowning jewel of Charles the Great's empire. There, the aging emperor spent his remaining years indulging his love of hunting and swimming in the pool he had built, which could accommodate up to one hundred guests. Named Aix-la-Chapelle, the magnificent fifty-acre royal complex was soon the standard by which all other palaces were measured and one that Judith's father, King Charles, had long coveted.

Judith had never seen Aix-la-Chapelle, although she had heard her father often speak of it in reverent terms. In the early morning, on the outskirts of the palace city, the company hid their camp within a secluded area of forest, hoping to remain undiscovered until they received an assurance of welcome from King Lothar. Felix removed his writing materials from his baggage and drafted a missive for Judith, requesting an audience with her cousin. He rolled the parchment, and Judith used her signet ring to seal the melted wax. Then Felix changed his traveling attire into clothes worthy of a court ambassador and rode off toward the palace.

The sun had passed its zenith by the time Felix returned, waking the weary travelers. Lothar's response was promising but not assured. King Lothar had heard of their flight and offered them lodging for the night in the guest house on the perimeter of the palace. However, he wished to meet with Baldwin and Judith personally in the morning before deciding whether to offer any further assistance.

Felix slept while Judith and Hemma, for the first time in weeks, changed attire to reflect their status of royal lady and attendant, and Baldwin donned his armor. When they had broken camp, Felix led the way to Aix-la-Chapelle. For Judith, the ride to King Lothar's palace complex required an enormous leap of faith. If they were not well received, she was uncertain where to turn next.

I feel a hypocrite," Baldwin confessed the following morning as he waited with Judith to see King Lothar. "Everyone proclaims King Lothar a villain. If there were any other choice . . ."

Judith nodded in agreement. "In truth, I do not really know my cousin Lothar. However, I am grateful that he is receiving us in his private apartments and not in the great council hall where our presence would certainly cause others to gawk."

Judith squeezed Baldwin's hand when the keeper of the door motioned them to enter. The scene in the exquisitely decorated sitting room was surprisingly familial, reminiscent of Judith's own childhood. At the far end of the room, a dark-haired young boy of six or seven years played with a younger child, supervised by two women, while Lothar sat next to a strikingly beautiful woman with lustrous black hair and startling green eyes. Judith could see how Lothar had fallen under Waldrada's spell.

"Cousin Judith, Count Baldwin, we were pleasantly surprised yesterday to hear you had entered our kingdom," Lothar rose to greet them. He motioned them to be seated. "I understand you are in some trouble. Tell me what has happened."

Judith was glad of the chance to tell their story rather than be judged by what others said of them. When she finished her account, Lothar asked probing questions of both before turning his attention to Baldwin.

"The steps you have taken to protect the woman you love are understandable. But you have chosen a dangerous path in challenging a king's power. If I had sensed any greed or ambition in you, I would have refused my aid. But I do not. I will offer what assistance I can."

Lothar then turned to address Judith.

"As for you, cousin," he smiled wryly. "I wish I had been as courageous as you and resisted my father's pressure to marry Theutberga. Waldrada and I were already in love at that time. As you know, I have spent many years trying to undo a decision that was made for me. If you wish, you can be married here in the Palatine Chapel. I will have one of my bishops perform the ceremony."

Judith looked at Baldwin, who grinned back at her. "Thank you, cousin. We would like that very much!" Judith responded.

Then, Waldrada joined the conversation, offering to provide anything Judith might require in the way of clothing for the ceremony. Judith readily accepted. She had left most of her queenly robes behind to make room for the gold and silver she carried on her pack horses. After traveling disguised as a man for a month while fearing her father's retribution, she looked forward to focusing on something as ordinary as what to wear to her wedding.

Lothar and Waldrada offered to show them through the palace complex. When they arrived at the jewel-like Palatine Chapel, that was built in the shape of a cross, Lothar spoke with one of the bishops who promised to make the wedding arrangements for the following day. Judith asked that Felix and Hemma be allowed to marry there as well.

Baldwin and Judith returned to the guest quarters to share their joyful news with Felix and Hemma, who had nervously waited to hear King Lothar's decision. It occurred to Baldwin that his mother was right. King Lothar might not be the complete villain he had judged him to be.

We all have sins. Baldwin admitted to himself. *I had best leave judging to God. I am not particularly good at it.*

❧

For the third time in her short life, Judith awoke to the knowledge that it was her wedding day. Upon this occasion, however, her feelings were that of anticipation and joy rather than fear. Hemma helped Judith dress in robes of finely embroidered golden silk, a present from Waldrada and King Lothar. Judith wore the only crown she had retained—a simple, gold tiara that represented her as a princess of Francia.

Judith gave Hemma one of her best robes to be married in, and the two brides walked arm-in-arm past the massive marble pillars and mosaic arches through the bronze doors of the Palatine Chapel. Waiting at the middle of the three altars to receive them were both Baldwin Iron Arm and Felix. King Lothar and Waldrada smiled down on them from the second-floor vantage of Emperor Charles the Great's throne.

During the wedding and the following feast, King Lothar's servants moved Judith and Baldwin's belongings from the guest quarters to the west wing of the palace complex, where they had been given a suite of rooms. Hemma and Felix also had been given a chamber nearby. Lothar informed Judith and Baldwin that they could remain at Aix-la-Chapelle for as long as they wished. However, Judith wondered how long they would be able to stay, considering the pressure her father was certain to put upon King Lothar once their whereabouts were known. But for now, she was content.

At the conclusion of the feast both couples were shown to their new chambers. Approaching her own door, Hemma turned back and went to Judith. She had helped prepare Judith for her previous two wedding nights. Now, on her own wedding night, she was unsure as to what her responsibilities might be.

Hemma hesitated. "My lady, do you require my assistance?"

Judith smiled, knowing why Hemma inquired. "Not tonight, Hemma," she hastened to reassure her. With a twinkle in her eye, she added, "I will rely on the 'Iron Arm' of Count Baldwin. I think he will manage very well. What say you, my husband?"

Baldwin laughed. As if to demonstrate his capability, Baldwin Iron Arm lifted Judith in his arms, pushed open the door, and entered the privacy of their bedchamber.

CHAPTER XXI

SPRING and SUMMER 862

News of Judith's whereabouts and her marriage to Baldwin Iron Arm reached King Charles' court by the end of March. Hincmar wondered how the couple had remained undetected for more than a month on their journey to Lotharingia. Baldwin had outwitted them in the couple's elopement, in their flight, and now in their place of refuge.

Sadly, events had combined to ensure little cooperation from Lotharingia. In response to Lothar's request for a divorce from Theutberga, Hincmar had written and published to all clergy his treatise, *Divortio*. Arguing against divorce in any form, Hincmar's reasoning had strongly influenced Lothar's council of bishops to deny King Lothar's request. This drove a wedge between the courts of Lotharingia and Francia. The rift had grown larger with King Charles' recent attempt to seize Provence from Lothar's younger brother, Charles of Provence.

Without much hope of success, Hincmar wrote to Lothar at King Charles' request, pressuring him to return Judith to the care of her father, and Baldwin to the justice of his king. Meanwhile, King Charles began seeking an annulment of Judith and Baldwin's marriage.

"Whatever it takes, this marriage shall not stand." Hincmar promised his king.

The unfortunate news of Judith's marriage had been somewhat tempered by King Charles' military success against Weland's band, which had traveled up the Marne and ravaged Meaux, setting up camp in the abbey and destroying several bridges. King Charles' men had set to work repairing the damaged bridges upriver from Meaux and posted guards along the riverbanks. Downstream from Meaux, they built a barrier across the Marne, hemming in any retreating Viking longships.

Unable to use their longships, the raiders were forced to raise the white flag and accept King Charles' demand to leave Francia by the spring equinox. They also freed those they had taken as slaves and forfeited any treasure they had stolen. King Charles personally selected ten hostages from among the Viking leaders to be held until such time as the band fulfilled their promises.

Having suffered such a decisive defeat, Weland and his son lost the leadership of the large Danish horde, and most of the Danes moved on to Salomon's holdings in Brittany. Having lost their followers, Weland's family knelt before King Charles and asked to be made Christians, promising to assist the king in resisting attacks by other Danes.

King Charles began planning his summer assembly with increasing optimism. He now had a proven strategy for battling Vikings—the building of fortified bridges. He had yet to deal with his defiant sons and daughter.

A messenger from Archbishop Hincmar arrived at Aachen with a missive from King Charles. Lothar's servant delivered the scroll to the king, who was walking with Waldrada, Judith, and Baldwin in the extensive, intricately designed gardens at the heart of the palace complex. Delicate purple, white, and yellow spring flowers had enticed them to stroll along the garden's maze-like paths.

Lothar unrolled the scroll, perused its contents, and handed it back to the waiting servant. "Tell the messenger that King Lothar requires a few days to consider his response. I will call for him when I am ready to reply."

Lothar turned to address Judith and Baldwin. "It seems you have a decision to make. King Charles' tribunal has stripped Baldwin of his lands and title and has excommunicated both of you from the church. King Charles demands that I turn you over to him or risk suffering punishment myself. If I am found guilty of providing you sanctuary, I will also be in danger of anathema."

"What do you plan to do, cousin?" Judith had paled at the mention of excommunication and her concern was reflected in her eyes. She had known that the past halcyon weeks could not last forever, but she had hoped to delay this intrusion into the blissful peace that she and Baldwin had shared.

"The question is, what do you two plan to do?" Lothar countered. "You have risked everything to be together. If you are determined to remain together, I will do what I can to help you. The choice is yours. Return to your father and seek reconciliation with him and the church or fight on . . . and risk losing everything."

Baldwin responded without hesitation. "The choice is Judith's. If she wishes to return to face her father, we will do so."

Judith also responded quickly. "If we return to Francia, I will lose my freedom, and Baldwin might lose his life. I say we fight on."

Lothar laughed. "It seems, cousin, that being here at Aix-la-Chapelle has given you the spirit of our great-grandfather!" He then grew more serious. "Here is what I can do to help you. I will delay the messenger for several days—long enough for you and Baldwin to be on your way. By the time the messenger returns to your father's court with my answer, you will have been on the road for nearly two weeks."

"Where should we go? To Louis the German?" Judith wondered.

"That would only delay the inevitable," Lothar pointed out. "If you wish to have your excommunication reversed and your marriage sanctioned, you have a clear destination. Only one man can do that."

"Rome," Baldwin anticipated. "You are recommending we go to the pope."

"That is my recommendation."

"It is a journey of a thousand miles," Baldwin commented.

"True," Lothar acknowledged. "The journey there and back again is filled with danger, and you will have to wait for an audience with the pope. That will require the better part of a year. And yet, I envy you. My own journey seems endless. After seven years, I am still trying to move heaven and hell for the right to marry Waldrada."

Returning to their quarters in the palace, Judith and Baldwin sought out Felix and Hemma. "Judith and I must leave as soon as possible for Rome," Baldwin explained. "It is an arduous journey of some two months, full of danger and with no guarantee of success. If we make it safely through the Alps, we could be set upon by thieves, intercepted by King Charles' knights, or have our petition denied by Pope Nicholas and be left exiles in Italy. But this is something we must attempt."

"You, however, may choose to remain here," Judith's voice caught, revealing her emotion. "King Lothar has promised to provide you with employment should you choose to remain at Aix-la-Chapelle."

Felix looked at Hemma's earnest gaze and knew instantly what her answer would be. "We will leave whenever you are ready."

Beaming, Hemma added, "I have always wanted to see Rome."

The following day, Lothar sent a messenger ahead of Judith and Baldwin's departure to alert his brother, King Charles of Provence, to expect visitors. Provence would provide a much-needed resting point before the group made the perilous climb through the Alps with its icy, narrow paths and steep cliffs. Lothar's messenger would continue on to Italy as well and ask Lothar's brother, Emperor Louis, and his wife Engelberga to receive Judith and Baldwin at their palace in Pavia.

"Be vigilant," Lothar warned Baldwin as he wished them a good journey. "If King Charles intercepts you, it will most likely be at the alpine pass of Mont-Cenis. Saracens and brigands also frequent the pass. I have assigned six knights as escorts and guides on your journey. When they reach Rome, they will act as my envoy to petition the pope on my own behalf."

"How do you suppose Pope Nicholas will respond?" Baldwin asked.

"I do not know," Lothar admitted. However, with or without the church's permission, I *will* marry Waldrada by summer. People say terrible things about Waldrada as my concubine. She must be my queen and our son Hugh must be my heir!"

"You are also in a difficult position, cousin," Judith observed.

Lothar nodded. "There is strength in numbers, Judith. You and your brothers have married whom you choose. If I follow your examples and we all stand together, future royal children may thank us for fighting for their right to choose as well."

༄

The summer assembly at Pitres on June 1st buzzed with excitement over the events of the past few months. Every group Hincmar passed spoke either of the marriages and alienation of the king's three oldest children or of the king's success with the Danes. Hincmar grumbled silently. Although he could not deny that the rumors flying about the kingdom like persistent, annoying gnats had increased the nobles' attendance this year. *Gossiping like a bunch of old hens.*

King Charles' request that each man bring a cart loaded with building materials had piqued the attendees' curiosity. The king obviously had something vastly different in mind for this gathering. With great anticipation, the nobles gave King Charles their full attention when he called them to order.

"Lords and Bishops, my faithful friends, I am gratified by your presence at this, our annual assembly. Many of you have labored diligently this past year to maintain peace within your counties and provinces. To those of you who have done so, I say 'thank you.' I encourage the rest of you to follow their example

271

and be peacemakers throughout this coming year. Work to unite our kingdom in fellowship and labor for the common good."

King Charles acknowledged several within the assembly who had proven most helpful during the past year before continuing his remarks.

"You may have heard of our recent success against the Danes. This success has given us new hope, but it was achieved only through hard work and vigilance. I have asked each of you to bring a cart filled with building materials. This assembly, unlike any we have held before, will be one of accomplishment rather than mere speech-making. For the next several days, with our own hands we will construct a bridge with fortifications across the Seine. Once this fortified bridge is finished, I will order my knights to guard it to prevent further attacks from the longships."

He paused for the assembly's inevitable reaction. When the assembly quieted, the king pressed on. "The skill and spirit of cooperation you gain from working with this assembly will have a direct impact for good upon your individual holdings and provinces. You will learn how to build these fortifications on your own vulnerable waterways. Labor with me and I promise you will have my help in fortifying your holdings. Now, what questions do you have before we begin building a bridge?"

"Why are King Louis and young King Charles not here?" one noble demanded boldly.

This was a question Hincmar had dreaded. But King Charles answered it frankly.

"My sons and I have our differences. However, Queen Ermentrude and I met with young King Charles a few weeks ago at Meung. He assures us he is committed to maintaining order in Aquitaine. Our other differences will be resolved shortly. As for Louis, he has been temporarily wooed away by Salomon's promises. We aim to reconcile with Louis by the end of summer and with Salomon before the next assembly. Some of you have not always agreed with me. And yet, here we are, working together for a common purpose. I am certain Louis and young Charles will join us at our next assembly."

Once King Charles had answered all the questions from the assembly, he organized his nobles, and they went to work. In three days, they had successfully completed a bridge over the Seine and fortifications to protect it. Now, it would be up to the nobles to return to their holdings and see what fortifications they could build to protect their own waterways. Thankfully, no one had been foolish enough to ask about Judith's elopement.

৵

The Danes who left King Charles' kingdom at the spring equinox had not gone far, finding employment with the rival factions in Francia. Salomon hired twelve longships as mercenaries to fight for him against Robert the Strong. To counter Salomon's move, Robert paid 6,000 pounds of silver to hire the remaining Danes to bolster his side. An inevitable blood bath followed.

Louis, who had sought refuge with Salomon, was caught up in the violence. Salomon gave Louis command of two thousand Bretons and sent him to Anjou to attack the holdings of Robert the Strong's followers. Completely outnumbered and without Baldwin Iron Arm for support, Louis' men were slaughtered, and Louis barely escaped with his life.

Humbled, Louis reconciled with his father. However, incensed by Louis' role in Judith's elopement and angered by Louis' own unauthorized marriage, King Charles refused to restore him to his kingship in Neustria. At Hincmar's suggestion, the king granted Louis and Ansgard the ravaged county and abbey of Meaux to rebuild.

Queen Ermentrude, who had been devastated by the alienation of her children, was relieved to have contact again with both young Charles and Louis. Hincmar knew she wished to also have Judith restored to the king's good graces. However, the archbishop was determined to ensure that the young couple who had started this family rebellion would suffer the most severe punishment.

Hincmar's correspondent in Provence had sent word that the rogue princess was on her way with Baldwin to plead their case before Pope Nicholas. If Judith and Baldwin convinced the pope to reverse their excommunication and sanction their marriage, it would be much more difficult to overturn Louis' and young Charles' unauthorized unions.

Hincmar sent King Charles' Count Palatinate, Father Fulk, to make the long journey to Rome. Well-versed in legal arguments, Fulk would present the king's best case before Pope Nicholas and try to take Baldwin and Judith into custody. However, the result of that assignment would not be known for several months at least. Summer would prove a difficult waiting game.

When Emperor Charles the Great invaded Italy in the year 773, he used the alpine pass at Mont Cenis to cross over into Lombardy. Later, his son, Emperor Louis the Pious, endowed a hospice there—the Monastery of Novalesa. Now, Judith, Emperor Louis' granddaughter, gratefully rested in that peaceful monastery after the arduous ascent to the summit of Mont Cenis.

During their alpine climb they had encountered deathly cold winds, icy roads, sheer cliff drop-offs, and the risk of avalanche. However, Judith's greatest fear had never been realized. No sign of her father's knights had troubled their perilous journey. Grateful for the head start and the escort King Lothar had provided, Judith slept easily. On the following morning, they passed over into Italy.

Judith was not prepared for the teeming mass of merchants, diplomats, nobles, and clerics pushing forward from one station to the next as they joined the Via Francigena leading to Rome. They passed pilgrims, easily distinguished by their long, coarse tunics, staffs, and small shoulder purses, seeking miracle cures at the scores of saints' shrines along the way to the holy city.

More troubling were the men whose chains bore witness to their serious crimes, including that of murder. Well-meaning bishops sent these convicts on pilgrimage as penance, providing them with certificates for food and lodging from monks along the way and absolution in Rome upon completing the pilgrimage. The road to Rome also attracted frauds who forged certificates and put on their own chains or who pretended to be ill and in need of a cure in order to benefit from the generosity of others.

Pavia, a week's journey south from Mont Cenis, had been the capital city of the Kingdom of the Lombards until they were conquered by Emperor Charles the Great in 774. Now, Emperor Louis of Italy made Pavia his primary residence. The palace complex was renowned for its size and beauty, its mosaics, and its frescoes.

Judith had never met her cousin, Emperor Louis. The eldest son of Lothar I, Emperor Louis, was nearer the age of Judith's father. As a boy, Emperor Louis was raised in the court of Louis the Pious, who had made his grandson—his namesake—ruler of Italy.

Emperor Louis and his wife, Empress Engelberga, had been blessed with two daughters. And although Emperor Louis had done much to negotiate peace between the warring factions in Italy, with no male heir, his legacy was in jeopardy. Judith remembered hearing her father and Archbishop Hincmar speculate as to how his kingdom might be divided amongst his male relatives upon the Emperor of Italy's death.

The emperor and empress warmly welcomed Judith and Baldwin, addressing the challenges awaiting the couple in Rome.

"I will do what I can for you," Emperor Louis promised. "However, I do not know how much influence I still have with Pope Nicholas."

Empress Engelberga explained. "Four years ago, impressed by Nicholas' knowledge and piety, my husband successfully proposed Nicholas as the successor of Pope Benedict III. Sadly, Pope Nicholas' sense of his own importance has outweighed his gratitude for Emperor Louis' support, and he has caused real tensions throughout the Christian world."

"In what manner?" Judith wondered.

Emperor Louis explained. "Pope Nicholas has forgotten that for generations Frankish kings and emperors have protected, expanded, rebuilt, and prospered the church in Rome. Instead of cooperating with us, he is trying to build his own empire—a religious one that will subjugate all Christians under his rule, from the eastern church in Constantinople to the church in Ireland. He claims his word is law over every Christian—king or cleric. And he is quick to excommunicate anyone who does not bend to his will. One day, he will push things too far and force actions he may not like."

"Do you think he will listen to our request?" Baldwin showed his concern.

"Oh, he will listen," Engelberga assured him. "How he will rule is unpredictable."

"We will go with you to Rome and help you gain an audience with Pope Nicholas." Emperor Louis assured Judith and Baldwin. "Only be prepared. King Charles is sure to send his own representative to Rome to argue his case as well."

౨

Their three-week journey from Pavia to Rome took Emperor Louis' party through the lively coastal town of Piacenza on the border between the Kingdom of Italy and the Papal States. Five days later, they entered Luna, a port on the Tyrrhenian Sea known for its quarries of exquisite white marble.

Baldwin was surprised to discover that Bjorn Ironside had attacked Luna shortly after he left King Charles' kingdom two years earlier. Bjorn Ironside, along with his fellow Dane, Hastein, mistook the port of Luna for Rome, having never been to the holy city. Discouraged from mounting a frontal attack by the high walls protecting Luna, Bjorn gained entrance through trickery—pretending to be dying and seeking Christian conversion. The unsuspecting citizens of Luna allowed him entry.

Once inside the church, Bjorn leaped from his sick bed and fought his way to open the city gates. With the gates open, Bjorn's men sacked the city. Nearly two years later, Luna still mourned Bishop Ceccardo, killed during the attack.

As the party approached Rome, the walls of the Leonine City rose on a hill in the distance across the Tiber from the main city of Rome. Forty-feet tall with more than forty watchtowers, the Leonine City walls had been built a mere ten years earlier by Pope Leo IV with enormous donations from the Frankish kings. The walls encompassed St. Peter's Basilica with its monasteries and churches, the mighty fortress of Emperor Hadrian's Mausoleum, and the pilgrim communities that made up the Borgo. Pope Leo had commissioned this massive wall-building project to connect St. Peter's with the Aurelian walls surrounding the rest of Rome, protecting the sacred sites in this part of the city from marauding Saracens.

Entering Rome through the ancient arch of the Porta Aurelia, secured on either side by two watch towers, they passed a cluster of houses and several water mills before encountering the narrow, winding streets of Trastevere. This region of the city, on the west side of the river, contained opulent Roman-style mansions as well as dwellings of desperate poverty. The maze of irregular, unpaved streets eventually led to a bridge, the Pons Aemilius, where they could cross over the Tiber into the heart of the city. Baldwin and Judith planned to stay at Emperor Louis' mansion in Trastevere while they prepared for their audience with the pope.

The mansion was as elegantly furnished as the emperor's palace in Pavia. Larger than any other building on the street, its ornately carved wooden double doors opened into a large vestibule, where imperial guards prevented unwanted intruders from accessing the private areas of the mansion. Guests who made it past the vestibule entered the atrium, an open and airy courtyard with a pool, where rainwater drained into a cistern below. Sleeping chambers surrounded the atrium, and a passageway led to a kitchen, a banquet area, and a second courtyard with a tiled bathing pool and a meticulously kept indoor garden. Marble colonnades and statuary, frescoes, and mosaic-tiled floors provided the opulence befitting an emperor's dwelling.

Emperor Louis sent a messenger to the Leonine City to inform Pope Nicholas of their arrival. For several days, Judith and

Baldwin hoped vainly for a response. Baldwin would much rather have a mission to accomplish, a foe to fight, or a journey to conquer than sit and await a determination of his future.

Eventually, they received the good news that Pope Nicholas would grant them an audience at his palace in the Leonine City. Baldwin's elation was quickly tempered by the final piece of news. Their plea before the pope would be countered by Fulk, the newly arrived Count Palatinate of King Charles.

CHAPTER XXII

FALL 862 through FALL 863

Passing out of the city through the Porta Settimiana on the north side of Trastavere, Judith and Baldwin's party joined the steady stream of pilgrims, merchants, and clerics following the banks of the Tiber on the Via Santa leading to the Leonine City. Above the arched gate, which opened directly into the Saxon quarter, an inscription admonished travelers to "Admire the splendor of golden Rome."

Judith felt a rush of memories as they made their way through the Saxon quarter—built to look like a village in Wessex or Kent with its characteristic timber houses. Here and there were remnants of buildings still not restored after the great fire of 847 which had destroyed the Saxon and Lombard quarters and had threatened St. Peter's Basilica. All around them, Judith heard men calling out in the English vernacular, offering services to any Saxon pilgrims entering the Borgo. The escort Emperor Louis had provided guided them past churches, inns, and shops as they made their way toward the basilica.

The hill upon which the Leonine City was built once held Emperor Nero's circus—an arena for entertainments such as chariot races, mock battles, and the execution of Christians. The apostle Peter was said to have been martyred next to the Egyptian obelisk south of the basilica. On the west, the catacombs held the remains of many saints. On the north lay the pope's palace. Entry through five arched gates on the east led to the basilica's atrium, with its pinecone fountain welcoming the weary pilgrim and promising the spiritual refreshment of "living water" to those who continued into the basilica.

Built over the tomb of the holy apostle, the massive St. Peter's Basilica was the ultimate representation of what church and state could unite to create. More than 400 feet long, 200 feet wide, and 100 feet tall, the church was designed to cause emperors and peasants alike to worship in awe. The basilica's aisles were lined with row upon row of marble and granite columns. Those brought from Jerusalem had the spiral formation characteristic of Solomon's temple.

The walls and ceilings were adorned with mosaics and frescoes depicting biblical and historic events while the light reflecting off the omnipresent gilding in the ceilings and furnishings bathed the basilica in a rich golden sheen. Judith was especially moved to see the large reddish-purple slab of Imperial Egyptian porphyry where her great-grandfather, Charles the Great, knelt to be anointed as the first Holy Roman Emperor.

Upon entrance to the papal palace, a bishop ushered the party into a lavishly appointed waiting room. Count Fulk stood at the far end of the room, conferring with two legates assigned permanently to Rome from King Charles' court. Dressed in a black cassock representing his clerical endowment, Fulk glanced up as Judith entered—his eyes calculating, and his brow furrowed in deep concentration.

Sensing Judith's tension, Baldwin squeezed her hand. "Whatever Pope Nicholas decides, we will remain together. That I promise you." Judith clung to that promise as they awaited their audience with the pope.

After some time, the bishop returned. "Follow me," he motioned to Baldwin, Judith, and Count Fulk, "Pope Nicholas is expecting you." Hemma and Felix and the rest of Count Fulk's party remained behind.

The pope's audience chamber reminded Judith of one of her father's throne rooms. However, the pope had provided benches for those waiting until they were called. Pope Nicholas presided from his throne, resplendent in a scarlet choir dress, the silver hair visible beneath his red skull cap testifying to his nearly six decades of church service. Feeling a bit shaky, Judith and Baldwin gladly collected their thoughts when Pope Nicholas called upon Count Fulk to speak first.

"Welcome to Rome, Father Fulk," Pope Nicholas began. "I understand that you are here in your official capacity as Count Palatine for King Charles' court. I have had the opportunity to read the missives you brought from King Charles and Archbishop Hincmar, but I wish to hear from your own lips why you are here and what it is you are seeking."

Fulk appeared not much older than Baldwin. Bolstered by the weight of the law and his royal commission, he spoke confidently.

"I am honored, Your Holiness, to represent King Charles, who seeks redress for the wrongs he has suffered at the hands of Baldwin Iron Arm. As a father and as a ruler, King Charles has the right to determine whom his daughter will marry. That right was taken from him, stolen by someone he had placed in a position of trust within his own family. Upon entering the royal service, Baldwin Iron Arm took an oath to serve the king faithfully. He betrayed that trust and violated the laws of God and of man when he stole Queen Judith away from the protection of her father and took her to himself. He is a condemned criminal and must be brought back to Francia to receive punishment."

Pope Nicholas prodded, "I understand punishment has already been meted out. Is this not so?"

"Only in part, Your Holiness," Fulk explained. "A synod excommunicated Baldwin Iron Arm and stripped him of his lands and his title. As support for that decision, I cite Pope Gregory, who said that any man who steals away a widow and marries her should be declared anathema."

"So, Baldwin Iron Arm has been stripped of his heavenly blessings, all his worldly possessions, and his ability to obtain more. And yet his crimes are worthy of further punishment?" the pope sought clarification.

Count Fulk hesitated briefly before continuing. "King Charles believes Baldwin Iron Arm is guilty of treason and worthy of a traitor's punishment. It is the king's right to impose such a penalty, and justice demands it. If Baldwin Iron Arm is not fully punished for his crimes, others will be emboldened to commit similar crimes. King Charles hopes and expects that you will allow me to take Baldwin Iron Arm and Queen Judith into custody immediately and return them to face justice. The law must be satisfied."

"A traitor's punishment, you say. You are perhaps speaking of exile, blinding, even execution?" Pope Nicholas waited for a response from Fulk, but the count said nothing. After an awkward moment of silence, the pope continued.

"Thank you, Count Fulk, for your excellent argument on behalf of your king. I now wish to hear from the accused criminals themselves. Baldwin Iron Arm, come forward."

Judith pressed Baldwin's hand tightly before he rose to defend himself. She wondered how he appeared so calm when the charges and the punishment looming before him were so desperate. Pope Nicholas stared at Baldwin for some time as if trying to take the measure of his character before questioning him.

"Baldwin Iron Arm, I have been told that you are under the protection of Emperor Louis," Pope Nicholas probed.

"We are his guests, at present," Baldwin acknowledged.

"You have also requested this audience. Why is it you are here, and what is it you want of me?"

"Your Holiness, I understand that my actions in helping Judith escape from the palace at Senlis appear treacherous to King Charles. For this, I am truly sorry. I have always held the king's regard and trust as a prized possession, and losing his trust is the biggest regret of my life. However, I also love his daughter Judith. We seek your sanction of our marriage and a restoration of our membership within the church." Baldwin hoped his voice and countenance did not betray his depth of emotion.

"Was this marriage done with proper consent?" Pope Nicholas asked.

"Judith's brother, King Louis of Neustria, gave written consent. We were married by a bishop of the church in Aachen before our excommunication." Baldwin answered.

Count Fulk arose, unable to restrain himself. "It was for her father to consent, not for King Louis, who had only just attained his majority two months prior."

Pope Nicholas was unruffled by the interruption. "Thank you, Count Fulk. I will take your legal argument into consideration when I deliberate. You may be seated." He turned toward Baldwin. "Count Fulk claims the law is on King Charles' side. Do you disagree?"

Baldwin's response was measured. "Unlike Count Fulk, I am neither eloquent nor trained in the law. However, I believe there is a difference between God's law and man's law. Man's law looks at a man's actions and seeks to impose justice. God's law looks at a man's heart and applies mercy wherever possible. I have been accused of betraying my oath and my king. In my heart, I have always been faithful to King Charles. I am not a traitor."

"How, then, do you justify your actions?" Pope Nicholas demanded.

"My oath was of two parts. I vowed to be faithful to King Charles, and I also vowed to protect his wife and his children with my life. For six years, I have devoted all my purpose to serving the king and protecting his son, King Louis. When the king's daughter Judith needed and wanted protection from her father, I could not deny her that protection without breaking my oath."

"Are you blaming Judith for your actions?" the pope wondered.

Baldwin's face flushed scarlet. "No, Your Holiness! I only wished to explain my reasoning in deciding to free her from her confinement at Senlis."

"Perhaps it is time I heard from Judith," Pope Nicholas replied. "You may be seated, Baldwin Iron Arm. Judith, I would like you to step forward."

Baldwin extended his hand, helping Judith rise. Judith drew strength from the warmth conveyed in that brief touch. Baldwin had done his best for them. The rest was up to her.

"Ah, Judith," Pope Nicholas' voice was not unkind. "You have found yourself the subject of much controversy and excitement in your short life. Perhaps this controversy is not to your liking. Has it been difficult for you?"

"Yes, Your Holiness," Judith responded carefully. "I do not wish to be at odds with my father or my church. I love them both."

"But you also love Baldwin Iron Arm. Is that what led you to defy your father?"

"Not really, Your Holiness," Judith admitted. "My experience as Queen of Wessex taught me a valuable lesson. I decided while I was yet queen that I would not agree to another marriage arranged by my father, should the occasion arise."

"I am surprised. What valuable lesson could possibly teach you to defy your father?"

"During some very dark days in my second marriage, my prayer book and the holy scriptures helped me realize that love—not politics—should be the bond between husband and wife or parent and child. I learned that love cannot be forced. It must be freely given. I do not believe a merciful God looks down with joy upon a marriage if the only fruit of that marriage is misery and pain."

"Do you wish to be restored to the church?"

"With all my soul!" Judith responded passionately. "And I desire the same for my husband."

Pope Nicholas bowed his head in silence for several minutes of deliberation, while Judith remained standing, not daring to hope.

Finally, Pope Nicholas nodded. "Step forward, Count Fulk and Baldwin Iron Arm. I have reached my decision. The choice before me is a choice between justice or mercy, between punishment or forgiveness. If we mortals were to receive justice alone, without mercy, none of us would fare well. Knowing that God also requires both justice and mercy from *us*, I have decided to err on the side of mercy. I have decided to deny Count Fulk's request to take Baldwin Iron Arm and Queen Judith into custody, and I am reversing the excommunication of both Baldwin Iron Arm and Judith of Francia. I do not find their actions worthy of anathema."

"Thank you, Your Holiness!" Baldwin expressed gratitude for both of them, seeing that Judith was overcome with emotion. "This means so much to us!"

Pope Nicholas smiled. "I will also send a missive to King Charles seeking a reconciliation between the king and Judith and asking him to restore your *benefices*, Baldwin Iron Arm."

The pope turned to Count Fulk. "You have carried out your commission honorably, Count Fulk. I will have my written responses ready for you to take back to King Charles in a few days' time. I will inform the king that you represented his interests well."

Count Fulk did not appear happy, but he bowed his head in acceptance.

Pope Nicholas concluded the audience with a parting reminder for Baldwin and Judith. "Even if the king is willing to reconcile, we will not know his response for several months. The waiting will be difficult but remain hopeful. I will send for you as soon as I receive word."

Upon Judith and Baldwin's return to the Imperial mansion in Trastavere, Empress Engelberga suggested that they use their time for the next several months exploring the monuments of the city of Rome while waiting for word from Francia.

"Rome," she explained, "is like no other place in the world. The city, at the height of the empire, housed more than one million people. Now, most of the city is abandoned, and the population is closer to thirty thousand."

"Why did so many people leave?" Baldwin queried.

Emperor Louis provided an answer. "A combination of several things. When the empire broke apart, Rome no longer drew large numbers of foreigners or foreign trade. This, combined with government corruption, collapsed the city's economy. Also, Rome's endless wars had damaged many of its aqueducts, while most of the remaining aqueducts simply fell into disrepair. People cannot thrive without water."

Empress Engelberga added, "Here in Trastevere, the aqueducts provide ample water for our reduced population. You will also find small clusters of people yet living where they can earn money from those visiting the city's abandoned monuments and basilicas. The areas connected with the papal states, such as the Lateran Palace, are also population centers. However, much of the city is abandoned. You will see for yourselves how empty this once great city has become."

Throughout the summer and fall Baldwin and Judith, along with Felix and Hemma, explored the great sites of Rome. They visited the baths at Caracalla, the great Coliseum, the Forum, and dozens of monuments and basilicas. Touring the remnants of the greatest empire the world had known was impressive but sobering.

Felix summed up everyone's feelings one afternoon. "Whatever man creates does not last. I only hope God has done a better job of it."

℘

The summons for a second audience with Pope Nicholas did not come until the beginning of December. Judith eagerly broke the papal seal on the scroll and read aloud the long-awaited missive. The pope had received an envoy from King Charles. They were to meet Pope Nicholas at the Lateran Palace in the heart of Rome.

Judith and Baldwin were impressed by the façade of the Lateran palace with its glorious mosaic of Christ the Omnipotent. Inside, a bishop conducted them through the basilica. When they came to the apse, the bishop took special care to show them the gold and jewel-toned three-part mosaic portraying Christ at the center, commissioning his apostles to go into all the world to preach the gospel. On the left, a seated Christ bestowed keys upon Peter and a labrum upon Constantine. On the right, a seated St. Peter presented the stole to Pope Leo III and the standard to Emperor Charles the Great, indicating the Frankish empire's responsibility to protect the church. When the bishop finally ushered them into the audience chamber, Pope Nicholas was waiting for them.

Pope Nicholas' expression was stern, his brow furrowed. "I have not received the response I had hoped for," he admitted.

"King Charles is adamant. He is not ready to forgive either of you. What is your plan now?"

Baldwin had given the matter considerable thought for the past several months. "Your Holiness, I am a knight who has served King Charles for more than six years. If I am no longer allowed to serve my king, my preference would be to serve his brother or his nephews. However, they have all signed treaties agreeing not to employ each other's displaced knights. It is not to my liking, but without other options, I must seek employment among the Danes. I have had occasion to cooperate with some of them during my service to King Charles and have reason to believe I will be welcomed amongst them."

Pope Nicholas shook his head sadly. "That would be most unfortunate for you and disastrous for King Charles and Francia."

Turning to Judith, the pope asked, "How do you feel about joining your husband in service to the Danes? Are you ready to give up the life you are accustomed to for life with him in a wild and hostile land?"

Judith did not hesitate. "I am ready, Your Holiness."

"You are a curious couple," Pope Nicholas smiled. "Not everyone is so steadfast. I am inclined to make a second attempt on your behalf. I am sending Bishop Radoald and Bishop John of Cervia to Francia on a different errand. I will send with them missives asking all the bishops in Francia to encourage your father to reconcile with you. Who else might have influence with your father?"

"Archbishop Hincmar and my mother have the most influence on him," Judith responded.

"Then I shall write missives on your behalf to them as well," Pope Nicholas assured her. "Baldwin, it might also serve you well if you include a formal apology in the form of a missive to King Charles."

Baldwin agreed and added, "Words are not adequate to express our gratitude!"

"Do not thank me yet," Pope Nicholas remonstrated. "We will not know the success of my efforts for several more months."

Judith hastened to offer her appreciation. "Your Holiness, no one could do more for us than you are doing. Whatever the outcome, we must accept it as God's will."

Pope Nicholas paused to consider before speaking. "Above this room is the Sancta Sanctorum, or Holy of Holies—my private chapel. To reach this chapel, one must ascend twenty-eight steps on one's knees, with full devotion and prayer. In the Sancta Sanctorum is a sacred image of Christ. That image was begun by St. Luke—but it was finished miraculously by angels. There is a parallel here. I have begun a work on your behalf. We must pray for the angels to finish it!"

∾

Archbishop Hincmar was in the uncomfortable position of being at odds with the pope. He had urged King Charles to take a strict stance with Pope Nicholas regarding Baldwin and Judith. Now, the pope had sent personal missives to all the bishops in Francia requesting their intervention with King Charles on behalf of the disgraced couple.

Pope Nicholas had also sent Radoald, Bishop of Porto, and John, Bishop of Cervia, as legates to meet with King Charles personally on behalf of Judith and Baldwin. They brought with them gifts for King Charles and Queen Ermentrude as well as a personal message for the queen. The pope had requested that his two legates remain with King Charles' court at Soissons for an extended visit before returning to Rome.

The legates had also brought a missive for Hincmar seeking his help with the reconciliation. The pope's entreaty caused him to grumble. *Judith and Baldwin must have bewitched Pope Nicholas!*

Hincmar had always believed that strengthening the kingdom would strengthen the church as well. Now, Pope Nicholas was asking him to weaken the king's authority by showing mercy to those who had stolen the king's power. Thus far, King Charles and Hincmar had agreed over the serious breach in both custom and law represented by Judith and Baldwin's elopement and the unsanctioned marriages of his eldest two sons. Hincmar hoped that King Charles' resolve would not falter under mounting pressure from Pope Nicholas' agents. The archbishop did not like pitting his king against his pope, but he could see no alternative.

The council room was aglow with ethereal spring sunshine shimmering through its large windows as Hincmar entered for their daily meeting. He quickly hid his disappointment at seeing the two papal legates joining the king's council. *What mischief are they up to?* he wondered as he took his place at the table.

King Charles began. "I have invited our two legates from Pope Nicholas—Bishop Radoald and Bishop John—to join our council today. They will address us a little later. Archbishop Hincmar, have you anything to share with us?"

Hincmar knew he would be facing off with the two representatives of Pope Nicholas. He began setting the tone for the coming battle.

"With the recent tidings that Baldwin Iron Arm is considering allying himself with the Vikings, I have written to all the Dane leaders who now call themselves Christian to let them know that anyone who gives aid to the rebel, Baldwin Iron Arm, cannot be allied with our kingdom or our clergy!"

"Does that include Pope Nicholas?" John Scotus wondered aloud.

Hincmar glared at him, refusing to answer the provocative question. "I have also received a report that other Dane chieftains may be interested in becoming Christian, following the example of Weland and his family. We hope for more baptisms later this year."

"An interesting development," King Charles agreed. "I hope they are sincere. What news have you of young Charles in Aquitaine?"

"My sources tell me that young King Charles, wrongly influenced by the rebel lords of Aquitaine, has helped them seize Toulouse. The poison of rebellion seems to be spreading from Aquitaine to Septimania." Hincmar summed it up.

"I am sorely disappointed in young Charles' lack of understanding," the king complained. "I will call him to account. If he refuses to come to his senses, I will not hesitate to march against him."

"Young Charles' age renders him easily manipulated," John Scotus ventured. 'However, I believe he will eventually see reason."

"I hope you are right in this, John Scotus," King Charles replied. "Since none of my children have come to their senses regarding their unfortunate marriages. That brings us to Judith and Baldwin and the reason for the presence of our legates from Rome. Bishop Radoald, Bishop John, I understand you have a message for our council from Pope Nicholas. You may share it with us now."

Bishop Radoald rose to address the council. "King Charles, thank you for this opportunity to speak with you on a topic Pope Nicholas holds close to his heart. The pope is aware that Baldwin's breaking of the law requires punishment. However, Pope Nicholas asks us to remind you that a Christian king must also show mercy to the penitent. We have here a missive from Baldwin Iron Arm admitting that he wronged you, professing his desire to be reconciled, and offering his pledge of faithfulness."

Bishop John handed the rolled parchment to Bishop Radoald who passed it to King Charles. Hincmar was incensed at the obvious manipulation of his king's emotions. He could see King Charles' face soften as he read the missive. King Charles was too often ready to forgive–a quality to be admired in a Christian but one that did nothing to deter future offenses. Not waiting for the king to finish reading, Archbishop Hincmar rose to challenge Bishop Radoald.

"The writings of Pope Nicholas himself argue that there must be penance before pardon. King Charles simply demands the return of his daughter and penance from Baldwin." Hincmar pointed out.

"You are correct in quoting Pope Nicholas' preference of penance before pardon," Bishop John conceded. "However, the pope believes that Baldwin Iron Arm has been sufficiently punished."

Hincmar decided to press his point. "Baldwin Iron Arm did not steal money from the king. Such a crime could easily be repaid. How can Baldwin make recompense for such a crime as he has committed unless he returns the king's daughter and faces the most severe punishment? And if Pope Nicholas supports Judith and Baldwin's right to marry, what of Lothar and Waldrada? You have also been sent to Francia to formally oppose their marriage. But are they not two sides of the same coin?"

Bishop John arose, taking passionate exception to Hincmar's questioning of the pope. "King Lothar's divorce and marriage are not questions for this council!"

"Every case that comes before Pope Nicholas is unique," Bishop Radoald asserted in a calmer manner. "The pope asks you to carefully consider. Baldwin Iron Arm is a highly skilled knight, well-schooled in the methods, strategies, and weaknesses of this kingdom. What harm might come to Francia or the church if you force such a powerful knight to join the pagan and lawless Danes?"

King Charles stood and threw the parchment scroll upon the council table. "If Baldwin Iron Arm seeks to threaten my kingdom . . ."

"I do not believe that is what is happening here." A soft and cultured voice made itself heard from the doorway.

In the midst of their heated discussion, no one had noticed the entrance of Queen Ermentrude, who made her way to the council table. "The missive I have received from Pope Nicholas speaks of the great love Baldwin Iron Arm has for Judith and she for him. I believe Baldwin acted impulsively out of concern for Judith's confinement at Senlis. His actions were wrong, but his heart is true. And the two of them refuse to be parted. Do you really wish Baldwin to take our daughter to live among Vikings? Would it not be better to use him to strengthen our borders *against* the Danes?"

Hincmar and the Roman bishops took their seats as the queen approached her husband.

"My husband, you have often chosen mercy over justice. I have admired your willingness to give others a second chance. At the conclusion of this council, you will ask your advisers to voice their opinions as to whether you should pardon Baldwin's offenses against you. I would like you to count my voice with those who would urge you to grant Baldwin Iron Arm a second chance to prove his faithfulness."

King Charles looked deeply into the eyes of his queen. "I can promise nothing. But your opinion is important to me, and I have noted it."

Queen Ermentrude nodded and left the room as quietly as she had entered. Hincmar felt a knot form in his stomach. King Charles' face did not reveal it, but the archbishop knew—even before the king asked the question of his council—that the queen's opinion would carry the day.

⁊

In August Pope Nicholas sent word to Judith and Baldwin that the angels had completed their miracle! King Charles had agreed not only to accept Baldwin as a son-in-law but had also restored his lands and title! Baldwin and Judith would be sent north to Flanders to defend Francia's borders against the Danes.

The return journey from Rome to Francia took Judith and Baldwin until October to complete. It was a joyful one as they anticipated reconciliation with family and a second wedding—one sanctioned by both the church and Judith's father. King Charles had arranged for them to marry at the Church of Saint-Eusèbe in Auxerre upon their return, as he would not recognize the wedding performed in Aachen. However, he refused to attend the ceremony.

Brilliant changing colors on the willows, oaks, and beeches within the city of Auxerre displayed their magnificence on the morning of Judith and Baldwin's wedding as if they, too, granted their approval. As Hemma dressed Judith in silken robes, she remarked, "Four weddings in seven years seems quite extraordinary for a young woman who has just achieved her nineteenth year. What will the next few years bring, I wonder?"

"Certainly, no more weddings!" Judith laughed. "And this ceremony, miraculous as it may be, does not really count. Baldwin and I have already been married for more than a year. I only hope it satisfies my father's wounded pride." After a pause, Judith added, "I wish he would come to the church."

"Give him time. The depth of his wound shows how much he cares for you both," Hemma reasoned.

Judith's hand gently traced the swelling of her stomach. "If the child I carry is a son, we will name him Charles, after the king. I hope my father will see how much we care about him as well."

"All will be forgiven once you are settled in Flanders. King Charles admires those who succeed against the Danes. And no one is better at dealing with the Danes than Count Baldwin Iron Arm." Hemma reassured Judith.

Judith smiled and hugged Hemma. "An enormous task awaits us in the wilds of Flanders if we are to defend our borders. I must ask Baldwin to show me how to use a sword. No Dane shall lay a hand on you, Hemma. Baldwin, Felix, and I will make sure of that."

"Can you promise that no more bears will attack us in Flanders?" Hemma teased.

"That remains to be seen," Judith laughed. "But first, we have one final wedding to accomplish."

With Hemma's preparations complete, Judith joined the processional. She smiled as she took her brother Louis' arm. Together, they made their way to the chapel in Auxerre, where Count Baldwin Iron Arm waited.

❦

Three weeks later, Judith and Baldwin stood before the remains of a ruined Roman fortress, largely abandoned except when used by Viking raiders. A few huts making up the small farmer's market were all that remained of Bruges' once thriving coastal port. Baldwin had brought Judith here to share his vision of building and renewal. He hoped their new beginning in Flanders would be reflected in a new birth for this ancient ruin.

Baldwin put his arms around Judith, providing her warmth from the winter chill rising from the ice-encrusted Roya River.

"I know it does not seem like much. But this is what you traded your crowns for," Baldwin observed wryly. "What do you think of your new kingdom?"

Judith laughed. "A little drafty at the moment."

"True," Baldwin acknowledged. "But next year at this time we will have torn down that old ruin of a fortress and have used the materials to begin building a better one."

"You have big plans for this place?" Judith asked, already knowing the answer.

"I do," Baldwin admitted. "I had always hoped that someone would rebuild Bruges and make it the city it needs to be. Marius says that someone has to be me."

They stood in silent contentment for a while before Baldwin added, "Your father is correct in thinking his daughter married beneath her station. However, I intend to build a magnificent fortress here with outer walls and gates to defend Flanders against the Danes. We will have an enormous great hall and our own private chapel. It will be suitable for a queen."

"A countess," Judith reminded him.

"A countess, then," Baldwin smiled. "Bruges will also become a proper town, with a cathedral. And we will once again establish trade–even with Wessex–if you so desire. In my vision, poor, destitute little Bruges will become famous for its great beauty."

"When do we begin?" Judith shared his excitement.

"We will spend the winter planning the construction. But first, I must organize the landholders to defend against any attacks by the Danes in spring." Baldwin lifted Judith's chin to look into her eyes. "I have been speaking of my dreams. But what does the queen desire?"

Judith's thoughts turned to Graveney. She had found peace and strength within its walls. At the time, she had believed that peace came from her ownership of the land. Now, she knew it came from having the freedom to choose her own path.

Her life had been one of miracles thus far. Perhaps it was not too much to expect one more. Together, she and Baldwin would defend their borders from the Danes. Together, they would build a great city. Together, they could accomplish anything!

"The queen says she is quite content with not being queen."

⁋

FINIS

AFTERWORD

This book covers seven eventful years in the birthing of modern Europe. With minor exceptions, the people and events depicted in this book are taken from historical records. I was lucky enough to find annals, correspondence, and several actual conversations recorded at the time. There is no written account that Baldwin was present at all the events in which he appears. However, as Louis' companion, and for the purpose of telling the story, I have included him at the events involving Louis. This afterword is a summary of what happened in the main characters' future lives.

JUDITH AND BALDWIN IRON ARM

Judith and Baldwin had three sons and two daughters. Their eldest child, Charles, died in infancy. Judith appears to have maintained contact with Alfred because Flanders and Wessex enjoyed a thriving trade after Alfred succeeded to the throne of Wessex. And their son, Baldwin II, married Alfred's daughter, Aelfthryth. Whether Judith died in 870 or whether she simply did nothing further to interest the chroniclers is a matter of speculation. However, as the first queen to have been consecrated, Judith's ceremony provided the pattern for every consecration of a European queen thereafter—including Queen Elizabeth II.

Baldwin was extremely successful in repelling Viking attacks on Flanders. He remained a loyal follower of King Charles until Charles' death in 877. Baldwin's name is also on a list of those who declared their loyalty to Charles' successor, King Louis "the Stammerer." Baldwin became ill in 879 and retired to the monastery at St. Bertin, where he died a few months later.

KING CHARLES (Historians refer to him as Charles the Bald)

Convinced that mystical power was bestowed by consecration with holy chrism, Charles had Hincmar perform the sacred rite for Queen Ermentrude in 866. He hoped Ermentrude would bear him another son whose right to rule would supersede that of Louis, with whom he was bitterly disappointed. Ermentrude gave birth to their tenth and final child in 864 - a girl they named Godehilde. Ermentrude died in 869 at about 46 years of age.

At the death of Ermentrude, Charles married Richilde of Provence. Hincmar consecrated her, at the request of Charles, who was still hoping to find an heir to supplant Louis. Richilde bore five children, but only one child, a daughter, survived beyond infancy.

When his nephew Lothar died, Charles divided Lothar's kingdom with his brother, Louis the German, but fell short of achieving his greatest desire to own Emperor Charles the Great's palace at Aix-la-Chapelle. King Charles was consecrated Emperor in 875 upon the death of his nephew, Emperor Louis of Italy. When Louis the German died in 876, Charles made an unsuccessful attempt to take over his brother's kingdom. Charles died of illness in October of 877 at Mont Cenis on a return trip from Italy.

King Charles "the bald" was probably not bald. No picture or statue of him depicts him as bald. The origin of the name given to him by historians is not sure. One tradition says the nickname came when he shaved his head in an act of pious submission to the church prior to the pope's arrival at Compiègne. This was remarkable to the Franks, who prized long hair.

LOUIS (known to historians as Louis the Stammerer)

Louis and Ansgard had two sons and three daughters. However, King Charles eventually had their marriage annulled in 875. He then forced Louis to marry Adelaide of Paris for political advantage. Louis was crowned King of Francia by Archbishop Hincmar at Compiègne in October 877, shortly after his father's death. Louis died in 879 and was succeeded by the two sons he had with Ansgard: Louis III of France followed by Carlomann II, both of whom died young and without issue. Louis' son by Adelaide, Charles the Simple, then succeeded to the throne.

YOUNG CHARLES (historians refer to him as Charles the Younger, or Charles III of Aquitaine)

In 863, King Charles pressured young Charles to give up his marriage to the widow of Count Humbert. In 864, young Charles, always ready to play a prank, jumped out and startled a member of his hunting party, who reactively hit him in the head with a sword. Young Charles suffered a head wound from which he never recovered and died at the age of eighteen.

LOTHAR II

The battle over Lothar's unsanctioned marriage to Waldrada came to a climax when, in August of 865, Lothar capitulated rather than be excommunicated by Pope Nicholas. He allowed Theutberga to move back to the palace at Aachen but could not tolerate her presence. Miserable, Theutberga herself petitioned the pope for an annulment, but her request was also denied. By the time Pope Nicholas died in 867, Lothar and Waldrada had five children together. Refusing to abandon his quest to legally marry Waldrada, Lothar set out for Rome to petition the new pope, Adrian II, who refused to take up the matter.

On Lothar's journey home to Lotharingia, he became ill with a fever and died in Piacenza. Lothar had fought for 14 years to have a marriage to Waldrada sanctioned by the church. However, his children with Waldrada were never recognized as legitimate heirs, and his kingdom was divided between his uncles—King Charles and Louis the German.

EMPEROR LOUIS OF ITALY

In 865, Pope Nicholas excommunicated archbishops Gunther and Theutgaud, relatives of Waldrada, whom Lothar had sent to Rome with a decree from the Lotharingian bishops granting Lothar a divorce from Queen Theutberga and upholding his marriage to Waldrada.

In a show of support for his brother Lothar, Emperor Louis laid siege to Pope Nicholas in St. Peter's Basilica. Pope Nicholas went without food for two days. However, when Emperor Louis suddenly became ill with a fever, Empress Engelberga intervened. Fearing that her husband's fever was God's retribution for beginning the siege, the empress brought about a reconciliation between her husband and the pope. Emperor Louis died in 875 with no male heir. King Charles took control of his kingdom.

ARCHBISHOP HINCMAR

Hincmar was arguably the most prolific and influential writer of the ninth century. In addition to creating the first consecration ceremony for a queen, he wrote many theological, philosophical, and instructive tracts throughout his long career. His treatise, *Divortio*, influenced the church's attitude restricting divorce for more than a thousand years.

Hincmar's relationship with King Charles suffered after the events surrounding both Lothar and Judith's marriages. He came in conflict with Charles and with several popes on various other matters but continued to serve as the king's adviser until King Charles' death in 877. Hincmar went on to serve Louis "the Stammerer" and his sons, Louis III and Carlomann II. Hincmar died in December 882 at the age of 76. He was succeeded by Count Fulk as Archbishop of Reims.

ALFRED (Known to historians as "Alfred the Great")

Alfred became king upon the death of his older brothers, Aethelberht and Aethelred. Despite being afflicted with what appears to have been Crohn's Disease from his late teenage years on, Alfred was able to strengthen the kingdom of Wessex against increasing Viking attacks. He revived education within his kingdom and became a noted scholar, authoring several books and translating a number of classical works. Alfred established a strong trade with Judith and Baldwin's Flanders. His daughter Aelfthryth married Judith and Baldwin's son, Baldwin II. Beloved of his people, Alfred laid a foundation that would eventually lead to an educated and united England, earning him the title of "Alfred the Great."

POPE NICHOLAS I

Pope Nicholas' relationship with the Eastern Orthodox Church in Constantinople soured when he excommunicated their leader, Photius, in 863. A synod in Constantinople in 867 returned the favor and excommunicated Nicholas in 867, causing a complete severance between the two Christian churches. Nicholas died later that year.

Under Nicholas, the power of the Bishop of Rome became supreme over all Christians in the Western church—clergy and layperson alike. His reputation for standing his ground in ecclesiastical matters, as well as his missionary efforts and his personal piety, caused him to be known posthumously as "Nicholas the Great." Nicholas I was declared a saint by Pope Urban VIII in 1630.

ROBERT THE STRONG

After his reconciliation with King Charles in 863, Robert remained faithful. A powerful warrior, he died fighting an army of raiders led by Viking leader Hastein at the Battle of Brissarthe in 866. His two sons, Odo and Robert I of France, ended the rule of the Carolingian empire and began the reign of the Robertian Dynasty in France. Robert is also the great-grandfather of Hugh Capet, founder of the Capetian dynasty.

THE BEAR OF BRUGES

With its death, the bear of Bruges won a place in history as a symbol of the city of Bruges and its founders—Baldwin and Judith. The bear's image can be seen on buildings in the city. Both Belgian chocolates and beer have been named for him.

FELIX AND HEMMA

Felix and Hemma are purely fictional characters. King Aethelwulf did employ a Frankish secretary named Felix, but I could not find any details about him. Hemma was necessary to the story because Judith escaped from the palace dressed as a servant. I believe that Judith must have received help from her own personal servant who would have had to assist her and be willing to risk punishment by so doing. Although Hemma is purely fictional, the story she tells Judith of the Viking attack on St. Wandrille and the slaughter of surrounding settlements up and down the Seine was very real.

ACKNOWLEDGMENTS

I am grateful to my husband, Rod, and my son, Richard, whose patience, feedback, and encouragement throughout the extensive research and writing process kept me going.

Many thanks also to my wonderful beta readers: Rachael Nelson, Lani Green, Lei Anne Ward, Amber Duncan, and Brianne Cowan. Their valuable and insightful feedback made this book so much better than it started out!

I would also like to express gratitude for incredible historians such as Janet L. Nelson, Pauline Stafford, and many, many others whose work I relied heavily upon while researching the fascinating world of the Carolingian Empire.

A native of San Diego, California, D. H. Morris has lived on four continents and traveled through many countries. She has four children and eleven grandchildren and currently lives with her husband in Kansas City, Missouri. She graduated from Utah State University with a Bachelor of Arts degree in Theatre and Choral Music education and pursued graduate work in English at USU and law at the University of Utah. She is also a published playwright.

As a descendant of Judith and Baldwin, the author discovered their intriguing story while doing genealogy. This inspired her to spend years researching everything about the 9th Century – including food, politics, travel, war, education, clothing, jewelry, religion, holidays, marriage customs, and medicine. She loves talking about this remarkable time in history when Europe was being formed and countries were fighting for their very existence. She is available to meet with book clubs and other groups. You can contact her at dhmorris00@gmail.com.